YAMIN

YAMIN

A NOVEL OF A DEMONIAC

JEFF KEENE II

WordCrafts

Yamin
Copyright © 2023
Jeff Keene II

ISBN: 978-1-957344-65-2

Cover concept and design by David Warren.

Published by WordCrafts Press
Cody, Wyoming 82414
www.wordcrafts.net

To my mom Genie who loved reading,
nurtured my passion for books,
and who would have adored this story.

Yamin ran uphill on the dusty winding path connecting the great lake's shoreline to his home. His shoulder-length dark-brown hair shot droplets of sweat as it whipped back and forth. He passed several merchants carrying baskets of fresh fish to the city of Hippos at the top of the hill.

His father, Eber, followed far behind at a much slower pace.

Yamin's muscles ached from the morbid chore he had been given earlier. His infirmed parents put more responsibility on him than those of other fifteen-year-old boys. He had even become proficient at baking bread and laundering clothes. The weaker they became, the more skills he gained. Because of that, he learned to hate learning.

The only work he didn't despise was with the family boat. Before his parents had been stricken, he spent his days on or by the sea, honing his abilities for when he could venture out alone.

The disease had spread quickly through the region east of the Sea of Galilee where his family lived for generations. Decapolis, a league of ten free city-states under the umbrella of Roman authority, was often attacked by illnesses spreading from all directions. The King's Highway stretched from Arabia in the south to Damascus in the north. This major trade route brought more than just goods from faraway places. Darkness often followed.

It took his uncle first. Since then, Yamin had been expected to take up the slack in daily duties. And the work seemed to never end.

Yamin's uncle and father co-owned a fishing vessel. Although they worked on the freshwater sea, they also traded in fishing nets and traps, selling their handcrafted wares at the local markets along with fresh and salted fish.

Now that his parents had both taken ill, and his mother become bedridden with the same incurable ailment as his uncle, Yamin's duties to support the family kept him busy from before sunrise to after sunset.

He entered his family's one room cottage. The pungent scent of excrement curled his nose.

"Mother." He breathed rapidly as he approached where she lay. Traveling uphill from the shore to the house was a challenge when walking, let alone running.

He sat on the bedside with trepidation and gently squeezed her thin, cold hand. No response. He remembered how these hands often made his favorite meal of lentil soup with chicken. Yamin used his sense of touch to analyze his mother's skin.

His gift of perceiving objects like trees, rocks, and, oftentimes, parts of his father's boat with his fingertips gave him a better understanding of them. They were not real until he could touch them. The ability revealed itself when he was a small child and caused a stir in the community when onlookers stared at his outwardly odd behavior of touching everything as if listening through his fingers.

Since his mother became ill, the meals he and his father shared were frugal and consisted of bread, olives, and pickled sardines. The family's aging boat sat in dry dock once again due to increasingly necessary repairs, so fresh fish remained costly.

He continued to stroke her hand, the loose skin moving over tendons and bones. Yamin gathered as much information from this tactile experience as his mind could handle. He noticed how his mother's breathing, shallow and raspy, had worsened since yesterday.

If only I could give her some of my breaths.

He studied her. She had suffered a drastic loss of weight these past weeks and appeared to be nothing more than a lumpy fold of linens under the bed coverings. Her seemingly bodiless head stuck out on one end and facial bones, once hidden behind healthy cheeks, now protruded giving her a corpse-like visage.

He tried again to stimulate a response. "Mother. It's me, Yamin." His voice cracked and throat tightened as he choked back emotions.

No reply.

"Father was right." Tears welled. "These *are* your last breaths. I didn't want to believe him. That's why he called me back so early before sunset."

Today's only chore had consisted of nothing more than digging a shallow grave for his dying mother. *I didn't think it would be so soon.*

Descended from Jews, Yamin's ancestors had been heavily influenced by Hellenistic culture. Having held on long to their ancestral beliefs, his family now worshipped a myriad of pagan gods along with the Hebrew god, Elohim.

He glanced at the humble altar his father had carved into the mud wall. A small, worn, stone idol of Neptune stood on the uneven surface along with a misshapen, wooden, fertility spirit, a bundle of herbs, and a small, well-used candle. *Useless.* Yamin's faith in all gods had waned.

Eber entered the house several minutes later. He forced his words through labored breaths. "I . . . I'm sorry, Yamin." He leaned against the doorway frame with both hands and bent slightly to rest.

Lit from behind by the bright sky, his father looked like a great spindly spider sitting in a web. "The walk . . . from the shore . . . seems longer . . . every time I make it."

I'm losing him too.

Yamin's father had lost his appetite, then weight, and suffered bouts of fever and coughing fits producing blood.

Just like Mother. Yamin's sorrow slowly transformed into anger. *My family is dying in front of me, and there's nothing I can do.*

He got up from his mother's bed and pounded his fists once on the wall. Flecks of dried mud, loosed by his rage, clinked softly on the hard clay-ash floor.

"Why?!" Tears streamed down his cheeks. He turned to his father. "Why is this happening to us? Are we cursed?"

Eber entered and took the place where Yamin sat moments ago. He clutched his wife's hand in his then turned slowly toward his son.

Yamin walked toward the altar. The idol stared at him with empty eyes. It seemed to beg him to ask for its mystical help. Yamin had done so in vain many times before. And for what? *How can I tell father my faith has diminished?*

"You have a right to be angry. It's not fair." He coughed, trying to control the severity of the spasmodic hacking. Upon gaining his composure, he continued. "But we are not cursed, my son. We are just—unlucky."

"I don't believe in luck, father." Yamin balled his fists, ready to strike the wall again, and took a deep breath. He stared at the idol.

Its empty eyes stared back.

He reached out and gently laid the statue on its side. "I no longer believe . . . in anything." He could not turn to face his father and half expected an object to hit the back of his head as punishment. He let out a great sigh.

To Yamin's surprise, his father did the same as he stared at his dying wife. "Maybe the gods *have* forsaken us, but we have done nothing to cause them to *curse* us."

Yamin turned to face him. "After uncle died and mother first got sick, I started to doubt. Why would anyone who lived a good life and worked so hard have to endure so much loss—so much pain?"

"I have no answer for you, my son." Eber slouched.

"Then I'll answer for you. *There are no gods.*" Yamin gazed blankly at his mother's gaunt face from across the room. He could not be here when the inevitable happened and darted from the house toward town.

Eber got up slowly to watch his son leave. He hung his head low. *How can I leave him alone?*

He recognized his own illness and had done nothing but pray to the gods in vain. *Time for more drastic measures.*

He had heard rumors about a physician who had some success in curing ailments such as his. The healer lived on the other side of town at the end of the main road. It would take quite a bit of exertion to make it there before sundown.

He was tired. So tired. But he had to do something. He could not leave his wife now, so he decided to rest and wait for Yamin to return. Then he would ask his son to join him for the trip.

Eber lay next to his wife, coughing as the fluid in his lungs adjusted to his supine position. He took her hands in his once more and squeezed them to find any signs of life remaining. He listened to her labored breathing and knew at any moment she would give up her fight.

2

Yamin's tears had dried by the time he reached the outskirts of Hippos. The scent of seared pork emanated from within the city's walls. His stomach growled.

The town sat high upon a hill overlooking the sea. From the elevation, the western shore cities of Capernaum to the north and Tiberias to the south stood out across the darkening waters. Silhouetted against the dimly lit sky, the outlines of their synagogues and wealthy resident palaces appeared as strange square mountains. The twilight of mid-winter glowed with a yellow-orange light.

Yamin breathed deep letting the humid air fill his lungs. The dry summers paled in comparison. He entered the town from the western gate and walked to a public rainwater cistern. Bending over the large basin, he used his hand to draw the liquid to his mouth. Yamin spit water and choked on the half-swallowed remains.

His best friend Dar appeared next to him. Laughing, the young man slapped him on the back. "You all right?"

Yamin gained his breath. "Yes. Thanks a lot." He coughed once more. "Dar, what're you doing out here? Thought you'd be home eating supper."

"You know my father." He cleared his throat and let a scowl spread across his face. "'I'm caught up in a piece of work I just can't leave at the moment.'"

Yamin smirked. "You sound just like him. But you must admit, he is 'the best sculptor in Hippos.'"

Aristocrats around Decapolis often hired Dar's father to create custom statues of all sorts of objects, from deities, to bowls, to bowls with deities on them. He also made many smaller items to sell in the market, mostly diminutive figurines adorned with his special accessory, mother-of-pearl.

"Hey, I'm his apprentice." Dar shoved Yamin knocking him off balance. "I plan on being just as good too."

Yamin quickly recovered. "Fine. But now you're avoiding *both* of your parents. Aren't you?" He was dodging his parents too, but for far different reasons.

Dar sighed. "Mother's irate for being kept waiting. But she knows Father has deadlines."

Yamin appreciated Dar's ability to distract him from family problems. He patted Dar on the back, and a cloud of dust rose into the air. His cough returned. "What *is* all that?"

"Snail shell dust. Father's making a set of finely sculpted handles for a physician who lives on the other side of town."

"Handles? For what?"

"I . . . don't know, exactly." Dar curled his fingers to resemble the claws of a monster. "Probably for the tools he uses to slice into his victims." He gnashed his teeth.

"Not funny." Yamin turned with a frown and walked toward the center of town.

Dar followed. "Sorry. I mean patients. Too close to home?"

Yamin shrugged. *Change the subject.* "What's something like that worth?"

"The handles? Quite a bit, I imagine. But without your father's donation of the shells, the cost would be a lot more."

Yamin stopped walking. "What donation?" He recalled the fun he had collecting those baskets of shells last summer.

At the time, his father had thought differently. "Yamin, help with these nets instead of playing with those?"

"I'm *not* playing. These are worth money." Yamin pushed the basket aside and heeded his father.

I thought he threw them overboard.

Dar answered. "The shells. My father gave him some small statues in trade and—"

"He didn't take any payment?"

"I think your father traded them in turn. At—at least that's what my father told me."

They strode down the central road toward Dar's townhouse. Yamin tensed. *Mother dying. Praying to stupid gods. Trading shells instead of taking much needed money.* He did not know if he could take any more.

"You all right, Yamin?"

Yamin waved off the question. It had nothing to do with Dar.

They walked in silence for a while down the colonnaded main street of Hippos, the *Decumanus Maximus.* The single row of buildings on each side occasionally opened to the sides by way of narrow alleys leading to less opulent housing. Behind the rows, the hillside sloped downward on all directions forming a natural defense against attack. Some of the outlying villages had houses consisting of white-washed mud and thatched roofs. But not within the city's walls. And none were like Yamin's house near the lake, constructed, in part, of animal dung.

He sniffed out of curiosity. The recent rain and humidity allowed the pungent pastoral odor to hang in the air near his house. But not in the city of Hippos proper.

They passed a wide alleyway leading to the sculpting shop, its front visible by the large white statues on either side of the entrance. "Want to try and save your father from any wrath your mother might dish out tonight?"

"I've tried once. He's on his own now."

Farther into town, the buildings took on a statelier look. Yamin admired their cleanliness and spaciousness. *Why can they live like this when I'm forced to live in manure?*

Rising two, sometimes three stories up, flat-topped roofs and large courtyards became the norm in the central area of the small city. These housed the wealthy citizens and aristocrats of Hippos, made of marble with granite columns of Greek influence.

Yamin craned his neck to get a better glimpse of the luxury he so coveted. "Do you ever see any of the town's leaders?"

Dar paused to grab Yamin's arm and pulled him along. "They stay closed off behind their courtyard walls and only come out to enter the central marketplace."

Yamin studied the homes with wide eyes and scowled at their lavishness. His family had always been sustenance anglers. The licensing fees forced upon them by Roman officials, the purchase of flax for nets, and the wood for the upkeep of the boat forced Yamin's parents to live in squalor compared to citizens here. Dar lived here. He had a two-story home and a room to call his own. Something of which Yamin only dreamed.

"How's your mother?"

Dar's question caught him off guard, and he stopped walking. He could not look him in the eye. "She's dying. Father says she won't make sunrise."

"Then—why are you here instead of down there?"

Yamin squeezed his eyes shut and took a deep breath. "I just need to be away. That's all. I've said my good-bye."

Dar kicked a rock from the road. "Want to join us for dinner? You know, while you're . . . being away?"

Yamin let out the breath he held. He was thankful Dar did not push the subject any further. "Of course. Especially after weeks of nothing but pickled fish."

They picked up their pace.

When they arrived at Dar's house, his mother's stern look gave way to a smile. "How pleased I am to see you, Yamin." She embraced him and kissed both of his cheeks. "Welcome. And when we are done, you can bring some to your parents. I'm sure your father would appreciate it, since . . ."

Her sheepish look broadcast her sorrow.

Yamin knew she understood his pain. Everyone had lost someone they knew or loved when the illness hit the region. He lowered his head and smiled. "Thank you."

Dar's mother turned toward a portable clay stove fueled with charcoal. The fire also served to warm the house, as the winter air had begun to cool with the setting sun.

Dar's father entered, covered in more dust than his son earlier.

His wife turned quickly from her chore. "Sophus, go back out and wash before coming in here."

Yamin produced a thin smile. He remembered when his parents could laugh at such things. *I wish* they *were my parents.*

At mealtime, the family, including Dar's four-year-old sister and Yamin, sat on mats around the cooking pots and used bread as scoops to get at their food. They had a low table reserved for more formal guests. Wine, beans, and boiled chicken made up the rest of the meal. Yamin devoured every morsel and thanked his hosts with almost every bite.

He would have joined Dar's family more often, but his parents strictly forbade him. His father was fond of saying things like, "I don't want to burden any other family with another mouth to feed," or "We have plenty of food right here." Plenty of the same food Yamin despised compared to what others were privileged with.

Envy did not always fill him, but there were times when he wished his parents had more money so they could have a nicer house, varied food, and a better fishing boat. Oh, and chickens.

Conversation was expected, but a constantly full mouth kept him from it. Yamin realized he came across as a rude guest. He sat up and swallowed his latest bite hard. "Did you know—" He searched the family's faces to insure their attention. "—that just to the north, in Gergesa, they raise herds of swine?"

Dar stared at him and mouthed, "What are you doing?"

Yamin continued. "I remember eating pork when I was younger. My father and uncle worked more then and had more money."

Sophus played along. "We *all* had more back then, son."

"I want a pig, Father." At least Dar's little sister showed excitement for Yamin's story.

Yamin smiled at her. "There was a festival in Hippos."

Sophus put his wine down. "Oh, Saturnalia. I know this story. Several Roman officials—oof!"

Dar's mother elbowed her husband in the ribs. She smiled. "Continue, Yamin."

"Yes, you're right. They traveled south through Decapolis and stayed in Hippos during the winter solstice. They brought many slaughtered and live pigs."

"I want a pig, Mother."

She shushed her daughter.

"The smell of the cooking meat coming from town was more than any of us down by the shore could bear."

Dar caught on. "What did your parents do?"

"They joined in the public festivities, of course. They sacrificed a suckling pig."

Dar's father raised his wine glass proudly. "A traditional gift to an earth deity. We did the same." He finished off his drink.

"That meat tasted so good." Yamin's gaze wondered off until he sensed the others staring at him. "Oh, but—nothing like this chicken." He stuffed another bite into his mouth.

Dar's father chuckled. "You know, that smell traveled all the way across the lake to the Jews in Tiberias."

Dar guffawed. "No wonder they hate us."

Everyone laughed except Dar's little sister. "Are we getting a pig?"

After dinner, Dar's parents allowed him to walk Yamin to the edge of town where the western gate opened to the slopes below. Darkness covered the hillside, and a cloud-shrouded crescent moon provided the only light to guide Yamin home. They paused at the gate.

Dar broke the awkward silence. "I wish there was something I could do to help you."

"Didn't you say your father's customer is a physician?"

"Yes. But your family— They can't afford to hire a physician, can they?" Dar's tactfulness needed fine tuning.

Yamin sighed. "There must be some way to pay him. What if

I struck a deal? Free fish for the season." He shook his head. "Or something like that?"

"It might work. I've heard of him accepting all sorts of payment." *Just like Father.*

"Why don't you meet me here in the morning and we'll go to his house. It's on the other end of town. The worst he could say is no."

As Yamin walked home in the chilly night air, he hoped there may be one more chance to save his mother and father from meeting his uncle's fate. *That doctor has got to be better than praying to stupid gods.*

3

$\mathbf{Y}$amin woke the next morning to an uncommon chill. *I know I placed the coverings over the windows before going to bed.*

"Father?" With his eyes still shut, he smacked his lips. *Not used to all that wealthy people food.* "Did you forget to add to the fire last night?" No reply. "Father?"

Yamin looked around the dimly lit room. "Where is everyone?" The sharp ring of rock striking rock entered the house. "No."

He jumped from his straw-filled sleeping mat and bolted for the door. Running around the house to the side facing the shore, he stared in shock as the early morning light revealed Eber placing the final stone upon his mother's burial site.

He walked slowly toward him. Eber's labored breathing could be heard from many steps away. Yamin stood motionless over the grave.

Eber prayed.

Yamin stopped him mid-sentence. "It's no use, father. Prayers have never worked. No god wants to hear about our troubles." He went around to the side of the grave. A tiny depression in one of the rocks held a minute amount of burning incense. "Good-bye, mother. Thank you for being here—when you could."

Yamin walked with his head down toward the shoreline and stopped at a small knoll overlooking the sea. The temperature had dipped below normal for this time of year, and grey streamers of evaporated water rose into the air from the calm glass-like surface. Yamin thought it a fitting phenomenon. He likened it to earthly spirits ascending from entrapment after being freed from their sufferings.

I wish I could be free from all this pain.

He turned his head toward the grave. In a matter of days his father would likely succumb to the disease now decimating his health.

"The doctor!" Yamin ran back to his father and told him about his idea. A tinge of hope returned to his voice.

"Son, I had the same idea last night after you left."

"We tried prayers. We tried poultices."

"We even tried that healing circle your friend Dar's mother suggested, remember?"

They both chuckled momentarily at having been through that experience.

Eber continued. "Remember, she used the bowline of my boat to make that circle? And then her husband brought that lyre he carved out of a tree branch?"

Yamin laughed. "It sounded like a sick cat!" But the amusement soon turned to tears of sorrow.

Eber put an arm around him while stifling a phlegm-laden cough. "Come on, son. Let's go see that doctor."

They stopped at the house to grab some bread and cheese. Eber feigned an attempt to eat his share but Yamin caught him hiding the food in his robes. He gave his father a chastising look.

"I plan on eating it … later."

Yamin had to shorten his strides to allow Eber to keep up. The uphill serpentine climb taxed a healthy person's muscles. Having aches due to a feverish state and weakness made it almost intolerable. Often Yamin had to support his father physically during the trip.

As they approached the steep slopes of the city, they passed through the necropolis. Carved into the hillside, it held the remains of burial tombs built for the wealthiest citizens of Hippos. Limestone and marble sarcophagi laid scattered across the surface. Yamin could not help but compare his mother's rudimentary resting place with these opulently carved crypts. His brow furrowed as he pulled Eber aggressively up the hill.

When they reached the top, Eber desperately needed to sit and rest before entering the narrow open gate leading into the city's main street. A stone guard tower stood on their left and looked unoccupied.

"I'm going to fetch you some water from the cistern."

It was the same one he had drank from the night before. But this time a man dressed in fine robes briskly exited the tower and impeded Yamin's access.

The man's disdain for Yamin came through his tone. "You cannot drink from here."

"Why not? I drank from it last night." Yamin's rudeness matched the man's evenly. But he decided to back off before being kicked out of the city as a troublemaker.

"There are new rules due to the illness spreading through town. You, and your . . . Who is that? Your father? He seems infirmed." The man raised his voice. "Is it true?"

"That's why I need the water." Yamin had no patience for this man's fearful foolishness. He decided the time to impress him with manners had passed.

"Only citizens of the town who have not been cursed with illness can drink from the public cisterns. Go find water elsewhere, *caenum!*" The discourteous man pointed in the direction from which Yamin had come and kept his arm and finger outstretched until Yamin moved away.

Yamin mumbled under his breath. "Superstitious imbecile. Call me filth? I ought to . . ."

He headed back to his father. "Rest a while longer. I'll keep searching."

Eber laid back against a great rock near the roadway. He only nodded.

Yamin shook his head and frowned. "You should have let me help you with mother's grave this morning. You're so weak, we can't go on."

Eber coughed violently in response to the chastising. After

gaining some control, he replied weakly. "You dug it. I had to do my part."

"Be right back." Yamin bolted past the water watchman, now troubling another beleaguered traveler who had entered the gate.

Yamin knew Dar's father worked close to the edge of town and sought out his shop. Sophus shared a sculpting studio with several other artists to save money. His family was not poor. But to maintain their well-to-do lifestyle, certain challenges needed to be overcome. Even though Decapolis and the city of Hippos were under autonomous rule, the local leadership took every chance to overtax their citizens.

Yamin knocked on the large door of the studio but no one answered. *Maybe it's too early?*

"Hallo!" Someone called from inside with a voice much deeper than that of Sophus.

"Hallo. Um . . . hallo!"

He waited. The only reply came in a series of loud crashes from within. He was about to walk away when the door swung wildly open revealing an enormous man covered in grey dust and chips of stone. Yamin took several wavering steps backwards. The man wore a leather kilt-like garment and sandals, but nothing more. He held a hammer in one hand and a chisel in the other.

"What do you want?" His booming voice caused several towns-people on the main road to stop and peer down the alleyway.

Yamin stood tall in the face of the imposing artist. "My friend Dar's father works here, and—I need some water—for my father. You see, he's ill, and we're trying to get to the physician on the other side of—"

The hulking man turned on his heels without saying a word and disappeared back into the building. He returned shortly with a sizeable clay jar full of water. He thrust it into Yamin's arms almost knocking the air from him.

"*Oof.* Thank you?"

The man grunted and closed the door.

I'll be sure to thank Dar's father the next time I join them for dinner. He turned and walked toward the narrow gate. He prided himself for having been successful and strutted down the main street. The bystanders quickly lost interest and continued with their business.

After resting and drinking their fill, Yamin continued to escort his ever-weakening father to the physician by way of Dar's house.

Dar waited outside when they arrived a few minutes later. "Good morning." His short curly hair reflected the sun's light.

Yamin stepped away from Eber to analyze his father's ability to stand on his own. "I was beginning to think you forgot about us."

Dar stood to meet Eber's gaze. "Good morning to you as well, sir." He then turned back to Yamin who had begun walking again. "I was waiting at the gate earlier—until that crazy water guard shooed me away. I thought you'd be earlier."

"Same trouble here." Yamin wanted to say his father's slow pace had kept them.

As they walked, Dar approached Yamin from behind and pulled on his robes to slow him. They let Yamin's father walk a few steps ahead to set the pace. He whispered in Yamin's ear. "Have you thought of a way to pay the physician?"

Yamin turned slightly and whispered back. "She died last night."

"Oh, I—I'm sorry."

Yamin let a moment pass and answered him solemnly. "Other than a fish deal? No, not really. Maybe I could work for him and pay off the debt?"

"I don't think you could work for the healer *and* do your father's work."

Dar. Ever the realist.

Dar revealed a handful of copper coins engraved with the image of the city's guardian goddess, Tyche, riding upon a horse.

The money was minted particularly for this city. Every time Yamin took a boat trip across the sea, people always knew where he lived when they used that coinage to purchase goods.

"Thank you, Dar. I'll take these when we get there, all right?"

Eber stopped. "What? Why are you thanking Dar?"

Ugh, I didn't want him to become suspicious.

Dar stepped ahead. "For—dinner last night. He thanked my parents enough already."

Yamin looked at his friend wide-eyed. *Stop talking.*

Eber gave the same look to Yamin but continued shuffling ahead without speaking.

Yamin knew his father would have chastised him, but his weakness prevented it.

Passing the centrally located forum and basilica, the boys stopped at the market. They were only a short walk to the physician's residence now.

"I need to rest—for a little while." Eber sat, nearly collapsing at the market's edge.

Roman officials gathered in the forum, parading around in their fancy robes atop the carefully arranged rectangular flagstones making up the floor of the open-air facility.

Colonnades of gray granite columns surrounded the meeting place on three sides. They gave the forum an impressive and ostentatious appearance. The pillars supported sloped roofs used to create shaded areas between the colonnades and the fronts of buildings erected around the forum.

Yamin knew Dar frequented this site. But he typically shied away from such displays of aristocracy, preferring the busy life surrounding the two port facilities on the lake. Even though the ports were controlled by the city, life was simpler there. No tedious bantering about legal issues and other administrative affairs down by the shore. *Just a few entertaining fish stories.*

Dar seemed to notice the apprehension on Yamin's face. "Let's go. It's not much farther."

"You could tell, huh?"

Dar nodded. "Not your favorite place, I know."

They hurried away from the growing crowds of the urban center. The physician's house was within site, and Yamin felt his father's steps quicken ever so slightly in anticipation of the expected help awaiting him.

Dar knocked on the ornate door. A sign with inlaid mother-of-pearl letters adorned it.

MEDICUS
AIGLE

Dar half-turned to tell Yamin what it said. "The goddess of good health."

Yamin could not read. He gave Dar a diminutive smile and nod.

Medicus meant the man within was a physician. The Latin inscription was for the Roman citizens. *Aigle* referred to the Greek goddess of radiant good health. An attempt to bring in patients from all walks of life, especially those with pagan philosophies. Those who could read, anyway.

Yamin motioned toward the door with his head for Dar to knock a second time, all the while supporting his dreadfully exhausted father. Much to the surprise of both boys, a beautiful young woman answered the door before Dar had a chance to knock again.

She wore soiled servant's clothes made of beige linen. But that did not matter to Yamin. Her dark mahogany hair coiled out behind her head from under a series of crossed braids in the front. He thought it looked like the hardened pitch his father used to seal the boat planks. Shiny, smooth, and with a tinge of russet.

He ogled her until Dar snapped him out of his trance-like stare. "Yamin? Yamin!"

"Oh, right." He blinked his eyes rapidly. Yamin suddenly wished he had bathed before leaving the house this morning.

"You'll have to forgive my friend here." Dar leaned toward her and whispered loud enough so Yamin could hear him. "He doesn't get out much."

Even Eber produced a weak smile. But instead of letting out a laugh, he coughed violently, this time producing blood. He tried in vain to hide his red sputum in a rag he carried.

"Oh, my," said the young woman. "We've seen this far too often.

Bring him around back and through the courtyard gate. I will summon the doctor." She closed the door.

Yamin's heart leapt. He interpreted the woman's familiarity with his father's symptoms as a good omen. *Nothing more than a minor setback to father's health. He'll be back on his feet in no time.*

4

When they entered the small courtyard of the physician's home, Yamin's hope turned to despair. A dozen men, women, and children, all ill and feverish, lay spread out within the walled enclosure. Some were on low mats of straw, others on wooden tables, and still others on the bare ground.

Several servants, including the attractive one who greeted them at the door, busily tended to the patients' needs.

The physician soon revealed himself as he exited his home, his robes surprisingly clean. Yamin thought after seeing the young woman that the doctor would look equally worn with the marks of his trade.

The gray-haired man cradled several ornate jars in his arms. He placed them gently upon a centrally located table that served as a workstation for the staff. Some of the contents spilled onto the doctor's robes, and he uttered an expletive. "I just changed."

The doctor looked up and down the table, seemingly impressed at the variety of tools at his disposal. Instruments of all shapes and materials were laid out upon the wooden surface. Some even appeared to be made of gold, at least in part.

As he moved, his arched posture and wattle of loose skin beneath his chin defined his age. The doctor's gratitude turned toward his servants for following his specific directions. *He seems pleasant enough.* But could he heal his father?

As two of the servants, instructed by the physician, guided Eber to an empty table near the center workstation. Yamin and Dar witnessed two other servants carrying off a limp and motionless corpse that had just occupied the same space.

They watched as the physician tended to Yamin's father.

"What is your name?" The healer inspected Eber's eyes.

"Eber," said Yamin's father weakly.

"How long have you been coughing, Eber?"

The boys did not wait for the answers and walked back toward the courtyard gate to sit against the wall and wait. Yamin had no stomach for such business. Nor did Dar.

Once, while assisting his father, Dar sliced his finger with a sharp iron chisel. The site of the wound made Dar pass out. He awoke to his father's enormous colleague standing over him—laughing.

As for Yamin, cleaning fish guts was one thing. Prying and poking around people's bodies was another entirely.

"His name is Kheiron," said Dar as he counted the coins in his hand. "He's a good customer of my father. Always pays on time."

"You think he'll ask for his payment now?" asked Yamin apprehensively, watching his friend and counting along with him. "If that's not enough, I can still make the fish offer."

The young woman who greeted them approached.

Yamin straightened up but did not stand to meet her. Her beauty struck him and had the same effect now as when he first laid eyes upon her at the front door. She reminded Yamin of how his mother looked years ago when still healthy. Her skin was smooth and free of blemishes. And her eyes—they looked as if they had seen so much but still held a youthful innocence. He remained mesmerized.

She met Yamin's gaze and asked gently, "You're his son, yes?"

Yamin nodded, unable to say anything.

"What's your name?"

She forced him to speak, and he stuttered his reply.

"Yamin, can I talk to you . . ." She looked at Dar and then back to Yamin. ". . . alone?"

Yamin stood and followed her to the other side of the courtyard.

He looked at each patient as they walked. At one point they were forced to step over a young man who lay upon the ground, muttering in a combination of languages, some familiar to Yamin and others he had never heard before.

Having lived near the Sea of Galilee in Decapolis, Yamin had been exposed to a multitude of foreign tongues and dialects by travelers. He recognized a few of the sick man's words as profanity in Greek, Latin, and Aramaic. He wanted to ask the nurse about that odd patient but decided not to repeat what he heard to the young woman. His recognition of common languages would not impress a resident of Hippos, anyway.

They stopped at the courtyard wall. Yamin glanced back at Dar who casually flipped coins and caught them in his other hand.

She spoke with a stern tone. "Your father is gravely ill. Master Kheiron is doing what he can, but as you can see . . ." She made a sweeping motion with her arm across the courtyard.

Aides constantly moved from one sick person to another, changing linens, giving water, and administering whatever the doctor's jars contained. *Was it some sort of oil?* A fire burned off to one side.

She continued. "And there is the matter of your form of payment."

Yamin reached into a small pouch attached to his belt and retrieved a single copper coin, the only currency his family had. "My friend over there has ten times this."

"Oh, dear. The doctor usually accepts only silver and gold currency."

Yamin looked down and his face reddened. His only option was to sell his services in exchange for his father's health. He reached deep within and mustered up the courage to speak. "What—what is your name?"

"Althea."

He had watched her mouth move when she spoke. *Beautiful.* He mouthed her name back.

"Are you all right?" She let out a small chuckle.

Her question caught Yamin off guard, and he snapped out of his trance. "Yes. I—I need you—Althea, to ask Kheiron if he'll accept the payment of—my servitude instead of the full cost." He tried to sound grown up, professional. But it came across as boyishly charming.

His sudden bravado brought a smile to Althea's face. "I'll go ask. He's been known to accept payment in other forms before. Go back to your friend and get the money you say he has. That'll help me convince the doctor to accept your proposal."

Yamin ran back the way he came and leapt over the blasphemous man.

The man reached out and grabbed Yamin's ankle with great force.

Yamin fell flat on his torso knocking the air out of his lungs and causing his vision to whirl.

The seemingly ill man rolled off his thin and soiled bedding to come face to face with Yamin in the dirt.

Their eyes, a head-length away, locked in a stare sending chills down Yamin's spine.

With a gravelly, ethereal voice the man spoke to Yamin in Greek. "You want her—don't you?" His breath smelled of rotten meat, and his teeth, those remaining, were blackened and broken.

Yamin could do nothing but listen and gasp for air as spasms plagued his diaphragm.

The man reached out and put his hands on Yamin's cheeks, grasping his head firmly. "You want what your friend has too. You want, and you want, and you want!" The man's screams sprayed saliva onto Yamin's face.

Their locked eyes broke contact as Kheiron and two others pulled the demented man away.

All the while, the man continued to holler wildly. Before they could control him, he stood and ran into the nearby fire. His robes quickly caught flame. He continued to run and scream, this time right toward Dar.

Dar dropped his coins and jumped to his feet. With nowhere to escape, he cowered behind his own arms and squealed. When nothing happened, he slowly opened his eyes to find the man had run out of the courtyard gate and into the streets, still on fire.

Everyone stood with mouths agape.

Finally, Kheiron spoke. "It is best we let that one go. His ailments are beyond my abilities to heal."

Yamin had no idea what *ailments* the doctor referred to. It certainly seemed that whatever bothered him before was now a lot worse after being on fire.

"Are you hurt?" Althea bent to help Yamin up from his spill.

"I'm fine." He was shaken up but did not mention it. He patted the dust from his robes. "What was wrong with that man?"

Before she could answer, Kheiron walked up and answered for her matter-of-factly. "He was possessed."

Yamin and Althea replied in unison. "Possessed?"

"I've seen similar cases before when I served the Legion in the Roman Army. But that was long ago when I was a much younger man. An apprentice under another physician."

Dar responded first to the doctor's incredible diagnosis of the madman. "You've seen *possessed* people before? Possessed with . . . a spirit other than their own?"

"Oh, yes. It's not something I prefer to talk of, however. Some would think me mad for evening mentioning it. But after what we all just witnessed—well, I guess we'd all be called fools if we tried to share it outside these walls, yes?" Kheiron peered through the gate as his attendants secured it. "All of them, with their gods. They say they believe." His brow furrowed. "But when any incident even hints at the supernatural, they turn their backs in disbelief." He turned to Yamin. "What was he saying to you, anyway? He ran away screaming something that sounded like, *wanting everything*."

Yamin came to grips with what the allegedly haunted man had said to him and hoped no one else heard his accusations of envy. His cheeks flushed. "I—I don't know. It was all garbled."

Dar finished picking up his coins. "How can you be so sure he was possessed? What makes you think he wasn't just crazy?"

"We all see what we want to see," said Kheiron. "Or better put, what we *allow* ourselves to see."

"Master?" It was Althea's turn to question him. "I have been working with you for over a year and have never heard you speak of such ailments. Do you think we'll see any more of him—or any others?"

Kheiron looked toward Eber in deep thought for a moment. "Demons are the peddlers of the spiritual world, my dear. They knock on your door, enticing you with their wares." He then turned toward Althea, Yamin, and Dar and continued sternly. "But you must resist by not answering. A *no soliciting* sign is not enough. Action must be taken to avoid their temptations." He walked back to care for Eber.

Yamin and Althea turned to console a clearly distraught Dar.

Dar's voice shook. "I thought I was done for."

"You're lucky," said Althea. "Yamin didn't see this, but that man was never headed for you at all. He was running toward the patient to your right. You covered your eyes and Yamin was still trying to catch his breath in the dirt. But the man on the table rose and yelled, *Messiah saves!* The flaming man then turned and ran through the gate."

"Messiah?" asked Yamin. "Who's Messiah?"

Althea shrugged her shoulders.

They walked over to the now unconscious man. His shallow breaths filtered through overgrown facial hair. Pallid skin clung to his bones.

"Just like mother had been," said Yamin quietly. *And now father.*

"Your mother has this illness, as well?"

"She did . . ." He glowered at her. "Until last night, when she died." Yamin let out a deep sigh. He swung around, searching for Kheiron, then raised his voice and spoke with malice. "Is there anything your doctor can do for my father? Or will he end up like these others, wasting away until there is nothing left but skin and bones?"

Yamin's pulse quickened while his inhibitions lessened. Those around him seemed the easiest targets. His mother had died, his father was too weak to even walk home, a madman attacked him, and he was about to sell his freedom to pay for services that might not work anyway. What else could go wrong?

Althea stood clearly taken aback. She sighed. "He will do his best." She turned and walked away, leaving the boys with the unconscious man.

Yamin watched yet again as someone he had feelings for left him. *What is* wrong *with me? I'm as cursed as my parents.* He wondered how much longer Dar would continue to be his friend if the situation continued to get any worse than it was already.

5

After waiting and getting no immediate reply from Kheiron about his offer, Yamin and Dar left with Althea's promise that word would be sent before long.

Dar waited until they had walked well away from the physician's home to speak. "My parents will want to know how things went?"

Yamin stopped and looked at Dar. "How do you think they'll respond if we tell them what we saw?"

Dar turned and walked again. "My thoughts exactly."

Dar's mother greeted them with a smile. "Yamin, you're welcome to stay until you feel well enough to head home." She returned to her chore of preparing dinner. "Kheiron is a fine physician. You know, when Dar's father broke his finger last winter, he was home before sunset and—" She slowly turned toward Yamin and showered him with a look of embarrassment.

Yamin managed a weak smile.

She continued working but spoke to the wall. "Not the same, is it?"

Yamin shook his head. After being rude to Althea earlier, he would control his anger. Keeping his mouth shut proved a successful way to accomplish this.

"I'll go fetch some water." She rested her hands on both boys' shoulders as she passed by. "Why don't you three start dinner without us?" She motioned for Dar's sister to join them.

Shortly after, there was a knock on the door.

Dar opened it to reveal one of Kheiron's male servants.

Yamin's head dropped. *Not Althea. My fault.* Considering how he treated her, it was no surprise.

The young visitor was all business. "I have been sent to inform you that the payment of eleven copper coins and an order of fresh fish twice weekly for two months will be sufficient payment for the medical services Master Kheiron is providing."

Yamin did not know whether to celebrate or curse his situation further. He should have been pleased with the chance to make payments in his own way. But there was still so much at stake. Would he be able to provide the expenditures? Could he work the family boat alone? Was his father going to get better?

Early the next morning, the boys ate breakfast while describing the previous day's events to Dar's parents.

Waking up at Dar's house was nothing new for Yamin. Over the years, he had spent many nights there enjoying what the wealthy had to offer. The softer beds, better food, and everything seemed easier. They even had interior plumbing. Why did *he* not have these things?

Yamin's mind dwelt on their rare relationship. Most wealthy citizens of the city did not care to associate with those of the lower class. It would be social suicide. But Yamin and Dar proved different.

When the boys were much younger, around five, Dar's parents took a short holiday at the lake. They had no interest in traveling far, and certainly not to a town like Tiberias. They only wanted to hire a boat for a few hours to tour the lake and give their young son a new experience.

Nearby, Yamin helped his father and uncle in the minimal capacity that a five-year-old could. He would fetch tools or hold a board. Any simple job to expose him to the skills needed to become a fisherman like his father.

Their boat had been pulled onshore for repairs. This used to be Eber's father's boat, so keeping the aged vessel seaworthy challenged them.

Eber reached into a small, worn, leather pouch at his waist. "We're out of nails."

Eber's older brother gave a dismissive wave without looking up while working on the port side. "Send Yamin to fetch them."

"Yamin, go to the dock and bring back the sack of nails."

Yamin nodded and ran off eager to help. When he reached the pier, he heard splashing from below and moved to investigate. He found a young boy struggling to stay afloat and choking on water. Already a strong swimmer, Yamin jumped in without hesitation, grabbed the boy's arm, and pulled him to the shallows.

A pair of panicking adults ran to the shore to join them.

Since then, Dar's parents had been forever grateful. The special circumstances causing their lives to intertwine had been enough to convince them to allow the boys' friendship to continue despite the overly segregated society. They showed their appreciation by always including Yamin when he visited their home.

At breakfast, Sophus finished his water and handed the cup to his wife for a refill. With a furrowed brow, he spoke to Yamin. "Considering what you've endured, it's good not to become the physician's servant, yes?"

Dar agreed. "Thank the gods."

Yamin swallowed his last bite of food hard. "The gods had nothing to do with it, Dar. I think it was Althea who helped convince Kheiron. Even though I could've been nicer."

"Well, you put your faith in man. I'll put my faith in the gods."

After breakfast, Yamin shared his idea with Dar. "I'm going to put my father's boat back in the lake."

"Are you sure it'll float? I mean, he hasn't taken it out in quite a while, right?"

"I'll do my best. I want to start making good on my deal with Kheiron as soon as possible. And that's the only way to make it happen." He only half-believed he could pull it off alone.

After thanking Dar's parents for their hospitality, Yamin made his way home. He sent word with Dar to inform Kheiron he would deliver the fish and check in on his father within the week.

"I'd come and help, but—" Dar motioned toward his father's studio.

Yamin nodded and turned to leave through the city's gate. *Like Dar needs the money.* But would Yamin be able to carry out this chore alone?

Within an hour he returned home to gather supplies and then arrived at the boat. He knew what still needed attention to make the vessel seaworthy. The only other task was to get help with getting the boat back into the water. He could set up rollers by himself, but it would be foolish to attempt the move alone.

Before starting, he took a step back and studied the aged craft. It spanned slightly wider than an average man's height and nearly three times as long. Eber, his uncle, and his grandfather before them had all been experienced boatwrights. But they lacked proper raw materials for the boat's upkeep. Cleverness and the determination to keep it floating had been enough—so far.

From a distance, one would think the mottling on the surface stemmed from poor eyesight or the way the sun's light reflected from the water onto the slick wood. But upon closer inspection, it was the many types of lumber used in its original construction and in the years of subsequent repairs to the hull that showed their true colors.

Yamin's grandfather had constructed the boat from timbers salvaged from other abandoned boats. He also used locally available, yet substandard, wood. Cedar was the most prevalent, while other sections replaced after his grandfather's death were pine, jujube, and willow, with oak for fasteners. Pine sap sealed the seams but bitumen pitch, a tar-like substance derived from the Dead Sea region, lay smeared over the whole underside.

It took Yamin the remainder of the day to exact the last of the repairs to the hull and the single mast that had softened at its base due to rot. Since he had no wood, new or used, to fashion a different mast, nor any money to purchase another, he simply sawed off the bottom and reinstalled it into the old mast box.

A little shorter, but it'll do the job. He smiled at his ingenuity.

Several of his father's fellow fishermen came over to watch. Yamin ignored them until they spoke.

"Your sail won't fill with enough air if you do that."

Another said, "You know what they say about fishermen with short masts."

The men laughed and pointed at Yamin.

A surly angler with a dirty scarf wrapped around his forehead approached as Yamin finished up. "The narrow width of the base will cause the box to crack after long."

To preserve what little pride he had left, he answered the man without glancing up. "I know."

"Then what do you propose to do about it?"

Yamin could not answer. Instead, he smacked his mallet on the hull. "Just leave me alone, Baniy."

"As stubborn as your father."

Baniy had always been one of Eber's most bothersome competitors. Everyone competed, but Baniy seemed to always be close by, and Yamin didn't trust him.

Eber would throw his net over the side, and there Baniy sailed with his boat. Yamin would be sent to purchase flax for net making, and there Baniy stood buying the last of it. Yamin's mother would sell fish at the market, and there Baniy was yelling louder to sell his.

Baniy wanted to partner with Eber after Yamin's uncle passed, but Eber would not have it. This made Yamin's work harder. But if Baniy did not get his way, Yamin remained satisfied.

Night fell upon Yamin's work, and he had to stop. His plan to take the boat out as early as possible and try his hand at fishing for the first time alone had gotten off to a good start. But getting the boat into the water remained a task to tackle at sunrise.

Yamin woke at dawn to an empty house. Only the second time he had done so in his lifetime. He could not allow his fear of being alone to hamper his efforts at helping his father. Breakfast would wait.

He approached the shore, but his father's boat was nowhere to be seen.

6

Yamin's heart pounded, and he found it hard to swallow. His only option to pay for his father's medical needs had vanished.

I'll kill whoever did this.

He marched off to the port where his father often docked his boat. It took only ten minutes to walk south. He made it his goal to ask everyone he met if they had seen anything. But first, the portmaster's office.

Before he saw a single person, there the boat sat, docked where his father usually kept it, tied up and remarkably afloat. Yamin swept his head from side-to-side searching for the responsible parties. Finding it intact made no difference in his level of outrage.

Baniy exited a small stone building that served as the main port storage. Several other men, all acquaintances of Yamin's father, followed Baniy out. They watched Yamin with mischievous grins pasted upon their haggard faces.

"You found it," bellowed Baniy. The other men laughed in unison.

Yamin sneered. *Not funny.*

"Come now, Yamin. The men felt sorry for Eber's loss and illness. They wanted to help his son."

Yamin remained unmoved. He shouldered his way past Baniy and stomped toward the dock.

Baniy and the others followed him. "We moved it while you slept. Come now. Don't be angry."

Yamin bounded wildly into the boat and almost toppled overboard.

More laughs. Great.

He untied the lines and shoved off, the whole time ignoring the men. With little breeze to aid him, he had to oar the heavy water-soaked boat away. The men continued their chaffing as he struggled to put distance between them.

He nearly exhausted himself getting out of earshot of his hecklers. When he could no longer hear them well enough to discern their taunts, Yamin allowed himself a respite from the oars. He sat in silence, breathed deeply, and focused on nothing but his disdain for those men who had teased him.

A breath of cold wind swept the calm water and spilled over the side and into the boat.

"You hate them."

Yamin froze. He scanned the gloomy horizon searching for the source of the ghostly statement. He turned his head slowly, first to port and then to starboard. He craned his neck over the edge to see if anyone held on to the boat from within the water.

Nothing.

An uneasy hour passed while he fiddled with the nets and rigging waiting for that strange voice to return. Yet it had not uttered another word. The morning mist cleared enough from the surface of the lake for him to see a meaningful distance. The fog of contention had cleared in his mind as well. A small number of boats passed in the distance, some fishing and others transporting goods. Otherwise, he sat alone, his own thoughts occupying his mind.

He closed his eyes and let out a long sigh celebrating the solitude. Normally, his father would be on the boat with him, barking orders but at the same time making the casting and hauling nets far easier. Only once before had he taken the boat out singlehandedly but was severely chastised for it.

As a child of ten years, Yamin had heard stories of pirates coming inland from the Great Sea to the west to hide their loot in and around the lake. His father forbade him to succumb to such tales. The temptation proved too great. Yamin managed to sail an hour north before his father's acquaintance apprehended him. He had been told to lookout for the runaway treasure hunter.

Eber's fishing nets varied in size depending upon the species of fish sought. Yamin purposefully packed one of the smallest yesterday in the hopes he could handle it alone. The flax fibers chafed his fingers as he gathered up the tattered ends. He folded it perfectly over his arm. Its aged coarseness triggered heartrending childhood memories of him and his mother sitting on the shore, mending the nets on a warm summer day.

He hoisted the net above the port side of the boat and cast it into the still water. It slipped down into the inky depths. To his horror, he realized he had forgotten to secure it to the boat.

As the net slid from view, Yamin grabbed the gunwale with one hand and jumped into the water reaching wildly for the sinking net's line. He caught the end of the rebellious rope but it was heavy. He had just enough strength to hold on.

"Need any help over there!" A deep voice called from across the water.

Yamin did not answer. He strained to secure the net but found nothing to tie it to. He looked across the boat and found the only cleat to be on the starboard side. Grunting, he pulled himself around the stern and to the starboard gunwale. He haphazardly secured the line to the worn wooden fastener and pulled himself inside, falling onto the deck, gasping for air.

The mariner who called out had now made his way over and pulled alongside. Yamin looked up.

Baniy peered over the edge. "Lotta boat for a young man."

Loves to state the obvious.

Baniy's complexion, dark and wrinkled by many years of exposure to sunlight, revealed his maturity. His deep brown robes made Yamin wonder if they had gotten that way from filth or if they had aged the same as his skin.

Yamin sat up with a sigh. "I can handle it. I grew up fishing with my father, remember?"

"Your father, huh? You would have thrown him overboard with your net if he were here." Baniy laughed intensely at his own gibe.

Can never resist a laugh, no matter how it makes others feel. "Leave me alone, Baniy. Can't you see I'm working . . . to make *him* better?" Yamin stood to haul in the errant netting from the starboard edge, a side of the boat he would use for casting nets from now on.

"A valiant effort." Baniy remained alongside Yamin's boat until the netting had been hauled in. "Could help you a while, if you'd like." His yellow teeth reflected the morning sunlight, transforming beauty into repulsion.

Yamin wrestled with the net, now wet and heavier than before. "I'm—afraid—I don't have the time."

"Time," remarked the old sailor. "A lot can be said about time." He sat in his boat and looked out upon the now clear air above the sea.

"Oh?" Yamin now held part of the net in his teeth while trying to untangle it. *Come on, stupid net.*

"Yes. Take yourself, for example. A boy with all his years ahead of him who says to an old sailor like me that he *doesn't have the time.* Now, if those words came from someone like your father— Well, I think you get my point."

Yamin replayed what Baniy said inside his head, pausing only a moment to do so. *Mother doesn't have to worry about time anymore.* "What are you talking about? If I could make the day go any faster, I would. Then I'd have all the fish I need to pay my debt. So, if you'll be on your way."

Baniy gently shoved off and left Yamin alone. Struggling or not, he would do this by himself.

After more trial and error, Yamin got the hang of the net and even managed to pull in a few fish before sundown. He returned to shore to deliver his catch to the doctor, save one for his own meal. The temptation to wait until morning waned, as the deal to deliver fresh fish, not day-old fish, prevailed.

He trekked all the way up to the town and to the doctor's home. He knocked on the door.

Althea answered and greeted him with a diminutive smile that turned quickly to a frown.

He closed his eyes for moment. *Don't say anything embarrassing.* Holding up the basket of fish, he opened his mouth to speak.

She saved him the effort. "Come quickly. It's your father."

Instead of sending him around to the courtyard gate like last time, she guided Yamin through the doctor's house. He had never been in such an ornately decorated home before. Statues and stone vessels of all shapes and sizes festooned the walls and floors. Did Kheiron bring something back from everywhere he traveled around the known world? Or were these payments from patients without gold like himself? He wanted to stop and peek inside each one to see what treasures they held, but the drive to get to his father outweighed his curiosity.

Lying silently on the table where he had left him days ago, Eber exhibited the same shallow, labored breathing as his mother had just before her demise.

"What happened? I thought—I thought Kheiron could heal this type of illness."

"Your father was too sick for the doctor to stop it from taking him. He doesn't have much time."

Baniy.

"I smell fish." A voice called from inside the house. Kheiron exited. "Oh, young man. I did not know you had arrived at this late hour." He looked at Althea and motioned for her to join him.

Althea walked to Kheiron, and they both reentered the house, leaving Yamin alone.

The light from the courtyard fire flickered upon the walls. Another patient's cough broke the silence. How could it have come to this point? How did he lose his entire family so quickly? For a moment he wished he would get the sickness and join them all.

Eber snapped awake. His eyes searched for something familiar.

"I'm here, Father."

His weak voice issued forth. "Yamin . . . my son."

"Yes, Father." Yamin took his hand. Its softness contradicted what he remembered, as a slippery substance now coated them. It had the consistency of olive oil but far more fragrant, more pungent.

Eber whispered. "I waited for your return. I need to tell you—" A coughing fit interrupted his speech, and it nearly sent him into unconsciousness. Yamin turned to call for Althea, but his father stopped him. "I gave up, my son. I'm sorry."

"What are you talking about? You were always there for Mother and me."

"I don't want . . . to be a burden."

"You could never be—"

"Ever since your mother grew sick, I knew I would be next. I . . . I wanted to be next. It was . . . too much for me to handle." His feeble breathing caused Yamin to lower his ear to his father's mouth to make out his words. "You have to leave here, Yamin. Leave before the illness takes you too."

Yamin straightened. "I can't leave. Not now. I've struck a deal, Father. For your treatment."

"My son, you were always . . . so . . . sincere." With that, Eber gave his last breath.

"Father?" Yamin backed away from the now lifeless body.

The wood fueling the fire shifted. Lighter-than-air embers drifted into the sky above the courtyard walls.

Althea approached and placed her hand upon Yamin's shoulder with a gentle touch.

He did not react.

"I'm so sorry, Yamin."

"He gave up." Yamin's eyes welled with tears. "He just gave up on me." His throat tightened. He had already lost his faith in the gods. Now his faith in humanity was exhausted.

"Yamin, I—"

Yamin soft voice grew bitter. "Tell the doctor he'll receive his fish as agreed upon." He turned and hastened through the courtyard gates.

7

A month of fish deliveries passed before Yamin spoke to anyone with purpose. He spent most of his time across the lake near Capernaum. Seven warm springs fed into the water just south of the city making it the prime fishing spot for the winter months.

With winter came the cold. Flakes that typically stayed in the higher region to the east had found their way to the shore twice during the past month.

Although the snow did not remain past noon, it made preparing the boat a challenge for Yamin. New to these conditions, his fingers numbed while untying the moorings. He shook his hands in vain to warm them.

On a typical day, more than 200 boats worked the lake. His competition was fierce, but Yamin had gained some legitimacy. His determination and small successes inspired his competitors.

Baniy lumbered toward Yamin from the portmaster's building. He remained true to his meddlesome nature, regardless of the weather conditions or Yamin's level of proficiency. "I could save you a lot of trouble with your lines. Your hands would be warmer too."

Yamin remained true to his hardheadedness. *Can you just stay away from me?* He turned from Baniy then breathed on his hands to warm them.

Baniy bent to untie the boat from the dock. Before Yamin could stop him, he re-secured the boat to the mooring with a knot Yamin had never seen before. "Other knots, perhaps ones your father taught you, are terrific for warmer weather. But this one allows a quick untie with a swift pull from just one hand. See?" Baniy grabbed the end of the rope and yanked. The lines slid past one another with ease and the knot fell apart.

Yamin drove an expressionless look at him. "Thank you."

"Not even the frost of a winter morning can slow you down now, yes?"

"I said, *thank you.*"

Baniy laughed off Yamin's rudeness and returned to prepare his own vessel.

After a particularly long day on the lake, Yamin made his way back to port to unload his meager catch of sardines. Although his fishing skills had improved, he had to learn to pull in catches as his father and uncle had done. He drew close to shore.

Dar waited for him not ten steps from the very spot where Yamin had rescued him all those years ago. Dar never went in the water since, but sometimes came to the lake with his sister to visit Yamin. This time he was alone.

"Dar! This is a surprise." Yamin tossed the bow line around a pole but stayed in the boat. "Are your parents nearby or did you sneak away again?"

Dar smirked. "You're not fooling anybody, Yamin."

Yamin nonchalantly threw fish from the day's catch into a worn-out basket on the dock without making eye contact. "What do you mean? I'm paying off a debt and trying to survive out here."

"You haven't been to see me in a month, yet you pass by my house twice a week. I know you're grieving, but don't punish me because of it."

"What do you know of grief? You sit in your nice house, eating your fancy food—with your family. All I have is myself and this old boat."

"I thought *we* were family, Yamin."

Yamin paused for a moment. Foul words rose from within and forced themselves upon his tongue. But he clenched his teeth, kept his mouth shut, and continued working.

Dar moved the basket of fish making it harder for Yamin to continue. "I'm not sure if you've heard the news, but there haven't been any new cases of the disease since . . . since your deal with Master Kheiron. My father thinks—"

Yamin swung his head toward Dar. "I don't care what your father thinks!" Saliva sprayed into the water as he spoke.

Dar flinched and stood silently while Yamin kept working. "Goodbye, Yamin." He strode off, then turned once more. "Oh, I paid off your debt to the doctor. I guess you have no more reason to come into town." He walked toward the city.

Yamin opened his mouth to speak but turned back to his catch. *What is* wrong *with me?* He slammed his fist down upon a small fish that had fallen onto the seat. The creature's scales sloughed off into his hand and its belly split open squirting innards onto the boat's hull. He rubbed the scales between his fingers, trying his best to truly see the texture. But the sensation eluded him.

"*More.*" The menacing voice seemed to come from every direction.

Yamin swept his head around. He was alone, save for a few fishermen several boats away.

He continued to feel the dead sardine. It seemed . . . duller than usual. This only made him angrier. He smashed the fish again, and again, until nothing but a bloody pulp of raw fish paste remained.

Some of the other men stared his way.

"What are you looking at?" snarled Yamin as he threw an unmolested fish in their direction.

The onlookers scoffed and went about their business.

Several months passed. The short and stormy winter gave way to warmer days on the lake. The spring brought storms too, but gentler than those of winter.

The fishing improved in some areas, but Yamin still hesitated to try the coast directly across the lake. Fishermen from Tiberias controlled that area, and he already experienced, on more than one occasion, the inhospitable response offered to any who trespassed on their waters.

While sailing one morning around the Tiberias coastline, the winds blew counter to his direction. Yamin needed to tack back and forth or give up altogether and head east toward home. Before making his decision, the poorly fitted mast box finally cracked in the strong breeze. His sail listed to one side, and the wind blew him right into waters he dared not go, even when his father had captained the boat.

Within minutes, two fishermen in separate boats approached him from the west with the wind at their backs. Their disdain for him rang out as they yelled across the water.

"Ahoy, pagan! Go home, heathen!"

They threw stones at him.

"Go to Hell for living without Elohim!"

"Sheol take you for worshipping other gods!"

He tried desperately to secure the mast with forestay and backstay lines. Every time he came close, a rock would hit him. *They carry rocks in their boats?*

The Jewish men sideswiped his boat as they passed.

Yamin almost fell overboard but another pomegranate-sized stone struck him in his ribs and knocked him back.

Two more boats approached.

Could this be the end? He wildly flung anything he could at the boats. His tools, baskets, anything not tied down.

Another stone made contact. This time on his knee.

"*Kill!*"

The ugly speech he heard months ago filled his ears once more.

He swung around to see if someone had climbed upon his vessel. No one. In a blind rage, he lifted the heavy anchor above his head in an effort to throw it at the nearest boat.

"Yamin, stop!"

He lowered the stone.

The two attacking boats turned and fled.

He recognized the new arrivals as Baniy and another fisherman from Hippos.

Blood trickled from Yamin's forehead stinging his right eye. He dropped the anchor on a folded net. His vision blurred as he fell into the bottom of the boat.

8

Yamin woke in a one-room workplace. He looked around from the straw mat where he lay. *This isn't home.* The mud brick hut he found himself in had no feminine influences. His head throbbed. He tried to sit up but his stomach rebelled.

A table with scrolls, a lamp, and a scribe's tools stood in the far corner accompanied by a solitary chair. A large wooden cabinet with shelves was the only other piece of furniture in the room. It rested against the wall to the right of the doorway. A single window above Yamin let in bright morning light. A roughly drawn map of the lake and its harbors hung on the wall, pierced by rusty iron nails—the same fasteners used in boat building.

He tried to sit up a second time. "Oh, my head."

Baniy's familiar voice issued from the entranceway where he leaned silhouetted against the jamb. "Better stay put, for now. You took quite a blow. No thanks to those *skybalon*."

Just past Baniy, the humble building overlooked other various port buildings and the southern stone jetty supporting the docks below.

The gruff, aged portmaster pushed weakly past Baniy and entered the room. "No need for such vulgarity, Baniy." He lowered himself into his chair. "How much longer?" The city-appointed position of portmaster was one lasting until death. The current master was not far from the end of his appointment.

Baniy entered after the portmaster. "I'll take him home as soon as he feels well enough to walk."

"Take me home? No one has to take me home. I can go myself."

Yamin made a third attempt to right himself but almost vomited from the vertigo.

After making a note on a scroll, the portmaster stood. Before he left, he turned to Baniy. "Make it quick. I'm too busy for this." He nodded once in Yamin's direction. "Sorry about your father." He turned and exited.

Once alone, Baniy took advantage of the empty chair and sat facing Yamin.

Yamin wanted nothing more than to leave and be alone. But Baniy always showed up. "What do you want from me, Baniy? My father often spoke of your meddlesome behavior in his affairs. Have you come to be *my* shadow in his absence?"

"Oh, I'm flattered you've come to realize I've been a part of your life for so long." He rested his heels on the table and smiled.

Typical. "All I want is to be left alone, with my own thoughts. Why can't anyone understand that?"

"Your own thoughts. Ha!"

Yamin's head tilted to the right. "What did you say?"

"I said, I'm flattered."

Yamin tried to shake off the emotion suddenly overtaking him. It felt as if someone invaded his personal space, stealing the little comfort afforded him. His skin crawled. The only other person in the room was Baniy.

Yamin craned his neck. "Is there someone outside the window?"

"There are many people outside, as always. Are you all right?" Baniy put his feet down and straightened up to see through the paneless window.

"I don't know." Yamin tapped on his temple with the heel of his palm. "I think I'm hearing voices."

"Probably because you took a stone to your skull." Baniy put his feet back up. "You know, if I had left you alone out there, you'd be floating belly-up in the lake, and those Tiberian *skybalon* would have either scuttled your father's boat or taken it for their fleet. I would have abandoned the pathetic thing." He chuckled.

Yamin ignored Baniy's comment. *I really was fortunate.* He took a deep breath. "Thank you, Baniy."

Baniy's eyes widened. "You're welcome. But I must say my debt is now paid." Baniy pulled a knife out from under his belt. He cleaned his nails of what seemed like a year's worth of filth.

"Debt?" Yamin sat up once again and rubbed his temples. "What debt? Who would you get into debt with?"

"Your father, before he died, came to me right before your mother was laid to rest." Baniy flicked some grime from the tip of his blade. "He said, 'Baniy, I want you to watch over my son when I'm gone. He's still green and will need someone . . . experienced around.' He then gave me what I can only assume was all the money he had left to seal the deal."

Despite his headache, nausea, and the knot on his forehead, Yamin launched himself from his mat. He immediately fell to the sandy wood floor and spewed vomit at the portmaster's feet as he reentered.

"Get out. Both of you!"

Baniy dragged Yamin outside.

Yamin broke free from Baniy's grasp and crawled toward the water. Upon reaching his boat, he rolled off the dock and onto the sail and netting that lay crumpled inside.

Yamin looked up once more.

Baniy dropped a handful of coins into the boat. As each coin struck the bottom, shivers resonated through Yamin. *You left me. You left me to him.*

Baniy shook his head slowly and walked away.

The crippled vessel served as Yamin's home for the next two nights until he felt well enough to make the short trip back to his house.

He stayed ashore for two weeks. He had lost the desire to continue his father's business after being attacked. He needed to come to grips with his anger at his father. *How could he ask someone like*

Baniy to watch over me? What was he thinking? We could have used that money to pay the physician sooner.

He wanted nothing to do with this place—his home. Everywhere he looked, memories assaulted him, reminding him of what he had lost. *Too much pain.*

Over the next few days, he took anything of value and sold it. The shell of a home he left behind would never be occupied by anyone else. It was dilapidated and aged. *More like cursed.* He wanted to burn it down to save others from having to look at it.

"No. That will draw attention."

He refused to look around this time. Instead, he closed his eyes. *Must be in my head. Yes, only in my head.* He opened one eye. No one. "Time to go."

He talked himself into leaving the region altogether. Or was it the voice telling him to leave? When he was healing, his dreams often contained an elusive presence, guiding him through unknown waters toward places he had never seen before. Maybe he was now listening to that voice. *So much the better. Anything to get away from here.*

Before turning from his childhood home forever, Yamin reached out to touch the dried mud wall and timber forming the single doorway. The wood's rugged surface splintered under his caress. He broke off a small piece. Trying his best to sense the texture, his mind wandered. Visions of far-off places and strange people filled his mind and clouded his perception. Things that would allow him to forget what he lost here. Confusion and distraction were just what he needed.

Yamin squeezed the splinter hard. The sharp end penetrated the skin of his finger, and he winced. Pain. *At least I can still feel that.*

He dropped the splinter into the dust beneath his feet, no longer caring if he could feel it or not. *My time here is over.*

The whispering voice intensified. *"Yes, it is."*

9

Yamin felt better, at least physically, so fixing the mast box took little time. He only had to make it across the lake, then dump his father's boat when it hit the shore. He left so early that the other mariners had not yet arrived at the port to start their day. Yamin wanted neither questions nor anyone to know where he went. His only desire—to disappear.

A tinge of dismay floated into his mind as he looked toward the city. *Dar's probably still asleep.* Yamin knew he had mistreated his friend. *My woes are not his fault.* Although, it did not make him feel any better that Dar would wake up soon to a family and a hearty meal. Regret turned readily to envy, and Yamin turned away from all he knew.

The air, already warm, hung still over the Sea of Galilee. He scoffed at his misfortune and grabbed the oars from a neighbor's boat. He had thrown his at those Tiberian bullies weeks ago. The cool, damp surface of the oar's blades provided no new meaning for him. The dark cloud now smothering his inhibitions, also deadened his once powerful sense of touch. A shadow in the form of a voice. He placed the oar in its holder. *Just a piece of wood now.* A tool with no more soul or history than the impermanent, temperate haze surrounding his boat. He traveled tactilely numb through the world around him.

Having powered a boat made for two grown oarsmen for several months, Yamin's muscles had grown accustomed to moving the vessel along at a suitable pace. He shoved off from the dock as several fishermen approached to make ready their own boats.

Yamin saw Baniy arrive just in time for him to disappear into the thick morning mist.

Within an hour, a small breeze picked up from the north. He hoisted the square mainsail as best he could with the poorly situated mast. The gentle wind caught the cloth and pushed the boat at an awkward angle westward. He figured he would have to tack at least three times to land on the shore between Tiberias and Capernaum. *Anywhere, as long as no one's around to see me abandon it.*

Sailing on the great lake challenged even seasoned mariners. Used to the sudden changes in wind patterns, Yamin considered himself such a person. He planned to use his skills to get hired onto a merchant vessel that would take him onto the Great Sea to the west and as far away from here as possible.

The lake had mountains on three sides which often caused the breeze to shift direction without warning. In the morning, at this time of year, cool air usually came from the north. By the early afternoon, the wind would cease completely for about an hour. When this happened, the water looked as flat as a sanded boat plank. Yamin would use this time to mend nets and sort fish into baskets, as well as enjoy a small midday meal in peace.

Imperceptibly, a delicate breeze from the west brought ripples seen in patches on the lake. When the sail caught this zephyr, a rare smooth sailing could be obtained on the shiny surface for a few miraculous minutes.

Yamin recalled with fondness that feeling when the perfectly trimmed sail allowed him to fly over the water's surface. His heart would race. He tried to remember how the wind felt on his face.

The current north wind provided nothing like that now. He heard it. He saw its action upon the sail and on the surface of the water. But he no longer *knew* the wind like he once did. The feeling diminished as he craned his neck toward the bow.

After those few minutes of smooth sailing, the wind would change so drastically that whitecaps developed upon the entire lake. This is how he felt now. A tempest raged inside of him that he could not control. Yamin allowed it to intensify, acting upon every thought popping into his mind. And like the wind, accepting it and using it to his advantage seemed the only option. Fighting what nature threw his way only bred futility.

His anger toward the Tiberians who assaulted him also grew as he sailed closer to their city.

"Go."

That voice. The same voice that addressed him before. He purposefully discounted it as the wind and stayed his course.

But the grudge he held for those wicked men prevailed. He squeezed the tiller, wringing it within his grasp.

The voice urged a second time. *"Go there."*

Clearly not the wind. Someone spoke to him. But Yamin knew pulling into the harbor at Tiberias would certainly hamper his travel to the Great Sea. He fought the prodding voice and turned a few degrees northward. Confronting those fishermen would only remind him of what he tried to leave behind.

"Go!"

Yamin uncontrollably seized the tiller with both hands and turned the boat drastically toward port. The full force of the northerly wind hit the sail at a ninety-degree angle. The boat heeled and nearly capsized.

The voice that only gently urged him earlier had now taken control and forced its will directly upon him. He knew he did not want to go to Tiberias, but he headed there, nonetheless.

He grunted as he tried to fight off the force directing his hands. All his energy only served to keep the tiller still and on course to Tiberias. Surges of anger coursed through his limbs. "If those *skybalon* get in my way, I'll kill them." Turning the frustration toward something tangible was the only way he could vent his rage.

Before long, he entered the waters controlled by the Tiberian fishermen. Unfamiliar boats floated nearby. One of them headed toward him.

"Ram them." The voice filled his ears this time, not just his mind.

"Did *I* say that?"

He would certainly sink if he succumbed to the command. He father's old boat would never withstand the force of a collision. Only wooden shims held up the mast. The only thing keeping the hull together was pitch.

"No!" His voice traveled over the water and attracted the attention of the men who had yet to see him. With all his might, he fought the impulse burning within and pushed the tiller back toward the north.

Rocks and dry grasses dotted the shoreline ahead. Yamin glanced over his shoulder. The boat he nearly collided with now followed close behind. The effort from fighting the voice squeezed and twisted his innards into painful knots. He winced and bent at the waist.

The landing site, now too close to Tiberias, provided no chance for a clandestine departure. This left little time for Yamin to gather his supplies and make it to an inland road leading west.

The hull scraped upon algae-covered rocks and stopped abruptly short of the dry beach. The force broke the already weakened mast box. The pole and its rigging crashed down onto the bow cracking open seams in the hull. Water rushed in.

Grabbing his sack of food and a set of robes once belonging to his father, Yamin leapt from starboard into the shallow waves. He turned to grab the anchor stone but remembered that he no longer cared what happened to this boat. He ran ashore.

The fisherman who had followed him yelled epithets from their boats.

Yamin's desire to disappear outweighed the temptation to return with his own verbal bombardment. Without looking back, he hastened up the slope leading away from the lake and toward the Great Sea.

10

A well-worn path ran along the rocky shoreline. Scrubby brush and trees lined both sides. The unwanted shade provided little help in drying Yamin's robes. A two-hour walk stood between Tiberias and the port city of Taricheae to the northwest.

Yamin turned his head to look over the water but snapped it back when the voice returned.

"There's nothing there for you."

He had to accept its presence. No proof existed to show this to be a temporary aberration. Somehow, he knew it was not.

The actions of the possessed man in the physician's courtyard all those months ago still haunted him. The man's screams conjured a fear that had crippled him and his friends.

Maybe possession is an incurable disease and he contracted it. It sure ended badly for that man.

Was he possessed? Had an evil spirit entered him? Or was he just crazy?

Yamin kept his eyes glued to the trail for the entire hike.

The strong smell of pickling spices, mixed with the lakeside's earthy scent, met him just before arriving in the city. His stomach growled. He quickened his pace despite aching feet.

Cliffs rose on his left. Shallow caves pocked their surface. A small outskirt village beneath the cliffs bustled with activity. He had seen these bluffs from afar while on the lake and now understood how first-time visitors to Hippos may have marveled at their height above the water.

Taricheae was known throughout the Roman and Greek world for their excellent pickling process. Large quantities of fish shipped south supplied Jerusalem during yearly feasts. Barrels of their smoked and pickled sardines were also transported around the Great Sea. Some even ended up in Hippos. Yamin only sampled them when at Dar's house. He typically ate his own catch.

He followed the lakeside road into the city and found an out-of-the-way nook against an aged building along the tree-lined main road. There he rested in the shade and ate some of what he brought along.

Many people came and went along the thoroughfare connecting the lake town to regions west. They ignored him for the most part.

Yamin smiled. "So far, so good."

The voice returned, hissing and gurgling. *"They'll know you soon enough. Know us."*

Yamin answered the voice for the first time. "I've never been this far west in my life. It's impossible for anyone to know me."

A woman walked by with two children and glanced his way. She squinted when he finished talking to himself.

Yamin winced and shook his head in defeat.

"Reputations are valuable commodities. My reputation is anarchy."

The incident on the lake with the Tiberian fishermen entered his mind. He closed his eyes. Anger seeped up from within. If only he could reach inside and rip the voice from his mind. He opened his eyes to strike.

He was alone.

A pair of larks chirped their way through the branches of the oak trees above his head. Late afternoon sunlight filtered through those same limbs into his nook. The beam's yellow spots danced with the shadows of leaves on his knees. The smell of pickling spices carried by the sea breeze lingered. His anger abated. He heard his own breath. Calm. His ability to control it remained—for now.

His father taught him that Taricheae had a prosperous ship-building trade. He also said their family had always been too poor to afford much of anything from here for his own vessel. Other than a used forward keel made from Lebanese cedar, Eber never bought another thing for his boat from here, or anywhere else for that matter. He, his father, and his brother made anything else they needed by hand, or they scavenged parts from other abandoned boats found along the shoreline. When a tenon snapped, a timber split, or a peg rotted, the men fashioned new ones from scrap or raw materials.

From what Dar had told him, artisans abounded here too. But Yamin never ventured inland enough to see if shops like that existed. He scanned the area. Vendors sold clay sculptures and pottery along the roadside, much of which depicted sailing and fishing related themes. Others displayed jewelry made of varied materials including glass, stone, and even gold. Being a port city where production, travel, and commerce were at the heart of its existence, the eclectic themes of both Jew and Greek presented themselves in the artist's work—colorful mosaics, floral patterns, and inanimate objects, for the most part.

Yamin debated staying put for the night when he overheard a conversation through the crowd. Two young men sat nearby enjoying the evening meal.

"... hear they are hiring at the port?" said one man.

"... the pay ... can make in Tiberias or Capernaum," said the other.

Yamin stared at the remains of his meager meal. He had no idea how far the Great Sea lay from here but assumed he would need at least a few days' worth of food for the journey. Heading down to the port to seek out work seemed easy enough. He should be able to earn enough in a week for more than what he needed.

The next morning, he woke at dawn. Sleeping on the hard ground made his muscles ache. A tinge of regret surfaced for what he left behind. The soft bed at home or even the fishing nets on the boat had provided cushion enough for a good rest. He shrugged it off. *Not worth it.*

Several men already stood in line outside the portmaster's door when Yamin arrived. Before long, the two he overheard yesterday joined behind him. He had no idea what the job entailed, only that they sought able-bodied men.

The murmurings grew louder as they waited. The sun had risen and reflected off the water onto the group of prospective employees. The wood door creaked open on rusted iron hinges, and the first man was finally ushered inside. It closed with a slam.

Yamin stood eighth in line.

It felt like an hour for Yamin to get to the door. The queue behind him ran fifteen men long. Every one of them looked older and more seasoned. Perspiration dotted his forehead. He could not guess at what waited for him behind the doorway.

Men laughed from within.

This isn't funny. I need to go west. Was it his demon pulling him or the desire to escape the pain? Maybe both.

After an excruciating delay, a thin pale man of perhaps forty years escorted the last interviewee out and invited Yamin inside with a flick of his bony finger. He trembled in his robes as he spoke. "Sit."

Two seats presented themselves. One near the portmaster's table and another next to the door. Yamin looked back and forth at the two.

The pale man rolled his sunken eyes and pointed to the rickety three-legged stool nearest the table. "Here."

Other than the stool, the one-room building looked almost identical to the portmaster's office in Hippos. *Does a rule exist requiring portmasters everywhere to have a set amount of square space and only certain kinds of furniture?*

"We need boat builders." The gruff portmaster's scroll-strewn desk muffled his voice.

Is there another rule requiring all port masters to be bad-tempered? He craned his neck to look over the pile of papyrus and found the shortest man he had ever seen.

Yamin slumped and looked away. "I have—some experience."

"Some?" The master stood, stepped out from behind the table, and looked Yamin over. "They call me Nanos. Take a good look." Nanos turned once in place.

Yamin widened his eyes as he heeded the portmaster's command. Dark brown ink marred Nanos' nearly bald head, as well as his stubby fingers. His light-pink woolen cloak hung over a simple linen tunic and leather belt.

"How old are you, boy?"

"I'm sixteen. I grew up fishing and repairing boats." He pluralized boat to sound more experienced. In truth, his father's boat had been made from many different boats.

"But have you ever worked in a yard? Commercial boats, boy?" Yamin hesitated.

"Lie to him."

Yamin uttered an obscenity at his demon under his breath.

"What did you say?" Nanos walked in front of the table.

The pale man moved closer.

"Nothing," he said quickly. "I mean, I . . . I . . ."

"Lie!" The demon's voice echoed in his head.

"I have experience." Not directly dishonest. But the absence of the truth still counted as a lie.

"You're too young, boy." Nanos turned around and sat behind the scrolls once more. "What experience could you possibly have that would benefit my business?" He dismissed him with a wave of his hand and returned to his ledgers.

The pale aid then moved to escort Yamin out.

"Please. Wait." Yamin rose from his tiny stool. "I've lost everything. I—I just need work. *Any* job will do."

Nanos stood and looked him over again. He spoke as he wrote on a small piece of scroll. "I wasn't supposed to be a dwarf, you know."

Yamin watched and wished he could read the note.

"They tell me my mother, while carrying me inside, looked upon another dwarf, and that is how I came to be." Nanos rolled up the scroll and tied it with a string. "I had lost *everything* once, even before I was your age." He handed the scroll to Yamin over the pile of parchment. "Take this to the other side of the harbor. To the pickling works. Maybe *they* can put your boat-building skills to good use."

Yamin looked at Nanos, at the scroll, at the pale man, and then back to the portmaster.

Nanos boomed from behind the scrolls. "Go."

Yamin jumped back into the stool and knocked it over.

The pale man escorted him to the door.

As Yamin walked away he heard the pale man order the next in line to enter.

A pickling factory? he said to himself. *I told him I had experience building boats, not pickling fish.*

The men in line chuckled.

He turned and leered at them.

The power of his maniacal visage immediately weakened the men's sense of humor. They turned away and straightened their line.

Yamin walked with slow strides, kicking small rocks from his path. *What did I do wrong in there?* He kicked a larger piece of limestone and stubbed his toe. He winced. Would he make enough money anywhere in this port city to continue?

The pickling and smoking works consisted of a series of buildings on the northern side of the harbor. Many wooden barrels lay stacked outside. Their aged and cracked surfaces stood out, while others in a separate pile appeared to be newly manufactured.

Several men worked around the buildings. Some carried baskets of salt. Others sawed and shaved planks of oak.

Yamin's unfamiliarity with the strange wood they used didn't deter him. They had stacked it in tall piles off to the side of the work area. Although oak trees grew here, shipbuilders used other types of wood. And oak was only used as a fastener in his father's boat.

These coopers, or barrel-makers, seemed engrossed in their work. He watched for a moment, searching for someone free enough to ask a question.

After a minute, one of the men walked toward him to add wood to a fire.

Yamin brushed his hair with his fingers and straightened up. "Can you tell me who's in charge here?"

"Who's asking?"

The brawny man's beard impressed Yamin. It reminded him of his uncle's beard, curly and dark. Sawdust littered his whiskers.

"I'm looking for work." Yamin thrust out his hand to give him Nanos' scroll.

The man laughed haughtily without taking the note then pointed to the building nearest them.

Yamin followed the man's lead, walked past the workers, and entered the structure.

Empty.

Soon after, the bearded man he just met walked to the door and stood at the threshold.

"How old are you, boy? Nanos has now taken it upon himself to send me *boys* to build my barrels, yes?" He reached out his hand to take the scroll.

Yamin handed it to him.

He opened it.

Yamin had the feeling he already knew what was written. He thrust out his chest. "I have *years* of experience working with wood."

"We don't build boats here . . ." He looked at Yamin expectantly.

"Yamin. My name is Yamin, son of Eber." He stammered and fiddled with his robe. *Why did I use* his *name?* "I'm from—I come from the east."

"I am Allown, owner of this facility."

"I'm willing to learn." A hint of impatience clung to Yamin's words.

"Most men come to me with no experience. All right, I'll give you a chance. You'll work as an apprentice under Vlasis."

"Apprentice? You mean, work for free?" A forlorn expression spread across his face.

Allown laughed. "Of course, young man. You don't think I am going to hire you for a denarius when you've never built a cask before, do you?" He waited for an answer. "I'll provide meals and a place to sleep until you've proven yourself. A couple of weeks should be all you need."

Yamin shook his head in disbelief and looked Allown in the eyes. He clenched his teeth. "I *have* experience. Just show me what to do and I'll do it."

Allown squinted thoughtfully at Yamin and took a deep breath. "I'll tell you what—Yamin. I don't like your insolent tone." He turned toward the door. "But I'll give you one chance. You show me you can build a functioning barrel by the end of the day tomorrow, without help, and I'll start paying you." He looked at Yamin fiercely. "But if not, you can seek work elsewhere, and the apprenticeship offer is invalid."

"All or nothing, huh? I agree."

"See you tomorrow then?" Allown exited.

Allown watched Yamin leave the building, expecting the young man to keep walking, perhaps never to see him again.

Instead, Yamin turned and talked to one of the workers who shaped the staves of wood that made the sides of the barrels.

He continued to study Yamin as he worked with that cooper through the entire process of shaping the staves and joining them together under an iron hoop.

For the next hour, Yamin moved through the succession of workers while Allown observed in amazement from a distance. The final step involved making the heads, or tops and bottoms, of each barrel.

The cooper showed Yamin the method. They had to be custom fit to each barrel made.

In the end, Yamin experienced the entire process before the sun had set.

The workers filed out of the workshop for the night.

Allown was impressed with Yamin's determination. *Maybe his attitude will change.*

11

A dry-docked fishing boat served as Yamin's bed. The familiar smells and sounds of harbor life allowed him to sleep straight through the night. He leapt over the side without checking to see if anyone watched and relieved his bladder without caring again.

He walked toward the strong scent of pickling spices and arrived at the barrel-making facility before anyone else. He started by shaping raw pieces of oak into barrel staves. That would prove his worth to Vlasis and Allown.

When Allown arrived, Yamin had already finished shaving and piecing the staves for one barrel and had begun joining them with an iron hoop.

Allown approached. "You know, that metal comes all the way from Ptolemais."

Yamin grunted while trying to fit the hoop over the staves. "Really? I—I don't know where that is." *I don't care.*

"You've never heard of the greatest seaport in Galilee? Ha!" Pointing to the west, Allown continued. "It's a full day's walk from here."

"Well, I've *heard* of it. I just didn't know this metal came from there."

Allown leaned against a stack of oak. "Great metal working industry there."

Vlasis approached, and his face lit up. He spoke with a heavy lisp reminiscent of a snake's hiss. "I'm sshhocked." He chuckled when Yamin struggled slightly.

Allown left Vlasis with Yamin.

Vlasis reached over to help.

Yamin bumped him away with his hip and grunted. "I can do this—by myself.

"Fine. But sshhomone ought to teacchh you sshhome mannersshh, boy." Vlasis went about constructing a new barrel from scratch, several strides away.

By midday, Yamin's standoffish behavior had successfully annoyed every cooper along the manufacturing line. Their glares and whispers irritated him in return. Everyone attempted to help, but he had something to prove. He would show them all, whether they liked him or not.

He only had two more steps to complete his barrel. Beads of sweat dripped from his forehead and stuck his tunic to his back.

Without stopping for the midday meal, as the other men had, he continued in rebellious fashion to complete his first barrel.

Allown stood by as Yamin hammered the chime, or top iron hoop, sealing the head of the barrel until it could be used for pickling fish later. "You've done well, Yamin, son of Eber."

Yamin curled his lip. "Don't call me that."

Allown looked at Yamin and shook his head slowly. A frown grew where a proud smile was moments ago. "I have bad news and I have good news. Which do you want first?"

"I see no bad news." Yamin continued to work no longer making eye contact.

"That's part of your problem, impudent young man."

Yamin stood upright and glared at Allown. His cheeks grew warm.

"You see, something's bothering you—eating you up from the inside. Before I can have you working for me—really, before anyone who I know in this town will hire you, you'll need to modify how you conduct yourself with others."

"*Strike him.*"

The voice. *No, not again. Not now.* Yamin's eyes darted back and forth searching for the source. He answered it aloud. "No."

"No?" Allown stood in amazement. "You will *not* be changing how you treat your coworkers? Your employer?"

"Strike . . . him . . . now!"

Yamin stood stiffly trying to fight the urge to raise his hand. He took a hesitant step forward. His fist seemed to rise with a mind of its own.

Allown took a step back, looked over Yamin's shoulder, and nodded at someone once slowly.

From behind Yamin, a strong pair of arms wrapped themselves around his, pinning them to his sides. His legs flailed in a vain attempt to kick his assailant.

Vlasis carried Yamin to the facility's boundary and threw him to the ground.

Allown walked up next to Vlasis. "Here's the good news." He threw a denarius at Yamin as he lay upon the ground covered in the dust that clung to his sweaty skin.

Yamin stood, spat at the coopers, and cursed them. He bent to pick up the money.

Without warning, the force inside released him.

Yamin heard diminishing laughter as he regained control over his limbs. Shock spread across his face. *How could I have let that voice control me? Ruin my only chance?* He gazed at the men, blinked twice to govern the tears that welled up, then tore wildly down the road and away from the harbor.

The duality penetrating his mind wore on him. Yamin ran until he got to the nook in the wall where he spent his first night in the city. He plopped onto the ground, curled up, and wept.

His mother's face swept through his thoughts. Childhood memories of his parents stabbed like sharp knives in his gut. Visions of Dar's family sitting around the table eating a meal sent his mind whirling.

What is wrong *with me? Am I going mad?*

The voice answered him. *"Yes, you are."*

"Shut up!"

Others on the road had been victims of Yamin's curses as he

ran through the town. They ignored him for the most part. Some followed him to see what he was about. As they witnessed this breakdown, they stepped back to give him space.

"*I'll never shut up.*" The voice grew kinder. "*I am part of you—Yamin.*"

"No. No!" Yamin wrapped his arms around his head and tried to block out the voice.

"*You know me, Yamin. We met at the doctor's home, remember?*"

Yamin froze. He *had* heard that voice before. *The man who was— possessed.*

"It can't be you. I—I can't . . . You can't be a —"

"*It is. You can. I am.*"

Yamin sat up. He knocked the back of his head on the wall. "Who are you?" He banged again. "What are you?" Again. "Get out." Again. "Get out!"

"*I am Ashchuwr.*" And then silence.

Bystanders gathered around Yamin's nook trying to determine the source of the ruckus.

A small blood stain on the wall behind his head made an older woman gasp. She pulled her veil to her face and scurried off.

Having a momentary reprieve from the demon's taunting, Yamin stood and staggered to another location to avoid the judgmental faces.

After having found a vendor and spending his entire denarius on food to last him the next day, he fell asleep without any more outbursts from Ashchuwr.

Yamin's dreams, however, were littered with dark whispers. Utterances in blackness of blasphemies against the Hebrew god and someone named Jesus.

12

The hike across the hills proved challenging. But a force other than himself now drove Yamin. After speaking to several people during his stay in Taricheae, all of whom regretted starting a conversation, he discovered if he traveled due west, he would eventually hit a major Roman road leading to the port city of Ptolemais.

He passed through several small towns on the way. He found the road in Selame. Which led to Sogane, followed by Saab and Chabulon. At Chabulon, the Great Trunk Road took him directly to Ptolemais. Strange hints of humid sea air increased with every step as he strode.

The Great Trunk Road served as an important trade route, and the Romans had taken excessive care in building it for that purpose. Its grandeur awed Yamin. He had never seen a road made from interlocking blocks of what he likened to a stone-like mud. Even the *Decumanus Maximus* of Hippos paled in comparison. Carts of all sizes, pulled by people and animals from lands he had only heard of in legends, passed him in both directions.

As he approached the city, the last vestiges of twilight faded as blackness blanketed the coast. Waves crashed on the beach below the road but he failed to grasp the vastness of the water laying offshore. The wind's speed did not warrant the size of the waves he heard. He would understand soon enough what was meant by the name, Great Sea.

The familiar sour scents of a busy port city welcomed him. Ptolemais, like other large seaports, served as an urban center of industry and trade. If Taricheae had been any indication of what to expect here, Yamin arrived unprepared. The innumerable buildings separating him from the docks belched plumes of mysterious aromas unparalleled in his previous experiences.

As he walked, he recognized pickling and smoking facilities, shipwrights, suppliers of leather, rope, and shipping containers, as well as numerous other trades, including slavers and brothels.

"*Go to them.*" Ashchuwr stirred as well.

Temptation gripped him. If he were not moneyless, he may have succumbed to the enticement. He forced himself on toward the water's edge and found a relatively quiet place to stay the night on gritty damp ground between two small boats that had been pulled ashore.

He thought of his father's boat and what he had done to it. His chest tightened with guilt. The anxiety caused by his unfamiliar location and the decision he soon would make made it hard to fall asleep.

Yamin's dreams were filled with the same ambiguous opacity as every night since leaving home. Something called to Ashchuwr, drawing the dark spirit across the Great Sea. The images fueled his own desire to head west in search of something . . . anything to forget where he came from. Was the longing his own or the desire of the demon within?

Hatred filled him. His parents had abandoned him. His best friend refused to understand his pain. And all those who hated him—from the Tiberians to the dockmasters—he spit in revulsion at their memories and allowed Ashchuwr to curse the ground he rested upon. Dawn could not come soon enough.

The morning brought a ravenous hunger. Yamin's stomach vibrated with a long, low growl. His ability to sense his environment through touch had diminished and other urges, more related to desire, now intensified. His senses drew him to places he knew he should avoid.

When a woman passed him on the street, accompanied or not, he lusted after her uncontrollably. He uttered profane and disgusting proposals as he worked his way through the streets downhill to the docks. When the object of his desire, or her male counterpart, threatened him, Yamin scrambled away. He tried to resist but Ashchuwr grew too strong as his spirit continually intertwined with Yamin's.

To his left, long breakwaters spread across the harbor protecting moored vessels from proud seas. The early summer weather provided a warm morning breeze from the west across the water and around a formidable guard tower located between the two jetties. Yamin had seen this tower the night before, but only its light peering from its top serving as a beacon to warn unwary sailors of the rocks laying beneath the shallow surface. He had dismissed it as a lamp on an anchored boat's mast.

Many Jewish citizens resided here, as evidenced by the numerous synagogues Yamin passed. Their foods lured him.

"A quick grab here. A little sleight of hand there."

A powerful urge to enter a home with an open door and swipe their breakfast right from the table nearly overcame him. He pushed on.

A market presented itself in his path.

Ashchuwr's timing proved flawless. *"Perfect."*

"No! I—mustn't steal."

The first of the early morning catch had just arrived and the scent of scaled and shell-bearing creatures filled the air. The market stretched ahead and the meal choices were numerous.

"Why? You're hungry, are you not?"

Yamin could not argue. He reached out from under his dusty robe and groped a fish lying in a basket. The preoccupied merchant did not see Yamin's almost seductive caress of the dead animal. The mucous coating stuck to his fingers but produced no emotion. It felt sticky, slimy. The scales lifted beneath his fingernails and the fish reacted with a post-mortem involuntary slap of its tail. Yamin started.

"Hey!" The sleep-deprived fishmonger swiped aside a stained brown curtain separating the back of his stall from his oceanic wares. "You buy. If not, leave."

Yamin hastened to the other side of the marketplace. Before leaving, he grabbed a large handful of snails from an unwary salesperson's basket and sped toward the water's edge. He sat down as the pilfered shellfish poured out of his robe and onto the sand. He had no desire to cook them. He only wanted to eat. He cracked them open one by one on a rock and slurped the still writhing creatures into his mouth.

Several citizens saw him as they walked along the seaside road. They screwed up their faces in disgust and whispered to themselves. Yamin cursed them and went on eating his ill-gotten breakfast.

Ashchuwr laughed. *See? Delicious.*

A few minutes of walking brought him to the harbor's edge. Several large merchant vessels sat moored on a long wooden dock. Crowded around them were anchored several formidable military ships. Yamin had never seen their like before.

Rows of long oars stuck out of the sides of the Roman naval boats. It reminded him of a porcupine that had wandered into his house years ago. And like that surprise nocturnal visitor, these members of the Imperial attack fleet were equally unwelcome by many here in Ptolemais.

The sun had risen above the buildings and lit up the ships and their crews. Soldiers pushed droves of slaves onto the ships to serve as the muscle to propel them. He loathed them all. The soldiers for their mistreatment. The slaves for their weakness. He almost yelled an obscenity, but to his surprise Ashchuwr stopped him. Poking the beehive would not help him with his goal.

"There he is!" A woman yelled from the street uphill of the docks.

Yamin turned to find the target of her accusation.

To his shock, she pointed directly at him. "*He* stole from the market! There!"

Yamin contemplated running but soldiers rapidly surrounded

him. Ptolemais was the center for Roman naval activity in the area, so there was no shortage of men.

He considered his options.

"Looks guilty to me." One of the soldiers pointed. "Chewed snail still clings to his whiskers."

Two others standing downwind of Yamin recoiled slightly when they caught a whiff of his unwashed body.

Ashchuwr ordered. "*Say nothing*."

Yamin reluctantly complied. All he wanted to do was board one of those merchant vessels and sail west.

Ashchuwr desired nothing less.

Finally, something they agreed upon.

13

Hallo!" A well-dressed sailor called from the dock. "What goes on here?"

N*ow what?* Another witness who saw him steal? *Curse you, Ashchuwr.*

A Roman Decanus, leader of the soldiers, answered first. "This boy has been accused of stealing, as evidenced by the filth around his mouth." He waved off the sailor. "It is none of your concern."

The Decanus motioned to his soldiers to seize Yamin, surely meaning to exact swift punishment.

Yamin poised himself to run when the bald sailor spoke again. "This boy is in my charge, set to serve upon my vessel for a personal debt previously obliged." The man's light brown face held a peculiar symmetrical mustache so short it could have been drawn on with charcoal.

Yamin had never seen this man before. What was he talking about?

The Decanus took a step toward the sailor and stuck out his chest. "He transferred that obligation to the Empire upon his decision to steal from the citizens of Ptolemais."

"Stealing? Not stealing." The sailor walked next to Yamin and put his hand on his shoulder. "I asked him to retrieve a fresh snack for me from the market and swiftly return, as my ship needs to be underway within the hour. I guess his hunger got the best of him." He squeezed Yamin's shoulder.

Yamin nodded slowly. He felt the instinct to act dumb.

Unconvinced, the Decanus gave no orders for his men to release Yamin.

Seeing this, the sailor continued. "You see, the boy, he's not very smart. He's done things like this before. I thought he had learned his lesson last time. I sent him with a coin to pay." He turned and spoke directly to Yamin, slowly and in Greek. "You forgot to pay again, didn't you?"

Yamin nodded and hung his head attempting to show a remorse he did not feel. Anything to avoid being made a slave—or worse. He did not know this sailor's intentions, but he knew it must be better than what the soldiers had in store.

"Then show me this coin you have, boy." The Decanus reached out with an open palm. "You'll have to pay to make amends before I can release you to . . ." He turned to the sailor. "Who are you?"

The sailor stepped in front of Yamin.

The soldiers backed away and released their grip on his arm.

"I am Adjo, Captain of The Lukka." He took Yamin's hands in his and bent slightly to meet his eye. "Give the coin to the kind soldier, boy." He spoke slowly. "The—coin."

Captain Adjo turned and gave a coin to the Decanus.

The soldier ordered his men to leave. "Captain Adjo, take more care from now on by sending only competent hands to retrieve your goods. This one won't get a second chance."

After a moment, Yamin spoke to Captain Adjo, albeit looking at the ground. "I didn't need any help."

"Oh?" He spoke Greek with a strange accent Yamin had not yet heard. "It seems that without me, you'd be in the galley of a naval ship and headed for certain death."

Yamin dug down deep. "Well—thank you." He turned to walk away.

"Not so fast." Captain Adjo grabbed Yamin's shoulder and spun him around. "Where do you think you're going?"

"I need to find work on a ship." As he spoke, Yamin realized who he spoke to and changed his tone.

Ashchuwr spoke for him. "*I need to go west.*"

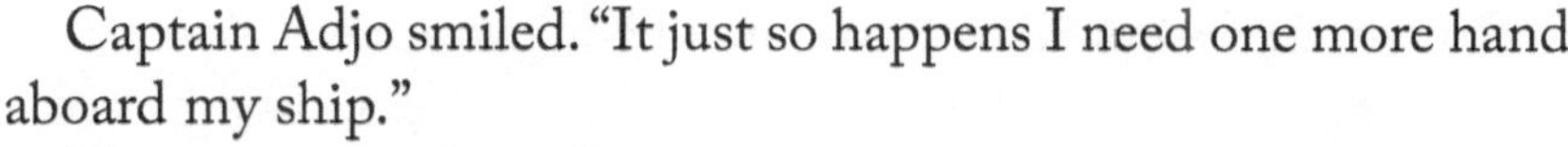

Captain Adjo smiled. "It just so happens I need one more hand aboard my ship."

"Are you going west?"

"We are as far east as one can get in the Great Sea. West is our only choice, young man."

"Then you've found a new hand."

"You know, I don't even know your name."

"It's a good thing the soldier back there didn't ask you." Yamin continued to walk without divulging his identity.

Captain Adjo stopped.

Ashchuwr.

Yamin shook off Ashchuwr's suggestion. "Yamin, son—just Yamin."

On the way to the docked merchant vessel, Captain Adjo filled Yamin in on what their journey entailed. As a frequent visitor to this port city, The Lukka often carried in its hold a plethora of goods including grain, wine, metal products produced in Ptolemais, and even barrels of pickled and smoked fish, of all things.

Yamin screwed up his nose at the mention of pickled anything.

"We carry these to Rome and then return with amphorae filled with garum."

"Oh, I like fish paste." For the first time in a long while, Yamin smiled. But it quickly receded when he remembered where he last had the privilege of tasting such a delicacy. He wanted the memory of Dar to disappear forever.

As they approached the ship, Captain Adjo's fifteen men worked on the deck preparing for departure. Their cargo had already been loaded.

The Lukka was a twenty-meter cargo vessel with the capability of carrying a near 100-ton payload. It possessed a rounded hull and a curving prow and stern. The single mast held a clean, rectangular, linen sail hanging loosely furled to a single yardarm stretching far above the deck.

Yamin stared wide-eyed. He had never seen such a display of maritime engineering as this transport vessel.

Roman in design, The Lukka had been fashioned from a mix of cypress, pine, and oak wood. It was the first detail he noticed. "I've not seen a boat with this much oak."

"Being Egyptian, and not overly fond of Roman themes, I made significant modifications to the ship's structure over the years since I acquired it. Do you see the figurehead?"

Yamin eyed the length of the ship to no avail.

Captain Adjo chuckled and pointed. "There, on the bow."

Yamin nodded at a carved human head being crushed in the jaws of a lion.

"That is purely Egyptian." Captain Adjo stood with hands on hips.

"It looks like something my uncle . . . Well, legends I've heard about pirates."

Captain Adjo chuckled and his voice rose over the background noise of the dock. "Pirates, you say?"

A group of Roman soldiers looked his way.

"Those outlaws haven't been seen on the Great Sea since Pompey's navy wiped them out nearly a hundred years ago." Captain Adjo looked toward the soldiers and waved once out of respect. "No, that carving is just a tribute to my ancestors who fought off the Sea People thousands of years ago along the Egyptian coast." He turned and continued with Yamin's pre-boarding tour.

The exterior, like many of the ships docked here, was covered in black pitch to seal out the sea and create a surface unfavorable to the growth of marine fouling organisms such as barnacles and their kin. An angular stern was built up above the rounded transom and sat higher above the water than the bow. On top of the stern sat a cabin rising above the main deck. Below the cabin and under the main deck was the galley and two small berths—one for the captain and the other for his second-in-command, or whomever the captain chose to privilege at the time.

"The crew, that includes you, sleep wherever you feel comfortable. On the deck or among the cargo."

They boarded using an ingenious draw bridge serving as a gang plank. Yamin soon realized this was no ordinary spartan ship. Carved on almost every vertical surface were ancient hieroglyphs. The gunwales, bulkheads, and even the mast were covered in the decorative, Egyptian sacred writing. Paintings of temples, cities, and sea creatures of all shapes and sizes accompanied them.

Yamin stood wide-eyed but inclined to hold his tongue. Ashchuwr's vile way of seeing the world did not allow for the enjoyment of artisanship such as this. This ship would serve as a means to an end that Yamin would only begin to understand when he reached the destination Ashchuwr had already chosen.

He leaned upon the gunwale. His hand rested on the wood. He scraped at the artwork with his fingernail until a small chip peeled off. When no one looked, he flicked it over the side and into the water below. A sinister grin grew on his face.

Ashchuwr was pleased.

14

The number of times a crewman almost crushed a hand or became entangled in the ropes astonished Yamin. When they reached open water, he released the breath he had been holding and felt gratitude that the task of shoving off fell to others.

What seemed like near mishaps to him had been the well coordinated actions of seasoned mariners. Captain Adjo led as a proper ship's captain and had hired only seaworthy hands. These men worked in unison, as if a rhythmic percussion drove their movements.

As they passed by Yamin in blurred motions, scents of hyssop and jasmine mingled with the pungent odor of perspiration and tar pitch.

What were they doing onshore to make them smell like that?

Captain Adjo asked Yamin to step aside and observe carefully. "You'll need to lend a hand when we reach port again." As he barked orders, he shot occasional glances in Yamin's direction, as if scrutinizing his newest recruit. He moved closer. "They use the beat of the drum deep within the belly of that warship to provide a tempo for their work."

That's where it's coming from. Yamin found the vessel far off the starboard side and slowly nodded to the faint beat reverberating from inside its sleek hull.

"Intriguing cadence, yes?" Captain Adjo listened with Yamin for a moment. His inflection darkened. "The men they just put on those oars will most likely be dead within the month."

Yamin's eyes widened.

"You see, the slaves you saw earlier—the ones being loaded into the Roman ship's hold—they were taken from the poorest part of the city. Male citizens too far in debt with taxes to avoid the terminal sentence of propelling a warship at inhuman speeds. Or as punishment for a crime."

Yamin turned away and looked out over the vast sea ahead. "You mentioned our next port. When will that be?"

Captain Adjo gave several more commands as his men made minor adjustments to the sail when the ship came about. "That depends upon *Mare Nostrum*."

"Mare Nostrum?" Yamin watched the warship turn to a more northerly track. Its battery of long oars broke the surface of the rippling sea in unison.

"Our Sea. Well, not *my* sea. In the sense of ownership, the Romans believe they have over its vast waters."

Yamin shook his head slightly in disbelief. "You mean, they think they *own* this sea?"

"Yes, they do!" The captain made a sweeping arc across the horizon with his hand. "The Roman Empire. Certainly, where you come from— Where, exactly, do you come from?"

The dreaded question of origin.

Ashchuwr answered inside Yamin's head. *"You must have known he would ask."*

Yamin almost forgot Ashchuwr's presence with all the novelty. "My experience with sailing comes from an inland sea. The Sea of Galilee. Perhaps you've heard of it?" Yamin sensed unfamiliarity from Captain Adjo. *How could a captain of the Great Sea know of my lake?* He turned away with a reddened face. "It has been called other names, as well. Sea of Chinnereth? Lake of Gennesaret?"

"No doubt a beautiful body of water. How does it compare to this?" He nodded toward the vast open water laying before them.

Yamin ignored his question but could not ignore the implied ownership conveyed by Captain Adjo's gestures. "I'm a Roman citizen, you know." He was not overly proud of this designation but felt he should be honest about his residency before Captain Adjo made any assumptions. "They controlled the lake where I grew up, but I never heard of them—*owning* it. No military vessels like that, anyway." He thrust his chin toward the diminishing vessel then lowered his eyes toward the water.

"Did your family pay taxes for using the water?"

"Yes."

"Was their work regulated by laws passed to you by those in charge?"

Yamin turned slowly to Captain Adjo. "Well, yes."

"Then they owned your lake, too."

"But this?" Yamin held out both hands, palms up. "How can they own something so great? So enormous?"

A small gust hit the ship from the north heeling the vessel slightly and causing some of the freight stacked in the central open-air hold to settle.

Captain Adjo pointed to two of the men. "Secure those!" He turned back to Yamin. "I've asked the same question many times, young man."

"Do you pay taxes to them?"

"When I have to." Captain Adjo chuckled. "Every port in the sea is controlled by them."

"And you have laws to follow too, no doubt."

"When—" He looked at his men and cracked a mischievous smile. "—necessary, yes." "But we are the sort who have a set of laws all our own."

The men tilted their ears toward the conversation.

Captain Adjo put his arm around Yamin's shoulders.

Yamin squirmed under the weight. The sound of the beating drum was long gone, and the drab shoreline faded into the distance. The sea lay before them, continuing into a blue-green eternity.

"This Great Sea, as you are so fond of referring to it, has always provided my ancestors with the freedom to live as we please and to prosper as we see fit." Captain Adjo took back his arm and turned to face the men. "I comply with the Imperial regulations when necessary." He glanced knowingly at his crew who had now collected around himself and Yamin. "But we have a long history with *Wadj-wer*, or the Great Green."

"*Yes.*"

"You have heard of this name?"

Did I say that out loud? Ashchuwr! Yamin looked wide-eyed at Captain Adjo and the surrounding crewmen. The hieroglyphs and strange colorful ship art appeared to dance around them. *Ashchuwr, what are you doing?* Beads of sweat formed on Yamin's upper lip.

Captain Adjo frowned. "I choose my hands carefully, Yamin. Regardless of their backgrounds, they must show a loyalty to me and this ship. The Roman swine do not control us. The emperor will not impugn any authority over what I can do on the waters of my *Egyptian* ancestors." He raised his voice and called out over the sea. "I am a son of the Pharaohs! I am Adjo!"

His proud acknowledgment fell silent, absorbed by the salty air and waves. In the awkward lull, the captain nodded to his men.

Two of them grabbed Yamin's arms and held him securely.

Yamin panicked and allowed the demon free reign. But his fierce struggle proved no match for the muscled deckhands manhandling him toward the side of the ship.

Overpowered, even Ashchuwr knew when to yield. *"Resisting will only stop us from our goal."*

The man his right held up Yamin's arm. "A fighter. I like dat Cap'n."

Yamin turned to look at him. His deep gravelly voice complemented the strange patterns of scars across his chest, neck, and face. It was as if the branches of a tree had grown within his skin. The diverging deformity even traveled through the man's left eye, visible behind a translucent cloudy lens.

"What you lookin' at, boy?" He pushed Yamin against the decorated gunwale and, with the other man's help, held him securely. The dancing symbols continued their eerie spectacle.

The men lifted him off his feet. The dark water splashed menacingly against the sides of the cargo-laden ship.

The other men laughed until Captain Adjo raised his hand and silenced them. The hieroglyphs froze as well.

Yamin feared his admittance of being a Roman citizen meant certain doom. His knees weakened, and he lost control of his bladder.

The men, barefoot, quickly let go of him and recoiled in disgust.

The others laughed again.

Captain Adjo ignored the puddle and glared at Yamin. "Yamin. You have a choice to make. Forsake your citizenship to the Imperialist regime and vow to be loyal to *this* ship and its Captain."

"There's a choice?" He was not sure if he or Ashchuwr had spoken.

The men laughed once more.

Captain Adjo remained grim, stared at Yamin, and waited for a response.

Yamin straightened and spoke with choppy words. "I pledge my loyalty to the ship and its captain."

"It's a binding pledge, mind you. There are only two ways to be released from its fetters."

Yamin did not care. He wanted to get as far west as possible. As far away from where he came from as he could. *Whatever bonds they place I will deal with if the time comes.*

"We *will deal with it.*" Ashchuwr gave no cognitive assistance in making decisions. At least none Yamin detected. Only an indescribable urgency led him along an unfamiliar path. A dark path revealing itself in pieces when Ashchuwr allowed it.

Glad that was in my head this time.

Captain Adjo continued. "Those two ways are death or banishment."

Yamin thought of numerous ways one could die while serving on a ship such as this, including murder. But he was uncertain how banishment could ever happen. He did not ask.

Captain Adjo reached out and grabbed Yamin's forearm.

Yamin followed suit to bind the agreement.

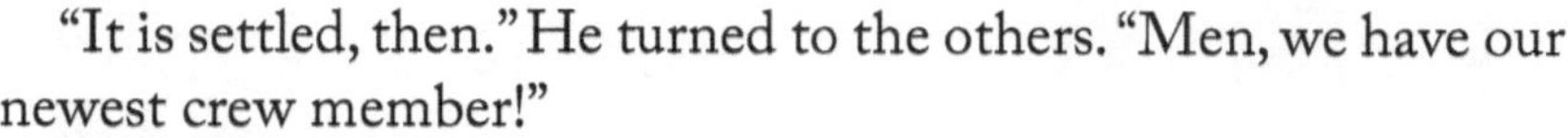

"It is settled, then." He turned to the others. "Men, we have our newest crew member!"

They cheered in unison.

The scarred man shoved a worn rag and bucket of seawater into Yamin's arms. "You can start by cleanin' up dis mess."

Yamin took the well-used supplies and bent to follow orders. As he scrubbed, he listened to Ashchuwr's chants.

"*Wadj-wer. We know. We know.*"

The demon pushed him to follow orders and avoid confrontation. It was Yamin who wanted to strike out in anger at the men who frightened him. Instead, he kept it pent up. He sensed Ashchuwr's contentment about their current situation. And both were pleased to be underway.

But how long would this mutual gratification last?

15

A man sat facing Yamin on a white marble throne in an open-air shrine. Or was it a woman?

Yamin could not tell.

The androgynous figure appeared to be composed entirely of water. As the form shifted in place, ripples pulsated along its torso and extremities.

The structure Yamin peered into reminded him of a worship hall built just outside of Hippos, dedicated to idolatry and ritual sacrifice. He stood on the threshold. His legs locked preventing his entry. Behind him lay the expanse of the Great Sea. In front, the watery visage of a spirit. Or was it a god?

"There are no gods." He forced his right leg into the opening and took one step forward.

The viscous entity rose from its stone resting place and materialized in front of Yamin.

He froze.

"*Wadj-wer.*"

Ashchuwr's ecstasy as he spoke the water spirit's name sent a chill up Yamin's spine. His demon's ardent anticipation made it feel as if he met a long-lost family member. No, a lover. The desire to connect physically with it now tangible. Irresistible. Yamin lusted for it too.

"Mother?" Yamin had not felt any connection this strong since her death. She had been the only person he ever loved with this much fervor.

The rippling spirit now had breasts and a swollen abdomen. Before Yamin could say another word, Wadj-wer's belly split open, and a dark vaporous shape emerged. It entered Yamin's chest and penetrated his soul, interweaving with Ashchuwr's dark form.

Yamin woke with a start.

The scarred man had doused him with water. This roused him from a deep and fitful sleep atop the cargo in the central hold. "We're near." His loud but monotone voice completed the task.

Yamin gathered his wits, and his sarcasm. "Thanks, Fulgur." He blew water from his nose onto the decking and followed Fulgur up to the deck.

It had been almost three days since meeting this strange man. But this was the first time he had the courage to ask him about his unique disfigurement. "Where *did* you get those scars?"

Fulgur, unperturbed, pointed to the sky. "Da gods."

Typical superstitious answer. Fulgur's matter-of-fact reply bothered him. No one on board this vessel had come forth with information. Yamin almost gave up his inquiries when Fulgur volunteered some useful insight.

"I once served da Imperial navy under Varus. We tried to capture part of Germania. Got ambushed by barbarian tribes. Before da battle ever began, a great tempest formed above da would-be battle ground. Lightning struck da mast of our ship. Then it hit me."

After Yamin recovered from the initial shock of hearing more than one sentence from him, he asked, "Hit? *What* hit you?"

"Lightning, of course!" He pointed to the strange vein-like scars on his neck. "Da gods marked me for da rest of my life. I believe they meant to tell me I was destined for something greater dan dying in dat worthless battle."

Yamin used a rag to wipe the water from his face. He then spit repeatedly onto the flooring when he discovered it had already been used to wipe the deck. "So, you never had . . ." He spat once more. ". . . a chance to fight, then?"

"I woke later tied to da mast dat broke off from da lightning.

One of my shipmates must've realized dare fate and attempted to spare my injured soul from da same."

An orange and white cat with black spots leapt from the deck onto the sacks of grain in the hold. Yamin saw a flash of matted gray fur beneath its paw. "Who owns that pest?"

"What's da matter? Not like cats?" Fulgur reached out to stroke it but the cat jumped away with its prey secured between its jaws. "Emu helped himself aboard Da Lukka two years ago while we docked in an Egyptian port. Captain Adjo was instantly enamored and insisted dat every crewman treat him as one of dare own."

"Never been a cat person. Prefer pigs, myself." *To eat, that is.* "At least it gobbles up the vermin that climb on me all night."

Yamin and Fulgur joined the crew on deck.

Captain Adjo waited for all hands to be present before speaking. "Men, we have fought hard to maintain our way of life among the myriad of Imperial statutes imposed upon us. The high times of our ancestors' methods of acquiring fortunes has been virtually erased from existence. But we have not forgotten their struggles. We have never denied their sacrifices nearly one hundred years ago when Pompey—"

The ship rounded the southwest tip of the island of Cyprus. A series of rocks jutting out of a clear blue sea near the shore drew Yamin's attention away from Adjo's speech. He had no idea, nor did he care for, what Captain Adjo ranted on about in front of the men. Instead, he let his mind wander to those jagged rocks pummeled by the waves.

Ashchuwr joined him, adding his own obscure sense of wonder. "*Wedj-wer. Wanassa.*"

Yamin was tempted to ask his stowaway spirit what it spoke of when Emu snapped him back to the present.

The cat jumped into Captain Adjo's arms and hissed ferociously at Yamin.

Captain Adjo took this as an encouraging portent. "Even our feline protector can sense it, my friends."

The crew laughed.

Yamin remained stoic and took a step away from Emu. His stomach growled painfully with a tinge of nausea.

"She doesn't like us." Ashchuwr laughed at the obvious. *"She can see me."*

Yamin looked at the men in fear. *Can any of* them *see?* He needed a break from the ship, its crew, and that annoying cat. *Dry land and to be alone.*

"Alone?" Ashchuwr seemed to be waiting for this. *"You have never been alone. Nor will you ever be."*

"What do you mean!" Yamin's cry startled the men.

They all turned to look at him.

Captain Adjo seemed delighted Yamin asked such an obvious question, although the inquiry had not been meant for him. Yamin forced a sheepish grin.

"Men, our newest hand wishes to know of what we are discussing." The men laughed again. "This is our last port before undertaking a new mission. We'll need everyone to be at their sharpest."

"*New* mission? I thought we were transporting grain and goods from Ptolemais to Rome."

A few men chuckled, but the rest turned serious.

"We will reach Rome in time."

Yamin suddenly became aware he needed to know more about what he was now part of. His brow furrowed, and his heart thumped heavily. Thankful he had just peed over the side of the ship; he now listened intently as Captain Adjo spoke again, silencing the chuckling men with a wave of his hand. "Yamin, recall how we met. I saved you from a fate worse than death—because you were a thief." He gave Yamin a brittle smile.

"I remember."

"It takes a thief to know another. Wouldn't you agree, men?"

Confirmatory grunts issued forth.

"As we pass Aphrodite's rock in the distance, we always use this time to remind ourselves of our true nature. Of where we come from and what our true purpose is on the Great Green."

Yamin thought for a moment then his eyes widened. "You're *thieves?*"

"No, no. We are merchants, friendly and fair." Adjo winked at the crew.

"Then, I don't understand."

"You will soon enough." Captain Adjo walked to the center of the ship and gave orders to prepare for a course correction. He turned back to Yamin. "We will be at the city of Paphos by tomorrow night. We could all use a little rest from our trip, yes?"

Yamin did not answer. Instead, he brooded about the captain's attitude and enigmatic ways. He hated him for his smugness and plotted to make him pay for the way he was treated. *As if I'm some plaything for the crew's amusement.*

"*Wait.*" Ashchuwr's order lacked encouragement.

Even my demon withholds information. This is growing old.

16

The port city of Pathos loomed in the distance like a polished fragment of marble set in a sheet of dingy brown leather. The setting sun's golden hues reflected off white buildings rising above the shoreline. Surrounding the city stood arid fields of tawny grass. The summer dry season had begun early leaving the land parched. If not for the constant supply of food from elsewhere, this city would starve.

Fulgur further explained to Yamin the island of Cyprus, particularly the southern half, had been subject to destructive tremors. Visible from the ship, some of the buildings' facades and pillars stood misshaped and crumbling.

"Earthquakes? Looks like a battle took place here."

Fulgur dispelled Yamin's misconception. "You'll see large cracks in da earth when we enter da city. The Cypriots are a peaceful people, but day must be upsetting dare gods to receive such punishments."

Yamin aided Fulgur in the docking preparations. Fulgur had taken to Yamin and acted as a sort of mentor. Yamin, always wanting to work alone, decided he could tolerate the strange man, at least for a while. The others proved less inviting. He figured the misfits could stick together easier.

Yamin scratched at his whiskers, now grown at least as much as a sixteen-year-old boy's beard could. He refused to keep it neat, as Captain Adjo recommended. He sensed the other men's resentment at his insubordination as they turned their backs to him whenever they had the chance.

Pathos was as modern a port as any other on the Great Sea. Due to their need for an easy cargo transfer, Captain Adjo dispensed with the standard offshore anchoring and used the process of warping instead, starting with the use of smaller vessels to offload and reload freight. Once this was accomplished, the warping process for docking took place.

Port workmen took a heavy line from the shore to the ship by a smaller boat. Once secured, they wound the line around a capstan, a large cylindrical pulley that spun horizontally. Iron bars jutted out from the capstan radially. Other shore hands pushed the bars around in a circle, winding the line tighter and tighter. This force pulled the ship into the pier. They used the same procedure to bring large vessels back out into deeper water by securing the ship's anchor at a distance.

The newness excited Yamin, and he beamed. Being the youngest on board, his jobs included cleaning decks, sorting lines, serving meals, fetching and carrying, and generally doing anything he was told. Being busy as a deckhand was the only thing keeping his mind off everything he left behind, as well as Ashchuwr. He dreaded going to sleep. That was when Ashchuwr acted up most and when his ability to protect himself from unwanted thoughts and memories worsened.

After they secured The Lukka and the final exchange of goods took place, Captain Adjo communicated alone with the portmaster's aide.

Yamin's lack of rest hampered his efforts at being overly useful in the movement of sacks and clay amphorae in and out of the cargo hold. He groaned with every twist of his back. His arms shook, and his legs quivered. His upper lip curled uncontrollably in spasmodic response to every piece of cargo he endured.

After a while, Captain Adjo noticed and reassigned Yamin to an easier task. "Take Emu below deck and lock her in my berth. I don't want her running off into the city and getting lost."

Yamin would rather have jumped overboard and scrubbed the

keel than handle that beast. But he welcomed the respite from heavy lifting.

Now, where's that skulking creature?

As far as cats go, Emu's elusiveness rivaled them all. She often scared Yamin by appearing out of nowhere. Yamin's curses could be heard across the ship, much to the amusement of the others. Often enough, if one ever needed to find the ornery feline, she usually hid under a crate or atop a lofty beam below deck.

Once, Yamin had reached for a tool he was sent to retrieve and put his hand on one of Emu's droppings. Had it not been for Fulgur's rapid response to Yamin's resulting tirade, Emu would have been fish food.

Emu had a likewise intolerance of Yamin. She occasionally did as any cat would and rub against one of the men's legs or even leap into their bed to sleep with them. But not Yamin. He learned quickly that attempting to reach out to the cat was foolish. The forceful hisses Emu emitted upon Yamin's attempts at getting close told him she was off limits to anyone harboring a dark spirit.

So how was he going to get the cat into the captain's berth without suffering deep lacerations? With all the noise on deck, the cat surely laid ensconced in the deepest recesses of the vessel. He also knew of her fondness for fresh fish. But the only fish he had on hand was pickled or smoked.

Taking a piece of each from the storage barrels, Yamin crumbled them up. The resulting scents permeated the air in the hold. It reminded him of his last meal with his father. He swore and threw each into its own basket.

"Here, kitty, kitty." His words hissed from behind teeth clenched like that of a predator's. "You weasel."

Waiting quietly for a few minutes was all it took for Emu to emerge from her hiding place. Being away from shore for so long meant her supply of rodents had dwindled. With a quick trilling *meow*, she leapt into the basket with the smoked fish and ravenously devoured the oily meat.

Yamin acted quickly. He placed a second basket atop the first and trapped Emu within. It was all he could do to keep the baskets closed, as the cat fought desperately for her freedom. The animal growled and hissed with such ferocity that Yamin almost threw it overboard.

"I'm not sure you don't have a demon of your own, cat."

Ashchuwr's demonic voice rang inside Yamin's head. *"Nothing so familiar on this vessel."*

The confirmation surprised Yamin as he approached Captain Adjo's quarters. He tossed both baskets angrily into the berth and slammed the door. The exterior latch clanked shut.

"You're the only…" Yamin inspected his hands. Blood trickled from his fingers. "…demon onboard, then?"

"Wait."

Yamin cursed inwardly at his demon's ambiguity. He ignored his wounds and hurried back to report his success to the captain.

When he reached the deck, the work had been done. Captain Adjo ordered the men to take their leave. They would stay in Paphos only one evening and depart first thing after sunrise. What the men did during the next twelve hours was up to them.

Captain Adjo shouted as they disembarked. "Stay out of trouble."

Yamin tried to hide his fingers when the captain looked his way.

Captain Adjo chuckled. "It appears she got the best of you, yes?"

Yamin replied coldly. "The task's complete, Captain. Although, you may find two slightly chewed fish baskets in there with it." He refused to refer to the cat's gender or call it by name.

"You've earned an overnight leave as well, boy. Remember, the people of Cyprus have no real security force on this island. Outlaws or wrongdoings severe enough to need the local authority's intervention are almost unheard of here. Not to mention The Lukka's reputation is at stake. So, keep your fingers off any merchandise. Besides, it'll give them time to heal, yes?" He chuckled and shooed Yamin along the gangplank and onto the dock.

"We'll be fine."

"*'We* will?'" Captain Adjo's eyes narrowed.

"Uh, yes. Meaning . . . the crew . . . and me." Yamin punched his thigh in a vain attempt at doing harm to Ashchuwr. His patience thinned.

The city he viewed from offshore was only a glimpse of what the capital of Cyprus comprised. Farther inland, the proconsul and other aristocrats lived in great mansions. These structures put those in Hippos to shame.

The sun had set only minutes ago. Servants lit large oil lamps to illuminate the main roadways. Dark and narrow alleys ran between most of the buildings. Every so often, the shapes of people lurking in the constricted passageways caught Yamin's eye. He wanted nothing to do with them. He only felt drawn to walk deeper into the city.

Ashchuwr had taken control.

Fulgur emerged from an alley after Yamin passed. Because of Yamin's odd behavior during the passage from Ptolemais to Paphos, Adjo ordered Fulgur to keep an eye on him. Fulgur had no intention of seeking prostitutes, like the other sailors, nor any other debauchery while on shore. Delighted to have the chance to do something different, he felt as if he was back in the military seeking out intelligence on the enemy.

He trailed Yamin and could not help but notice the boy's odd tics. Whispers and hand motions made it appear as if someone accompanied him. But no one was nearby.

Fulgur watched with pity as the occasional passerby crossed to the other side of the street to avoid Yamin.

One couple laughed and tossed their wine at Yamin. "We've an Abderite in our city!"

He growled at them and kept moving.

Snarl all you want, boy. But dare right. You do look like a fool. Why would a young man with no knowledge of this city walk with such purpose through its streets? Never stopping to talk to anyone or look at anything? *What're you up to, boy?*

17

The altar of Aphrodite rose beyond the city on the elevated hills above the sea. Its open-air architecture, encircled by three walls, stood in defiance to many other roofed temples dotting the island landscape. Its entrance was guarded by nothing more than bright, turquoise-colored wooden doors.

The cloudless sky had changed to an eerie grey-green, veiling the remaining twilight. It matched Yamin's mood—one of darkening despair and muffled senses.

He approached the holy site. Several cult priests worshipped here and walked about, but none seemed to take notice of Yamin. He approached the doors and gingerly pushed them open.

Once inside, voices echoed through the chamber. They communed in an unknown language. Whispers of darkness carrying malicious intent. Yamin had heard this tongue before, from the possessed young man in the physician's courtyard at Hippos.

Ashchuwr talked to another demon spirit.

To Yamin's surprise, he understood them.

"He can carry us . . . can serve . . . us." Ashchuwr spoke with certainty. *"I've felt it."*

"The others. They are far, trapped," said the new spirit.

Yamin's mouth moved. *"He is willing. His anger is great."*

"You are right. I can . . . feel it."

Yamin froze. He knew he carried a malevolent entity. But *serve* him? And *another? Yes, I . . . want to.*

Anything to drive out the memories. Anything to numb the

feelings. With his gifted sense of touch nearly gone, the sensation of love entirely diminished, wasted away only to be replaced with a new sense of purpose, albeit evil. *To be needed again.*

It felt almost like love but demented. The feeling he received from these two spirits was one of inclusion and necessity. It was a false sense, however. One that could never pay itself back except in pain and suffering. Anguish caused by knowing the feeling will never go away and no amount of attachment would help. To embrace it was like wrapping himself in a blanket to stay warm, only to find the blanket to be a coarse open-weaved net.

The sky opened, and rain fell around him. The sounds of people outside celebrating the short-lived deluge echoed in. The heavy drops struck the ground and formed small puddles upon the limestone floor releasing an earthy scent.

Yamin stood listening to the demons converse about him.

Walking, being led farther into the chamber, a large conical object presented itself before him in the center of the room. It stood half the height of a man and sat upon a marble pedestal making it just higher than Yamin's head. Its off-white color washed out any markings or writing. It was utterly smooth. The rain struck the upright support, but the object itself remained strangely dry.

He reached out to touch the boulder's surface. The expectation of tactile sensation barely a memory. Searing heat from the stone's surface entered his fingertips. A blinding light caused his eyes to shut tightly. It knocked him to the ground. He twisted and convulsed as an unseen force gripped and strangled his insides. The room blackened.

Fulgur ran inside when he saw Yamin collapse. He had not seen nor heard any of what Yamin experienced, only knew the boy had fallen unconscious upon touching the unusual stone.

A priest attempted to stop him by grabbing Fulgur's arm. Lightning flashed overhead revealing the branching scars on Fulgur's face. The man recoiled and gasped. "Demons. Demons in the sanctuary!" The priest ran. "The holy altar is under attack!"

"Dis isn't good." Fulgur lifted Yamin and carried him out into the town below.

Several citizens took notice and stepped into the road to watch as Fulgur proceeded briskly toward the harbor with a young man on his shoulder. The rain had stopped, and before long he had quite an entourage gawking and gossiping about what this strange behavior could mean.

"Is he kidnapping him?"

"Maybe he's sick."

"Should we summon the authorities?"

Yamin moaned, roused by the jostling movement. "What—what's happening?" By the time they reached the port, he gained consciousness. This enabled him to walk the rest of the way to the ship, albeit only slightly lucid and aware of his surroundings when they reached the deck.

Captain Adjo was the only one aboard and came up onto the deck when he heard the scraping of sandals on wood. He looked at the gathering on the dock of about fifteen people and whispered to Fulgur. "What happened? I told him to keep his nose clean. I told *you* to make it so."

"I watched him da whole time, Cap'n. He did nothing immoral. He spoke to no one, ate no food, and touched nothing. Well, except *one* thing."

"What? Did he desecrate something? Someone! He didn't grab a patrician's daughter, did he?" Captain Adjo grabbed Yamin by the collar. "*Did you?*"

Yamin's vision blurred, but he knew where he was and who spoke to him. He had a difficult time remaining upright. Forces were at odds within him, and he looked hungover from too much shore leave.

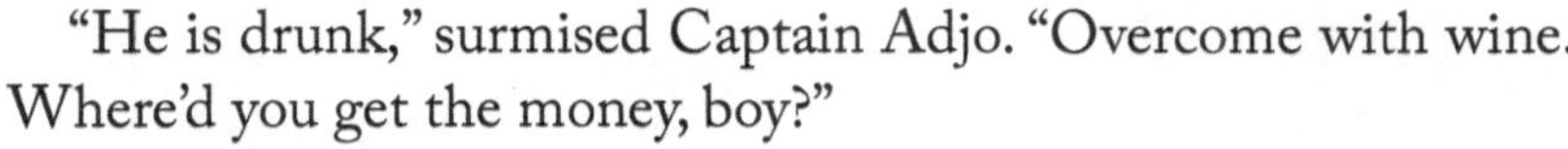

"He is drunk," surmised Captain Adjo. "Overcome with wine. Where'd you get the money, boy?"

"*We are* not, *fool!*"

The backhand smack Yamin received was meant as punishment only. A reminder of the captain's dominance. But it was enough to bring his own thoughts to the forefront of his mind and ask for forgiveness.

"It—it's the wine speaking, Captain. I meant no disrespect." He found lying to be the easiest way to appease the captain right now. *Covering up for these demons is getting old.* A constricting twist inside caused him to wince and clutch his chest.

"Rid me of his presence. I'll deal with him when he sobers up."

Fulgur escorted Yamin to the lower deck and dropped him on a sleeping mat. "You're *not* drunk. And I'll *not* lie for you again."

Yamin forced himself to thank Fulgur. "You won't have to. I'm back where I belong."

Fulgur turned to leave but stopped before climbing out of the hold. "What happened to you in dat shrine? Dat stone. It had some kind of effect on you."

"Don't know what you're talking about. I was weak from work and no food. That's all."

"I saw da stone, Yamin. I saw how da rain didn't touch it."

Yamin rolled over and ignored him. Nothing else could be said to convince the man what he had seen had been a figment of his imagination. If he admitted his spiritual affliction to Fulgur, he would surely be cast off the ship immediately. *Could* he admit it? Would the demons even allow him to?

He needed to press on. Others awaited his arrival. Others who required him.

18

"What's wrong with *him*?" Three men asked the same question as they returned one by one to the ship in the morning.

The early sun shone brightly upon the city and its port. Sea birds wheeled above and called to each other. Yamin cursed them under his breath, both birds and men.

"Someone had an interesting night of shore leave!" said a fourth. The men joined him in a chorus of laughter.

A fifth sailor approached and sat next to Yamin. Being the oldest deckhand on The Lukka, he looked as if he had seen a great many things in his travels. As he bent to sit, the joints in his knees cracked, and he let out a great sigh. He swept shoulder-length grey curls from his tired dull eyes.

Captain Adjo's call for all hands on deck entered through the open hatchway for departure.

The old sailor attempted to save Yamin from a punishment worse than any vestige a supposed alcoholic binge could produce. He spoke only loud enough for Yamin to hear. "Those who go down to the sea in ships, who do business on the great waters; they have seen the works of the Lord, and his wonders in the deep."

The words burned Yamin's insides as if he swallowed a hot coal. He sat up fast and struck his head upon a beam then fell back onto the mat and moaned.

The man peered into Yamin's teary eyes. A look of concern spread across his wrinkled face.

Yamin turned away quickly.

The man squinted.

"You have a spirit within you."

Yamin shot the man a piercing look.

"Yes." The man nodded slowly. "Those words from the Hebrew texts—that was a test."

Yamin opened his mouth and the new spirit spoke for him. *"What do you know of us, Emmet?"*

"*Us?*" Emmet contemplated. "More than one of you, then." He nodded again as if not surprised at all.

"*There will be* many *more!*"

Yamin tried to get up again but the blow to his head was right where he suffered a wound at the lake weeks ago. Coupling that with the actions of the tumultuous demons within caused him to fall unconscious again.

Emmet stood over Yamin and shook his head. He shuffled away to inform the captain.

Captain Adjo did not reply at first. He stood looking out the small window in his quarters.

"Captain, you know I've been around the Great Sea and beyond and have served with many." Emmet paced the captain's cramped quarters. "I know when a man is harboring—*unwanted* passengers."

Captain Adjo turned. "I knew the boy was weird, but malignant spirits, Emmet?"

Emmet stopped moving and faced the captain. He spoke with concern, not fear. "When I looked into his eyes, I saw it. A dull gray mist or fog surrounded him. The spirit spoke from within him. And that hellish leer upon his face— If he hadn't struck his head, I fear he would've struck *me.*"

"I will keep a close eye on him. I want to see evidence for myself before making any decisions about the boy. You understand."

"Of course, Captain."

"In a week, we stop in Crete. And another week, Malta. In

between we have our—rendezvous." He winked at Emmet. "Keep your observations quiet until I decide."

Emmet nodded and exited the cabin.

Four days passed until, much to Fulgur's dismay, the captain approved Yamin's return to full duty. The Lukka had been struggling against a strong headwind countering its progression. The task of tacking the ship in a zig-zag pattern to maintain their heading to the island of Crete took its toll on the men. Spray constantly wet the deck, and the sail needed frequent resetting. The men were on edge as Yamin recovered from his injury below.

On Captain Adjo's orders, Yamin only performed light duties, until now. He spoke to Fulgur without looking at him. "Bring him up here." An impatient snort followed his order.

Fulgur kept his distance from Yamin after what he had witnessed in Paphos. On several occasions, he exchanged knowing glances with Emmet, but they spoke nothing about the boy outwardly.

Emmet stood in Fulgur's way as he attempted to enter the forward hull. "This will not be good, Fulgur."

"What're you talkin' about?" Fulgur tried to push past the old man.

"You saw something, didn't you? On Cyprus."

He did not want to sound crazy without proof. "What do you know about it?"

Emmet stepped closer to Fulgur and whispered. "I saw it."

Fulgur's eyes widened. "You saw dat stone too?"

"Stone?"

Fulgur swallowed hard. *Great. He won't believe me if I tell him.* "What did *you* see den?"

"The boy is *possessed.*"

Yamin suddenly appeared.

The two men jumped inside their skins.

Yamin wore a wry smile and spoke firmly. "I understand I'm needed on deck."

Fulgur went to lead Yamin by the arm but decided against touching him. He locked eyes for a moment with Emmet and exited the hold.

Yamin met Captain Adjo as he snapped orders at the crew. "Brace about!"

The men worked at turning the single mainsail to the opposite side of the ship for the fourth time this morning.

"Let go the sheets and braces!"

The crew numbered fifteen but the ship could be sailed with eight experienced men. It was the loading and unloading of cargo in a timely manner that required the extra hands. The Lukka was slower with the extra men aboard and the cargo. But something else needed tending to so the vessel could be more efficient.

Captain Adjo smiled when Yamin approached. "Feeling better, I hope?"

Yamin nodded.

Fulgur and Emmet stood to either side of Yamin.

"I have an important job for you, boy." Captain Adjo walked to the side and looked over the edge into the water. "You do know how to swim, yes?"

Yamin's menacing laugh sent a visible chill through Fulgur. "A sailor that can't swim? What sort of question is *that* . . . Captain?" He spit the last word out.

Emmet cleared his throat. "I cannot swim. That's why I always carry this." He pulled out a small goat-skin pouch from under his robes. He put his mouth to it and blew air into an opening. It expanded to the size of man's head. He tied a string tightly around the opening and patted on the inflated sac. It produced a hollow thump.

Yamin stared incredulously. He then addressed the crew. "Is there anyone *else* aboard that can't swim?"

Two other men slowly raised their hands.

Yamin's taunting laugh incited some of the men to join him.

"Enough!" Captain Adjo grabbed Yamin's arm and pulled him to the gunwale.

Yamin's worn sandals slid across the wet decking.

"You're the youngest and greenest of my men. I need you to plunge beneath The Lukka's hull and scrape off the barnacles."

"What?" Yamin stepped back from the edge and bumped into Fulgur and Emmet.

Emmet's goat-skin life preserver fell to the deck, bounced once, then rolled to the other side.

"It's been quite some time since she's had a good scrub. How long, Fulgur?"

Fulgur looked up and thought for a moment. "Oh, last summer, I'd say."

"So, about a full year, then."

"A veritable reef, Captain."

"That's enough to slow us down substantially." Captain Adjo drove a serious look at Yamin. "We're not making good time. And if we don't make it to Crete in three days, and Malta seven days later, there will be dire consequences—for all of us."

"Malta. We need to go to Malta."

Yamin looked around. *Oh, good. That was in my head.* It was more than a day since he had heard from either Ashchuwr or . . . *What's that one's na—*

"Skylla." A female voice. Coarse and wraithlike but that of a woman, nonetheless.

Captain Adjo handed Fulgur a rope which he then tied around Yamin's waist with trepidation.

Emmet gave Yamin a small iron scraping tool shaped like a scythe, but with a straighter blade. He secured the tool to Yamin's wrist with a short piece of twine.

Captain Adjo shouted an order to bring the ship into irons, stopping its forward motion. The sail flopped in the wind and the men hauled it in, so Yamin could work in a slack current.

Yamin took a hesitant step toward the edge of the ship and looked over into the blue-green water.

"Your punishment for calling me a fool." Captain Adjo pushed Yamin over the gunwale. The line trailed behind him as he plummeted into the sea.

19

The Lukka skimmed over the sea after Yamin removed the bulk of living matter encrusted on its hull. He remembered the same smooth feeling, to a greater degree, from his father's small boat.

It took roughly three hours of labored scraping to satisfy Captain Adjo's scrutiny of Yamin's work.

Yamin repeatedly held his breath, dove beneath the ship, scraped until his lungs nearly burst for want of air, and resurfaced. Twice he thought he had done enough when the captain sent in a crewman to inspect his work. Only after the third inspection was he allowed to be hoisted back up.

Yamin now knew how fish must feel when pulled into a boat. Gasping for air and weakened from a fight, it took an hour for his quivering muscles to calm. His skin bore many scrapes and bruises from the ordeal.

Yamin relayed his experience to Fulgur and Emmet when they settled down in the open-air hold for the night. "Fish of all sorts swarmed about the hull. Some larger than myself."

"Dog fish," Emmet said. "Probably attracted to all the debris you dislodged."

Fulgur propped himself up on his elbows. "Sea dogs? Very dangerous. I couldn't have done what day forced you to do." He looked off into the distance. "Saw a pack of 'em eat a horse once."

Silence filled the hold until Yamin spoke again. "What would've happened if I had refused the captain's orders?"

Fulgur and Emmet glanced at each other. Neither responded.

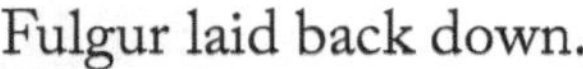

Fulgur laid back down.

"I mean, has anyone *ever* disobeyed him?" Yamin was sure one of his demons prompted these inquiries. The curiosity took hold of him too.

Fulgur leaned toward then and spoke in hushed tones. "I served under many masters, on land and on sea. Captain Adjo . . ." he swung his head to check for eavesdroppers. ". . . by far da strictest and swiftest in his punishments."

Emmet turned over from where he lay. "Don't misunderstand us, Yamin. Captain Adjo is also quite charitable. Take your situation, for example."

"So, he gives second chances?"

Fulgur sat up again. "Only when da first chance wasn't up to him. Gives him da advantage, you see. Creates loyalty, you see."

"That's how he collected this crew. We were all given second chances by Captain Adjo." Emmet looked up at the stars.

"What was *your* second chance, Emmet?"

Emmet thought for a moment. "It was a matter of life or death. I chose life." He rolled back over away from Yamin.

Yamin looked at Fulgur for an answer.

Fulgur also turned away.

"*It does not matter. We are going to Malta,*" the two spirits murmured in unison, only to him.

What is *Malta? And* why *are we going?*

Like his shipmates, his demons provided little information.

Yamin huffed. *Guess I'll find out soon enough.* He drew his gaze upward toward the ship's edge.

As the crew slept, the Egyptian designs on the gunwale swirled and pulsated as their patterns eerily reflected the starlight. He blinked hard and shook his head. The illusion ceased.

"It doesn't matter."

Pre-dawn arrived. A crewmember roused Emmett in the early hours to relieve the helmsman. Emmett's service on a prior vessel required nothing less. And that is why Captain Adjo had spared his life.

A Germanic named Sterno currently served as Emmet's navigator. His lighter skin reflected the scarce starlight by which he directed the ship's course.

Yamin's desire for answers drove him to follow Emmet to the deck. *Why is everyone so secretive on this ship? Are they truly plotting a course to Malta? We must find a way to get there! We will find a way to get there.* Yamin nodded to the voices as he watched from the edge of the hold as Emmet and Sterno interacted to steer the ship.

Emu scampered about near the men.

Emmet tossed a small morsel to the meddlesome feline.

The cat tore a chunk of flesh from the fish and chewed fast. Once she swallowed, she eyed Yamin and hissed.

Both men looked to see what had upset her. Their eyes locked with Yamin's before he sunk back into the hold to hide.

"Soon."

Yamin agreed.

Two days later, the Island of Crete appeared on the horizon. The men longed for another night of shore leave and performed their duties without any cajoling from Captain Adjo.

Emmet studied the russet clouds billowing toward them. "That is no ordinary storm, Captain."

Yamin looked up from his task of repairing lines.

"I thought not. It is summer, after all." Captain Adjo peered over the gunwale toward the south. "Dust. We better make haste."

Originally headed to the southern coast of the island, and recognizing their dilemma, Captain Adjo ordered a course change for a more protected harbor. "Starboard rudder! We make for the north coast!"

After a couple of hours, the sky to the south grew dark with the brown dust of the African desert. The Lukka's rigging groaned as the crew used every thread of sail to catch the wind. They still had a schedule to keep. Storm or no storm.

Captain Adjo steered them as far as he could before seeking safety in the coastal harbor of Amnisos. A course change meant no shore leave for the crew. "Remember our goal, men. There will be plenty of rest afterwards."

A series of grunts and obscenities issued from the men as they made ready to anchor The Lukka and batten down for the storm. They knew from experience not to protest too loudly, or the captain's fury would be worse than the weather's.

The dust climbed toward them like a cresting wave. The island served as a breakwater for the storm, forcing the wave of dust to crash upon them with the fury of a slave master's whip. The setting sun made the swell of arid particles look like a wall of venous blood.

As Yamin and the crew sheltered in the fore and aft holds, Captain Adjo remained in his quarters. The wind intensified. The sound of the sand blowing against the ship sounded like a million scarab beetles chipping away at dry bones. It was maddening.

The normally stalwart crew shivered in their skins.

"We'll be swallowed alive," exclaimed one man.

"The gods have doomed us," groaned another.

"Be quiet, all of you!" Emmet sat against the bulkhead taking deep breaths through a piece of cloth. The men followed suit and covered their mouths with whatever scraps of cloth they could find.

Yamin's demons felt some freedom in the bedlam and spoke out loud.

"*We can feel them.*"

"*Our brothers and sisters from the caves.*"

"*Nearby. On the island.*"

Yamin sensed the crew to be too occupied to hear, or even care. He spoke back to them. "What island? Is Malta an island?"

"*This island.*" They lifted his hand to point toward Crete. "*There are caves. Wonderful caves. Deep, dark, ancient.*"

Sand battered the ship with blowing sheets of stinging crystals.

"But the captain said we aren't going to the island."

The hatch above Yamin's head flew open. Lightning flashed in the cloud of dust over the ship.

Yamin's muscles tightened as fiery rage filled him. He frantically searched for a weapon, a tool, anything to inflict harm. His erratic movements attracted the attention of those nearby. He found an olive-sized barnacle that must have stuck to his robes when scraping the ship. He picked it up and fingered the sharp white plates of its shell. His lips curled back to expose a foamy, tooth-filled grin.

The men called out in terror.

"Get Fulgur!"

"And secure that hatch!"

Lightning flashed again, and the thunder it produced vibrated the ship. Fulgur clung to a beam in the opposite hold and prayed to his gods for the bolts to not strike him again.

A terrified crewman entered, his sweat-soaked face was smeared with fine, orange dust. "Come quick. It's the boy."

Fulgur forced himself to rise and followed the sailor to the forward hold. He stopped at the entrance. What he saw sent a shock of terror down his spine.

Trembling just inside the doorway stood six of the crew, their faces plastered with fear and disgust. Another bolt of lightning tore across the sky.

Fulgur cowered slightly and followed their gaze toward the bow where he found Yamin. Gashes covered his forearms. Viscous crimson stained his robes. The words on the wall, written in Yamin's blood, proved illegible and ran together with ancient swirling symbols he did not recognize.

Fulgur came out of his stupor and grabbed the man who summoned him. "Get the captain."

20

Yamin woke in bandages, and chains.

Crewmen toiled above sweeping and scraping layers of sand and dust from the deck. The ship was already under sail.

Captain Adjo shouted orders, angrier than usual.

"*Malta.*" Skylla's voice echoed in the empty space around him.

Ashchuwr stirred as well. "*They moved everything away from you. They didn't like your artwork.*" He cackled and howled.

Emmet appeared in the bright doorway. His clothes were still stained from dust. "The captain approaches."

Yamin sat upright. His arms stung, and he winced. The single shackle on his ankle clanked against the deck.

Captain Adjo charged into the hold.

Yamin jumped at his forceful advance.

He did not mince words. "Demons, is it?"

Yamin sat wide-eyed and mute.

"Fulgur told me the truth about that night on Cyprus. And Emmet— Well, Emmet has a sense for this sort of thing. And I tend to believe my men."

Yamin's eyes darted back and forth avoiding the captain.

Captain Adjo kicked Yamin's chained foot. "No answer, then? Maybe one of your spirits would like to reply?"

"*Malta.*"

Adjo recoiled slightly at the gruff voice emanating from Yamin's mouth. "What? What did you say? Malta?" He looked at Emmet and then back at Yamin with a slight tilt to his head.

"Who is asking?" Yamin shifted in place. *"We're headed there, yes?"*

"You know we are." Captain Adjo threw his hands up in frustration. "And what is this drawing you've made? With blood, nonetheless." He stepped close to the bulkhead.

"I don't—

"Wadj-wer." Two voices.

"You drew Wadj-wer." Captain Adjo touched the figure. It was the outline of a man filled with rippling water. "How do *you* know of this?"

"I don't know." Yamin looked at the floor. *"They* do."

Captain Adjo turned and spoke decisively. "Do you remember anything from last night?"

"Just—being out of control."

"Could you be—unrestrained again? If you wanted to, I mean?"

Yamin did not know how to answer.

Captain Adjo propped himself against a barrel across from Yamin. "This drawing is a portent. Do you know what that is, Yamin?"

"Is it something bad?"

"Ha! No, my boy." He held his arms out wide. "It means something *momentous* is going to happen." He leaned in to Yamin. "I will let you in on a little secret."

Yamin leaned toward him.

"Soon." Captain Adjo stood and walked out.

Ashchuwr and Skylla spoke in unison. *"Soon."*

Before Yamin reacted, Fulgur entered. "Da captain says you can be released now dat you're no longer a danger." He bent to unlock the shackle. "You aren't, are you?"

Yamin loosed the binding and dropped it after Fulgur unlocked it. "I'm fine," he huffed and walked out.

The men on deck stopped their work to stare as he exited. With a sharp look from the captain, they went about their business.

Yamin scanned the horizon. The sunrise provided a dark orange light thanks to the remnants of dust in the atmosphere. The island of Crete diminished behind them.

The demons tugged within him toward the disappearing shore.

But he felt a more powerful pull in the opposite direction. Nothing but sea extended before them, and the wind carrying the dust and sand yesterday now pushed them farther west.

Late the next day, another vessel appeared, headed east toward Crete. Yamin secured the line he held and turned to Captain Adjo. "Who do you think they are?"

He did not answer and instead turned to a nearby crewman. "Bhekizitha, go."

Bhekizitha's dark skin matched his somber, unspeaking personality. He wore a tight wrapping of linen on his head. As he climbed the mast, he whistled in tune with his steps. When he reached the top, he stood on the yardarm and looked toward the approaching vessel.

Tensions swelled as the distance between the ships decreased.

Yamin held his bandaged forearms. "Aren't you afraid they could be pirates?" The unknown vessel was almost upon them.

Some of the men waved as they walked portside.

Bhekizitha whistled rapidly three times and signaled with a circular arm motion.

Captain Adjo grinned and shouted in Egyptian to the men. *"Ehna han hamr'a!"*

Out came swords, daggers, and grappling hooks. The Lukka shifted hard to port to come alongside the other vessel. Yamin fell backward onto the deck.

Captain Adjo glared back at him and hollered, "Now is the time to lose control!"

The hooks found their marks on the gunwale of the other ship. The Lukka's crew leapt over and overwhelmed the unsuspecting men.

One of the other ship's men lifted a bow and loosed an arrow. The black arrow struck Bhekizitha as he climbed down the mast. The projectile entered his shoulder forcing him to let go and plummet a short distance to the deck. The impact shoved the arrow farther in and it sliced through the back of his tunic.

All Yamin could think of was how Bhekizitha said nothing

throughout the ordeal. Instead of gasping, Yamin guffawed. The grizzly scene and attack on his shipmates triggered the demons.

He sought out the enemy bowman who now targeted others of Yamin's crew—the crew that was to take him to Malta.

"Protect them." The demons called out through Yamin. *"Malta!"*

Yamin grabbed the yardarm line. The sides of each ship rubbed and crashed together like a set of monstrous wooden jaws. Splinters shaved off into the water. He ignored any urgency to hide and swung across the watery chasm, propelled by demonic vigor.

Captain Adjo watched his well-practiced men cleave the other crew into silence. But his attention fixed upon the wild being climbing and swinging toward his prey. He beamed as Yamin raced toward the enemy archer.

Yamin carried no weapons. The demons were all nails, teeth, and muscle—animalistic.

The bowman fired wildly as the visage of Yamin terrified all who witnessed him. The arrow whizzed by Yamin's head and sliced harmlessly into the sea.

Yamin pushed off with all four limbs into the air and onto the bowman. A bite to the man's neck forced a blood-curdling scream out of him. He cursed in Latin as Yamin tore at his face and gripped his head.

When it was all over, the man splayed motionless on the deck.

Yamin stood over him panting and sneering at his fallen prey.

Captain Adjo led the cheer and the men joined. *"Ehna han hamr'a! Ehna han hamr'a!"*

Yamin did not understand their chants.

Skylla offered a translation. *"Are you going to break your promise?"*

Captain Adjo approached Yamin. "Well done, boy. I knew I could count on you when the time came."

"Are you going to break your promise?" Yamin stood up taller and wiped the bowman's blood from his face onto his bandaged forearm.

Captain Adjo's laugh echoed between the two vessels. "You are certainly one of us." He turned to the men and cheered again.

The demons stirred and twisted within Yamin. *"One of us."*

Yamin groaned and bent slightly. "Are you going to break your promise, Adjo?"

Captain Adjo looked at him with a furrowed brow. His lips tightened. "What have I promised *you*? *You* are the one who owes *me* his life."

"Your promise to take us to Malta."

"Malta." The demons spoke in unison.

"That is where that ship came from, and that is where we are going." Captain Adjo's look of concern faded and he walked toward the crew. "No witnesses. No evidence."

Emmet, who had never crossed to the other ship, called from The Lukka. "Captain, you realize this was a *Roman* merchant vessel, yes?"

"The plan all along." He turned to crew. "Now, move!"

Yamin stepped toward The Lukka. A severely injured man lay at his feet. Yamin went to step over him as he coughed his last breaths.

The man gargled through a bloody throat. "Wait."

Yamin knelt to listen. No sooner was he overcome by the shock of the blow. A third spirit penetrated his soul from the dying man. Worse than the previous two, the force knocked Yamin onto the deck of the crewless vessel. He writhed and convulsed in pain.

The last thing he heard before consciousness failed him was Ashchuwr's hoarse utterance. *"Welcome, unexpected friend."*

21

A Lukka crewman reached over the gunwales of the two still connected ships and handed Yamin's limp body to Fulgar. "Now what? Can't trust him. Too unpredictable."

The other crewman agreed. "We should drop him overboard and pretend it was a mistake."

Captain Adjo overheard them. "And lose such a glorious asset? You saw how he performed today. What better weapon than the unexpected, yes?" He chuckled and turned to the other crewmen. "Set it ablaze and cut it loose!"

Fulgur carried Yamin to the doorway of the forward hold. He looked at the Roman ship as flames spread over the freshly oiled decking. The vivid paint on the carved image of Apollo at its stern melted into the sea. An injured man's muffled scream rode over the water with the smoke issuing from inside the scuttled ship's hull.

Fulgur placed Yamin on a sleeping mat and secured a shackle to his ankle. "Nothing we can do for you, Yamin." He looked at the young man's whiskered ashen face. "You're on your own now."

Yamin slept for two days of westerly travel. When he woke, he found himself again bound to the bulkhead.

One crewman stood watch at the doorway and ran out as soon as Yamin met his eye.

Yamin searched the room. A horde of unfamiliar goods

surrounded him. The hold had become cramped. A single brass oil lamp swung from the ceiling in the center of the room.

Within a short time, Captain Adjo, Fulgur, and Emmet entered and formed a semi-circle around him. A breeze of fresh salt air followed the men in.

It had been days since Yamin took in anything but dust and smoke-filled breaths. He inhaled deeply.

"*We smell it. Malta.*"

Yamin closed his eyes hard. *Go . . . away.*

Emmet handed Yamin a clay jar of watered-down wine. When he did not open his eyes, Emmet barked his name. "Yamin."

Yamin's eyes snapped open. He reached out and gladly accepted the drink.

"You're somewhat of a problem, boy." Captain Adjo paced in the narrow walkway. "Useful, yes. But too unpredictable to keep around."

Emmet sat on a barrel. His knees cracked.

Emu meowed from the entrance, and Fulgur shooed her away.

Captain Adjo continued. "You've been the center of discussion among the crew since our last encounter with that Roman ship."

Fulgur sat next to Emmet and spoke to Yamin. "Dees demons. You want dem in you?"

Bold question. Yamin dreaded this. Would he be able to speak of the demons outwardly? Would they allow him to have control and admit the truth?

The three men waited for an answer.

Yamin searched for the demons' desires. He placed each of them into the center of his thoughts.

Ashchuwr. Nothing.

Skylla. Still nothing.

Ashchuwr and Skylla spoke in unison. "*He is Jacobus.*"

"*I am Jacobus.*"

Yamin's eyes closed tightly again as the intertwining darkness squeezed his viscera.

"*We will allow you to speak freely—for now.*"

Yamin's eyes slowly opened and he looked at the three men. "I feel like a stranger in my own body." His voice quivered.

Emmet's face shone with compassion. "What can we do for you?"

Fulgur stood quickly. "Nothing can be done. He's cursed. And his curse'll be our downfall, unless—"

"Unless what?" Captain Adjo held up a silver ingot stolen from the other ship. "He is property. My property. And I will decide what's to be done with him."

Yamin straightened up. "Just get me to Malta, and I'll no longer be anyone's problem."

Captain Adjo pocketed the treasure. "And why is that? What awaits you there?"

Fulgur pulled Captain Adjo aside. "The men. They're frightened."

Captain Adjo turned to Yamin. "So, we leave him there? To what end? What if he turns on us? Tells the locals of our affairs? What then?"

"We . . ." Yamin cocked his head . . . "*I* will speak of you to no one. It's not our . . . *my* objective."

Emmet stood. "What *is* your objective then?" He looked around Yamin, as if seeing something the others could not. "What do they want?"

This time the demons replied together with an inhuman voice. *"Our objective is to be known."*

Emmet gasped and stepped back from Yamin. He made a strange sign with his hands, plucked a hair from his head, and burned it in the lamp's flame.

Captain Adjo turned to leave. "We drop him on Malta. Exiled as a noncompliant." He turned back to Yamin. "Remember when I told you there were two ways to leave this ship?"

"We remember."

"Consider yourself lucky it's not the other." Adjo blew out the lamp and exited the hold. The other men followed, leaving Yamin shackled and in the dark.

Emu reentered the hold, this time carrying a wet rat that must have jumped from the other vessel as the sea engulfed its burning hulk. A muffled growl followed by a hiss escaped the feline as it crept along the wall behind some crates, presumably to ingest its prey.

Yamin knelt and crawled slowly toward the distracted cat. The rusty chain holding him to the bulkhead had just enough length for him to reach out. He grabbed Emu by the scruff and yanked it from its meal. The sound of the cat's neck snapping energized the demons.

Yamin pulled at his fetters. The skin around his ankle tore. He would have to break bones to escape.

The demons needed him mobile.

He grabbed the chain and pulled with all his might. A powerful force rose within and spread to the muscles in his arms. The iron ring holding the links bent and spread. The chain snapped lose from the bulkhead sending Yamin flying backward into a barrel. His head rang from the blow.

The demons laughed. *"We are free!"*

Yamin grabbed the cat's body and stuffed it behind the cargo. He sat back against the wall. His hand fell upon a plate of dried fish and old bread. He ate furiously.

When he finished, he laid on his sleeping mat. His demons plotted.

"It will be useful."

"Yes. Keep it hidden."

"To cause anarchy."

Yamin woke late the next morning to the sound of chanting on the deck. He crept toward the doorway and peered through a crack to see the men gathered around the mast.

They droned deeply in one accord with long drawn-out vowels. *"A ka dua."* Their voices resonated through the ship's wooden structure as they repeated the saying over and over.

Yamin's demons stirred. They translated the ancient Egyptian for him. *"Unity uttermost showed."*

One of the men held a polished piece of quartz up to the sun. He bent and placed the object next to the mast where three Egyptian patterns had been carved into it. No, burned. The designs differed drastically from the others adorning the ship's artistry.

A beam of concentrated sunlight emanated from the quartz and struck the wood below the three hieroglyphs. The surface charred. Thin wisps of smoke rose and disappeared as they passed through the gathered men.

Yamin sniffed at the air.

Adjo addressed the men as the artist worked. "One hundred years ago my ancestors were the most powerful army of marauders on the Great Sea. They sought shelter in the high cliffs of Sicily and used those strongholds with ten thousand men to rule as they wanted. To take what they wanted." He drew his hands to his chest.

"Pompey and his Imperial navy drove them to destruction. But with this victory, our fourth in two years, we strike back in defiance against the tight fist of our Roman oppressors. We will not be driven into oblivion. Our gods will allow us to overcome in the face of tyranny." He held up a cup of wine, and the men joined his salute.

"To the gods! To Wadj-wer!"

Yamin crept back to his dark resting place.

No men other than the wounded Bhekizitha had slept in Yamin's hold with him for three nights. They had Bhekizitha placed near the doorway, far from Yamin's reach.

Light from a quarter moon shone through the open doorway. And no one guarded the entrance. Several hours had passed since Captain Adjo's speech, and the night's stillness encompassed the vessel.

He listened to the gentle squeak of the rudder as the helmsman kept The Lukka's course true, the sail flap as it caught bursts of wind from the south, and the water splash as the hull cut through its surface.

"*Soon.*"

Yamin wrapped his arms around his stomach as the demons drove him to act. He groped in the dark for the object, found it, and made stealthily for the door.

22

Bring him to me!"

The scraping and stomping of many feet on the deck above tensed Yamin's muscles. Upon hearing the Captain's irritable command, he reached behind to make sure he had secured the shackle ring. Bending it back in place took effort. The demons obliged with delight.

Two crewmen entered with Fulgur. They yanked Yamin to his feet while Fulgur unlocked the bindings. After their act of piracy, they had nothing to hide now and let their brutality surface with impunity. They shoved Yamin out of the hold and dragged him topside.

He squinted in the bright sunlight and curled into a fetal position on the deck.

The men shouted.

"I say throw the devil to the dog fish before he kills again."

"Keelhaul him. He's already familiar with the ship's bottom."

A few men laughed.

Fulgur stepped up. "How do you s'pose he carried out dis fiendish task?" He bent and grabbed Yamin's leg. Dark coagulated blood clung to his ankle. "Chained all night. I just unlocked him."

A crewman called out from the back of the group. "Siding with *him*, are you?"

Fulgur dropped Yamin's leg back onto the deck. "I've no sympathy for the curs'ed boy. Whatever he did in the past to invite dees demons to take up residence is beyond me."

Captain Adjo wrestled out the bent nail holding Emu's dead

body to the mast. His eyes welled with tears when the cat fell to the deck with a wet thud. He dropped the nail, and it clinked next to the carcass.

Emmet approached with a section of clean linen and held it out. "This is a terrible omen, Captain. Very bad luck. Something needs to be done."

Captain Adjo wrapped Emu tightly in the cloth, as if preparing a mummy for burial. He turned to Emmet and spoke softly. "How long until Malta?"

The men watched in silence.

"Two days, Captain. Unless the winds turn unfavorable."

Captain Adjo walked up to Yamin and held out the shrouded corpse. "I want to talk to the demons."

"Captain —" Emmet spoke, but the captain held up a hand to silence him.

Yamin writhed. *As if I have a choice.*

"Who did this?"

"*He who covets. He who lies. He who is . . . deceitful. This is who has slain the beast.*"

The crewmen took a step back when they heard the otherworldly voices proceed from Yamin's mouth with the lengthy hisses of a snake.

The captain, unfazed, snickered and half inspected his crew. "That could be any one of us."

"*We cannot leave this vessel, the boy. We need him . . . to be safe. It . . . was . . . not . . . us.*"

Fulgur stumbled over his words. "Cap'n, da boy . . . *day* . . . day speak truth."

"You are deceived, Fulgur. Am I the only one who can see?" Emmet stepped in front of the men. "Captain, I perceive what lies within him. The indwelling spirits of temptation. An aura of evil hangs about the boy. Whether he did this or not, he cannot be trusted any longer. If it wasn't him, then he's obviously corrupted another."

Captain Adjo looked deep into Yamin's bloodshot eyes. He

turned his gaze to Emmet. "Maybe *you* killed Emu, to make it look like *he* did it. Maybe *you* are lying because you fear the boy."

Emmet teetered on weak legs. "He—he's deceiving you, Captain. Can't you see that?" Emmet almost collapsed onto the deck but grabbed the gunwale to support himself. "It's the trespassers in the boy, clouding your judgement." He pointed a shaking finger at Yamin.

Captain Adjo spoke to Yamin. "Tell me why you must go to Malta."

Emmet cried out. "No, Captain! It is strictly forbidden to communicate with demons to acquire knowledge."

"And how do you know this? Who forbids it?"

"I have studied the Hebrew's Law. Moses—"

"Stop! Do not speak the name on this vessel of the magician who deceived my ancestors." Captain Adjo spat his words. "I do not recognize the false god of the Jews."

Yamin sat seething on the deck.

Captain Adjo motioned to him. "Lock him back up. We will abandon him, and whatever may live inside, for the Maltese to deal with."

"Cap'n," Fulgur whispered, "how can we trust him to not go to da authorities?"

"Leave that to me." Captain Adjo looked up at the sail. "The wind changes. Make adjustments!" He stomped back to his quarters with the remains of his beloved cat under his arm.

Fulgur pulled Yamin up and lead him back to the hold. He secured the shackle on Yamin's unscathed ankle.

Yamin stared at Fulgur's cloudy eye. "Can you see out of that?"

Fulgur replied coldly. "I see well enough."

"*Of that we have no doubt.*"

Fulgur bolted upright and backed away. "Whether I see dem or not, I believe what Emmet discerns. You fool no one."

"*Except maybe the captain, yes?*" Yamin produced an unsettling manic grin.

Fulgur exited with haste and slammed the hold's door behind him.

The demons laughed as he did so.

23

Oh, what a stench." The men who entered Yamin's hold two days later covered their noses with rags. They grabbed him up and unlocked his shackle. Gasping for fresh air, they stepped around the unconscious Bhekizitha and hurried Yamin out.

The sun had set. Yamin sighed in relief, for he had seen nothing in two days brighter than the narrow beams of light that pierced through the space under the door.

The last of the sea birds called overhead as they flew inland to their roosts in the fading twilight.

Men from the shore communicated with The Lukka's crew while they unloaded goods and took on fresh supplies for their voyage to Rome. This port on the northern coast of Malta was on a smaller island in a protected bay. Captain Adjo wanted to avoid the port on the south shore from where their previous encounter had hailed.

"Who's this prisoner?" A lean middle-aged portmaster with a full salt-and-pepper beard appeared from behind a stack of crates. "We don't accept prisoners at this port. You'll have to take him to the centurion." He pointed inland toward the Roman city of Melite.

"My man Fulgur will take him."

The portmaster put up a hand. "He won't see your prisoner now. It's far too late. It's a three-hour walk anyway."

"He's not *really* a prisoner."

"What do you mean?" He looked at Yamin's bloodied ankles. "You could've fooled me."

"This boy has taken ill—in spirit." Captain Adjo gave Fulgur a knowing look.

"Is he deranged?" The portmaster and his aid scrutinized Yamin.

The flickering light of a nearby fire reflected off Yamin's greasy skin. He stood tight-lipped and silent. His soiled robes and matted hair only helped support the captain's claim.

Captain Adjo took the portmaster aside. "We were attacked by pirates on the way here from Crete."

"Pirates? How did you escape with your lives?"

"Hard to believe, I know. We were two days out. They shot one of my men with an arrow injuring him badly. He is healing below deck as we speak." Captain Adjo's feigned level of sincerity grew as he spoke. "This boy was never the same after what he endured during the melee. He became enraged. Mad, really. If it were not for his ferocity, the brigands would have overtaken us. But he is now withdrawn and full of deceptions to trick himself into believing what he experienced did not happen."

The portmaster stood hard-pressed to maintain his composure. "A terrible tragedy, to be sure."

"Worse yet, he thinks *we* were the pirates. Can you believe that?"

The portmaster gave a half-hearted laugh.

His aid mimicked him out of respect.

"None on my vessel can help him."

"I suppose not." The portmaster turned to his aid. "He doesn't need the centurion. Take him to the local priests, for healing."

The aid wrestled his gaze away from Yamin and addressed his master. "Yes, at the temple. I will escort him there in the morning."

Captain Adjo spoke only to the portmaster. "Can't he take him now?" He held up a small animal skin pouch and jingled the contents within. "We need to be underway as soon as possible. Rome waits for no one."

The portmaster snatched the pouch and opened it. He poured the golden coins into his hand to assess their worth. He nodded in agreement.

The portmaster's aid took Yamin by the arm.

"One more thing." Captain Adjo held up Emu's mummified remains, now decorated with hieroglyphs and repeating geometric patterns similar to the weaves of an ornate basket.

The portmaster huffed. "What is *that*?"

"Do you know of a place where I can bury my cat?"

Yamin followed the aid to a wooden bridge connecting the port island to the mainland of Malta. A sturdy stone jetty of Roman design supported the base of the conduit.

"*He is deceptive.*"

"*Yes, like us.*"

Yamin succumbed to the demon's temptation to pry. "What's your name?"

The aid refused to look at him. "I don't care to know yours. Why do you care to know who I am?"

Yamin did not give up easily and spoke matter-of-factly. "I've seen jetties like this one before." A myriad of small rock crabs skittered into holes in the rocks. Their carapaces resembled a fine-grained marble. "But they were much larger where I come from."

Yamin winced and balled up his fists. '*Where I come from?*' *Really? Ugh.*

The demons snickered.

"Oh, where's that?"

"East. Far east of here." Yamin motioned with a loose arm in a general easterly direction.

"I am Heber." He kept walking, still refusing to look at Yamin.

Yamin's heart pounded before asking, "A Hebrew name?"

"That surprises you?"

"Only that we thought you were a Roman, or at least Maltese."

Heber continued leading Yamin up a gentle slope. "'We?'"

Yamin stopped.

"I only meant—"

Heber finally turned to study him under the remaining vestiges of diluted dusky sunlight. "*We* are both Roman and, at the same time, all Maltese." He began walking again. "Rome keeps its distance, and the authorities here like it that way."

Another hour passed before a small row of multi-level, beige, limestone townhomes rose above them to the left of the dirt road. Heber knocked gently on one of the doors.

After a moment, a lamp's light grew from within until it illuminated the edges around the door. When it opened, Yamin noticed a faintly painted Menorah on the upper right corner of its wooden exterior.

"These are your priests? Jewish priests?" Yamin took a step back. Images of the sailors who attacked him months ago flashed into his mind. His breathing grew heavy, and he tightened his jaw.

The priest in the doorway motioned to others inside, and they ran to help.

Yamin fell on the ground and thrashed about. *"Jews, pagans, Egyptians. What do they know of us?"*

The first priest pushed Heber out of the way.

Heber obliged by stepping aside. "His—his name is Yamin."

"Take him inside. And you . . ." He gestured to Heber with a nod. "Return to the port. Quickly. Before anyone sees you here."

The priests took hold of Yamin and wrestled him in, slamming the door behind them.

One of the holy men, a man not much older than Yamin, placed a scroll of velum between Yamin's teeth to prevent him from biting his tongue.

Yamin bit it in two, growled, and spat the pieces at him. *"Filthy Jew. Keep your god and his prudence away."*

The man stepped back as his eyes widened. "This is no normal sickness, Nathan."

Nathan, the priest who answered the door, knelt next to Yamin. "I agree, Abdown. Heber would have brought this boy to the pagans if it were anything close to normal."

They allowed him to convulse on the polished stone floor for several minutes until calming.

Abdown bent to pick up the two halves of scroll. He showed them to Nathan "Why did the boy say that?"

Nathan took one half and inspected the writing.

He read aloud. "They made him jealous with strange gods, with abhorrent things they provoked him. They sacrificed to demons, not God, to deities they had never known, to new ones recently arrived, whom your ancestors had not feared."

The demons within Yamin released a blood-curdling howl.

Yamin leapt up to run, but two priests blocked the only exit.

"Take him upstairs." Nathan grabbed a length of rope from the wall. "Hurry."

They seized Yamin and struggled to carry him. He slipped from their grasp several times as he fought their attempts.

Against one wall was a raised sleeping platform. They deposited Yamin upon it.

Nathan helped tie him down then led the men back downstairs. "He will calm down again. Do not speak of our beliefs to him or give him any information about who we are or what we do."

The men nodded.

"For now, I will go back up to gain as much information as I can before we act."

Abdown approached Nathan. "Rabbi, that boy's demons, they are raging."

Nathan put his hand on Abdown's shoulder. "They are not *his* demons. Know that they control him." He turned to walk back upstairs. "Demons I know. It's people who are insane."

24

The next morning, Captain Adjo woke well-rested. He had rid his ship of that nuisance and pled to his gods to take Emu into the afterlife. But his good mood declined rapidly as his crew argued loudly in the forward hold. He exited his quarters.

Fulgur approached. "Just coming to get you, Cap'n." His breath escaped him.

"What is it now?" His shoulders sank. "Don't tell me Bhekizitha died."

"Well, Cap'n—"

Captain Adjo entered the hold. The stench of death and excrement meeting his nostrils made him recoil. "Get this place scrubbed down before we set sail!"

Fulgur drew Captain Adjo's attention to Bhekizitha's last resting place.

Emmet, holding a rag soaked in hyssop flower oil over his nose and mouth, folded back the linen covering Bhekizitha. Several flies buzzed off.

All the body's internal organs, from the intestines to the heart, had been removed. The wounded shoulder had turned gangrenous, its telltale foul-smelling tissue spread down the arm and up the neck in blackened irregular patches like ink stains.

"It may not be of any consolation, Captain," —Emmet swallowed hard— "but it looks like Bhekizitha may have died from that Roman's black arrow before Yamin did *this* to him."

Fulgur pointed to the wall behind them.

Yamin had written in blood again, but this time something resembling letters.

Captain Adjo's eyes narrowed. "Where is he?"

Fulgur looked about the hold. "Could've hidden dem entrails anywhere in—"

"Not Bhekizitha!" He smacked Fulgur on the back of the head. "The boy!" Captain Adjo exited swiftly and dragged Fulgur by the arm. "Take two men and find him. You have until sunset to bring him back. And atonement will be swift." He swept his gaze around the ship as the crew readied for departure. "Emmet!"

Emmet appeared from behind. "Captain?"

"Inform the men we are holding over for the time being."

"Yes, Captain." Emmet turned to carry out his order.

"And, Emmet?"

Emmet turned back around.

"Find me someone to translate that writing down there."

"Yes, Captain."

"What do you mean, *He is gone?*" Nathan ran upstairs to find an empty bed.

Abdown lifted a piece of snapped rope and looked at Nathan wide-eyed.

"He couldn't have gotten very far. Search the area for any sign where he may have headed."

"If the Romans find him—"

"He will be dead before sunset." Nathan headed back down the stairwell. "I'm more concerned what will happen if the pagans find him."

Nathan's experience with possessed persons stretched back more than twenty years. Having received his formal priestly training from rabbis at a diasporic synagogue on Sicily when still a young man, he felt coming to Malta held meaning for him.

Malta had been known for its ancient cults and polytheistic worship. Exposing the people here to the one true God was at the heart of Nathan's calling. He had never been successful at ridding a person of a demon, but Yamin would make an excellent case study.

A fellow priest entered the townhouse. "Rabbi, we found his trail. It looks like he's headed south to Melite."

Abdown followed Nathan out. "There's no way he'll go unnoticed. He won't even make it there before being picked up by a patrol."

Nathan walked with Abdown to the end of the row of houses. "Take two men with you on the trail and bring him back. Speak of this to no one."

Abdown walked swiftly to meet the others.

Nathan returned to the townhouse. But before he entered, someone called from across the road. He looked. No one.

They called again. "Over here."

He turned to investigate the roadside. A Roman roadmarker stuck out of the shrubs. Behind it he saw a pair of legs with bloodied ankles.

"Yamin? Is that you?"

A whisper. "They are impossible to control."

Nathan took a step closer. He almost called out for the others but did not want to scare the boy away. "What would you have me do?"

"There is nothing—*you can do.*" The voice changed mid-sentence.

Nathan looked back at the house and up and down the road. No one.

"*We are leaving now. We have others who need us.*"

"Who? Who needs you?"

Yamin rose and walked down the hill into the small valley below and northward.

Great boulders and steep inclines lined that path. Nathan could not follow. He ran as fast as he could to the others, but they had already gone too far in the opposite direction.

Emmet returned to The Lukka by midday. He had with him a potential translator.

"What do you mean, you *might* be able to translate it?" Captain Adjo closed his eyes and took a deep breath. He pointed to the forward hold. "The men just finished cleaning but left the inscription."

Emmet escorted the woman around the various goods brought onto the deck when the crew cleaned.

When they approached the entranceway, the woman froze. "He was here."

"That is what I said." Emmet studied the elderly sage. She wore an eclectic gathering of robes made of different earth-tone fibers. Her head covering loosely shielded her thinning gray hair.

Captain Adjo walked up behind them. "What's wrong?"

The woman blocked the door with her back to the men. She held up her right arm. Her sleeve fell away exposing wrinkled, weathered skin on the back of her hand. A faded gray tattoo depicting swirling patterns of lines embellished its surface.

Captain Adjo stepped closer to Emmet. "Where did you dig this one up?"

"She comes highly recommended by the portmaster's aid."

Captain Adjo considered the woman's back. "You didn't answer the question."

"I had to go into the countryside. An hour's walk. There are some caves—"

"You brought me a cave woman?"

"Her people—they have worshipped their gods on this island for thousands of years."

The sage stepped into the hold and turned to look at Yamin's writing. "Those of my ancestors—before the Roman gods. Before the Greek gods."

Captain Adjo took out his coin purse and shook it gently. "You know it then?"

A man's voice answered from the doorway. "It is Canaanite."

She held out her hand and looked at the newcomer.

Captain Adjo placed one silver coin into her palm.

Emmet stepped aside to let the man in. "You did not need to come, Heber."

"Sacrifice." The woman's shrill voice echoed in the empty hold.

Heber crossed his arms and studied the drawing.

Captain Adjo chuckled at the woman. "I don't think more is necessary." He put his purse away. "One coin will do."

"I think she means *sacrifice* is the translation." Heber walked back to the doorway, unimpressed.

"That's all?" Captain Adjo raised his voice. "Nothing more?"

"Sacrifice." The sage seemed to deflate when she spoke the word again.

They exited the hold, and Emmet walked the woman and Heber to the gangplank.

Captain Adjo joined them. "Which one was the sacrifice? Emu or Bhekizitha?"

Emmet shrugged his shoulders. "I do not know, Captain."

They watched as Heber escorted the old woman out of the port.

"Either way, Heber now knows something went awry on The Lukka. And he is a Roman."

"We need to leave sooner than later, Captain. An investigation would certainly finish us."

"I know."

25

Again—from the line, *If you have a mind for it!*" a sing-song voice rose from somewhere behind the stage.

Abdown sat on a rock and watched in wonder at the open-aired structure, and the people therein. He never understood actors and their idolatrous performances. Yet, the players' tones and forced gesticulations intrigued him while he rested from his search for Yamin.

The actors continued.

"If you have a mind for it, or it gives you pleasure, I do permit it. Tie me up, bind me, scourge me. I recommend you, I give you my permission."

"If, hereafter, you should revoke your permission, when you are unloosed, I myself should be hung up for punishment."

"And would I venture to do that, to yourself especially? On the contrary, if I see you but struck, it gives me pain immediately."

"To me, indeed, faith.

"No, to me."

"I could prefer that to be the case. But what now do you wish?"

"Why need I tell a lie to you? I am desperately in love."

"My back feels that."

"Stop!" The thinly built director held up his arms, interlaced his fingers, and placed his hands on his head. "'Back?' It's supposed to be *shoulder-blades*."

"Why would Milphio feel it specifically in his shoulder-blades?" Alair lowered his mask to reveal a middle-aged man with a short

beard. He turned to his fellow actor. "You have to see the logic here, Callias."

Callias shrugged his shoulders.

The director walked up to the stage. "Because that's what Plautus wrote two-hundred years ago and that's what we are performing . . . *tonight*. The Governor is watching this performance in a few hours. It is his favorite play. Just stick with how it is written. No *ad libitum*."

Abdown smiled at the trouble the actors were having. As a Jew, he was not permitted to attend any theatrical performances. Anything Roman was an abomination to the rabbis. *Nathan would not be pleased.*

A man approached Abdown from behind. "Why would a Jew be watchin' a play?"

Abdown swung his head to see Fulgur standing proudly behind him.

Men held daggers to the throats of Abdown's two frightened fellow holy men.

Fulgur sat next to Abdown on the large stone perch. He motioned for his men to make the others sit as well. "I believe we're both looking for da same person."

"How do *you* know why I am here?"

"Because Nathan asked us for help."

Abdown sprang to his feet. "What have you done to Rabbi?"

"Please, sit back down." Fulgur looked around to see if anyone had taken notice. The actors continued to rehearse. "We're no one's enemy here. Well, maybe the Romans, huh?" He elbowed Abdown and chuckled. "Nathan is as you left him."

Abdown's brow furrowed, and he shifted away from Fulgur. "We thought the boy came this way."

"As did we." Fulgur watched the actors with Abdown. "You know, a lot of what you see on dat stage, da technology, comes from sailin' ships."

"What do you know of theatre? You're a mariner."

"Ah, a dumb sailor, huh?" Fulgur stood next to Abdown. "The systems day use to fly tings around involve counterweights. Blocks and falls." He allowed his hands to articulate the motions of these articles as he spoke. "Like da mechanics of sails." He looked at Abdown. "Not dat a Jew would know."

Abdown walked to his men. "Let's go."

Fulgur motioned for his men to back away and followed Abdown up the dirt path leading away from the theatre. "If da boy made it dis far, da Romans would certainly have captured him by now."

Abdown continued to walk at a brisk pace. "Agreed."

"What did da rabbis want with da boy anyway?"

"Rabbi thought he could—help him—in some way."

"Help him?" Fulgur laughed. "Do you know what he did on our vessel before being exiled?" Fulgur reached out to grab Abdown's shoulder.

Abdown swung around to meet his eye before Fulgur could lay a hand on him.

Fulgur bared his teeth. "He killed da captain's cat and gutted a man."

Abdown screwed up his face and swallowed hard. "His demons did that."

"You mean da demons *made* him do dat. He's lost control."

"How did you know the boy was taken to us?"

"Da portmaster's aid told us. He's a Jew too. But I suspect you knew dat already."

"Since I can see you are no friend of the Romans, can I trust you not to share that information with anyone else? We need Heber's news of their comings and goings at the port."

"As the ancients say, *Da enemy of my enemy is my friend.*" The vein-like scars on Fulgur's face crumpled into wrinkles under the force of his crooked smile.

They reached the apex of an outcropping of limestone. Abdown scanned the horizon. "He could be anywhere on this island by now.

A dog howled in the distance.

Was that a dog? Abdown shuddered at the strange humanistic sound. "I'm afraid I'll have to report back to Rabbi the bad news."

Fulgur stared toward the source of the bizarre cry. "Yes, and I to da captain."

26

Yamin reached the lowlands on the opposite side of the bay from where The Lukka was still moored. Azure water rippled in the distance, but the faraway ship escaped his vision.

Ancient temples dotted the landscape. As he traveled, men carrying baskets on the road ignored him. A woman and her two children strayed too close, so he withdrew into the shrubs until they passed.

One silent temple beckoned in the distance. Fighting the compulsion proved impossible. The demons within him grew more and more energized as he neared the timeworn structure. He served as the divining rod for their forceful will.

He stopped at the temple's entrance. One last effort of resistance spread down his arm. He placed his hand on a pockmarked rocky slab supporting the opening.

Stone. Nothing more than rough-hewn limestone. It felt no more real to him now than before he touched it. An absence of sensory input. A partial blindness brought on by his affliction.

An invisible fist wrapped around his innards tugging him forward. He looked at the ground. Footprints. Someone had recently been here. A pagan priest? Another tormented soul like him? Welcoming midday sunlight streamed through the entrance behind him, only to be snuffed out by the darkness ahead.

Inside the temple, a central cave corridor opened into an antechamber. An ancient mural decorated the walls and curved ceiling. Whirls and wavy lines, random diamond patches, and oval patterns painted dark-red swirled around him.

He bent low and crossed a narrow passage with two steps leading downward. He stood erect in a room carved from sandstone seemingly eons ago. Dim light still filtered here from the passageway behind.

The dank earthiness of dark places intermingled with a hint of flowery perfume his mother used to wear. Yamin's heart sank, and a lump formed in his throat.

His bare feet produced a pattering that resonated endlessly into the connecting caverns.

"The oracle."

"Deep they delved."

"It is powerful. Use it."

A semi-circular hole on the rear wall, the diameter of a man's arm, stood at the height of Yamin's mouth.

"Speak, and they will listen."

Yamin paused, then spoke into the rock's void. "I am empty."

His voice magnified a hundredfold and echoed throughout the entire structure. Had he uttered these words? Why? Bitterness, hate, resentment, anger, fear, and violence surged through him.

A flash of his mother dying. A glimpse of his father coughing blood. Dar eating at his family's table. Baniy laughing at him as he struggled with his father's boat.

He knew why.

"Fill me so that I may be whole again. I feel only torment. Come so that my senses may be restored. I am lost. Find me."

Many voices replied. Their terrible utterances made his insides tremble. *Even the demons are afraid.*

"Our earthly wisdom is sensual. We walk like a roaring lion, seeking whom we can devour. Give heed to us and listen to our doctrine. We are here. Seek us out."

He followed their whisperings as they guided him through many narrow and darkening passages which led down, down into the cold solid earth beneath the ancient island.

He straightened when he entered the next room. Only shadow.

Yet he could still see. Where blindness should exist, another sense permeated his mind, as if he had memorized the structure.

He did not need the light.

In the center of the large opening stood a circular stone altar. Grimy stains clung to its rough surface. Thick chains hung from above. Darkness hid their starting points. Cut out of the surrounding rock walls were layers of stone resting places with hollows scooped out for bodies. All empty.

Down he went again, stooping and crawling through a slender passage into another large room, rimmed with narrow slits in the stone walls. Thousands of skeletons laid piled high on either side of the chamber. He peered through one of the slits. Even more skeletons. Thousands more. Some had elongated skulls. Some piles were organized by bone type. Others laid haphazardly strewn about.

Yamin peered through another slit. An empty room. A thick, square, stone door, almost as tall as he, guarded its entrance.

A second passage opened on another wall.

"Go. It is not much farther."

He crawled into another passage, this one narrower and lower than the others. Yamin's sense of knowing diminished. How much time had passed since he entered the cave? Had he been here for hours or days?

He groped his way, pulled by the demons, until he reached a narrow ledge pathway about as wide as a man. A sheer drop that seemed to have no end opened beyond the ledge to the right. A wall rose on his left.

He stepped forward, staying close to the rock wall side. His foot knocked a small stone loose. As it fell, Yamin waited in vain for the report signaling an end to the abyss. None sounded.

He stopped, but not of his own will.

His demons spoke in harmony. *"They are here."*

Ghostly images of gangly ethereal beings emerged from an opening across the cave. They floated in single file along a narrow ledge below him, pouring from cracks in the walls as steam issues from a leaky clay pot. Too many were their number for Yamin to total.

He stared in disbelief as he clutched to the rock around the opening.

As the spectral multitudes passed along their path, each stopped and turned toward him. They raised their lanky arms in unison and beckoned him with their sinuous fingers.

Terror rooted Yamin to the spot. He moved his left hand on the wall to steady himself. He did not contact cold rock but something soft and wet. As it moved beneath his hand, a strong gust of wind came from the depths. The pressure swept him from the ledge and he fell into the inky darkness below.

The passage of time seemed to stop as Yamin plummeted forever downward. With each beat of his racing heart, the piercing penetration of dozens of demonic entities entered his vacant soul—a soul left void in the wake of overwhelming losses and perceived futility. Such was his experience, until Yamin could feel no more, and his body landed with a squishy thud at the bottom of a stony pit darker than the depths of Hell itself.

27

How old is this boy?"

The centurion's questions grated on Captain Adjo. "I don't know. Maybe sixteen."

The sun neared the horizon and still no sign of Fulgur or Yamin. The Lukka's crew stood by to cast off.

Emmet approached. "Captain, our daylight wanes, and the tide turns. If we do not leave within the hour, we'll have to wait until morning."

The centurion's impatience grew. "What would you have me do, Captain Adjo?"

Captain Adjo clenched his fists. He wanted justice, only to be harassed by the local authorities and the whim of Wadj-wer. "Prepare to—"

"Hallo!" Fulgur and his men called from docks.

A tight-lipped smirk spread across Captain Adjo's face. *At least he is back.* "Prepare to get under way, Emmet." He turned to the officer and spoke with haste. "Just a friendly warning about a crazy young man who now resides here—with you."

"You are leaving without this crewman?"

"As you are aware, sir, Rome waits for no one." Captain Adjo walked up the gangplank. "Cast off the spring lines!" He turned back to the soldiers on the dock. "Thank you for your inquiry into the matter. We'll be back in a few months if you have any further questions."

The distance grew between the dock and The Lukka. The crew kept busy as they used the outgoing tide to their advantage.

"Fulgur. In my quarters. Now."

Fulgur closed the door behind him. "Let me explain, Cap'n."

Captain Adjo's eyes cut through him. "Explain how you had one job and could not follow through." He slammed his fist on the wooden table. "Explain how that Roman pig found his way to *my* ship to question *me* about that boy."

Fulgur took a deep breath.

Captain Adjo sat in his chair.

"Cap'n, we found him."

"You found Yamin? Then why isn't he with you? If you tell me you took care of him without me—"

"No such ting, Captain. You see, we met up with a Jewish priest at da theatre."

"Why is this relevant, Fulgur? You went to the theatre? I should have sent Emmet. At least he would not have stopped for some Roman frivolity. Did you pay a visit to the local brothel as well?"

"Cap'n, please."

"Very well." He lowered his head and waved his hand for Fulgur to speak. "Continue."

Before long, Fulgur rehashed the entire story about talking with the rabbi and how he found Abdown. "T'was after, when we followed Abdown back to dare townhouse, dat Nathan told us da truth about what direction Yamin headed."

"So, you tracked him, yes? Again, Fulgur, why is the boy not hanging from the yardarm?"

"We followed his trail for an hour. We thought he was going to head right back to you. Instead, he led us to a temple of the Roman god Venus."

"Ah, Hathor. Yes."

"A local worshiper witnessed him entering da catacombs. We waited outside as long as we could before coming back before dark."

"He never came out?"

"'Da worshiper said he didn't even take a torch with him."

"I have heard rumors about the caves of Malta. I bet it was the demons that led him there."

"So, you've accepted da fact dat he's possessed. Emmet will be happy to hear it."

"I have also heard that foreigners who venture into them rarely come out alive."

"'Den maybe it's for da best, yes?"

Captain Adjo looked out his small square window at the waning island. "Yes, for the best."

Abdown waited outside the entrance to the catacombs until sunset.

Several pagan priests walked by and gave him a wary look.

He shifted in his seat and cleared his throat. Making eye contact with these people was the last thing he wanted to do, let alone speak to any of them.

One of them approached. "Planning on converting, Rabbi?" The man cackled away as he entered the foyer of the temple. Several minutes later he exited. "Still here, yes? Hoping for a sign from your god?. What do you call him? Yahweh?"

As he spoke the name, a ghostly whisper made of many frightened voices emanated from the temple entrance. Abdown could not make out what they said. A brief cold breeze followed it from the stone arch.

The pagan priest dropped to his knees, bowed his head, and raised his arms in the air. He uttered prayers in several different languages. His arms rhythmically swayed as he chanted.

Abdown watched the superstitious priest. He did not believe in this man's many gods. Only Elohim.

The sun set with a beautiful vermilion cloudscape. It took over an hour to walk back uphill to the townhouse. He left with the notion of returning tomorrow. Hopefully, Nathan would not be too upset.

Yamin woke at the last place he remembered being. The chasm that dropped below was quiet now and the air about him still. He crawled through the passageways and up stairwells and over piles of bones before seeing the moonlight shine through the temple's open entranceway.

All was calm. Then they made themselves known.

"We are ready."

"It's been so long."

"Where should we start?"

"Everywhere."

Yamin heard them all in his head. Jealousy, perversion, lies, heaviness, and bondage. They intertwined and writhed like a nest of serpents within him. Fear, error, pride, antichrist.

This last one confused Yamin. He asked them, "What is a—Christ, if we are against it?"

"No."

"Do not speak his name."

"He torments us."

"Make no mention."

Yamin wandered the countryside all night before finding a cave to the south in which to sleep. But the demons preferred the tombs within the cemeteries. They had been underground too long and wanted to be where they could inflict the most fear on others.

28

Yamin remained stranded on the island for many months. With their purpose for going to Malta fulfilled, he and his possessors, while awaiting their next calling, terrorized the locals almost daily. He screamed at the people when they visited their loved ones' graves. He stole food from their gardens and sometimes their tables. He snatched chickens and piglets from their farms.

Winter brought the Saturnalia festival. And the Maltese knew well how to celebrate the most popular holiday on the Roman calendar. Citizens donned colorful robes and decorated their homes with greenery. Yamin had more chances for mischief than ever and more opportunities at nicking food from those drunk on wine and otherwise distracted by riotous revelry.

Halfway through the week-long debauchery, the demons drew close to a village near the border of the cemetery. Yamin approached a window of a townhome and eavesdropped.

The family within played at choosing a mock king to feign rebellion against the normal Roman order everyone endured throughout the year.

The father spoke to a young boy of maybe eight years. "You found the coin in the cake, Octavian. You are now our *Saturnalicius princeps!*"

Yamin reached up and peered over the windowsill. His wild eyes reflected the light from the multiple lamps and candles within. He watched with envy as the mother placed a crown of leaves on her son's head.

The other family members genuflected and said things like, "Leader of Saturnalia, we bow to you," and "Lord of Misrule, do your worst."

Octavian yelped and jumped up and down, all the while with a big smile.

Yamin's stomach turned at the overenthusiastic merriment. *"We'll show them who's Lord of Misrule."* He yelped loudly from under the window.

Thinking their neighbors had arrived, the family ran to the front door to greet them.

Yamin climbed in the window, threw their food around the room, and set fire to the table. He grabbed a chunk of roast pig and leapt back outside, all the while crying out with piercing yelps.

Winter turned to spring, and the locals finally had enough of Yamin's mischief. The magistrate sent a citizen posse to put him in chains, but the demons broke him free during the night.

From time to time, Yamin had a modicum of control over the dark spirits accompanying his soul. Temptations to maim, rape, and murder pushed him with a force he could hardly hold back. He would satiate these urges by slaying a goat or cutting his thigh with a rock. The demons would abate for a time. They grew comfortable within Yamin. And he with them.

Winds from the south blew bringing with them the warm arid summer. The Romans learned of this young wild man, so the governor in Melita sent an eight-soldier unit, known as a contubernium, to halt Yamin's devilish escapades.

The decanus, Egnatius, was a young officer but accustomed to strange missions his centurion assigned him and his men. It became a joke among the other soldiers on the island.

The hike from Melita to the tombs took about three hours.

One of the soldiers held his hand up to the sun then dropped it at increments. He mouthed the number of times the width of his hand fit between the sun and the horizon. "Let's make this fast." He elbowed the soldier nearest him. "I want to get back to my wife before daylight ends."

The other soldiers chuckled.

The elbowed soldier squinted. "You don't have a wife."

"More the reason to get back to town, yes?"

The men laughed.

Egnatius swept his dark brown curls from his eyes and gave his subordinate a berating look. "We follow protocol. And be ready to spend the night."

The first soldier huffed.

"From the report I've received about this boy, he's hard to find. Especially when someone's looking."

The ancient temple on the south shore of the island served as a favorite haunt for Yamin. The frustrated locals knew this and pointed the soldiers right to him.

A disturbing howl spilled down the from hillside behind them.

The soldiers gripped their sword hilts and took up defensive positions behind the raised sarcophagi surrounding them. Egnatius gave a hand signal to stay put and be quiet.

Yamin walked down the hill toward the sea. He smacked each of the graves with the palm of his hand and cackled each time it made any damage to the crumbling morbid décor.

This was the midday routine relayed to Egnatius from those who submitted the complaints. He watched the boy as a hungry lion would an antelope.

Dusty threadbare robes clung to Yamin's grimy skin. A patchy, wooly beard covered his gaunt face.

It reminded Egnatius of a mangy dog. *How can this scrawny boy be a nuisance to anyone?* He stood. "The reports of his ferocity seem overrated."

His men laughed.

No sooner than their outburst began, Yamin disappeared behind a mausoleum.

The ancient necropolis spread out in all directions. Erosion on the southern shoreline caused several of the graves to hang precariously over the short cliff. The remaining monoliths, obelisks, and sepulchers covered the dry ground and hampered the soldiers' view.

Egnatius signaled for the men to fan out and create a semi-circle around their quarry.

Another hellish cry issued from Yamin's direction. Was he taunting the men?

"Go!" Egnatius led the men forward.

One of them produced a net. Another a club. And yet another a set of chains and shackles.

The soldiers closed the circle in. When they reached the spot at which they last saw him, he had disappeared. A jagged hole large enough for a child opened into the mausoleum's side. Bits of fabric and blood clung to the sharp edges of broken stone.

Egnatius cursed his luck. "No one saw him?"

The men shook their heads.

"Open it."

They stood to one side and man-handled the stone covering until it crashed and broke into several large pieces on the ground. When they looked within, a grizzly skull stared up at them. Half of the flooring had collapsed into a dark passage below taking with it the lower half of the skeleton.

"We'll set up camp here. Like a scared rabbit, he may circle around during the night."

The men grumbled but followed Egnatius' orders without delay. They gathered firewood and prepared for the evening meal of bacon, bread, and cheese.

The first soldier produced a bunch of fresh white grapes from their satchel.

One of the men snapped, "Where did you get those?"

Another thrusted out his hand. "Yes, give me some."

Egnatius laughed. "Better for producing *falernian* than eating raw."

"Hey, my wife grew these in our yard." The soldier popped

a grape into his mouth and threw one into the open mouth of his friend.

His friend thanked him with a nod and replied, "But you still don't have a wife."

They all laughed again.

"Not to mention Egnatius won't allow us to drink tree sap, let alone such a fine wine as *falernian*."

Egnatius squinted to see the man he left guarding the mausoleum. Diminishing twilight made for poor visibility. "All right, keep it down. There may be other holes where this scum crawls up from tonight."

29

A rooster's crow permeated the surface and found its way into the depths. Yamin stirred in the cool darkness on a limestone shelf. He knew the men still lingered out there somewhere, hunting him.

"They'll scourge us."

"Destroy the vessel, they will."

"The bird sounds delicious."

The demons' sudden release of their control on Yamin sent a shudder through him like cutting a bale of fresh straw free from it constricting bindings.

"Let the boy do it."

Their whispers faded off.

"If only . . . for a time."

His stomach growled. A matte gray beetle crawled across his knee. Yamin swept his hand over it and snatched it up. He ripped off its wings and gobbled up the rest with a satisfying pop and a crunch.

The climb back to the fractured mausoleum took little time and effort. Birds sang in the morning twilight. A faint pink sky rested over the horizon as he approached the opening. Yamin squeezed through the hole.

"Now!"

The coarse net following the stranger's shout dug into Yamin's skin and twisted his limbs into knots. It was meant not only for capture but for doing harm. Small thorns had been sewn into the twists of rope making it difficult for anyone to resist.

He fought but soon surrendered.

The demons provided no assistance. Yamin knew he would be killed if they took control. Their whispers had grown faint but their weight lingered.

The soldiers clamped iron shackles to Yamin's wrists and legs. The scars on his ankles from past incarceration issued new blood.

"He should walk, Egnatius. Why should we be made to carry the weight of this *stercus* back to Melita?"

Egnatius scoffed. "Weight? He's as thin as my grandmother." He swatted his hand at the men. "Walk him, then. Just hope he makes it back."

Over an hour passed before one of the soldiers sniffed the air. "I need a bath. This one probably hasn't washed in a year!" He kicked Yamin in the rear making him stumble. His chains clinked on the stony ground.

Noon arrived, and the late summer sun beat down on them as they climbed the high plateau to the city. Thick stone ramparts surrounded the entire capital and a dry, weedy ditch below added little security for a paranoid people.

Cemeteries lay outside the walls as well. The demons stirred as they wanted to inflict damage upon them, making Yamin's insides twinge. *That would certainly make us known.*

As they entered the city's main gateway, a grand portico supported by four ornate columns rose in front of them. This temple to Apollo was the largest building Yamin had ever seen.

Several parishioners loitered in the portico's shade.

"Where did they find him?" A stately woman stepped cautiously behind the man she accompanied. "Is he the one haunting the eastern end of the island?"

Not far past the temple stood a theatre. Noises from within piqued Yamin's interest.

Someone wearing a grotesque mask and colorful robes exited and lowered a ladle into a water cistern. Before the thespian took a drink, he froze and watched Yamin as the soldiers escorted him through the streets.

They walked on a stone bridge spanning a narrow shallow canal. The dark water sprouted several small islands of mud from its surface. Freshwater crabs busily feasted on the algae-covered muck.

The heat had stolen the men's energy. The links binding Yamin's limbs dragged along the road and attracted more onlookers as they made the final approach to the governor's townhouse.

Secured to a wooden pole in the middle of the street, Yamin awaited judgment. The rough-hewn wood pressed against his back and poked through his tattered robe into his skin. The desire to reach back and touch the aged and splintered surface no longer existed. Numbness prevailed.

The demons finally spoke, but only to Yamin.

"We were driven away from this pole before."

"Not again."

"Diminish. Diminish."

"Publius! Get back inside." A middle-aged man exited the house to stop his young son from getting too close.

A woman waited in the doorway to receive the child. She locked eyes with Yamin as she took the boy inside the regal home.

Egnatius cleared his throat. "Governor Gracilus, I present to you the offender."

Gracilus was slender with a few grey hairs scattered in his beard and temples. He approached but did not get close enough to leave the protection of the shaded stone walkway on which he stood.

"I see." He looked Yamin up and down. A slight breeze blew in his direction. He pulled the sleeve of his robe to his face and scrunched up is nose. "This . . . *stercus* is the source of all those reports?"

The guards chuckled under their breath. The one who berated Yamin earlier elbowed his comrade and stuck out his chin with pride.

Egnatius took a cautious step toward Gracilus. "He is wild, your Honor. With a strength mysterious to me. It took all my men to subdue him in the graveyard."

"The graveyard?" Gracilus guffawed. "As long as it wasn't a Roman one, who cares?"

Yamin stood as tall as his bindings let him. "I am a Roman citizen."

"What did he say?" Gracilus craned his neck forcing the top of his head into the sunlight.

Yamin withdrew, fearful his plea would be futile.

Egnatius struck Yamin with the back of his hand. "Answer the governor."

"*Answer him.*"

His voice cracked. "I—I'm from the city of Hippos in Decapolis. I'm a Roman citizen."

Gracilus stepped back into the shade. His wife peered out from the doorway behind him.

Young Publius, stole a glimpse from behind her legs.

"Is this true, Egnatius? We would not treat a patriot like this. Has he murdered? Has he raped?"

"He raped—a goat—sir." Egnatius looked at the ground sheepishly.

The soldiers chuckled under their breath.

Egnatius gave them a stern look.

Gracilus' wife gasped and retreated behind the door, slamming it.

"A goat, you say? Well, we can't put him to death for that. Can we?"

Egnatius grabbed Yamin's chains and held them up. "What would you have us do with him, then?"

"Decapolis, you say?"

Yamin nodded weakly.

"What image, then, is stamped upon the coinage of your fair city, boy?"

Yamin took a moment. It had been a long time since he gave currency any thought, especially any from his hometown. "A horse—sir."

"He seems harmless enough. Decanus, put him on the first ship east. Send him back to his own people so they can deal with him." He turned toward the house. "Maybe they will bathe him too."

The trip to the shore could not have been faster for the demons. They hooted and howled with glee to be leaving Malta.

Yamin had no idea why, as he wanted to go in the opposite direction. He did not care if the ship they put him on sailed off the face of the world and into oblivion.

Three hours later, they chained him to a bulkhead inside a Roman patrol ship. The vessel would shove off in the morning. They did not want to take any chances with Yamin, as Egnatius filled the captain in on what they endured during his capture. Had they only known the chaos he caused on his previous ocean voyage, they would have never accepted him as cargo.

Over the following weeks, twice Yamin broke free from his chains before the soldiers doubled up his bindings. They placed guards on him at all times.

Before the multitude of indwelling spirits, Yamin had not cared much about the passage of time, nor had he paid attention. Now, in the belly of this ship, he felt the passing of each second. With the pulsing of each moment, his thoughts ceased to be his own. It remained his only sense not depraved by the demons. He loathed it.

When they approached Sebastos Harbor, they carried Yamin up to the deck. Two great breakwaters jutted from the shore at Caesarea to create this manmade port in what would otherwise be open sea. Ships of all types came and went. A fleet of naval ships sat as if awaiting deployment for a distant war.

They hastily took Yamin from the military vessel and escorted him east over land. A contubernium of soldiers served as his chaperones. They kept to the main highways starting with the *Via Maris* leading them to the town of Galilee. Turning east and then north, they arrived at the town of Philoteria. The journey took three days.

Here, on the southern shore of the Galilean Sea and western shore of the Jordan River, many fruit trees grew. A Roman fortress greeted them inhospitably as they entered the city. Its ominous walls rose abruptly from the sparsely vegetated desert floor.

The sun sank to just above the horizon, and the soldiers wanted to go no farther. The decanus, being a seasoned warrior, was not accustomed to duties such as this. "I refuse to take him across river, let alone this pond they call a sea. Let's find dinner."

Yamin's stomach growled.

A cacophony of insect chirps erupted from the walnut trees above.

"Welcome to Kerakh, ancient city of art and—"The beggar cut his Greek greeting short as his eyes widened at the site of Yamin's gaunt half-naked frame.

"Save your nonsense for someone who cares, old man." One of the soldiers spat then pushed Yamin to the ground next to the wretched welcomer. He turned to his decanus. "What about the prisoner?"

The beggar wrinkled his nose and slid away from Yamin.

"I was told to escort a Roman citizen to a city on the inland sea. This city seems good enough." He tossed the shackle key to the soldier. "Leave him. The walk around this tiny lake can't be more than a couple of days. He'll be fine."

After being freed, Yamin crawled back out the gate as the contubernium walked deeper into the city. He followed the fortress walls to the water's edge and collapsed on the rocky beach. The warm water, driven by a westerly breeze, gently lapped upon his hand as he squeezed pebbly wet sand in his fist.

The sensation roused the demons but did nothing more than anger Yamin for its intangibleness.

"Chinnereth . . . we've been here."

"He is near."

"Yes, we feel him."

"Go home."

"No. Don't go there."

"Go . . . home."

30

Yamin woke the next morning with gut-wrenching hunger. The only morsels allotted him were the crumbs from the soldiers' meals over the three days it took to get here.

He had spent his first night of freedom since Malta on the beach under an inverted derelict fishing boat much like his father's. The town and its harbor woke with him.

A small dog sniffed around the outside of the boat.

Two adolescent boys called for it.

He scrambled out of the wooden shell on all fours and flashed his teeth. A low frothy growl issued forth.

The boys ran to their father's side and pointed to where Yamin had been. But when the fisherman turned to see, Yamin had departed.

The dog had vanished as well.

Satiated, at least physically, Yamin sought a route to the east coast, and Hippos. He knew not why. But he felt it had to do with something the demons said while on Malta. He asked again, "What is a Christ, if we are against it?"

Again, the demons flailed within him, like wild goats trapped in a box.

Blood dripped from his nose. He resigned to not knowing and further not wanting to know if this would be the result for even thinking about what it meant.

The demons' impatience urged him to steal a boat.

He met with resistance when the boat's owner brandished a sturdy filet knife then laughed at Yamin's impudence. Eventually, the locals drove Yamin away from the town to where the Galilee empties into the Jordan River.

Greenery surrounded him. Trees lined the banks, and reed-covered freshwater marshes spread in patches from one side of the river to the other. Yamin waded in and before long needed to swim to keep his head above water. Serpent-like motions propelled him forward as he forded the waterway to the western side. There the bank steepened. Once over it, he began the long hike along the southeastern shore and then northward . . . to home.

What waited there for him? He had spent all this time fighting to get away, and now these dark beings drove him back.

By midday, the summer heat hampered Yamin's progress. He longed for the coolness of the catacombs deep inside Malta. The comforting shade of a stand of gnarled oaks welcomed him, and he rested there until the sun lowered.

Jays swooped into the twisted canopy to pick acorns. Their raucous cackles reminded Yamin of demon laughter. Once a bird had possession of an elongated seed, it would fly to a nearby area of exposed soil and bury it. The demons reveled in immediately running to the buried caches, digging them up, and throwing them into the lake. The jays eventually caught on and dive-bombed Yamin's head making him move on.

Two hours later, Hippos stood in the distance. Marble columns and whitewashed walls reflected the golden setting sunlight and gave the entire elevated city an otherworldly look. Yamin kept to the shadows, afraid of who might recognize him. *Why are the demons pushing me back here?* The question plagued him. Thoughts of revenge and recompense pushed themselves into the forefront of his mind.

"*They have more than you.*"

"*Your mother . . . Your father . . .*"

"*It was their greed that . . . killed them.*"

Yamin crawled along the hillside beneath the plateau. The smell of cooking meat conjured a split-second memory of a suckling pig.

"You, there!" The voice pierced the silence from below. "Where're you going? Get down from there before you're hurt!"

Yamin laid on his belly with his head downslope of his feet. He peered out into the twilight to search for the voice's source. The water glistened as the setting sun sank below the horizon. The silhouetted buildings of Tiberias reminded him of simpler days. Days when he and his mother sat on the shore waiting for his father to return with a boat full of fish.

Grabbing at the earth beneath him, Yamin found a jagged stone. He raked it across his forearm. The memories of his childhood would soon fade. The sensation numbed the painful emotion.

Creeping in the shadows, he made it to the cemetery stretching alongside the road leading to the city's western gate. The demons helped push open a sarcophagus lid. Yamin slipped in and laid next to the withered dry corpse. Starlight twinkled through the narrow aperture above.

As Yamin slept, nightmares tormented him.

His old friend, Dar, appeared at the gate. "Yamin, where are you?"

Yamin opened his mouth to reply but he produced no sound. He tried again producing only a weak strained breath.

Dar reached out his right hand.

Althea stepped out from behind the city wall and took Dar's hand in hers. "He's never coming back."

Yamin tried to scream.

This time the demon's voices spewed obscenities at the handsome young couple.

The more Yamin cried out, the more they pulled him away from the city and downslope toward the lake. He clawed and scraped at the hard ground to no avail. Then he stopped.

"Yamin." His mother's muffled call came from inside his home.

The house was now a shell. The mud, once forming walls, now lay in loose piles around a frame of splintered wooden posts. The entire structure leaned to the west, ready to fall down the slope and into the lake.

"Yamin, where are you?" Her clear voice faded every time she repeated his name.

He struggled to run into the house, but his feet dragged as if weighed down by anchor stones. Yamin made it to the door. "Mother, I'm here."

Instead of his mother in the bed, a dark figure filled the space. As it breathed, its form rose and fell like a blacksmith's bellows. Tendrils of inky black fingers hung from all sides of the bed and entangled with the dry weeds now covering the floor.

One of the slimy coils reached for Yamin's foot.

He tried to move, but it was too late.

Its powerful grasp pulled him onto the floor and dragged him toward the rotten bed.

Yamin's heart pounded.

A light brighter than the sun engulfed the entire building. The entity occupying the bed shrieked in pain and withdrew its viny limbs.

Yamin stood in awe as he peered into the light. "You." His own voice rang clear and strong.

The blinding glow grew even more brilliant until it woke him. Yamin's borrowed crypt surrounded him and provided a welcome darkness from that horrid vision.

A songbird chirped from outside the cemetery.

Yamin stretched and pushed against the coffin's cold stone walls. He poked his head out of the opening.

"Ah!" A woman carrying a basket of pomegranates dropped it at the sight of him.

Yamin scratched and pulled at his matted dusty beard. He shook off the woman's surprise and jumped from the crypt to the rocky soil below. When he turned to find her, she had run uphill toward the city. He made quick use of her discarded fruit.

He looked up toward Hippos. The sun had just risen and the buildings above stood silhouetted by the saffron twilight behind them. *Should I go?*

The demons answered with ecstasy.

"Stay. We like it here."

"Go. You can find them."

"Leave this place. Before we are found."

The demons had never disagreed before. Yamin contemplated this while he sat and ate the woman's fruit. He watched the sun rise over the hill. Something elusive drew near. Something destructive. He felt the spirits' anxiety manifest as palpitations and muscle twitches. *Why are they in conflict?* He spat an errant stem onto the ground. *They're in upheaval.* He stared at a piece of the fruit's skin that had stuck to his leg. *Demonic indecision.* He took the partially chewed skin between his fingers. *They are distracted.* A momentary burst of texture brought long lost meaning to his barren psyche.

A figure appeared from the blackness of the cityscape disturbing his focus.

Yamin drew his gaze upon the man, ready to act if attacked. *She sent her husband to get us. We'll scare him off too.* Anger rose like an ocean swell within him.

"Or kill him."

He tossed a pomegranate at the man from behind the sepulcher. It struck another grave marker on the other side of the road with a squishy thud.

The man stopped to investigate. He picked up the pummeled fruit and looked around. After finding no one, he whistled a solemn but melodious tune and continued his trek downhill toward the harbor.

Yamin's curiosity grew. He followed the man from a distance until he reached the shore.

Fishermen readied their vessels for a summer's day of work on the great lake. Several stopped to look at Yamin as he followed the man. The remains of a tattered tunic hung over a soiled triangular loin cloth.

The man he followed walked out onto the dock and scanned the lake's horizon.

Yamin hid behind a nearby boat. *Dar? Can it be you?*

A woman exited the portmaster's building and joined Dar on the dock. She grabbed his hand. "He's not coming back."

The demons stirred. Old feelings surfaced, and Yamin could not contain them. Fear of loss. Hatred from circumstance. Anger at betrayal. Jealousy, regret, desire. *I'll stop them. He can't swim. We'll push him.* A wraith-like howl left Yamin's mouth.

All eyes turned to him.

He catapulted himself away from the boat toward the couple. Several pieces of lumber leaning on the boat's edge fell toward Yamin. One struck him square on the top of his head before he could get close.

The last thing he saw was his old friend Dar kneeling over him. "Yamin? Yamin, I can't believe it's—"

31

Yamin slept soundly. The demons reveled in their new accommodations and so allowed him that one luxury—on occasion. The chains binding him remained secure, for now.

"We'll be free soon."

"Yes, to ravage."

"To defile."

"They wanted us to go away." Yamin's throaty laugh echoed around the tombs northwest of Hippos on the shore of the Sea of Galilee. "Those men will pay."

He picked up a melon-sized rock and hacked at his chains. Flakes of gray stone ricocheted off the mausoleum walls and fell to the floor with a clink. Sparks shot from where the rock struck the iron.

The demons pulled, and the chain gave way. They leapt within him.

"Free!"

Yamin's skin crawled. He felt them tearing away at his consciousness, withering away his soul. Destroying the very definition of self. For now, their conflict of earlier had waned and combined with concerted determination toward one goal.

"We are hungry."

Lust and greed filled him. A red sky welcomed the sum of souls as if the very atmosphere attuned itself to their desires. They broke open the door to their apportioned lodgings and fled into the morning mist.

Several men watched as he left the prison-like tomb. They sounded the alarm by calling others to help subdue the maniac.

But the wild man was too fast. Too strong. The men could not contain him.

Yamin screamed for food. When none was given, he cut himself with sharp stones.

The locals were at a loss. They left him alone if he remained in the tombs and did not disturb their families. Just like on Malta.

The savage dined on grasses and mice, and he drank the tears streaming down his filthy face, filtered by his patchy whiskers.

One late afternoon, a great wind grew with haste and drove the lake's water into a churning mass of white. The local herdsmen watched as the maniac delighted in the anarchy. Sand whipped and water sprayed. Yamin danced on the shore in spasmodic random undulations, his threadbare coverings soaked.

Then it stopped as fast as it started.

Once the lake calmed, a boat carrying more than a dozen men approached the shore.

"Where are we?" One of the men jumped from the bow carrying a stone anchor. "Got turned around out there." He placed the anchor behind another rock on the beach and pushed it into the pebbly sand with his foot.

"Gadarenes," said another as he dropped into the knee-deep water. He joined the first man and looked up and down the coastline. "I think. See the cliff?"

A third man of sturdy build stepped off the vessel. His short beard and medium-length head-of-hair contrasted with the others. And he carried himself as if surer of his purpose.

The demons drove Yamin from the safety of the tombs to meet the new arrivals. He spied from behind a rock as they made their way from the boat to the beach. *Curious. They're not fishermen. Although, I may have seen one or two of them on the water—*

"He is here!"

"Take us to him."

"No, hide. To shadow!"

"Move. We must be known."

"*Yes, we are meant to known.*"

Yamin's approach began as a plodding walk which soon became an unbridled sprint to the shore. More confused then ever, he fell to his knees and writhed at the feet of the third man before any of the others could stop him.

The third man stood his ground and spoke. "Come out of this man, you impure spirit!"

Looks of incredulity spread across the other men's faces.

The demons recoiled with a force Yamin had never felt before. A sudden rush of consciousness struck him, and yet the spirits still spoke for him in unison. Their unearthly vocalizations spilled out onto the calm water. "*What have I to do with You, Jesus, Son of the most-high God? I implore You by God that You do not torment me.*"

Jesus stood his ground. "What is your name?"

Yamin's mouth contorted into unnatural shapes as they spoke through him. "*My name is Legion, for we are many.*" They made Yamin cower before this man they called Jesus. "*Also, I beg of you. Do not send us out of the country. No, not into the abyss.*"

Yamin looked frantically at his surroundings. His neck tilted sideways and his eyes fell upon a herd of nearly two thousand pigs feeding in the distance on the slopes. "*We ask that you send us into those swine, that we may enter them.*"

Jesus pointed to the herd without hesitation. "You have my permission."

Yamin fell to the ground on his back and thrashed about in quick rhythmic convulsions. He cried out as the now cooperative unclean spirits that had plagued him for almost two years left all at once as a multitude of sinuous streams of ethereous black vapor that smelled of sulfur and asphalt.

Yamin hollered with indiscernible emotion. Anyone looking on would have thought he was being torn apart from within but would not be able to tell if he was being tortured or tickled. His contorted facial features and writing body gave no one comfort who looked on. Yamin looked like he was dying.

The entire herd leapt in unison as the demons approached. Their stiff fur stood on end, and their bloodshot eyes grew wider than could possibly be imagine. As if controlled by a hive mind—like a flock of starlings or a school of sardines in the Great Sea—the animals started to run uphill. But when the demons found their targets, the animals turned on the tips of their hooves and ran violently down the steep slope toward the sea.

Squeals of terror rose from the throng of unfortunate beasts. As they trampled one another on their way to oblivion, tears streamed from their eyes, and saliva shook from their jowls. The earth shook from the stampeding horde as they leapt from the precipice into the churning water below. The sea turned a frothy pink, and one by one they pressed each other beneath the waves.

As the cacophony diminished, and the clouds of dust settled from where the drove of swine once grazed, the herdsmen who had cared for the swine fled in fear.

Yamin sat up and took a deep cleansing breath. He touched the ground and shook with emotion. *It—it's back.* His sensation of touch, and the information that came with it, had been returned. A great smile spread across his face, and he let loose a joyous laugh as tears streamed down his face.

One of the boatmen placed a clean robe around Yamin as he sat contemplating the world around him. The rough linen fabric rubbed upon his skin, and he fell in love with the sensation once more, as if newly born.

Jesus sat quietly next to him as he regained his senses and the realization of what just happened washed over him. The other men continued to make the boat secure and stood by waiting for Jesus.

Before long, the herdsmen returned with other men they had gathered from the nearby village and the countryside. They approached Jesus and marveled at Yamin's obvious improvement. Their eyes widened at the sight of masses of pig corpses floating along the shoreline.

Yamin turned to Jesus. "They're afraid of me."

One of the men pointed at Jesus. "He's the one who drove our swine into the lake to perish." He then directed their attention to Yamin. "And this filth. How did you do it? How did you put him into his right mind then make our herd behave that way?"

The other locals kept their distance, afraid to speak at all after what they had seen and heard conveyed to them by the shepherds.

The leader of the herdsman continued. "Please, leave us alone now. Go back to where you came from. Go anywhere but here. Our livelihood is destroyed. We've already informed the authorities. We don't want any of you here." He gestured toward Yamin with a shaking finger. "And take him with you."

Jesus complied and had his companions ready the boat for departure.

When they boarded and started to shove off, Yamin ran into the water and grabbed the side of the craft. "Please, Lord, I beg you. Take me with you." He glanced at the men waiting on the shore. "I—I can't stay here."

Jesus fixed his eyes upon him. Their bright green hue reflected the evening twilight. He spoke softly. "Go home to your friends and tell them what great things the Lord has done for you. And how He has had compassion on you."

The vessel slipped from Yamin's grasp, and he sank waist deep into the water. He watched as the boat departed and returned to where it had appeared out of the storm just a short time before.

The sun dipped behind the horizon as a burst of emotion erupted in Yamin's chest. He wept uncontrollably. Tears fell into the lake. With each drip that broke the surface, Yamin sensed a release of all that had weighed upon him since his mother's death. Begrudgery and resentment melted away.

Jesus' departing words clung to the forefront of his mind. *I must do as he commanded.* Yamin waited for a moment and surveyed the sensations around him. Having felt nothing but demonic presence for many painful months, all he felt now were the wet pebbles underfoot, the cool water on his legs, and the gentle breeze on his tear-soaked cheeks.

Go home and tell your friends . . . Jesus' words echoed in his mind. "Decapolis is my home. I will spread this story through all of Decapolis."

He fell into the water and washed the filth of the tombs from his skin and hair. Afterward, he left to find the men who had forced Jesus to leave.

Gone.

Looking southward, Yamin departed. Hippos and his friends awaited. *But will they accept me? Will they even recognize me?*

Nearly two hours later, Yamin reached the shore beneath Hippos. Darkness had spread. Not so welcoming as it had been in recent months. He knew this area well and found his old house despite the dimness.

Every step on his hike home provided ecstasy to his senses. A myriad of earthen textures beneath his feet sent chills up his spine. *I'm going to have to get used to this again.* He smiled.

Regardless of the image haunting his earlier dream, of which he no longer feared, the building still stood. Much to his delight, no one had taken up residence since his abrupt departure almost two years ago. Before stepping inside to investigate, Yamin reached out and ran his hand over the door's rough wooden exterior. He closed his eyes, and the material came to life at his touch.

He opened his eyes. *Everything's the same. Dar must have made sure of it.* He could not wait to search for him tomorrow. To let his friend know he was better. That he had been saved.

The moon rose and filled the open door with its light. The silvery glow spread like a mystical blanket on the earthen floor. Yamin shook the old linen on the bed.

Several desert mice fell out and scurried to hide elsewhere.

He pushed the window shutters open. A comfortable late summer breeze welcomed the first good night's sleep he had in a long time.

"Jesus, thank you for saving me. I will tell everyone I meet about your compassion. About God's compassion."

Yamin glanced to the small alter in the wall where his parents' idol once sat. He did not know if those other gods existed. The only evidence he had to the contrary was his own personal experience with Jesus today. This Jesus had said, '. . . *great things the Lord has done for you.*'

"The Lord did this for me." He looked at his sore wrists and ankles. "What did those other gods ever do?" A tinge of regret surged through him. *If I had only accepted the one true God before all this happened.* He looked at his parents' bed and vowed to never make that mistake again.

He laid down on his old sleeping mat under the window and covered up with the tattered bedding. More so, he found himself wrapped with a peace that surpassed his ability to understand.

32

Wake up."

Yamin stirred. He had slept so peacefully through the night. His current plans did not include waking.

"They're coming for you." The stranger shook him.

He turned over and squinted at the person standing over him. "Dar? What's wrong?"

"No time to explain. Come on."

Yamin swept his long hair from his eyes.

Dar helped him up, and they exited the house into the early light of dawn.

Men's voices from downhill caught up with them as they climbed the path to the plateaued city.

Yamin recognized one. "Is that Baniy?"

"Yes. And right now, he's not our friend."

"But he's someone I need to talk to. I need to tell him—"

"I'll explain when we get to my father's shop. Hurry."

Yamin slipped to the side of the road and ducked behind a rock. "Who are those men with him?"

Dar let out a frustrated sigh and joined Yamin. "Just know they mean to do you harm. They've been asking about you for a week."

"Who has?" Yamin turned to Dar and gave a sincere smile. "It's good to see you, old friend. Thank you."

Dar looked at Yamin and screwed up his face. "You need some help."

"The beard? It's a long story."

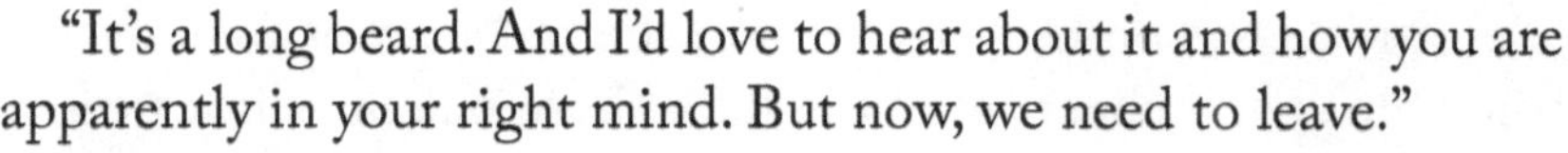

"It's a long beard. And I'd love to hear about it and how you are apparently in your right mind. But now, we need to leave."

"Just a moment more."

Yamin and Dar watched as the men entered Yamin's home.

A crash issued through the doorway, followed shortly by light gray smoke.

Yamin sighed. *So much for any remaining possessions.*

There was just enough light now to make out four men. Baniy was the only one who hurried back to the harbor when the ransack began. The other three exited the house and stopped on the road. One of them pointed toward Hippos. The man had a bald head and was clean-shaven— No. A thin mustache.

Yamin squinted. "Adjo."

"Yes, that's his name. So, you *do* know him. He and his men have been asking about you all over the place."

Yamin sat with a thud. He allowed a contemplative look to spread over his face while weighing his options.

Dar must have noticed. "What did you do that could've driven this man to hunt you like this? Everyone refers to him as, *The Egyptian.*"

"He's a pirate."

"A pirate? They still exist?"

Yamin looked back toward the house. Flames now licked the lintel where only smoke had been moments ago. "We need to leave."

"That's what I've been telling you. Come on."

Yamin let Dar lead him up the road. They passed the cemetery. Yamin searched his feelings but felt no pull toward the graves. He grinned and pulled in a deep breath of fresh air. Air he had not taken in for a long time.

Dar noticed. "Why are *you* so happy? I think those men want you dead."

"Like I said, it's a long story. And the ending's the best part."

"Well, your story seems to be taking a turn for the worse. Keep up."

Yamin's stomach growled. "Is your mother making breakfast? I miss her cooking."

A frown grew on Dar's face. "I've a story to share as well. There's some bread and cheese at my father's shop, if Aphra hasn't eaten it all."

Minutes later, after staying low and keeping their pursuers at a distance, they entered Sophus' workshop and closed the heavy wooden door behind them.

The two made their way to the back of the building and sat on the floor.

Sophus entered with water and some food. "You found him. Thank the gods."

Yamin looked at him with compassion. "There's only one God, Sophus."

Sophus looked at his son, wide-eyed.

Dar returned the look and slowly shrugged his shoulders.

Sophus sat with the boys without retort.

Dar moved next to his father. "So, now's the time to tell us where you've been, what happened, and why those pirates are after you."

Sophus handed Dar some bread. "Pirates?"

Yamin gave Dar a concerned look.

Sophus ripped off another piece from the loaf and handed it to Yamin. "And who is this *one* god you refer to?"

Yamin was only halfway through his story when Sophus' hulking associate, Aphra, entered the shop. He left the door open.

Sophus got up quickly and bolted the door. "What's wrong with you?"

"Too hot."

The man's deep voice resonated in Yamin's chest.

Sophus guided Aphra's gaze toward the boys in the back with a nod.

"Oh."

"Come. We need your help."

While Yamin finished the story, Aphra skillfully trimmed his hair and beard. His large rough fingers did not hamper his barbering abilities.

Sophus held up a highly polished copper mirror to Yamin's face. "Better?"

Yamin stroked his shorn beard and smiled. "Yes. Thank you, Aphra. I'm a new man—in more ways than one."

"Your story was worth the effort." Aphra plopped down next to Sophus. "This man, Jesus. He *cured* you?"

"Amazing. Yes."

Sophus scratched his head. "Who is *the lord*? Did he mean the Hebrew god?"

"The one and only." Yamin went to sip his water but instead pulled one of his own long curly hairs from the surface of the cup.

Dar wiped his mouth on his sleeve. "That's some tale, Yamin."

"I understand if you don't believe me. I wouldn't have believed it myself if it hadn't happened directly to me." Yamin stood. "When I left you all, I was so lost. Angry. Can you ever forgive me?"

Dar stood and walked next to Yamin. He put his hand on Yamin's shoulder. "We already have. But the current leadership would be most upset if you told them their gods weren't real."

"They'd kill you." Sophus poured more water for himself. "Or worse."

"What could be worse, Father?"

"Burying him alive, crucifixion—"

"They wouldn't crucify a Roman citizen, would they?"

"What he's saying is blasphemous, Dar."

Raised voices from the street penetrated the door. Sophus sent Aphra outside to investigate.

Dar sat again. "I remember that man at the physician's, the day we brought your father."

Yamin nodded. "Ashchuwr—it was the first one." A shiver ran down Yamin's spine.

The chill acted like a contagion and spread to Dar and Sophus. "My family prayed to all the gods for your father. Just as we prayed for your mother before she passed."

"As did we." Yamin's head drooped.

Sophus cleared his throat. "My wife got sick right after you left, Yamin."

Yamin's eyes widened. He looked at Dar. "You didn't tell me."

"You were unreachable. Even when out in your father's boat weeks before disappearing, you wouldn't listen. And recently, during your stay in the tombs—"

"You're right. I didn't care to listen. I was—preoccupied. I'm sorry, Dar." He put his hand on Dar's shoulder.

Sophus stared into the flame of an oil lamp on a nearby shelf. "We buried her last harvest season. Perhaps if we'd prayed only to the Hebrew god—"

Aphra returned. "The people are agitated, Sophus."

"What do you mean?"

"The wine seller says a murderer's on the loose in the city. A reward's been offered."

Yamin sat upright. "Adjo must've told the authorities about me."

"A murderer?" Aphra looked at Yamin and tensed.

"I—I killed his cat." Yamin's sheepish admittance was good enough for them. "Albeit under the influence of my possessors."

Dar stood. "Father, we have to get him out of the city."

Yamin stood also. "But I have orders."

"Jesus told you to spread the story of your salvation across Decapolis, yes?"

Yamin nodded. "Well, his exact words were, *to your own people*."

"And you are a son of Decapolis."

He nodded again. "I can't let these criminals stop me from that."

"Pirates, you say?" Sophus grabbed a small unpainted clay statue of a Roman foot soldier from a nearby shelf. "I know someone who would be interested to hear that."

33

Sophus knew Hippos' corpulent Governor Urbanus found little interest in the common man's plight. But when he came to the aristocrat that afternoon with astounding news, it captured his full attention.

"The swine! Why did none of my people relay this information to me?" Urbanus reached for the closest slave and grabbed the fabric on his shoulder into his fist. "Gather the council and have them meet me immediately. And inform Justus of this terrible report."

The servant ran off. Another replaced him at the governor's side.

Sophus continued. "Perhaps they feared you would not believe their story, Governor. I mean, pirates? Who could imagine such criminals to be this far inland from the Great Sea, let alone bold enough to attack Roman citizens directly?"

"After what Pompey did to them a hundred years ago, you would not think they would be so insolent." Urbanus signaled to a servant who brought wine. "Drink with me, Sophus."

Sophus obliged and glanced around the governor's opulent home. "I see you've made good decisions arranging the statues I crafted for you."

"They are adequate for my décor." He belched. "How did you come by this information?"

Sophus swallowed the contents of his glass and cleared his throat. "You—you wouldn't believe the coincidence."

Urbanus gave Sophus a disparaging look.

"I was coming back from a snail collecting trip."

"Snails? I love them." He smacked his lips and signaled to his servants again.

"I use them in my craft. And I witnessed the entire event."

A centurion entered. Ignoring Sophus entirely, he approached the governor's seat and saluted by holding his right hand at arm's length and parallel to the floor.

"Yes, yes." It appeared as if Urbanus' patience with mundane military formalities had worn thin. "Thank you for coming so quickly, Justus."

The servant reentered with a tray of snails and other delicacies, placing them on a table next to the governor's seat.

Urbanus indiscriminately scooped up a handful of food and stuffed it into his mouth.

Justus eyed Sophus before addressing Urbanus. "I checked on the story before arriving. It is true. The city's entire herd of pigs is now floating in the lake. All dead."

"We will starve!" He threw his hands dramatically into the air. Pieces of food spilled from his swollen lips. "What of the upcoming Saturnalia festival?"

"I ordered my men to retrieve the pigs nearest the shore. I thought perhaps they would still be usable. When we inspected them—they were tainted, my lord."

"Tainted? How?"

"A black soot clung to their jowls. That was the first clue. But when we opened them . . ."

Urbanus stopped chewing for the first time and spoke slowly. "Continue."

"The meat was riddled with worms and darkened. Not burned, just offensive. And the smell." His face contorted ever so slightly. "My men buried as many as they could gather."

"These criminals must be punished, Justus."

"If I could have some information before proceeding?"

The governor motioned toward Sophus. "Speak to him. He

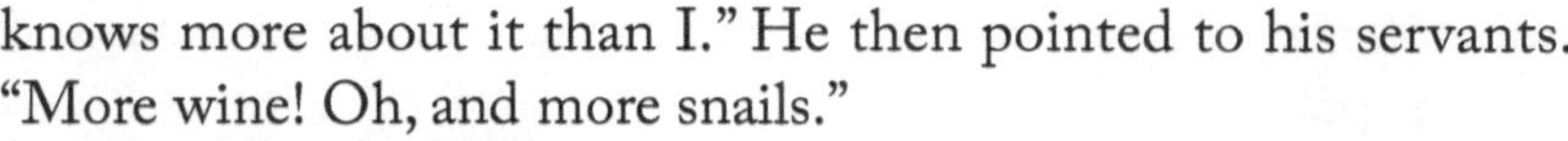

knows more about it than I." He then pointed to his servants. "More wine! Oh, and more snails."

Sophus bowed slightly as he took the governor's leave.

Urbanus ignored his gesture.

Sophus followed Justus outside to the courtyard. The sun shone brightly through a clear blue sky. Any signs of the storm that churned the lake so violently yesterday were now absent. A black and white woodpecker with a red nape knocked on a nearby olive tree.

"These pirates have been skulking about the region for weeks, Centurion."

They stopped near one of Sophus' statues. This one portrayed Saturn wearing woolen strips wrapped around its feet.

"How do you know they're pirates?"

"They are boastful, of course. The herdsmen heard them speaking of their escapades on *Mare Nostrum*. The leader's name is Adjo. They even burned a citizen's home down near the harbor."

"My men investigated that this morning. No bodies, no witnesses, and no one's complaining. We dismissed the hovel as abandoned."

"I have one witness. A Roman named Yamin, son of Eber. It was his house they burned. He had been sleeping in it only moments before the crime."

"He didn't report these men? Why?"

"He did. To me. And now I'm respectfully reporting it to you. Through the proper channels, of course."

Justus looked at Sophus askance. "Of course."

"I must return to my shop. If you need anything else, you know where to find me."

Justus nodded once and turned to leave.

"Still using snail shells?" Yamin held up an ornate fruit bowl inlaid with mother-of-pearl.

Dar took it from him and placed it carefully back on the shelf in his father's shop. "Yes, my first actual piece that's an order and not just practice."

Yamin produced a diminutive smile and nodded his approval.

Sophus entered and approached them after securing the front door. "It's done."

Yamin asked, "You reported them? How'd the governor take it?"

"Telling him the source of his favorite menu item is gone for the foreseeable future was enough to start things moving. The local guard is now informed and on the hunt for the culprits. I think if you keep a low profile for a few days, all of this'll come to an acceptable end." Sophus snickered. "Urbanus would probably call up an entire legion if he could."

Yamin's knees weakened, and he sat quickly on the floor to prevent falling into any of the fragile objects surrounding him.

Dar supported his back. "You all right?"

Legion. Not a term Yamin wanted to hear so soon. "This has just been—exhausting." He looked up weakly at Sophus and Dar. "Thank you for everything. I think I need to rest for a while."

"Dar, show him where to lie down."

Dar took Yamin by the arm and led him to a group of soft sleeping mats in the back of the shop. "We usually sleep here now, since mother's passing. Home doesn't seem the same anymore. We store father's supplies there."

"What about your sister? I haven't seen her since my arrival." Yamin laid his head down.

"We sent her to live with my uncle in Pella, south of here on the Jordan. She wasn't the same afterward. My uncle has his wife and two daughters. We thought it would be easier for her there."

"Family's always good. And now, Dar, you're my only family." Yamin closed his eyes.

Dar returned to the work area where he left Sophus.

Loud scraping came from the front of the shop where Aphra

moved large pieces of marble in preparation for chiseling. *I'm glad he works for us.*

"Dar, help me decide." Sophus contemplated what type of stone to use for a recent order.

Dar motioned to the back where Yamin lay. "He's sleeping."

"Good." Sophus wiped the dust from a piece of limestone. "Do you believe his story?"

Dar took a step back. "You saw him before he left. But since this Adjo person arrived, I believe him even more."

"Could it be true? There's only one god? The Hebrew god?"

"I know we prayed to all the gods in the past. But Yamin's a different person now. You heard it. His story is miraculous."

"We've seen nothing like it before."

"No, we haven't."

34

All signs pointed to one possibility. Yamin had returned to this place. To this town. Fulgur knew it, but the captain had gone too far.

Captain Adjo pulled Fulgur into the portmaster's office and slammed the door. The breeze created by the forceful motion stirred up an earthy pond-like scent from the corners of the musty room.

Fulgur screwed up his nose. He was accustomed to strong smells when accompanied by those of the salty sea. This town reeked of the unknown. Fulgur despised the unknown.

The captain must have noticed his discomfort. "Speak your mind, Fulgur." He sat abruptly in the chair at the table.

"We've postponed long enough." Fulgur paced the room. "We can't stay another week near dis . . . putrid freshwater hole." He motioned toward the lake. "We've shipments. Our competitors will soon get wind of our absence and fill the gaps."

"Emmet can hold the ship—"

"You've more faith in Emmet dan you should—Cap'n." Fulgur sat on the stool near the door, glanced at Captain Adjo, then averted his eyes.

"I understand your frustration. But we cannot let what happened go without the consequences deserved for the responsible party. The Maltese said he was brought back here. To Hippos."

"If we don't leave by morning—"

Captain Adjo stood and peered through the single window to the south. The late afternoon sun cast long shadows from the small buildings encompassing the harbor. He reached down to his belt. "We should have finished this before we even landed on Malta."

"We thought we'd left him for dead."

Captain Adjo pulled out Emu's severed tail and stroked it. "Not dead enough."

Baniy pulled his boat to the dock. Two men worked the nets with him. But when he saw Captain Adjo's man standing outside the portmaster's office, he hastened them away and left the vessel without cleaning.

No way around it. He had to walk right past the man on his way home. *Don't make eye contact. Just keep walking.*

"Baniy!" Captain Adjo stepped out immediately after Baniy walked past. "My friend, where have you been all day?"

Baniy stopped and slowly turned to see the captain approaching, arms up to embrace him.

"We came so far this morning but you left so quickly." Captain Adjo hugged him and kissed his cheeks. "Nearly flushed the vagrant out of his hole." He gave a hearty laugh.

Fulgur and the other sailor stood behind the captain, both inexpressive.

"Well," Baniy chuckled softly. "Have to make a living." He forced a smile and looked around at the boats. "You, of all people, should know what happens when you can't pay your employees."

Fulgur rolled his eyes.

"So much useful information you have provided, Baniy, over these past days of our . . . acquaintance. Tell me, did Yamin have any friends you can recall?"

Baniy looked at Fulgur and his companion. Their scowls and menacing stances unnerved him. "There may have been one friend of his—up in the city." He motioned to the road with his chin.

"Would you happen to know his name, or his family name, perhaps?" Captain Adjo put his arm around Baniy's shoulders and squeezed. "It would mean a lot to me." With his other hand he produced a gold coin and handed it to Baniy.

Baniy did not know Yamin had returned. *Easy money for a hopeless pursuit.* "His name is Dar, I think. His father's a sculptor."

"Very useful, Baniy. Thank you."

Too much. "I—I believe he's the personal sculptor for the governor of the city."

"Really? A person of such high regard spending time with someone as loathsome and vile as our boy Yamin?" He looked at Fulgur. "These citizens of Decapolis do keep strange company." He turned to Baniy. "Until we meet again."

Baniy turned and walked with purpose away from the harbor. *Yamin, I hope you're far away from here.*

Yamin slept all afternoon and woke around midnight to Sophus' snores. Another sound came from the front of the shop. Scraping noises. *Was Aphra working this late?*

He slowly rose from the mat and crept through the dark isles full of stone and pottery. He stepped on something soft and warm. Yamin jumped out of his skin.

Aphra pulled his powerful hand back toward his sleeping body.

Yamin tensed. *The sound was* not *from Aphra.*

Sophus slept only a step away.

Yamin whispered. "Sophus." He shook him and whispered a little louder. "Sophus, wake up."

Dar heard him first and called out in a groggy, panicked voice. "Yamin? What's the matter? Is my father all right?"

"Shh." Yamin reached for Dar and instead hit a wooden stand holding a set of chisels. The sound of iron on stone clanged and echoed for what seemed an eternity.

Everyone leapt from the floor and scrambled blindly until Sophus found a candle.

Yamin tried to hush everyone for fear of the sound he heard at the door. Once the cacophony resided, the scraping had stopped and they all stood confused and a little angry.

"Yamin, why were you skulking about at this late hour?" Sophus lit a lamp and sat on a stool against the door. "Probably woke up the neighbors too."

Aphra shook his head then drank some water from a large, simple clay vessel. He burped then wiped his mouth on his arm.

Dar sat on a block of stone. "You told us about the nightmares you had. Was this another?"

"No. Of course, not. My dreams are to abide by what Jesus told me. My mind rarely thinks of anything more. I heard what sounded like someone trying to get in." He motioned to the door behind Sophus. "I tried to wake you but—" He looked around at them then hung his head and rubbed his neck. "Sorry."

Aphra burped again. "Could've been cats. They come sniffing around at night."

Dar laughed. "Yes, looking for the source of that rotten snail smell."

Aphra gave a burst of hearty laughter.

Yamin chuckled. "My dad always cleaned them for you first, didn't he?"

Sophus leaned back against the door. "I could always count on him to—" Sophus suddenly arched his back and groaned. A grimace spread across his face. The sound of iron sliding against iron sung out as a bladed weapon withdrew from the door against a hinge. Sophus fell forward onto the dusty workshop floor.

"Father!" Dar rushed to Sophus' side. He tried to help him up and pulled back a blood-soaked hand.

The door burst open. Captain Adjo, Fulgur, and a third man stood in the road lit only by moonlight and the faint twinkling flame from within the shop.

Aphra grabbed a long iron file and lunged toward the men.

Before he could act out his revenge, twenty Roman soldiers flooded the street and surrounded the captain and his men.

Captain Adjo stood tall in the face of this new roadblock. He glared straight through the hulking, seething Aphra right at Yamin and smiled hungrily.

Justus stepped forward. "Relieve these men of their weapons."

Captain Adjo stood armed only with a long ornate dagger. Even in the dim light, Yamin made out the Egyptian designs on its golden hilt—and the fresh blood.

The third man panicked when the soldiers approached. He swung his weapon wildly and sliced a soldier's forearm. Two of the guard's short swords thwarted his attempt to run when they found their way to his abdomen. He grunted and fell to his knees. Blood leaked through clenched teeth as the villain collapsed onto the stony road.

Captain Adjo never took his eyes off Yamin, now protected by Aphra.

"Look what they've done." Dar held up his bloodied hand and tears streamed down his face.

Justus glared at Captain Adjo. "The governor will not be happy to learn you've murdered his personal sculptor, ship rat. First the swine, and now this? You'll be lucky to be alive to see the sun rise."

Captain Adjo did not seem to hear a word.

Fulgur stepped forward. "Swine? What're you talking about? We don't know about any swine."

Yamin remained silent. He looked back at Captain Adjo with the kindest look he could muster. *If only I could talk to him alone . . . and not be in danger.*

Captain Adjo finally tore his gaze from Yamin and addressed the centurion. "This is news to me as well. Who told you we—" He shook his head in disbelief. "What exactly was done to the swine?"

"The man you just murdered witnessed you speaking of the deed. And now that he's dead by your own hand, you have practically sealed the governor's decision in stone."

Fulgur raised his voice. "What decision?"

"To do what the Empire has always done to pirates. Crucifixion."

Yamin moved next to Dar and Sophus. *I have to speak to him before that happens.*

35

You need to rest, Yamin." Dar ladled hot broth into two clay bowls and brought them to where the others sat on pillows around a low table. "You're half the man you were when you left us."

"Ah, but at the same time, I'm twice the man spiritually."

Dar chuckled.

The morning twilight crept through slats in the courtyard door leaving long beams across the table's surface and their breakfast. Tiny specks of dust danced in the rays of light.

"Thank you." Sophus winced as he shifted his weight to accept the bowl. Captain Adjo's blade had only scraped his rib and cleaved off a piece of muscle. They were all thankful it was not as bad as it first looked.

Aphra dropped down between Sophus and Yamin with a vessel twice the size of theirs.

Yamin received the second bowl Dar brought and breathed in the intoxicating steam rising from within. The strong scent of rosemary brought memories of his mother's cooking. "Thank you, Aphra. This soup will do us all good. Especially since we got little sleep."

Aphra grunted. "You brought these men here and almost got Sophus killed."

"It wasn't his fault, Aphra." Dar approached with his own bowl and some bread. "You heard the story."

"A story I have to tell to Adjo and Fulgur as soon as possible." Yamin slurped his broth from the edge of the bowl.

"What?" Sophus dropped a hunk of bread in his soup, and it

splashed on the table. "After what they did to me?" He shifted and grimaced. "To your house? You want to see that maniac again? To *talk* to him?"

Yamin continued slurping broth nonchalantly. "Jesus wants me to. Therefore, I must."

Aphra finished his meal in several large swallows. The liquid dripped from his beard. "I will join you."

Dar remained standing. "No, I'll go with him. Aphra, you're—intimidating. The guards might not let someone with your . . ."

"You're scary, Aphra." Sophus had fished his bread from the broth letting the excess fluid drain back into the bowl. "In a good way."

Aphra's deep laugh produced little ripples that spread across the surface of Yamin's broth.

"It's settled then." Dar sat next to Yamin. "We leave right after breakfast."

A rooster crowed. Sophus listened for it to stop. "You better go sooner than that. They probably haven't much time."

Heeding Sophus' advice, Yamin and Dar left as the sun rose over the mountains.

Yamin had to work to keep up with Dar. His body still needed healing from all the abuse. He thought back to how his father walked this same street over a year ago for the last time. *Pain slowed* him *too. His was a walk to the end. Mine is a walk from the beginning.*

Yamin stood a little taller.

Two small stone cells in the tower at the western gate served as the town's prison. The structure also housed barracks, but many of the centurion's men slept outside in tents. Several mules bore bulky gear, and soldiers packed up others as Yamin and Dar approached.

Yamin stopped to draw water from the same cistern he had the night his mother died, but this time it was empty. He shrugged his shoulders and looked at Dar for an explanation.

Dar sighed. "This isn't Jerusalem." He reached in front of Yamin and released a small lever. Water trickled out slowly at first from a small hole in the stone wall and then in a steady stream. "We're not stuck in the past."

"When was *this* installed?" Yamin moved in and drank from his cupped hands.

Dar answered by pointing to a stand of ornate oak trees. He traced the path of an aqueduct running from the wall, behind the oaks, and eastward out of sight behind the city. "They finally finished it." He pulled the lever to stop the flow. "It sure helps during the dry season."

"Hey, you two!" A young woman with curly mahogany hair stomped toward them. "That water is reserved for the soldiers."

Yamin squinted hard at her. "Althea?"

"Wow. You've sure changed." She smiled. "Yamin, right?"

He nodded. Yamin's heart skipped. "You haven't changed at all."

Althea's olive face reddened.

Dar waved his hand dismissingly at her. "Since when is water for a select few? Shouldn't you be peeling scabs or something on the other side of town?"

Althea gave Dar a playful look of disdain.

Yamin chuckled nervously. *What's with these two?*

"As a matter of fact, I've been given the duty of tending to the soldiers while the doctor is traveling with one of the senators on special assignment."

"A woman? Doing a physician's work?"

Dar's defensive attitude perplexed Yamin. He could watch no longer. "I think she's perfectly capable."

Althea smiled again. "What brings you back to town? Last I heard, you were lost on the lake. That was over a year ago."

"A lot's transpired during that time." He glanced over at Dar and smirked. "Would you like to hear it?"

"I think I can sneak away for a while. The men are packing to leave, so I don't think I'll be missed."

"Good. Follow us."

Dar and Yamin lead the way to the tower.

Althea followed several steps behind.

Yamin turned slightly and whispered to Dar. "What could've happened in the year I was gone?"

Dar rolled his eyes as he mocked Yamin. "A lot has transpired during that time."

They both chuckled.

Two guards stood watch at the entrance.

Dar moved to address the men when Yamin stepped in front of him. "I wish to speak to the prisoners." He spoke in a hushed tone but with authority.

Dar's eyes widened.

Althea walked up behind them.

After a moment, the oldest soldier replied. "They'll be dead by midday. What difference can whatever you say make?"

"I have news that will—ease their passing."

"Your words will fall on deaf ears. These villains gave up their chance at anything *easy* when they rebelled against the Empire."

Althea shoved her way between Dar and Yamin. "I have been placed here, as acting physician, amongst your men in an official manner by the authority of your centurion and demand, respectfully, you allow these two passage within."

The older soldier glanced at his partner and let out a great sigh. He stepped aside, and the other followed his lead.

Tall narrow windows lit a holding area consisting of two small cells separated by a tight passageway. The sweet smell of freshly laid straw filled the air.

Fulgur sat on the floor of his small cell to the left. Captain Adjo sat in the cell to the right. Farther in, a flight of wooden stairs spiraled up into the tower, presumably, the barracks. Captain Adjo saw them first.

Yamin witnessed a momentary jolt of surprise quickly reverting to the hateful stare from the night before.

Fulgur had his eyes closed and started when he heard Yamin's voice.

"I'm sorry it has come to this." Yamin reached out his hand to rest on Captain Adjo's iron cell. The cold rough metal sent a shiver up his arm and down his spine. *I remember the bite of steel but not how it truly felt until now.*

Dar and Althea stood just inside the doorway, silhouetted by the morning light.

Yamin continued. "In part, I blame myself."

Captain Adjo still possessed Emu's tail and stroked it continuously without a word.

Yamin reached out to him again. "You're in pain. I once felt as you now do. Your family taken away. Your livelihood diminished. Your way of life fraught with loss and frustration. But there's another way."

"Demon! Get away from him!" Fulgur leapt at the bars and reached for Yamin. His fingers found the hem of his robe but Yamin pulled away in time.

Dar took a step forward but Yamin waved him off.

"Do I sound like I once did on The Lukka? I admit, I was never myself when we were acquaintances. I always had—unwanted company."

Fulgur backed away. "If you're gonna say your demons are gone, you'll have to convince me."

"That's my goal." Yamin sat on the straw-covered floor between the cells, crossed his legs, and shared his story.

Dar sat also. He bade Althea to join him and whispered in her ear. "Wait until you hear this."

36

Yamin knew the power his story held and looked into the eyes of everyone in the small room from time to time to gauge their understanding and acceptance. He noticed Dar's hand accept Althea's as she reached for comfort at one point.

All but Captain Adjo seemed outwardly moved.

Nearly an hour had passed before the guards interrupted. "It's almost time. You better finish up whatever you're babbling on about in there."

Yamin had just finished the part where Jesus departed back across the sea. "And Jesus said, *Go home to your friends and tell them what great things the Lord has done for you. And how He has had compassion on you.*"

Yamin looked at his friends again.

A tear slipped down Althea's cheek. She attempted to wipe it and realized Dar still had possession of her hand. She hastily pulled away.

Fulgur, now sitting, shifted in place. "We're going to die." He spoke to no one as he stared off into the darkest recesses of the room. "All my adventures. All my—*second* chances."

"You don't have to die alone." Yamin turned to the captain. He raised his eyebrows in anticipation of some sort of response to either his story or Fulgur's statement of the obvious.

Captain Adjo's death stare had contorted into one of loathsome contemplation. He opened his mouth to speak but no words emerged.

Fulgur stood and approached the bars. "I don't wish to die alone. What must I do?"

Captain Adjo stood. "My gods are the only gods, Fulgur. Do not listen to the lies from this boy. He speaks of forgiveness and salvation. The gods of my ancestors have promised everlasting life if only you follow your leader. Fulgur, *I* am your leader."

Yamin no longer saw Adjo as the proud captain of a mighty sailing vessel. He had become as plain as the rest of them. *The rest of us.* None were any more special than the other. All transparent as the air they breathed. A person was either missing God or had found God. Titles melted away. All that remained was the bareness they were born with. How they clothed that bareness was up to them. Covered in grace or smothered in a life of sinful acts.

Fulgur spoke with quivering breaths. "We're not sinless, Captain. Your gods speak of judgement. How can thieves and murderers enter without forgiveness? Do your gods offer forgiveness?"

"Then the goddess Ammit devour you!" Adjo gnashed his teeth and spit at Yamin and Fulgur.

The guards rushed in and pushed Yamin and his friends through the doorway and into the road. Shortly after, they escorted Adjo and Fulgur outside in chains.

Yamin followed them to the hills just below the city but above the tombs. Two roughly hewn crosses laid upon the rocky ground.

Althea stopped. "I can't watch this, Dar."

Yamin gave Dar a small nod.

Dar escorted Althea back up to the gate and out of Yamin's view.

The screams from the two pirates echoed off the city walls and back down to the great lake.

Yamin's heart sank.

Several citizens gathered to witness the barbaric death sentence be carried out.

"Blasphemers!"

"Traitors!"

"Pig thieves!"

Others spat and threw small stones toward the suffering men.

Yamin waited for nearly an hour before the ordeal ended and both men neared death.

Fulgur mouthed the same words over and over as his breath diminished.

Yamin moved closer to understand his utterances.

Adjo stared off toward the distant water. A tear rolled down his cheek.

Yamin flashed a diminutive smile when he recognized Fulgur's final words.

"I . . . believe. I . . . believe."

Adjo shook violently before becoming limp.

Fulgur appeared to fall asleep as he gently released his last breath.

The bittersweet success of Yamin's most challenging apology so far gave him an unexpected sense of hope. It also gave him clarity concerning what he might expect when he traveled throughout Decapolis. Some would hear. Others would not. Some would believe. Many would refuse. *Just as my heart was once hardened, so theirs will be.*

Yamin reached the top of the path and joined Dar and Althea. Dar had his arm around her shoulders.

Yamin sat next to Althea. "I have to leave soon."

All three stared off toward the distant lake.

Althea spoke without taking her eyes off the water. "Everyone must hear your story, Yamin."

Yamin spent the next few weeks recuperating with Dar and his father. At the same time, he helped Sophus with his healing and the workload of a prospering sculptor.

Yamin accompanied Dar on a visit to the harbor. They passed the charred remains of his childhood home in respectful silence.

As the shoreline grew close, Yamin paused. He knelt to pick up a handful of sand and small pebbles. A wave of welcome emotion spread through him. He sat and smiled.

Dar joined him. "You're leaving now, aren't you?"

"I still have a promise to keep." He let the sand fall through his fingers. "So, what's with you and Althea?"

A seabird cawed.

Dar ignored the question. "But this is where you belong. You've said it before." He repeated Yamin's words in a mocking tone. "'The sea is in my blood.'"

"Yes, we all belong somewhere. But the paths we take to get there must first be traveled."

Several fishermen talked nearby.

Dar harrumphed. "Some paths are rockier than others."

"Are we talking about Althea now?"

Before Dar responded, a man called out from the docks. "Hallo!"

"Baniy." Dar stood. "He's been looking for you. I've kept him away for obvious reasons." Dar took Yamin's arm to guide him away.

Yamin stood and smiled. "It's all right, Dar." He gently pulled his arm from Dar's grasp. "This will be even easier than Adjo, yes?"

"Even though he helped them find you?"

Yamin hushed Dar as Baniy approached.

"So, you've returned to us, then. You look a lot healthier than when you left." He poked Yamin's shoulder and chuckled. He looked at Dar. "You've been feeding him well."

Dar took a step between Baniy and Yamin. "What do you want, Baniy?"

Yamin did not wait for Baniy to respond. "I wanted to thank you, friend."

Baniy stood wide-eyed.

Dar did the same. "Well, that's a first."

Yamin turned to Dar. "What's that?"

"Baniy does not know what to say."

All three men laughed.

Baniy guided them to his boat, and they sat on the dock while Yamin shared his story.

Several other fishermen joined them at different parts of the tale.

Near the end, nine men sat listening as Yamin finished. He stood. "Most of you knew my father and have known me since I was a young boy. I'd never proven to be untrustworthy . . ." He looked quickly at Dar.

Dar gave him an approving nod.

". . . in my youth, but I am being honest with you now." Yamin scanned his audience to gauge their agreement. "If you believe, then go your own way and spread this story about Jesus. Tell all who you know, the one true God exists and those who trust in him will be saved just as I was."

One older man who stood in the back of the group threw up his hands. "You accuse us all of having demons, do you?"

Yamin's brow furrowed. "No, that's not—I didn't say that."

Another fisherman who had been sitting in his boat while listening stood. "You assume we all need to be saved, then. What makes you think this? You don't know who we are. Your father was the one who died and needed saving."

The temptation to become angry presented itself, but instead Yamin lowered his head in frustration.

Another man, this one a close associate of Baniy's, turned to the first man. "You've turned his words around. He wasn't speaking about that. Were you even listening? Maybe your guilt is making you deny his account."

Dar leaned over and whispered to Yamin. "We'd better go now."

"I think you're right." He slowly rose and allowed Dar to escort him from the harbor. Only when they turned and headed uphill did the sound of the men's arguing lessen.

Dar and Yamin walked in silence until they reached the site of the crucifixion weeks earlier.

Yamin stopped and put his hand on a nearby rock to rest. "Do you think it will be like that every time I tell it?"

Dar shook his head. "Well, the way I see it, it's been about half-and-half."

Yamin looked at his friend and then let his gaze drift to the ground. "You know, Dar, I never told you how trying the demons were. How difficult it was to have them in my head."

Dar looked at Yamin. "You never had to. I can only imagine."

"I heard them, just now, in the men's voices. The acceptance of sin, the blindness, the blame." He turned and sat on the ground with his back against the rock. "There was a time, just a moment really, when their voices no longer came from outside. A moment when . . . well, when it's within. It—*they*—became part of me, filling a void meant for another."

"For the Hebrew god, you mean."

"Yes. But it was more than that. Bigger, more worldly. Something's coming that will make what happened to me seem so small in comparison. I can feel it. The demons felt it too. They knew their destiny was defeat. The only thing they could do in the end was make themselves known before their destruction."

"It sounds like you pity them."

Yamin thought for a moment and shuddered. "As much as want to pity them I cannot. They were not people like us. They were pure evil. I would not wish upon my worst enemy what happened to me over the past two years."

"I'm sorry, Yamin. I can't pretend to understand what you endured."

"I need to know how to convey the enormity of what happened to me and how close I came to my end. Others won't believe unless I can." He turned and peeked around the rock toward the harbor. "I have to do better than half-and-half."

"Still, that's not too bad." Dar shrugged his shoulders. "At least they're talking about it."

"I hope it's enough." He looked to the sky. "Lord, I hope it's enough." *Some may have demons of their own.*

37

G et up."

Yamin shot from his sleeping mat.

Aphra stood over him holding a small lamp. "Come. You must leave. Quickly."

Dar waited by the back door.

"What's going on? What's all that noise?"

"Citizens, in the street outside. My father's doing his best to keep them there—for now." Dar ushered Yamin into the small courtyard.

"What do they want?" Yamin accepted a sack of food and skin of water from Dar.

"Apparently, your story at the docks has spread through the city already."

Dar led Yamin to a small gate in the courtyard wall. It opened to a narrow trail hugging the steep northern cliff of the city.

"Half-and-half, you say?" Yamin looked over the edge. Darkness greeted him. The cave on Malta flashed into his mind. "Looks like the disbelieving half is knocking on our door."

"Once we assure them you're gone, everything'll calm down. Now, get moving."

"You sure about this, Dar? It looks steep."

"Keep one hand on the wall, and you'll be at the bottom before you know it. We did this once as kids. Remember?"

Yamin slung the bags over his shoulder and took a wary step down onto the slender path. "That was years ago, in daylight, and we only made it halfway before crying."

"Come back to us, Yamin." Dar disappeared behind a gate whose locking metal hasp closed with a harsh snap.

Yamin worked his way down the steep cliff. Small rocks tumbled after every step. *One hand on the wall. One hand on the wall.*

A loud crash spilled over the cliff and echoed into the valley. Raised voices followed. *Dar?* Yamin paused. He heard nothing more than a falling pebble hit farther down.

The water skin slipped off Yamin's shoulder shifting his weight. This caused his foot to miss the path. Down he slid. He grasped the rocks where his feet had been a split second ago. The water skin and sack of food continued down without him. He heard the thud of their landing below.

Yamin clawed at the jagged stones and pulled with all his might to end up prone and out of breath on the ledge. There he lay until the early morning light filtered over the mountains and aided his final descent. Halfway down he found the errant provisions only scratched from their fall.

He reached the valley floor and turned to gaze upon the hilltop city from an angle he never viewed before. The polished stone buildings where aristocrats still slumbered shone in the face of the rising sun. Yamin sighed. *I hope Dar's all right.*

For the first time since before his mother's death, Yamin knelt and prayed. "Lord, you've sent me on a journey in the name of the miracle worker, Jesus."

He paused and imagined what the scene of his exorcism would have looked like from a bystander's point of view. He pictured clouds of ethereal darkness spewing from his mouth, and from the center of his chest, and from the top of his head. *That's what it felt like, anyway.*

"You pulled those spirits from within me, and I don't know how to thank you other than boldly following Jesus' command." He moved his right knee aside when a sharp stone dug into it.

Yamin opened his eyes. *I don't know how to pray.* He searched for any sensation to guide his words.

A hawk started its daily ritual with a great shriek that echoed in the hills and ravines.

Yamin shuddered and closed his eyes tightly. He dropped to his hands. Grass, jagged pebbles, and dry, wind-blown seeds littered the ground. He let them poke his palms until he sensed the fullness of their being.

"The land you're sending me to is full of people who'll be challenged to believe. I'm only a young man with a story that's," he shook his head slowly, "incredible. Look what happened back there when I tried." Yamin pulled up a bundle of grass. Its seeds fell to the ground. "Please make my words like these seeds. Let them fall upon the ears of those who'll hear. And direct my feet on paths that'll bring you glory."

He stood and turned south, as Sophus had told him, to find the Imperial road that would lead him to the second of the ten cities of Decapolis, Raphana.

The sun had crossed nearly the entire sky by the time Yamin reached the Hieromices River. The contoured land and warm light made traveling, even on the road, a trying feat. He welcomed the cool riverine landscape and stepped off the road to fill his empty water skin, and stomach, with its clear contents.

The Roman bridge spanning the river consisted of arching limestone rock reminiscent of other bridges he saw in the west.

As he stepped onto the viaduct, Yamin ran his hand over the low, gray, stone walls and stopped. He closed his eyes and let the last of the day's sunlight settle upon his face.

"Hallo!"

Yamin's eyes snapped open as adrenaline coursed through his veins. He reduced his profile and peered over the arching bridge wall at the silhouetted figure. *Lord, please don't let my mission end so suddenly.*

From the far side, a smiling man emerged from under the overpass carrying an armful of sticks.

Yamin straightened and half waved at him.

"The wood builds up against the rocks during the rainy season. Most people don't know to look there." The man reached the road and handed the bundle to a woman.

Yamin met him on the other side.

"I'm Oren."

"Yamin, son of Eber." It felt good for the first time he could remember to make that reference. He stood a little taller.

"My wife, Nitza."

Yamin smiled and nodded at the handsome middle-aged couple.

"What brings you out here in the middle of nowhere?"

Yamin followed Oren and Nitza to their campsite just off the road, but out of the way of any would-be travelers. "I'm going to Raphana."

The couple's oversized cart, laden with flax-fiber sacks, clay jars, and bundles of plant material stood at the back of the site guarded by two healthy oxen.

"And where are you coming from?" Oren placed two pieces of wood on the small smoldering fire.

Yamin searched his feelings before answering. No lingering shame. No desire for secrecy. Just freedom. "Hippos, my home."

"Oh, really?" Oren glanced at Nitza, raised his eyebrows, and grinned.

Yamin plopped to the ground not too close to the fire. He did not want to intrude. "You've been there?"

Oren cleared his throat. "Well, not to sound like we dislike your little city on the hill, but—"

"What my husband is trying to say is we prefer towns with less of a . . . pompous air."

The couple studied Yamin for a reaction.

Yamin tightened his lips and nodded slowly. "I know exactly what you mean." He smiled.

They all laughed.

Nitza removed the cover from a cooking pot that rested in the embers. Savory steam rose from within. "Would you like to join us for the evening meal, Yamin?"

A musky scent drifted into Yamin's nostrils and mingled with that of the food. He sniffed to gain more information but it eluded him.

"We're in the perfume trade. What you smell is our livelihood." Oren stood. "Come. I'll show you while Nitza prepares."

One of the oxen gave a short bellow in response to Yamin's approach.

He stopped moving.

"Don't worry. They're harmless. Have you no oxen in your town?"

"My family lived on the sea. Some people had them. We could never afford an animal so—stately."

"Stately?" Oren chuckled. "Did you hear that?" He patted the noisy animal on the rump. "He thinks you're *stately*."

The ox snorted and shook the cart.

After the tour and welcoming dinner, Oren retrieved a sleeping mat for Yamin from the recesses of his cart.

As they sat around the fire, the river's waters gurgled in the distance, and crickets chirped from the brush.

"We're on our way south for the winter to harvest a unique herb in the canyons outside Jerusalem. Why not join us?"

"Sounds intriguing. But I'm on a mission from God. Jerusalem's not part of that plan."

Oren chuckled. "'God?' Which god? There are many."

"He means the Hebrew god, Oren." Nitza addressed Yamin. "Yahweh, yes? Or is it Elohim?"

"Actually," Yamin shifted his position, "Jesus is the one who performed a miracle to save me, and it's *his* mission I undertake."

Oren harrumphed. "We've not witnessed anything miraculous in our travels."

Nitza corrected her husband. "Unless you consider sunsets, winter rains, the scent of healing herbs, and the birth of our only daughter." She winked at Yamin.

Yamin smiled. "Daughter? Have I missed something?"

Nitza's countenance darkened ever-so-slightly. "Pericope. She's married and lives in Jerusalem. We keep hoping to visit, but—"

"But our work insists that we travel to particular areas during the exact time of year. If we miss one location, we might very well miss our narrow window of opportunity to harvest." Oren reassured his wife. "We'll get there soon."

"It sounds like good timing is important in your line of work. Actually, my story is one you might be interested in then, as good timing was essential for it to happen."

The sound of hooves on stone echoed from the road on the far side of the bridge.

Oren doused what embers had remained after dinner and hushed Nitza and Yamin. He whispered. "Bandits."

38

Morning brought with it farewells. Yamin took leave of his newfound friends but not before accepting a sleeved outer cloak from Nitza. "For the coming winter," she said with a warm smile as she handed it to him. "I know it's very plain, but—"

"It's wonderful."

Oren walked Yamin to the road leading to Raphana while Nitza remained behind to pack up the camp. He had his own gift to bestow upon his new friend. One of wisdom. "The bandits we evaded last night are not the only dangers on this path, Yamin. Roman patrols are eager to bully travelers for taxes, and slavers are always in need of new labor. Be cautious."

"Thank you for your hospitality, Oren. I might already be another's property had you not been placed in my path."

"Placed by your god, no doubt?"

"I wish I had the time to share my tale with you, friend. You might think differently."

"Maybe, had we not needed to be silent for the remainder of the night. But for now, Nitza and I are content with the gods of rock, of plants, and those of the birds in the sky. They serve our needs."

"But without miracles." Yamin gave him a warm smile. "Goodbye, friend."

Oren returned the smile and bowed his head slightly as Yamin marched eastward.

Several hours later, Yamin approached the outskirts of Raphana. The settlement stood atop two hills, one to the north and one to the south. A saddle-shaped valley between the hills held most of the city's buildings, terraced to compensate for the hills' slopes. A stout wall surrounded the town and limestone temples of varied design rose from behind the ramparts.

Yamin compared Hippos, never in need of walls, to this Decapolis city and found it far more heavily fortified. *What makes them think they're more vulnerable than us? We're only a good day's walk from each other.*

He approached the western gate.

Merchants lined both sides of the road. Some peddled idols to the Greek gods Herakles, Tyche, and Athena, as well as an equal number of their Roman deity counterparts.

Yamin closed his eyes and took a deep breath. *This isn't going to be easy.*

A slender middle-aged man with short hair and beard to match reached out toward Yamin to present a toothy grin and a small clay statue of Fortuna. "*Aspádzomai*, stranger. An idol to restore your luck? Only one *quinarius*."

Yamin stopped. *As good a place to start as any other.* He looked into the man's eyes, ignoring his wares. "*Epainō*, kind sir. But I don't believe in luck, nor possess even a *quadran* to purchase such a *beautiful* piece of artistry." He scanned the man's booth for a moment. "Have you anything on your shelves—to restore a man's soul?"

The merchant lowered his arm to his side and stared wide-eyed at Yamin. "Well, that's the first time anyone replied to my sales pitch with such a serious question."

A well-groomed man dressed in simple but spotless robes stopped to listen to their conversation.

Yamin replied to the merchant. "Ah, but wasn't your pitch equally serious?"

The merchant harrumphed. "Ha! I've no time for such discussions. Go into the city and speak to a temple priest if you doubt your beliefs." He turned to another passerby. "*Aspádzomai*, stranger. An idol for luck?"

The well-groomed man tugged on Yamin's sleeve. "You'll get nowhere with this one."

Yamin pulled away. "What? What do you mean?"

"Come, you can discuss luck, and souls, and other serious topics with me if you'd like."

Yamin studied the man. "I am Yamin, son of Eber." Although the formality of his greeting was not necessary, he like referring to his father with such pride.

"I am called Nat. Where do you hail from, Yamin?"

"Nearby. Hippos."

"Really? I've been there several times. Although, my kind are not overly welcomed by your people."

Yamin stopped walking. "My people?"

"Forgive me. I did not mean to insult. It's just that Jews are—"

"Oh, I see. Please know I'm not one of *those* people. I believe in the Hebrew god, just as you."

"I thought as much, after hearing your awkward chat with Ulricus."

Yamin chuckled. "A sorry attempt at a conversion, I know."

"If you're looking to convert the citizens of Raphana to Judaism, then you certainly have your work cut out for you."

"Oh, not Judaism. I speak for Jesus. To tell everyone about the miracle the Lord God provided for me."

Nat lowered his stature and hushed Yamin. "Before too many hear what you have to say, maybe you should tell *me* your story first. Come. My synagogue is nearby."

Minutes later, Nat guided Yamin into a battered but organized structure adjacent to the inside wall and east of the gate. A circular wooden plaque above the door depicted signs of the zodiac with corresponding words for each pagan symbol.

Yamin could not read the words but recognized them as Hebrew characters. He did not give them much more thought before entering.

A large open room, supported in part by simple columns,

welcomed him inside. The floor consisted of a grand unfinished mosaic, similar to the scene above the door but far more detailed, centered in the space. A beam of light from a small dormer's window in the roof shone upon the artwork revealing a myriad of minute, colored tile chips. Some of the pieces sat arranged in loose piles around the perimeter on the artwork.

Nat spoke proudly. "You appreciate a masterpiece when you see one."

Yamin stepped back to avoid dishonoring the craftsmen or, even more, his host. He thought of Dar's father and the masterpieces of art he created in Hippos. A disturbing image of the swirling pictograms in the Maltese caves flashed before his eyes, and he had to catch his breath.

"Are you all right, young man?"

Yamin shook himself out of it. *Focus on Jesus. Focus on your mission.* "Yes, I'm—just tired from my travels."

"Come. Sit down. How absent-minded of my manners. I'll fetch some water." Nat motioned to a long stone bench lining the perimeter of the room.

Yamin sat and realized he hadn't eaten since the night before when Oren and Nitza had shared their dinner.

Nat returned with a pitcher of water, along with a small plate of grapes, figs, and bread.

"Your hospitality is greatly appreciated, Nat."

A young man entered the room from a doorway in the back. "Good afternoon, Rabbi."

Yamin straightened. "Rabbi?"

"I did say this was *my* synagogue, did I not?" He settled on the bench next to Yamin. "Perhaps now, while we eat, you can share your miracle story."

Yamin swallowed his water hard and cleared his throat. "I thought Jews did not believe in miracles."

Nat nodded slowly. "Hmm, being from Hippos, I can imagine a great many things you believe about Jews are incorrect."

Yamin thought for a moment. "Perhaps." He took a deep breath and began his tale.

Afterwards, Nat remained speechless. He rose from his bench and walked across the room stepping on the unfinished mosaic in his stupor.

Yamin studied him. This was the first time he shared his story about Jesus without having his friend Dar nearby for support. He clenched his jaw not knowing what to expect. Would this strange rabbi call the authorities and have him arrested? *Hippos all over again, and I only just started.*

Nat turned after his momentary contemplation. "An intriguing scenario, I must say." He moved back to the bench and sat again. "This Jesus. You say he removed your demons and sent you here to tell others how the power of Elohim is responsible?"

Yamin nodded.

Nat stood again. "Pigs? I can't think of a better creature." He called to the back. "Bricius, come here."

The young man who greeted the rabbi earlier appeared with haste.

"Spread word to the congregation. Our lecture this coming Sabbath will be given by a special guest."

Yamin's heart skipped a beat.

39

Yamin spent the next two days before Sabbath living in humble shared quarters at the rear of the small synagogue. He volunteered to help Nat with repairs and cleaning to compensate for the hospitality. He also joined small classes every day to learn scripture and prayers.

But reading proved a challenge Yamin did not want to spend time overcoming. So, he resigned to memorize what he could by listening and repeating.

After the morning meal, the day before his planned lecture, he entered the main worship area. A lone craftsman applied the finishing touches to the large floor mosaic. Yamin stood mesmerized.

The worker picked each piece of tile with utmost care. And when he had chosen the right color, shape, and thickness, he applied a sticky mortar with a tiny knife to the back and placed it in the floor with a slight twist to set it. The man then exited but soon returned with several rolls of thin straw matting. As he covered the mosaic with the mats, he answered Yamin's unspoked question without looking up. "We can't have people walking all over it until the mortar has set, and I've applied the glaze."

Yamin stepped closer. "Can you tell me what it all means?"

The man stepped back next to Yamin but kept his eyes focused on the floor. He cocked his head. "I don't really care. As long as I'm paid, I make what they want. I've learned not to ask too many questions."

Yamin took his answer to mean the artist could not read either. "But you know what the symbols are at least, yes?"

He looked at Yamin with a furrowed brow. "All citizens who call Raphana their home know these symbols." He returned to covering his work.

Nat entered from the back room. "Are you ready for your tour of the city?"

Yamin nodded then thanked the artist.

The man replied with a grunt.

Nat adjusted his robes and led Yamin outside. "We'll start with the perimeter—that's where we are now—and work our way to the interior where the grand temple to Athena stands."

Yamin stopped. "Athena?"

"Yes, although Minerva is what you may be familiar with. There are smaller ones for Hercules and Fortuna as well. Come." He motioned for Yamin to follow.

"I'd rather skip the temples, if that's all right with you."

Nat studied him for a moment. "All right, but the price is you have to tell me why."

They walked uphill, staying close to the inside of the city's wall.

Yamin felt the part of his story with the pirates on the Great Sea was not pertinent to Jesus' command. But at the behest of his host, he shared it with discretion. *No need to mention the gory details.*

Nat stopped at a building and reached out to place his hand on the wall of a moderately fine home.

It reminded Yamin of Dar's house in Hippos. He squinted. *I wonder if he sees with his hands like I do.*

"I was born here." He chuckled. "The experience you just shared opens my eyes even more to what happened to my own family."

"Are they still in the city?" Yamin craned his neck to see inside the darkened interior through the partially open doorway.

"No, no. They left long ago." Nat pulled his hand from the beige stone and wiped the dust on his robe. "I am all that remains." He led Yamin away, this time toward the center of town.

"What happened?"

"Driven away—by the idolaters." Nat pointed his chin at the stark white columns now lining the street. "Their influence was too great to overcome. Too powerful to battle without a miracle."

Yamin likened the houses to the aristocrats' opulent dwellings in Hippos. "Driven away? Because they were Jews?"

"No. Because they were overzealous."

Yamin sensed regret and a tinge of anger in Nat's words. "Is that why you use pagan symbols at the Synagogue?"

"You mean the mosaic."

Yamin nodded.

"It's the only way they permit me to stay in the city." He stopped and looked toward the immense structures dedicated to the pagan gods of Rome, now directly on the road in front of them on the *Cardo Maximus.* "Only when I merge the two, have I found success in gaining proselytes."

"Proselytes?"

"Well, not so much gaining Jews as gaining God-fearers."

Yamin's brow furrowed. He could not help but think the task Jesus gave him would be more of a challenge the farther he got from home. "Tomorrow, when I give the lecture—"

"Tell them exactly what you told me, the way you told me. Leave the converting to the professionals."

The next morning, cool humid air cascaded through the only window in Yamin's tiny room, harkening winter's imminent arrival.

Before rising completely from his sleeping mat, he got to his knees and prayed. "Lord, you've led me here in the name of Jesus, to spread the news of my miracle to others." He paused and sighed. "There will be many who won't believe." He paused again and fell backwards to sit against the wall.

Nat appeared in the doorway. "Talking to Elohim does not have to be a chore."

Yamin stood quickly. He felt his face flush. "I've struggled to say the right thing. I'm not used to talking to a god—I mean, Elohim—and actually believing that he's listening."

"Come. I want to introduce you to some people."

Several other small rooms made up the rear of the synagogue, including a meeting place with two dark wooden tables pushed together and surrounded by short backless stools. Shelves housing numerous scrolls, jars, and sacraments lined the walls. Two bright decorative oil lamps hung from the center of the ceiling above the tables.

Four older men sat at one end of the tables, all dressed in similar fashion to Nat. Bricius, the young assistant whom Yamin met upon arrival, stood to the side, presumably awaiting orders.

"Allow me to introduce you to my council of elders."

One of the four stood out immediately as the peddler he met outside the gate upon arriving to Raphana.

Ulricus stood and smiled to greet him. "We meet again. Blessed be you who enters." He then grabbed Yamin by the right hand and pulled to kiss him on the cheek.

Yamin's wide-eyed stance made the men laugh. "You'll have to explain yourselves."

Nat welcomed him to the table. "And that is why we've invited you to sit with us, young man."

Yamin sat between Ulricus and Nat.

Nat offered him a small variety of breakfast foods including apples, bread, and figs. "I've only shared with the elders that you've an interesting tale to tell. Nothing more."

Yamin thanked Nat for the food and popped a fig into his mouth. He looked over the men once more and stopped at Ulricus. "But you were selling idols of Roman gods."

"Fishing." Ulricus took a swig of watered-down wine. "Surely you can understand that reference, being from Hippos."

You have no idea. Yamin cleared his throat. "You were working in tandem." He looked at Nat, smirked, and shook his head. "And I'm the fresh catch?"

Nat chuckled. "Not the exact sort of fish we normally set our nets out for."

"What sort would that be?"

Ulricus spoke. "Why, the lost, my boy. But you turned out to be not so lost as oddly enlightened."

"'Oddly enlightened?'" Yamin looked at Nat. "I thought they hadn't been told."

"Oh, Ulricus only knows of the question you asked of him at your first encounter." Nat looked at Ulricus. "What was it again?"

"'Have you anything on your shelves to restore a man's soul?'" Ulricus smiled. "Not the standard reply to a sales pitch, wouldn't you say?"

Yamin chuckled. "No, I suppose not."

The other men snickered as well.

"And what of the idols you sell?"

"A two-fold endeavor: fishing and income to support our cause. With every sale comes an invitation to our Sabbath service." Ulricus turned to his neighbor and elbowed him. "Unless that customer is a local official." He snorted out a laugh.

Yamin gave him a chiding glance.

"Words speak louder than idols can." Nat stood and walked to the end of the table. "Normally we seek those with less of a spiritual understanding. But some catches are more surprising than others."

Yamin searched the men's faces for a sign of what came next. Would he be allowed to leave? Or was he now part of these holy men's schemes to convert unwary travelers into God-fearers? Not too bad a notion, but also not what Jesus commanded him to do.

Nat continued. "You see, some fish are harder to catch than others. Take fishing in a lake, like the one you are from, and compare it to fishing in a river, like the one you crossed on your way here. In the lake, the same fish pass day by day and grow wary of your nets. These are the people of Raphana. Set in their ways, they go about their business avoiding our open doors and welcoming words.

"But the roads leading to our city are like rivers, bringing travelers from faraway places who perhaps have never heard the name Elohim. These fish are easily persuaded and now make up the majority of our synagogue's assembly."

Ulricus raised his hand. "I am one of those converts." He smiled proudly.

"We have a plan of attack and a certain way with our words when outside the gates in the public eye. But when you asked about restoring souls, well, we needed to proceed with caution."

Another of the elders spoke. "We could be arrested for blasphemy by speaking against the pagan gods openly."

"It is only because of our *discretion* that the authorities tolerate our presence at all."

Yamin looked at Nat. "That's what happened to your parents."

Nat nodded slowly and returned to his stool next to Yamin. "Yes. But unlike them we have found ways to integrate their pagan beliefs so conversions are easier to tolerate."

"The mosaic."

"Yes, and many more." Nat raised his glass. "But now, share with us your story once more in preparation for your lecture soon."

Ulricus straightened. "Yes, what have you to enlighten us?"

Yamin swallowed a bite of bread and relayed his story for the fifth time. As he spoke, the words he chose painted a clearer picture than the last telling. His intonations and hand gestures aided in the audience's understanding.

The men listened in awe as Yamin wove demonic possessions, high seas adventures, and Jesus' miracle into a compact narrative of salvation and enlightenment.

The men sat without speaking for some time after Yamin finished. He looked at Nat for a signal on how to proceed next.

Nat provided none. He simply scanned the elders allowing them time to digest what was just given them. After a moment, Nat rose. "Yamin, will you excuse us. We have much to discuss."

Yamin stood. A sense of foreboding grew in him as he thought about what happened in Hippos after sharing his story there. He nodded to the elders and walked out to the main hall.

Several men had already arrived. Some sat on floor mats around the covered mosaic and several on the perimeter benches.

A wave of anxiety surged through Yamin's innards. *Still, it feels better than demons pulling at me.* He filled his lungs with air. *You can do this. Jesus commanded. He believed I could do this.* He sat in the dark corner near the back of the room, closed his eyes, and released the breath.

Nat returned to his seat. "I know what you're thinking."

All four men answered at once.

"He's mad."

"He speaks of a prophet."

"Could it be Messiah?"

"Demons into pigs? Ha!"

Nat held up his hands. "Gentlemen, please. We need to come to some sort of agreement about his story before letting him tell it in there." He motioned to the main hall. "Yamin told me of the division it created in Hippos when told only to a group of fishermen. You know what could happen here if it were told to the wrong sort of ears."

Ulricus stood. "Yes, we must be in consensus when questions arise. What do we tell them when they ask who this Jesus is?"

The other men stood and spoke at the same time.

"Yes, when they ask of miracles?"

"And what of demonic possession?"

"Is this *Lord* he mentions truly Elohim?"

Nat stopped them again. "They will think him the god Vejovis, *The Savior*, if we don't offer clear guidance otherwise. Ulricus, what do you say?"

Ulricus paused and looked toward the empty doorway. "A savior is exactly what the people need to hear about. Either way, his story has exceeded our expectations, and the people will ask for it to be told again and again. We can use that."

"Exactly." Nat motioned for the men to join him. "But we must be cautious. There is a fine line between keeping the people's interest and scaring them back into the arms of Fortuna."

40

Nearly thirty men had gathered in the synagogue when Nat and the elders entered the main hall. Several women stood just inside the doorway to the main entrance's vestibule. Others intermingled with the men sitting around the mosaic on mats or along the perimeter benches.

Yamin never expected this many. Did Nat and the elders let the congregation know there would be a guest lecturer this morning? Perspiration built under his arms and around his neck. *Biggest audience yet. Lord, help me.*

In the hall's air lingered a faint but fresh woody smoke. Yamin had learned they chose this incense due its recognizability in the local pagan temples. Frankincense and other familiar costly essences were saved for the holy temple in Jerusalem.

Nat greeted the crowd in Hebrew, following every sentence with its Greek translation. "Shalom. Peace and Good morning."

Most of the congregation answered in Greek. "Peace, blessing, and good morning."

Nat, along with the elders, chose members of the congregation to participate in the service. He then sent the attendant to notify the chosen members of what part of the service they would perform.

After several benedictions and eulogies were spoken, other members read from the law and the prophets. All were spoken in Hebrew then translated into Greek.

Nat then introduced Yamin. "Men of Raphana, and you that fear the Lord, listen to the sermon."

All eyes fixed upon Yamin. A tendril of smoke stung his eyes and tears welled up. He blinked them away and spoke.

The words fell from his mouth upon the audience as a drenching rain feeds drought-stricken plants. Eyes widened, necks craned, and backs straightened, as if his words provided sustenance to those who listened. He'd only told the story five times before, but it felt like he'd been telling it for years. After all, it was *his* story, but would soon be *their* story.

No one spoke for many moments after he finished.

Nat broke the silence with a benediction intended strictly for Yamin. "Strength and blessings."

Everyone in the congregation replied with a hushed, "Be strong and mighty."

Yamin looked to Nat for any sign of praise, or disapproval.

Nat rewarded Yamin with a quick smile and motioned for him to return to his seat on bench.

Before Nat could open the floor for questions, a man dressed in dark fine robes, who had been sitting near the entrance, quickly stood and exited. Few noticed, save for Nat, Yamin, and Ulricus.

A cacophony of inquiries flew from the congregation. Nat pointed to a man in the front. Yamin scooted on his bench as far into the shadowed corner as he could. He eyed the back door.

"How do we know he speaks the truth?"

Several others who had vied to comment seconded him. Everyone silenced, waiting for Nat's answer.

Nat stated only what Yamin thought was the most obvious truth. "We do not."

Murmurs spread through the room.

Nat held up his hands to silence them. "But a story such as this—one so extraordinary that it begs questioning—can be used to teach, and to critique, and to train righteousness. Clearly the Lord of which he speaks can only be the one true God. Some call him Zeus, some Jupiter, and others, like ourselves, call him Adonai or Elohim."

Questions flew from the energized crowd.

"If there's only Elohim, then who's this *Jesus* to perform such a miracle?"

"Apollo."

"Vejovis."

"You mean Asclepius, the savior? I do not think so."

"And why not? Why can't this Jesus be the Savior? Or at least *a* savior. He healed that man, brought him from the land of the dead back to the living."

"He said he had evil spirits within him, not that he was dead."

Yamin could take no more. He slinked out the back door as the discussion gained in fervor. Even in his quarters the sounds of the men bantering proved too much.

It might be time to move on already. I've planted the seeds. Let's see what the Lord will do with them.

He drew a rudimentary map in the dust on the stony floor. He knew little of the area he planned on going to next and fought off the temptation to include anything west of the Sea of Galilee. He chuckled when he included the precarious cliff trail behind Dar's father's workshop. It looked like a snake trying to weave its way through tightly packed reeds.

Nat entered.

Yamin had been so deep in thought about his next destination he did not hear the silence now present in the main hall. "That went as well as I expected."

"Oh, it went far more than any of us expected. Did you hear them, Yamin? They could not stop talking about your story and its meaning."

"And that's a good thing?" He thought everyone should take his experience at face value. There should be no need for interpretation.

"Yes, yes. You see, most Sabbath lectures are about relationships between polytheism and monotheism. How the natural world shows this. It's all based upon the Scriptures, of course. Very monotonous, really." He waved his hand dismissively. "But this is the first time we've heard of someone experiencing an encounter with a prophet, such as this Jesus."

"I see." There was no more Yamin could say or do to help Nat and his congregation understand what they heard. "I'm not sure who Jesus is either."

"If there were one word you could use to describe the man, what would it be? Don't be hasty. Ponder the notion."

That's an easy question. "Savior. He's my Savior."

Nat produced a wide smile. "I would have chosen no other word myself. And that is how we will share your story with others who come our way." He scanned the room. "It looks as if you've gathered your belongings. Leaving us so soon?"

"I must continue in the morning, if I'm to follow my *Savior's* directions."

"That is disappointing, but I understand your need." Nat turned to leave but stopped at the doorway. "You know, there is one other rabbi in Raphana, but he holds service in a less traditional manner than I. His Sabbath lectures are held in the villages and fields surrounding the city. If you are willing, I will send him a message to meet you at the gate tomorrow morning. He'll guide you toward Capitolias. I assume that is your next stop?"

Yamin nodded. "If it's nearby, and part of Decapolis, then yes."

"It's closer to that city than your trip from Hippos to here." Nat stepped out the door and called for the attendant.

The young man appeared winded. "Yes, Rabbi?"

"Go find Ardown. Tell him there's someone special to meet at the east gate just after sunrise."

The attendant hurried off.

Yamin left alone at dawn after a farewell from Nat. As was the custom, Nat did not allow him to leave without first receiving a parting provision. Yamin reached out to accept a scroll of parchment. "What's this? Directions on how to pray?"

Nat chuckled. "No, not exactly. Although, that would have been an excellent second choice."

Yamin opened it to reveal a beautiful map of the region, including all ten cities of the Decapolis and the roads between them. His home city of Hippos had been exaggerated by purple ink. "Very kind. Thank you, Nat."

"Now, on your way. Mustn't keep the rabbi waiting."

Yamin walked toward the city's western gate where he entered a few days ago, his head buried in the map.

Nat called to him and pointed to the east. He mouthed the words, "That way."

Yamin rolled the map back up and secured it in his linen sack.

As he walked, Raphana woke around him. Citizens exited their homes, women and servants started kitchen duties, and the men, some dressed in fine white robes, walked briskly toward the center of town.

I'm happy to not be headed that way. The political affairs of aristocrats never interested him anyway.

He heard a passerby utter the words *pigs* and *demons* in the same sentence.

Already? How could word have traveled so quickly through the town?

As he turned a corner, the western gate opened a hundred steps in front of him.

Several men, gathering bundles of twigs, argued as they worked. Yamin had to walk past them, so he picked up his pace.

"... could it not be Apollo? Clearly, he is the son of Jove."

The other man whispered forcefully. "Be quiet." He watched Yamin suspiciously until he passed. "The Hebrew god, Elohim, is said to be responsible."

Yamin shook his head. *The only information that traveled this fast by the lake was when Baniy shared my misfortunes with the other fishermen. These people must be desperate for some good news.* He regretted not being able to stay longer to see the outcome of these discussions. But if it were anything like what drove him from Hippos, he had been right to play it safe.

The arched gate and formidable walls posed no hazard to Yamin's escape. *They have enough to contend with amongst themselves, let alone what might come at them from outside.*

"Are you the one with whom I'm to meet?"

Yamin blinked twice at the plainly dressed man who stood before him. "Nat? Your clothes. But how—"

The doppelganger smiled and shook his head. "Rabbi Nat is my twin brother," he whispered. "He's the uglier one."

41

Yamin had never met twins before. Yes, he knew they existed. After all, the Roman Empire started with the twins Romulus and Remus. Once, he thought he had seen twin girls running down the *Decumanus Maximus* in Hippos. But Dar assured him they were just cousins.

As they walked from the gate, Nat's brother introduced himself. "My name is Ardown. It was not always this. But things have not always been the way they are now."

"So, you don't preach in the city?"

"Oh, I used to. Did my brother mention anything?"

"Only that his family didn't quite fit in there."

Ardown laughed then extended his arm towards the surrounding fields and wilderness beyond. "*This* is my synagogue."

Yamin looked off into the distance and spoke under his breath. "Not unlike my own."

Ardown's eyes widened. "Come, let's walk. You can tell me all about it."

By the time Yamin completed sharing his story, they had walked past a sprawling cemetery, several fields of different grains, and stone-walled terraces for storing irrigation water.

They stopped where the road crossed a dry streambed about an hour's walk east from the city gate.

Ardown bent to pick up a handful of sand and smooth pebbles from the ground. "It's been a very dry season. Your story might just alleviate the drought."

Yamin almost asked, *How can my story bring the rains?* But soon realized Ardown had referred to something else. Something spiritual.

Ardown stood. "Are you aware that the very notion of a twin birth is looked upon as unnatural?"

Yamin frowned and shook his head.

"My mother almost died giving birth to Nat and me. The woman assisting with the labor ran from our house when she saw a second head on the way. My father paid a hefty sum for her silence. My parents then convinced others I was the son of my aunt who died in childbirth to avoid accusations of adultery. It was hard enough being Jews."

Yamin tried to understand how this had anything to do with the account he just shared.

"I've used my story with others to spark belief in the one true God. Apparently, the creation of two lives simultaneously is not compelling enough an argument for his existence. But your story —one exposing the *salvation* of a life in bondage from utter darkness—that will convert."

Yamin lightly nodded in agreement. He looked up at the late morning sun.

"Ah, but you must be on your way. I can share your story then, with others, that is?"

"Of course. But before I depart, there's something I need from you."

Ardown thought for moment. "Anything within my power."

Yamin reached into his sack and produced the scroll. "How do I read this map?"

Capitolias could be reached before sunset, according to Ardown. He told Yamin he had made the trip many times because, "The roads between cities do not judge, and the traveler is more willing to listen."

Yamin was not sure if that was because travelers were more bored or because they had the potential to be more lost than someone who stays put. He walked with purpose as he contemplated the aphorism and studied his new map. Although he could not read, he now recognized the names of the cities in Decapolis by their positions. The only other map he had ever seen was one of the Sea of Galilee on the wall of the portmaster's office. This one proved far easier to understand, thanks to Ardown's guidance. Surprisingly, Adjo never used a map.

Distant clouds thickened and curtains of gray rain cascaded on the hills to the north. *Canatha is getting drenched right now.* He looked at the scroll again and nodded—his next stop after Capitolias. The rest of the Decapolis cities lay to the south. It would be a long trek through cold weather if he did not wait out the winter in these two nearby cities.

Yamin spent the rest of the day's sunlight on the road to Capitolias. The concentration of fellow travelers increased as he approached the outskirts by dusk. He wondered why many families traveled away from the city at this late hour. He studied the parents' worried faces.

A young woman and younger boy, who Yamin perceived to be her brother, wept over a bloodied man on the side of the road.

What's happening here? Yamin stopped and took in the dismal display of depravity. Why were these people being treated this way?

A scream from farther ahead. Several men stripped a young couple of their personal belongings and ran off the road into the fading light.

"Stop!" Yamin called for their return to no avail.

Roman soldiers stood in the distance by the main gate of the city. They either chose to remain ignorant of the crimes being committed or had instigated them in the first place.

Yamin approached a cistern still many steps from the city's walls. He found a family resting there and filling their water skins. He asked for information while filling his own goatskin bladder. "I've not seen anything like this before."

The father, a man about twice Yamin's age with streaks of gray in his hair and beard, answered. "They are cleansing the city of non-believers. Easier than crucifying us all."

Yamin glanced up to the city's wall. Soldiers paced the ramparts while others expelled more citizens from the gate. "Non-believers? You mean Jews?"

"Everyone. The governor ordered—"

The wife pulled on her husband's sleeve. "Don't, Meshek. He might be ..." She motioned to the guards at the gate.

Yamin caught on. "I assure you I'm *not* aligned with their beliefs."

The man took his wife's hand in his. "Then you better leave with the rest of us. They've made it very clear by slaughtering the first ones to stand up to the exile order. Many of us had businesses. My livelihood—" He broke down.

His wife pulled her husband to a standing position and grabbed her two young children. She then looked at Yamin with sorrowful eyes before walking her family away.

Yamin felt like he needed to help somehow. But what could he do? He called to them. "Watch for bandits. I saw some along the road."

They did not acknowledge his warning and walked sadly away.

His shoulders sank. *I'll get nothing accomplished if I try to go in there and tell my story, except maybe ending my story.*

He finished filling his water skin, then rummaged through the small abandoned market for any scraps of food. He found a few pieces of dried fruit and sifted some wayward almonds from the dirt. Finally, in the bottom of a partially crushed basket, he discovered one brown egg. Its shell had the smallest crack, but it was still intact. *Thank the Lord.*

"Hey, you!" Two soldiers approached from the gate. "Leave this area at once!"

Yamin fled as visions of his capture by Roman soldiers on Malta fueled his pace. He looked over his shoulder.

The guards did not pursue.

Yamin slowed and peered into the waning twilight for a hidden spot to stay the night. *Soldiers, bandits, refugees. At least it's not raining.*

42

Yamin rested a little when a light rain forced him to move back onto the road in the hours before sunrise. His failed attempt at checking off another Decapolis city bothered him. He then recalled Ardown's words about travelers being more willing to listen. *Maybe this was meant to be.*

The rain dissipated not long after it started. Yamin gave thanks for its stopping before soaking his robes through to the skin.

After walking slowly for a couple of hours, sunlight filtered its way over the eastern horizon. A strange plume of thick yellow smoke twisted through the orange atmosphere far in the distance. Yamin had seen smoke of all kinds over different locations. But this seemed different. Ominous and unnerving.

He soon forgot about it when the sun's light washed the sky clean and gave him opportunity to see numerous people walking along the road, most northeast with him. Some had carts full of goods and effects, and others carried supplies in their arms.

He stuffed a portion of his meager sustenance into his mouth and sidled up to a man sitting in a cart with two families in the back. He swallowed hard. "Good morning, sir. Might I interest you—"

"We don't want to buy anything. Leave us be."

Yamin smiled, attempting to lighten the man's mood. "Then it's good that I'm not selling anything."

"We don't have any alms. Step away from my cart, *phlyaros.*" He spat the insult.

Yamin stopped and let the cart continue. *Never been called that before. At least not in Greek.*

Another man and woman, both about his parents' age, walked up behind him. The woman greeted Yamin with a kind voice. "I've been called worse."

Yamin turned. "I'm thankful someone on this road has manners. Hallo, I'm Yamin."

"I am Rena. This is my husband, Sabinus."

Yamin walked beside them as they passed yet another family resting on the roadside, obviously battered by their forced removal from the city. He said a quick prayer for them in silence. He stopped when he realized Rena watched him.

She produced a diminutive smile. "It appears as if the Hebrew god ignored his people this time, yes?"

"In my experience, he won't ignore you if you're ready to accept his presence."

"Is that what happened to you?"

This is an inquisition. Better be careful or she'll turn me in. "Don't all gods need your acceptance before they can move in your life?"

"In my experience, the gods will do what they want whether you're ready for it or not."

Yamin recalled his encounter with Jesus. *Was I ready for his intervention?* He had been under the demons' influence for over a year. He was tired. So very tired. Had he given up all hope back then? *Some of these people look as if they've quit. Will Elohim intervene? Perhaps, if it suits his plan. After all, didn't Jesus use me for the Lord's work when I felt useless and hopeless?*

Sabinus spoke for the first time. "Why don't you follow us to Canatha? The rules in one city don't necessarily apply to a neighboring one."

The man's voice seemed too upbeat for the situation. Was there something he knew that Yamin did not? "It was the next stop on my mission. I can always come back here . . . when things calm down."

Rena's face lit up. "Yes, you can stay with us. But you must tell us of this mission you are on as payment."

"I am happy to share my story. After all, that's my mission."

Sabinus screwed up his face. "Your mission is to tell tales?"

"Oh, Sabinus." Rena patted her husband's arm. "Let's hear the man out first before making any judgements."

Yamin smiled. *Ardown was right. The roads between cities don't judge.* Yamin spent the next hour sharing.

Unlike others whom he has spoken to, Rena and Sabinus commented many times during his narrative. They interjected with gasps of shock and questioned every decision he had made. At times, he felt as if they acted overly dramatic as a sign of welcoming. Was it their way of building trust to draw him in to some nefarious scheme? Or were they simply that entertained?

They even applauded when Yamin finished.

"Is there no more," asked Rena. "That was quite an adventure."

"Yes." Sabinus beamed. "It approaches Virgil and Homer as an epic tale. But what happened between the pigs leaping off the cliff and now? How did you get all the way out here? Have you told anyone else this story?"

"Well, no one that has been interested enough to hear anything past Jesus' miracle."

Rena and Sabinus asked simultaneously. "Miracle?" They chuckled at their perfect timing.

Yamin was not amused. "Yes. What else would you call it?"

Sabinus frowned. "Well, many attest their god can heal and cast out demons."

Yamin suspected they were baiting him. *Maybe they're fishing too.* "I've not known any other god to do anything except ignore those who give them attention." He thought back to the idol on the shelf in his parents' home. How many hours had they dedicated to kneeling, sacrificing, and praying, only to be neglected in their time of need?

"It seems like a good time for us to tell *our* story. Don't you think, Sabinus?"

"That's why we made this trip in the first place, my wife." He motioned with his head back toward Capitolias. "It obviously didn't go over well back there."

"You two didn't start that in the city, did you?"

Rena put her hand to her chest and looked shocked. "What, us?" She winked at Sabinus. "Now, what gave you that idea?"

Sabinus returned the wink. "From where do you hail, young Yamin? Rena and I are from Heliopolis in Syria."

"I was born in Hippos."

"Oh, the Decapolis city on the lake."

"You've been there?"

"A few years ago. But, just like Capitolias—"

Rena elbowed her husband. "Let's just say the leaders of Hippos were even less open to new ideas about theology."

"What *are* your ideas? I'd like to hear them."

"You see, Sabinus, travelers *are* more open-minded."

Now it was Yamin's turn to express an enigmatic chuckle.

He thought his story took a long time to express. But this couple had him beat. They did not complete their theological diatribe until after noon.

Rena and Sabinus took turns explaining that in Canatha they worship at the Temple of Theandrios, a local and ancestral god. They took him from Heliopolis when other gods grew in favor. The city's chief administrators exiled all believers in Theandrios. They described how their deity, this god-man hybrid, had been worshipped in towns and villages around Mount Hermon, just west of Damascus.

Sabinus spoke with pride. "We discovered his existence while traveling for business."

Rena's eyes widened. "Yes, we overheard talk of a man traveling around Galilee and performing miracles. We knew it must be Theandrios. But when we started talking to others about it—"

"You were driven away."

"Right. But we knew each Decapolis city is autonomous and self-governed. We hoped one of them would accept us, beliefs and all."

"Canatha?"

"Exactly. We were surprised a temple for Theandrios already existed there."

Yamin thought for a moment. "How long have you been here?"

"Only a few months. Since early summer."

Could it be? Could their rumors of a god-man be about Jesus? Yamin did not want to draw any conclusions and scare away potential believers before having the full story, so he changed the subject. "What's your business? I mean, what do you do?" He sighed when they looked at him askance. "What I mean is, what business are you in that made you travel in the first place?"

"Let's just say we're couriers."

"You carry messages? Isn't that usually done by someone on horseback?"

"We're the cheaper—"

"And more *selective* version."

"Selective?"

Rena and Sabinus gave each other a knowing look.

Sabinus nodded to Rena, giving her leave to explain.

"Are you sure, Sabinus?"

He nodded almost imperceptibly.

Rena looked at Yamin. "Do you know what a zealot is, Yamin?"

He thought for a moment. "I know what the *word* means."

Rena looked at Sabinus.

Sabinus returned an encouraging expression.

"I can see you've not traveled to Jerusalem recently."

Sabinus chuckled under his breath.

"There are many kinds of zealots. I assumed you may have heard of the Jewish ones. We are not them. Simply put, anyone who rebels against the Roman occupiers and their emperor is a zealot."

Yamin listened intently. He did not want to speak too soon. After all, he was a Roman citizen and never felt an aversion toward the emperor's rule. "We never had any of those in Hippos. Not that I know of, anyway."

Rena continued. "The story you've sworn to spread about Jesus—I hate to break the news to you, Yamin, but they would consider you a zealot, as well. They'd crucify you if they knew the lies you've been spreading."

"They're *not* lies!" *That didn't come out well.* Yamin's stomach tightened, and his heart raced. He thought about everyone he had told so far. How many belief systems had he clouded? How many people would go home and argue with their parents and neighbors about what god to honor at suppertime? He *had* been rebelling against the Empire. "Sorry about that. I guess there's some truth in your accusation."

Rena replied unvexed. "Oh, we're not accusing you of anything. Are we, Sabinus?"

"No, not at all. Perhaps that was too negative a term, Rena. After all, we're creating an ally in a land full of adversaries." He smiled at Yamin.

Yamin halfheartedly returned the expression. "Let's say I agree with you. You believe there's one god, Theandrios, who walks as a man performing miracles. I say that I've met this man, and his name is Jesus. Are we in agreement, or are we in contestation?"

A pondering look spread across Sabinus' face. "I'm not sure. Our courier roles allow us to act in the name of Theandrios causing dissension in other cities against Roman rule. Your role, as storyteller in the name of this Jesus, gives you permission to do the same."

"But causing dissension is not my goal."

"No? Then just by chance that's what you've done with your story?"

"I haven't told you about my experiences with my story telling."

"We've been doing this long enough to know that if you've told *that* story in Hippos, in Raphana, and to anyone else, the results were probably similar to what Rena and I accomplished back there in Capitolias."

"So, that *was* you back there."

Rena placed her hand on Yamin's shoulder. "We welcome the company, Yamin."

43

Yamin's approach to Canatha produced no further incidents, save for several ailing citizens along the road about ten minutes' walk from the city's western main gate.

A woman rested on a rock while asking passersby for alms. She produced a phlegm-laden raspy cough after her plea.

Yamin could not help his stare while following Rena and Sabinus. His mother had developed the same sign not long before her passing. He shrugged it off as coincidence until more residents exhibited the same symptoms, or worse. Some were so badly off they lied unconscious, faces ashen. *Are they dead?* He looked around at the other travelers then glanced at his companions. *No one seems to care. Not even them.*

He tore his gaze away from the sickly and focused his thoughts on something he could change. Would anyone listen to his story in this place? Perhaps, with Rena and Sabinus' influence, he had a chance to spread hope instead of this dreaded disease that seems to have taken hold of all Decapolis. *How far did its effects reach? Across the whole of the Empire?*

From behind Canatha's hefty wall, a stone tower reached into the sky farther than any Yamin had seen before.

Sabinus stopped him. "Impressive, yes?"

Yamin closed his mouth after he realized it was agape. "It reaches to the heavens."

"That it does." Rena stepped next to Yamin, putting him between her and Sabinus. "And it houses our god."

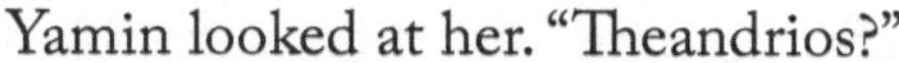

Yamin looked at her. "Theandrios?"

Sabinus nodded. "Our savior. Well, when he's not walking around the countryside healing people and expelling demons." He winked at Rena.

Yamin wanted to see the tower up close. He had to know if Theandrios had anything more in common with Jesus—with the Lord, Elohim.

The gate stood guarded only by loitering citizens. Several greeted Rena and Sabinus kindly as they entered.

One conspicuously dressed man with exceptionally curly hair reprimanded them. "Returned from your rebellious mission already, have you?" He stroked his beard which snapped back into place like a coiled snake.

Yamin wrestled with the thought that he had seen this type of attire before. *But where?*

The couple ignored the man and continued guiding Yamin into the city.

Another man, dressed in pure white robes, folded so that part of them covered his head, addressed them from the shadows. "Sabinus." He motioned for them to come nearer.

Yamin followed.

The man led them down a narrow, filthy alley to the back of a textile shop. A buzzing sound grew louder as they rounded the corner.

Yamin stopped as a thousand black flies flew into the air and swarmed. He covered his nose with his hand. "Oh, mmm." His actions proved futile as the pungent scent of rotten shellfish stung his nasal passages.

Sabinus imitated Yamin and took a step back from the hooded man. "Ugh, it smells of fleece twice dyed in purple, Amphion. And fleece smells bad enough to begin with." He gagged.

Rena turned and hurried back to the street. "I can't, Sabinus. Not on a good day."

Amphion, unfazed by the stench, inspected Yamin. "Sabinus, who is this?"

Sabinus coughed once before gaining his composure. "Do we have to do this here, Amphion?"

"If you want to avoid being overheard, yes."

Sabinus expelled a sigh then reluctantly drew in another breath. "This is Yamin. He might just supply us with a testimony we could use for major support."

"You trust him?"

Tears welled in Sabinus' eyes. He nodded.

Amphion raised an eyebrow. A large fly landed on the apex of his hood. He ignored it, looked at Yamin, and spoke to Sabinus again. "When does he plan on sharing this—testimony?"

"Tomorrow, the soonest. We made haste from Capitolias and are exhausted. The people were less enthusiastic than even the last time we visited."

"You are playing a dangerous game. I can't keep covering for your absences. If you recall . . ."

Yamin had a hard time paying attention. He gave thanks that his gift for sensing the world through touch did not extend to his sense of smell, because this one seemed to be touching his brain. It clung to the lining of his throat. Breathing through his mouth made it worse because now he tasted it. He had been around rotten fish before, but this was something far more concentrated.

He suddenly felt the two men staring at him as the lane in which he stood started to spin.

They swept him up from under his arms and shuffled him out to the street.

Rena leaned against the front wall of the building taking in long purposeful drafts of air.

After a moment, Yamin came to his senses. "Sorry about that. I've worked in pickling and shipping and never smelled anything *that* strong before."

Amphion harrumphed. "Between the both of you, I think we've drawn more attention than if we'd stayed out here."

Sabinus turned to him. "Tomorrow?"

Amphion nodded, spun on his heels, and walked briskly in the direction of the tower. His white cape-like robe caught a breeze from the gateway.

Yamin searched the flow of air for any scent to help mask the lingering stink on his person.

Sabinus did the same. "I think we'll need more than a gust of cool air. Come. Before the twilight fades."

He and Rena led Yamin east along the inside of the wall. Within minutes, they approached the doorway to a modest three-story dwelling.

Yamin, now more hungry than nauseous, hoped dinner waited within. Dar's mother always had food on the table in their urban home. A dim orange light filtered through the spaces in the door, and the sound of clinking pottery echoed from inside. Yamin's hopes escalated.

"Welcome to our home, Yamin."

The door swung wide. Inside, people moved about busily performing chores. A middle-aged man carried a small bundle of cooking wood from another room and dropped it at the foot of a large clay baking oven where two older women prepared the evening meal. Two more women, around Yamin's age, sorted linens in an adjacent room.

One of the younger women ran out to the main area. "Mother. Father." The back of her hand brushed Yamin's face as she reached to embrace both parents.

The sensation of soft skin on his cheek triggered an intense memory of his mother. He moved his hand up to touch the point of contact but stopped himself before anyone saw. Yamin assumed she just misjudged and tried to shake off any inappropriate impressions. It had been so long since he had any positive physical contact with another person, let alone a girl.

"Melita, this is Yamin." Sabinus stepped aside.

Melita released her hold on her parents and studied him. "Who have you brought home now? Another convert?" She ever-so-lightly wiped the back of hand on her robe after looking him over.

Yamin smiled sheepishly, suddenly conscious of the dust on his feet and robes.

Sabinus walked toward the large table in the middle of the room. "Yamin is a special case, my dear."

"Special?" She now looked only into his eyes. "Special Yamin." She smiled.

Her exuberance enchanted him, just as Althea had in Hippos. But things differed now. Desires of the flesh—hunger, sleep, sex—seemed muted, reduced in importance compared to the mission imparted to him by Jesus. Those cravings had been all his past demons cared about, possessed by their own lack of inhibition and self-control. He stood here a new man, ready for anything this world could rain down upon him. Even a flicker of flirtation from a beautiful woman.

But was this attraction something more? His heart skipped a beat. What was that? And was there room for it with what Jesus had laid upon him?

"Leave him alone, Melita." Rena helped one of the women near the oven with a large wooden bowl of roasted vegetables. "You'll learn all about him soon enough."

Sabinus sat at the table, and several others joined him. "Yes, daughter. Come and join us. We've much to share."

Yamin enjoyed this venue. Sharing his story in an intimate manner with a small group of avid listeners proved far more fulfilling than to a crowded room surrounded by the formality of religious leaders and their talented detractors. And every group differed in their acceptance of his carefully measured-out episode. Even this one.

Melita hung on his every word. The other women remained respectfully silent while several men sounded their opinions of Yamin's perceived shortcomings in his story. Demons proved the most annoying distraction—one Yamin had thought was behind him for good.

"What did it feel like? You know, to have all those spirits inside?"

Another asked, "Yes, was it like vipers writhing around?" He made twisting motions by intertwining his forearms. "Or more like if you had swallowed glass?"

"Why couldn't you resist them? Were they physically or mentally overpowering you?"

"Are demons the ghosts of the dead or something else?"

Yamin tried his best to answer simply and quickly. After all, he knew very little about the hows and whys of subject, other than what he had experienced. He had no lessons in the spirituality of demonic possession, no guidance in the process of exorcism, and certainly no understanding of the origin of demonic supernatural beings, other than being *from Satan*.

His greatest insight came from the knowledge that no matter how far down a dark path one may have wandered, there always existed a chance of returning your spirit into the light. "All one must do is believe in the healing power of Elohim." And in the end, that is the message he shared with these inquisitive men. It was the first time he added such a closing statement to his discourse.

Yamin paused after their barrage of inquiries. He stared into the orange flame of an oil lamp on the table before answering. "Of your questions, I can only say this. There are so many in this world who've lost their way. So many who've chosen to take an unworthy path in their lives. Some had circumstances beyond their control that helped these dark decisions. Mine were loss of loved ones, ridicule, and heartbreak. These opened the door to anger, jealously, and, ultimately, hatred. In turn, another door opened. A door one never wants to open to the wrong influence. The door to your soul. If not filled with light, the darkness will certainly find its way in. And once it gets hold, you will do unspeakable acts. Terrible and certainly unforgiveable by most."

He scanned the faces of his small audience. "I sense some of you already know of what I speak."

Silence gripped the room. None of those who had bombarded him with questions could speak.

"You don't need to have a legion of demons within you for an occasion of salvation. Jesus told me, through his actions, to tell you all that is needed is desire to change and a willingness to let your soul be filled with the Lord's love. Once you've started along this path, you'll find the darkness no longer has a chance. And forever it will dictate your fate."

"Intriguing arguments from an illiterate and untrained individual." Amphion strode in through the open door. Lamplight shone down from the ceiling illuminating the sharp curves of his cheeks and nose giving him a skull-like visage.

Sabinus stood. "No need for such baseless accusations here, Amphion. Besides, I thought I told you that you'd hear Yamin's evidence tomorrow."

"Oh, I only caught the tail end of his, what I can assume from your looks of amazement, gripping fantasy. Demons? Soul-saving? Adonai? Ha! He speaks of something more suited for the stage than for reality. It's blasphemy."

Yamin felt a cold chill down his back when he realized this city would accept his story no better than the others. He wanted to get up and run. But where would he go? The rest of Decapolis lay to the south and winter was upon him. He had to make the best of the current situation. Maybe biding his time would be the wisest decision.

Sabinus spoke through clenched teeth. "We had a deal, Amphion."

Before Amphion replied, Yamin stood and cleared his throat. "Perhaps you've misunderstood, sir." He held his hand out to Sabinus. "My gracious host and his family provided a wonderful meal and clean robes. In payment, I supplied entertainment. That's all. Take it as you will." He sat down with his back to Amphion and sipped his wine. A bead of sweat formed on his forehead.

Melita offered a silent smile.

He half-returned the expression. Her realization of his anxiety calmed him.

"Well, then. You see, Amphion?" Sabinus chuckled. "Our guest was simply amusing us with a colorful anecdote."

Amphion replied with a drawn out, "Yes." He turned to exit. "I look forward to your entertaining portrayal tomorrow." The shadow of the night swallowed his figure as he departed into the street.

Dinner ended abruptly, and Rena allowed Melita to show Yamin to the guest quarters. She stood in the doorway as he secured his meager belongings to a wood peg on the wall. "I, for one, thought your tale was amazing."

Yamin was not sure if she meant amazing as in *extraordinary* or amazing as in *bizarre and far-fetched*. "Thank you for your kind words."

"What does that old Amphion know about it anyway?" She picked at a loose flake of plaster on the wall. "I've heard his renditions about gods and their fantastic deeds more times than I can count. He never agrees with father."

"Never?"

"He doesn't even believe Theandrios should have the authority we give him."

Yamin's mind reeled. *What could they have in common then? Why are they associates?* Yamin vowed to discuss this with Sabinus first thing in the morning and certainly before sharing his story with anyone else here in Canatha. "If I may ask, where then does Amphion's loyalty lie?"

"With the Emperor, of course." She turned to leave. Her curly brown hair bounced as she traipsed off.

That confused Yamin even more.

The next morning brought the smell of cooking meat on cool air through the open window in his room.

Sabinus entered. "Are you ready for the day?"

Yamin straightened his new robes. "If that scent is any indication of what's being served for the morning meal, I am."

Sabinus grimaced. "Well, we'll just have to see about that."

When the men entered the house's main room, no food lay on

the table. Yamin brushed his hair back with his hand. "Everyone busy with chores?"

"We'll eat later. He handed Yamin a piece of yesterday's bread. "If you're hungry eat this. Come. We've much to discuss."

They entered the courtyard where the household gathered around Rena.

". . . information, we must be on our guard. You all heard Amphion last night."

Yamin had a feeling this talk concerned him.

She continued. "And the travesty that poisons our air this morning is a sign of why caution must be taken."

Deep lines formed on Yamin's brow. *Travesty? Sign?*

Rena must have noticed and addressed him. "Yamin, rest assured your story is good news to our ears. Those who hold to the principle that Theandrios walks among us even now have our hearts lightened and our passions energized by its telling. But it has incensed the local administration." She pointed to the narrow column of smoke rising from the center of the city. "What they've done to Ernestus this day is proof of their intolerance of our beliefs."

A wave of nausea hit Yamin's stomach like hot lead.

"If we're not careful, they'll burn us all."

I did this? People are being killed because I lived? Yamin's knees weakened.

Sabinus grabbed his arm to support him.

Yamin sat on a small stool. He took a deep breath and spoke into his hands. "Lord, you've given me an impossible task. How can I proceed any further without the panic and chaos it creates?"

The courtyard gate burst open. A dozen Roman soldiers, swords drawn, poured in and surrounded the small group in a semi-circle.

Melita's friend screamed. Melita took hold of her hand and comforted her.

Amphion followed behind the soldiers. He stood where Rena had been moments ago. He held out an open scroll. "I hereby declare the governor's latest order for the immediate cessation of any group congregating within the city's walls to worship, make sacrifice to, fabricate idols of, or discuss the belief in any gods but those sanctioned by the Emperor Tiberius, on this thirteenth day of October." He handed the scroll to Sabinus.

Melita balled her fists. "Why did you kill Ernestus?"

Rena motioned for her to step back and be quiet.

"Bite your tongue, mistress." Amphion addressed everyone. "He was already imprisoned for publicly denouncing the Emperor's divine status in front of the magistrate. Examples must be made."

The rising tension made Yamin wonder if any of them would make it through the day.

Amphion ordered the troops to leave. He motioned for Sabinus to approach him.

Sabinus tugged on Yamin's sleeve. "You'll join me."

Yamin's legs felt like immovable stone. He forced them to cooperate and shuffled after Sabinus to meet Amphion at the gate.

Sabinus whispered to Amphion. "You better have an explanation."

Amphion scanned Yamin, and his countenance melted. "You know as well as I there is nothing that can be done—for the moment. We are treading on dangerous ground here. And the information our new friend carries with him is more powerful than we could have dreamed."

Yamin tried desperately to make sense of the situation. Things were not so complicated in Hippos. Or were they? Maybe he had not stuck around long enough to see.

Sabinus placed his hands on his hips. "Then what shall we do with him?"

Amphion looked Yamin up and down. "Step back from your escapades for now. And keep this one's mouth closed, at least until things settle down and the magistrate has other problems to focus on."

"So, do nothing."

"Unless you want what happened in Capitolias to happen here, yes." Amphion swung around and walked away.

Sabinus closed the gate and escorted Yamin back to the group. "That two-faced fool. He won't be able to keep this up much longer. Looks like you'll be staying with us for a while, young man."

44

The winter months passed slowly. Plentiful rains blessed the land, and the residents showed their appreciation all season by holding celebration after tedious celebration.

Yamin had experienced his share of festivities in Hippos. Not as many as Dar's family, but enough to know one party is not too dissimilar from the next. He needed to finish his task and move on.

Yamin had hinted to Melita within the first week of his stay he had no interest in her other than friendship. He could not afford to be distracted by her beauty and charm, no matter how much it hurt him to say so. "If we had met any other time, Melita."

"What about the future?"

"The future?" His abrupt realization that his mission would someday come to an end stopped him in his tracks.

"Yes, after you've visited all of Decapolis. I can't promise I'll be available for that long, though. I've many suitors, you know."

Her outward flirtations ceased, and she kept her distance, as long as Yamin remained in mixed company. Therefore, he worked hard to spend the majority of his time with Sabinus and Rena helping with chores and daily discussing various topics, including theology and local politics.

A month had passed before Yamin finally learned what his hosting couple meant by *couriers* and how they made a living that way to pay the taxes on this house and afford the bare necessities. Tithes from their fellow believers at the temple of Theandrios generated part of their income.

Amphion supplied the rest, and that was where the discussion of politics always took a sideways turn.

One day in late January, Amphion caught Sabinus and Yamin strolling near the temple. He traveled alone, and his robes looked as if they had not been changed in several days. He approached them in a frantic manner. "Come quickly."

Distant shouts echoed through the streets. Yamin's heart raced as a group of soldiers worked their way through the crowd. He looked at Sabinus for a sign of how to proceed.

"We haven't done anything lately, so don't worry, Yamin. Go and fetch Rena and the others from the marketplace, and meet us back at the house."

Yamin nodded and did as his host ordered. He felt all the sneaking around, clandestine meetings, and anti-government discussions had finally caught up to him and his friends.

Rena spotted Yamin and called him to join them.

Melita accompanied her and flashed a bright smile at his arrival.

Rena swatted her arm. "Oh, leave him alone for once. Besides, you know whose eyes are on you."

Melita popped an olive into her mouth and spoke while chewing it. "He's too old. And too loyal to the establishment."

Yamin's wide-eyed stance snapped the two out of their banter. "Please, Sabinus needs us home. Quickly."

Rena shoved coins into a vendor's beefy hand. She then led Yamin and Melita home. When they arrived, the others of the household had already gathered around the main room's table. Amphion sat alone at one end.

Sabinus handed him a cup of wine. "It'll calm you down. Now, tell us what happened. Were those soldiers looking for *you*?"

Amphion swallowed a large gulp and put the cup down. "Yes, but they don't know it's *me* they are looking for."

"Well, that's a relief."

"For now." Amphion gave Yamin a quick glance. "It's time for someone to do what he came for and then move on."

Thunder rumbled in the distance.

Yamin's stomach tightened as a wave of apprehension passed through him.

Amphion continued. "You know I travel as you do, often to places more dangerous for our people than I send you."

Sabinus nodded.

Rena sat next to Amphion. "You went to Jerusalem."

"Indeed. Our brothers' fight is crucial there. But it was what I learned of another that drove me back here with haste." He looked again at Yamin. "I misjudged your story for fiction and ask your forgiveness."

Yamin looked at Sabinus and the others. He simply nodded lightly at Amphion. He still did not understand why this man held so much importance to Sabinus and Rena's cause. But one thing was clear. Amphion played both sides, and Yamin was not yet sure what side this man favored more.

"Wait, you've not yet heard me tell it."

"I heard more than I let on that first night you arrived. And Sabinus was correct. It was the spark we needed here in Canatha to move forward with our plans to strengthen our cause."

Yamin's face flushed as his frustrations grew. He looked at Sabinus and Rena. "You knew this?"

They nodded. But the compassion in their eyes gave Yamin the sense they harbored no wicked intent. There seemed to be much more going on here than anyone had led him to believe these past months.

A flash of lightning lit up the room as dark rain clouds blotted out the remaining afternoon light. Heavy drops cascaded on the outside walls. One of the female residents rushed to shutter an exposed window.

Yamin earned his turn to sit at the table. He plopped down, and the chair creaked beneath his thin but sturdy frame. "Let's have it, then. I feel there's much I need to know before this night is over."

Sabinus chose two men to summon several others who joined them at the table.

Melita helped prepare the evening meal with the other women of the house, but remained within earshot of the table.

Amphion surrendered the privilege of speaking to Sabinus with an extended, palm-up hand. "It's your house."

"Yamin, you spoke of a savior who wanders the countryside, travels with an entourage, and heals in the name of the Lord."

Yamin nodded.

"And we've discussed numerous times how our god, Theandrios, could very well be the same man."

Yamin could not take the tension. "Get on with it, then. What aren't you all telling me?"

"Amphion found more evidence of the same in Jerusalem." Sabinus turned it over to Amphion with a nod.

Yamin shook his head. "Are you saying Jesus and Theandrios are the same person?"

Amphion sat upright and seemed to have gained back some of his haughty composure. "There is a great upheaval in Jerusalem. Zealots, Essenes, Jewish leaders. They all work against Rome's occupation of the city, but not in unison. They clash with each other more times than with soldiers. This unrest helps our cause as well."

"How?"

"Most of Rome believes the Emperor is a god-man. That his whole family are gods."

"This is common knowledge throughout the Empire." *Get to the point already.*

"Do *you* believe it?"

Everyone in the room stopped moving and waited for Yamin to reply.

Yamin thought how best to answer. He had been sure if anyone heard his story they would know where his loyalties lay. A dangerous assumption and one already causing more contention than he had imagined possible. "It's true. At one time I agreed with my parents and friends to accept this. It took the loss of loved ones, denouncing faith in all gods, and my own internal trials to become something more than just a disciple of that which others follow blindly and without reason." He looked at the many formless scars on his forearms. "Jesus gave me reason and eyes open to the truth."

"And that, my friend, is where our two ideologies harmonize."

Lightning struck nearby, and the resounding thunder shook the table. The scent of wet dirt wafted in and mixed with muted aromas of bread and cooked vegetables.

"Just not with the city's leaders."

"And now you know our plight."

"It still doesn't explain why you, out of all of us, are being sought by soldiers. I thought you were a cult priest, an authority here in Canatha."

"And you should have. It was the only way to earn the trust of the magistrate and give lenience to allow Theandrios' temple to remain standing in the city. Our cause needs a home."

Sabinus interjected. "You see, Yamin. After the last turnover in governors, edicts from Rome fortified the worship of certain gods within city walls and weakened support for others."

"But aren't Decapolis cities autonomous, free to worship whom they please?"

"To a point."

Amphion continued. "Yes, and that point is drawn in the sand the moment one mentions any man's divine standing beside the almighty Emperor Tiberias."

"And that's what you did?"

"While in Jerusalem, I heard rumors of a man called Jesus traveling in the north. There was mention of him healing the lame, calming storms, and even resurrecting the dead. I could not hold my tongue as I traveled back here as fast as I could to bring the news that Theandrios walked among us. As I approached the city, guards waited at the gate interrogating everyone about where they've been and where their allegiance lay. Several travelers were brought into custody after not answering fast enough or without sufficient perceived conviction in their voices. Somehow, word traveled faster than I."

Yamin nervously flicked his thumbnails. Was he safer inside the city, or was leaving now his only option? A tinge of regret passed as soon as it arrived. He would never trade his meeting with Jesus just to avoid the dangers of tomorrow. No one else could have saved him from what seemed a doomed existence of sinful servitude. If he died tomorrow serving Jesus, it would have been worth all the effort. And then there was Melita. As much as he tried to ignore his feelings for her . . .

Sabinus turned to Yamin. "It looks as if you'll not have the chance to share your story with a larger group like we had planned."

"You'll have to relay the message for me, when the timing's right."

Sabinus nodded and smiled. "I will speak of the man who wanders the countryside and serves a higher being."

Rena reached across the table and took Yamin's hand. "Why not stay? Join our cause."

He met Melita's eyes and frowned. "A generous offer." He wanted to say his cause and theirs were only coincidental at best. Their god was still not Elohim. "You've all been so welcoming and kind. But my mission is one of travel, not a stationary nature." He turned to Amphion. "What will you do now?"

"I'll need to change to avoid suspicion. I must make excuses for being gone so long as it is. I will do what I can with the temple leadership to delay immediate action. Pray it is enough to diffuse the situation."

Amphion put on fresh linen robes provided by the household then cautiously exited through the front door. Yamin could not help but notice how his stature and sense of purpose remained the same as when he first met this man months ago. He sensed there was something spiritually askew with Amphion and could not bring himself to trust the man.

During his stay in Canatha, Yamin's spiritual awareness had grown in sensitivity akin to his keen sense of touch. He did not believe it at first. *How can I have the power to sense deceit in others?* He'd dismissed it as superstition until his intuitions had proven right several occasions in a row.

While escorting Melita to the market weeks ago, a task he found to be more enjoyable every time he did it, a man approached them, his arms laden with fine fabrics. "For the lady." His voice reminded Yamin of a poorly made shofar. But it was not the stranger's tone that prompted suspicion. It was his eyes. Something about the man's gaze gave Yamin a creepy feeling, a feeling first sensed when encountering the demonic man in Hippos. But this time he did not fear it, as if an impenetrable shield appeared between him and the man. One that did not exist before he met Jesus.

Melita gravitated toward the temptation without hesitation.

Yamin guided her otherwise. "Let's wait. I remember seeing a wider selection at the other end of the market." His desire to protect her grew strong.

As Yamin retired for his last night in Canatha, visions of what the road held in store plagued his ability to rest. He worried about how his new friends would fare with the recent loss of religious freedom. If he were to ever visit this city again, would Theandrios' tower still stand? Would Melita forgive him for abandoning her friendship?

He drifted off to a fitful sleep only when he focused his thoughts on where he had been, rather than where he was going. In his mind, he traced the path from his childhood home to the docks on the great lake. Every stone and bush, each a virtual landmark serving to guide his steps.

Finally, the sound of another approaching rainstorm lulled him to a deep slumber. Little did he know, the storm carried with it forces beyond his control. Dark forces bent on his destruction.

45

"Melita?" Yamin thought it a dream. "What are you doing?" He pushed himself up from his bedding and rubbed the sleep from his disbelieving eyes.

Melita stood, breathing heavily, inside his room wearing only silken undergarments.

Yamin surveyed his clothing to make sure it had been left intact. He then did the same to Melita. He had never seen so much exposed skin on a woman before. "Why are you in here—and dressed like *that*?"

Melita shushed him. She hid behind the closed door trying to listen to the voices coming from the main room.

Yamin grabbed an extra tunic and heavy winter robe and handed them to her. "What—"

Melita covered his mouth with her hand and mouthed, "Thank you," before quietly slipping on the garments.

Yamin whispered, "What's going on out there?"

"He lied. Amphion. He's been lying all along."

Yamin craned his neck to the door.

"—late for any further leniencies. Because you are Roman citizens, you will be given the opportunity to publicly renounce your belief in any *god-man*—this wandering Jew your new friend is so fond of spreading rumors about."

Rena spoke through tears. "What of our plans, Amphion? Your trip to Jerusalem? It was all a ruse?"

Yamin and Melita swung their heads toward the window

when screams rose from the street out front. They turned back to listen.

"—to draw out those who needed to be reminded of the behavior befitting that of a Roman citizen. Oh, my trip to Jerusalem was also necessary. Rumors are far worse than facts. They are pervasive and corrosive. When I confirmed their ubiquity throughout the province of Judea now matched that of Decapolis, I knew I had to convince the magistrate to enforce change. Unfortunately, that change had to come to you first."

Yamin wondered why he did not hear Sabinus arguing as well. Visions of him lying bloody on the floor flashed before his eyes. He was suddenly reminded these were Melita's parents in peril. He took her hand in his.

Melita squeezed back.

Rena continued in a rebellious tone. "What happened to our freedom to worship who we pleased? Did you *ever* believe, Amphion?"

"True, autonomy has its benefits. But conservative values have their advantages. And someone in my position just has more to gain from them. I chose the side with more power."

Rena gasped. "Please, let us leave. We won't tell anyone. We'll even leave Decapolis all together. Yes, we'll travel east, far from here. We won't bother any—No!"

Melita moved to open the door.

Yamin blocked her path and grabbed her shoulders. He gave her an intense look of concern and shook his head. He whispered, "We have to leave," then motioned to the window.

The second story room proved little challenge to climb down to the narrow passage below. Scuffling and grunts came from the street. Yamin and Melita moved to the corner of the house to spy.

The house's occupants knelt in a line on the muddy street. It did not appear any were harmed, beyond a bump or scrape. About twenty soldiers stood with swords drawn to keep them from bolting.

Rena spilled from the front door to join the others on her

knees. Two guards followed. They dragged the unconscious Sabinus between them and dumped him face first into the muck next to Rena.

Rena scooped up his head.

He moaned.

Yamin felt a wave of relief from Melita. "What should we do? They've got your family."

Melita thought for a moment. "My parents won't get themselves killed. Not if there's any chance to start again elsewhere. They'll do whatever Amphion tells them. If not, they'll never see tomorrow." She looked at him. "But I've got to get *you* away from here. Amphion, that traitor, sees you as the reason this all came to pass. He'll make an example out of you like he did Ernestus. Being burned alive would be better than what they'll do to you." She stood and pulled up Yamin with her. "Come."

They turned the corner and peaked over the wall into the courtyard. "It's clear." Melita ran through the gate toward the house.

Yamin called in a loud whisper, "No, wait, Melita."

She stopped at the back entrance where a supply of sandals lay. She scooped up a pair then sunk her finger into the mud. She scrawled something on the back wall and ran back to him. "We've a long journey ahead."

"We?"

"I'll come back when this has calmed. Besides, now I'll have you all to myself." She shot him a wicked smile and pulled him in the direction of the nearest city exit.

Before they reached the gate, it was clear that guards still stopped travelers from entering.

Yamin pulled Melita to the side. "At least Amphion was telling the truth about something."

"It looks like they're only stopping people from entering. Look." She pointed. Farmers and tradespeople exited the city freely. Only a single man carrying nothing was stopped and questioned. He presented something small to the soldiers, and they let him pass.

"We should be fine. You have your tessera, yes?" She produced a small ivory tile stamped with the image of an eagle and Latin words he could not read.

Yamin held up his hands, palms up, and shrugged his shoulders.

Melita sighed. "*Charagma*? No?"

"I *know* what it is. I just never needed one before."

She huffed.

"Well, my family never held the same status as yours. In Hippos, I was, *the fisherman's son*. And later, *the fisherman*. I've gotten this far without one. Hey, wait a minute. Where were you hiding that? In your . . ." He blushed.

Melita giggled. "We keep some in a small bowl by our sandals so we don't forget when we go out." She looked around. "We'll have to find you one before we can safely leave."

As they turned, a man towered before them, backlit by the morning sunlight.

Yamin and Melita gasped.

The stranger spoke calmly. "Perhaps I can help."

"You." Yamin instantly recognized him as the man in the familiar clothes months ago when he first entered the city with Rena and Sabinus.

"We don't need anything from the likes of you, Yareb." Melita pulled Yamin around the man.

"Melita, wait." Yamin stopped and spoke to the stranger. "I recognize your robes. I've seen them before."

"He's a Jew, Yamin."

"Not just any Jew, Melita." Yamin looked at Yareb's clothing and motioned on himself where the man's tasseled sash crossed his midriff. "You're a priest. I saw men on Malta wearing robes like yours."

"Malta?" Yareb's long, gray-streaked beard moved in waves when he spoke. "You've traveled farther than I ever have, young man. I'd be willing to hear about it. That is, if you have the time."

Melita pulled Yamin's sleeve. "No, not really. Come on, Yamin."

"Wait, Melita." Yamin sensed no malignant tendencies from the man. "What harm could it do?"

"He hates my people. We call him *The Scolder* because he sits and waits for us to pass by and does nothing but admonish."

"Hate is a strong word, Melita." Yareb's caring tone calmed Yamin. "Chastising poor judgement is a behavior your parents display toward you from time to time, no? They certainly don't hate you. Besides, I've come to learn your friend here and I have something in common. Come, we can get to my lodging quickly."

It was Yamin's turn to tug at Melita's sleeve.

She scoffed, rolled her eyes, and followed the men.

Yareb expertly avoided the soldiers and curious onlookers as he led them on a serpentine path to his home. Yamin expected a structure like Nat's in Raphana. Instead, they met with a hovel attached as an addition to a sturdier pottery shop. To his surprise, the interior provided a welcoming environment.

Yareb cut through the darkness with ornately designed oil lamps hanging from the ceiling by brass chains. Tiny round pebbles littered the packed dirt floor. A small bed, a table with scrolls and tools of a scribe, and inset wall shelving rounded out the room. The most striking feature of this home was its interior walls. Large, whitewashed sections, each with adorned with colorful, elaborate scenery, clashed with the muted earthen color of baked clay bricks.

Yareb caught Yamin admiring them. "Please, sit."

Yamin and Melita sat on mats in the center of the floor.

Yareb dipped his finger in a shallow dish of oil and marked each of their foreheads.

Melita looked at Yamin then wiped her forehead with her sleeve.

Yareb shot her a look of surprise.

Motioning to the walls, Yamin drew Yareb's attention away from Melita's rudeness. "Did you make these drawings? I've not seen anything like them before."

"I did. Do you know the stories they portray?"

They both shook their heads.

Yareb adjusted the cushion beneath him. "Then I propose a trade. You tell me your story, and I will share with you the meaning behind these images."

One more chance before I leave. "Agreed. And thank you for helping."

"You are welcome. According to Elohim, hospitality is more important than prayer."

"Is that where our commonality lays? With Elohim?"

"An astute fellow." Yareb reached for a tray with cups and a pitcher of water. He placed it between them. "Indeed, whispers from the west have permeated the fabric of our diverse Decapolis society. And I've been listening. Some of what I've heard mentioned a newcomer to this city who speaks of a relationship between Elohim and a savior who walks among us."

Yamin looked at Melita.

She shook her head. "It wasn't me."

A pensive look covered Yamin's face. "Someone in your household, then?"

"Doubtful. They're all too loyal to the cause. Besides, you and father walked through the city discussing theology openly for months. Anyone could've gleaned information from your discourse."

"Exactly how I came across it."

Yamin closed his eyes and sighed. *One more lesson learned.*

"Over those months, I kept myself close to your father, listening when not speaking of the scriptures in the public areas to small groups willing to hear."

"Even father didn't do that. It was only allowed within the temple itself. How do you do it without getting accused of blasphemy?"

"Well, you see, it's like—"

"Fishing." Yamin smiled.

"Exactly."

Melita shot Yamin an incredulous glance.

"Something your father told me."

Yareb smiled. "How about some food while Yamin elucidates?"

In record time, Yamin's words flowed. He noticed that even

though Melita had now experienced it twice, she sat mesmerized. *Maybe some will need to hear of it more than once.*

When Yamin finished, Yareb stared at his artwork. By now, the morning sunlight filtered in through the partially open doorway giving the nearest outlined whitewash a sublime radiance.

Yamin saw it too. "What's that drawing?"

"The Ark of the Testimony. The holy receptacle of the Spirit of Elohim."

"It glows." Yamin stood and approached the wall.

"I used gold leaf, just like on the real one." Yareb smiled proudly.

"Where's this kept?" Yamin reached out and ran his finger along the edge of the virtual vessel. "I would like to see it."

"No one knows. It vanished when the Babylonians conquered Jerusalem over five hundred years ago. When the ark was captured by the Philistines, outbreaks of tumors and disease afflicted them, forcing those pagans to return it to us—to the holy temple in Jerusalem."

They looked in wonder for a few moments before Melita spoke. "How can you afford to dress as you do and buy gold leaf when you live in such squalor?"

Yamin spun and glared at her. "Melita!"

"It's all right, Yamin. I would have asked the same question myself had I been on the outside. Although, I would have been more—diplomatic—in my verbiage."

Melita averted her eyes. "Sorry."

"Not long ago, I had my own synagogue here in Canatha."

Yamin returned to his seat next to Melita.

Melita's regret turned to frustration. "Let me guess. Amphion."

"His predecessor, actually. It was the rule of Augustus that allowed for more acceptance, as the Province of Judea had just been annexed by Rome. How long ago was that now? Nearly forty years. But since Emperor Tiberias' rule, the shackles on our freedom become tighter and tighter. The local pagan cult seized my building in the name of the Emperor, and I was forced to live like this. They blamed it on the growing rebellion in Jerusalem. But I knew they wouldn't tolerate us for long."

"Why don't you leave? Start over elsewhere? It's probably what her parents will do—when they get out of this mess. The city of Tiberias is directly across from my home on the Sea of Galilee. There's a large Jewish population there. You could come with us and—"

He held up his hand. "That is most kind, young man. Most kind." He stared at the two-dimensional ark on the wall.

In the time Yareb talked, the sunlight had partially drifted to an adjacent illustration of a large ship without sails. On its deck stood a single man extending his arm up to either release or capture a small bird, perhaps a dove. A rainbow crossed the sky over an island in the distance.

Yareb continued. "At times, your story of this man Jesus, along with other reports from the west, brings to mind pieces of scripture. The Book of Isaiah speaks of the eyes of the blind being opened, the ears of the deaf unstopped, the lame leaping like deer, and the mute shouting for joy. There is also something about a man honoring Galilee, traveling by way of the sea in the Book of Daniel. You've given me much to contemplate, Yamin." He stroked his beard.

"It seems to be the effect with every telling. But something's missing. I mean, when people hear, nothing comes but contestation. Is there an ingredient to storytelling to get them to believe Jesus is truly of the Lord?"

"If I knew the answer to that, I wouldn't be resigned to stay here."

Yamin scanned the room. "It's more than I have."

Yareb thought for a moment then gave a closed-mouth smile. "And that may be enough for now."

Yamin's brow furrowed. "What's enough?"

"Your story. It is more than what the lost people have. Don't you see? Changing people's minds is one thing. Changing their beliefs is entirely different. You have the personal experience of a man, who claims to be given power by Elohim, performing an unprecedented miracle upon you and you alone. Faith is not derived so easily by secondhand tales. I, for one, do not believe sirens exist just because an ancient Greek tale tells me they do."

Melita shifted in her seat. "My parents once took the word of others to worship only the *Dii Consentes*. Only when they learned about Theandrios, did they move away from the many to the one. And now you allude your Jesus, our Theandrios, is of another god, your god, Elohim? This brings us back to multiple gods and confuses me to all ends."

"Everyone's journey is an individual one, my dear. At least you have your parents. Some of us, like Yamin, have nothing but their story. Perhaps, by its influence, your beliefs will shift yet again. Perhaps all of ours will in time." He turned to Yamin. "Your story has the benefit of mentioning the Jewish God. I know it will help me with creating God-fearers, if not some true converts." He stood with a few grunts. "After all, we've not heard of a true miracle for many generations."

Yamin and Melita stood too.

Yareb placed his hand on Yamin's shoulder. "And it's about time." He smiled. "Thank you." He looked at Melita. "Both of you." He produced a small clay disk and handed it to Yamin.

Yamin held it in the light of the doorway. "I can keep it?"

"I don't plan on doing any traveling. I'll let them all come to me." He laughed.

Yamin stored the tessera in a loose pocket he fashioned in the front folds of his robe. He hoped it would provide safe passage through this dangerous region of Decapolis and prayed cities to the south possessed a more welcoming spirit.

46

Melita's plan to exit through another gate farther south failed when they found it guarded with cantankerous soldiers. "We better take our chances at the western gate."

Yamin nodded. On the way, he checked that the tessera remained secure in his pocket. Though not fond of storing items in his robe, he found it easier than fishing through his leather bag and incensing the guards. He made a conscious decision to stow it afterward.

As they approached, several men held a discussion with of a mixture of cult temple guards and Roman soldiers. They took turns interviewing pedestrians and those on carts. A line formed while Melita and Yamin sized up the situation.

"Act as if we think nothing's wrong. No one's looking for us. Can you do this, Melita?"

Her eyes widened. "Maybe we should pretend to be a young married couple."

Yamin screwed up his face. "I don't know if we can pull that—"

"Sure, we can. Listen."

The line moved quickly as travelers were either turned back and detained or allowed to pass through the gate and out of the city's walled enclosure.

Melita whispered. "I recognize one of the temple guards." She stepped out of line and pulled Yamin with her.

"So? What's wrong?"

Melita waited for the person behind them, an older woman carrying empty baskets, to move ahead of them in line. She whispered, "Just getting the timing right. Oh, and forget the married story."

Sweat formed under Yamin's arms despite the chilly air. His mission depended upon getting past this obstacle, and he felt unsure about putting so much trust in a girl who made it known she liked to take chances by acting on impulse.

The old woman before them passed without difficulty. Everyone who made it through the gate picked up their pace and stood a little taller, most likely due to a release of stress.

The temple guard addressed them with annoyance in his voice while the soldier had his back turned to speak to another. "State your business." His face lit up when he saw Melita.

"Hallo, Camillus."

The soldier at the other side of the exit half-turned when he heard her overjoyed voice.

Camillus' face reddened. "Uh, Melita. What—what are you doing here?"

"Just taking a walk with my friend. Are you able to join us?"

He huffed. "I wish, but I'm on duty. Besides, it's not safe today. Especially . . ."

Camillus' voice faded off as Yamin's thoughts drifted. *What's she doing?* Yamin flipped his tessera over and over in his pocket. *Keep calm. Must keep calm. Father Elohim, allow us to pass so I can continue the mission you've placed before me. Please make Melita say the right—*

Camillus stopped chatting and focused on Yamin. "Why are his eyes closed? What's wrong with him?"

Yamin snapped to attention and whipped out his tessera. "It's mine."

Melita buried her face in her palm.

Camillus chuckled. He looked back at the growing line of impatient and nervous people. "Get out of here, Melita." He gently pushed her through the gate. "And take your strange friend with you."

The soldier half-turned again after verbally abusing an elderly couple and pushing them away. He scowled at Camillus.

Camillus smiled cheekily. "I was once her suitor."

The soldier grunted and turned back to his duty.

Melita's face reddened as she walked abreast of a speedy Yamin. Neither looked back.

Many minutes passed, and Yamin's stomach grumbled. When under the influence of his possessors, this would have driven him to do unspeakable acts to satiate his desire. Now, he chose to act only to comfort his unlikely companion. "You must be ready for the morning meal."

Melita surveyed their options. "We're hours from the market outside Capitolias." She motioned behind her. "And we're not going back there." She sighed. "Didn't you have a plan for where you're going after leaving us?"

"South." He produced his map. "See?"

Melita took it. "Oh, I've never seen one of these before. I mean, father often carries an *itineraria*, but that's just a list of stops along his courier routes. What is *this*?" She placed her finger on a wavy line intersecting the path to the west.

"The River Hieromices."

"I've never crossed it." Her eyes grew wide. "Will you take me that far? Farther?"

Yamin's appetite waned. *This mission is mine. Well, it* was *mine.* How was he to answer her? Was she part of Elohim's plan?

They stepped off the road to allow a rickety cart to pass. Its driver grumbled at them as his donkey-drawn transport creaked by.

"What do you want, Melita?"

She looked up from the map, clearly confused by the severity of his question.

"What I meant was, how far did you plan on going with me? My decision on what to do next depends on your answer."

She handed him the map and adjusted her shawl. "Let's find some food first. Then we'll discuss it." She stepped off the road and onto a perpendicular footpath heading south.

"Wait. I didn't mean— Where are you going?"

She did not answer.

Yamin ran to catch up to her and fell in the loose soil with a thud.

Melita turned back to help him up. She attempted to control her laughter unsuccessfully.

"Very funny. I'm still recovering from our escape."

"Oh, that?" She scoffed. "My family's been in worse situations."

Yamin tilted his head and shot her a look of disbelief.

"All right, maybe not *that* bad. But close."

"I'd love to hear about it. But first, where're we going? Capitolias is that way." He pointed west along the Roman road.

"There's a small settlement less than an hour's walk south of here where my parents have friends. You might like them. At least it'll be someone you can share your story with, yes?"

Yamin had to give it to her. Maybe she *was* destined to join him. "Lead the way."

"And Charis makes the best porridge."

They hiked through fallow millet fields and stands of dormant fruit trees.

Yamin broke a small piece of dead branch from an apple tree. He caressed the bark between his fingers and closed his eyes to take in the sensation. He imagined the taste of an apple from this tree at the peak of ripeness. Several orchards grew in the hills surrounding Hippos. As a child, he was chased out many times by protective farmers. He smiled at the memory.

"Does touching things help you see them better?"

Yamin's eyes snapped open. "What? Oh, yes." He chuckled and handed the brittle twig to Melita. "Touch connects me to the object in a very personal way to make it seem more real."

Melita broke it in two and rolled one of the halves between her thumb and forefinger. "It's no more real to me now than it was a moment ago."

Yamin produced a quick close-mouthed smile. "Well, it's how I make sense of my surroundings in a way. I've been told it's a gift."

"Strange gift." She dropped the sticks and looked down the winding trail. "Come on. It's just around these rocks."

They circumnavigated several outcroppings of red-brown rock before reaching the settlement a quarter-hour later. An exceptional amount of smoke rose from several places among the houses.

Yamin squinted. "That's a lot of fire for making porridge."

"Charis?" Melita started to run toward the fires.

Yamin grabbed her arm. "Wait. It's too dangerous." He scanned the area.

An arm, blackened by smoke, waved from behind a pile of smoldering debris.

Melita broke off from him and ran toward the person.

Yamin followed.

<h1 style="text-align:center">47</h1>

Melita ran toward home as fast as her legs could carry her. Stains covered her. Tears on her face. Blood and soot on her clothes. Regret and worry on her soul. Why had she let Yamin go off alone? *How could he just leave me?*

She struggled with the idea that he abandoned her in the midst of what they had found. After having spent months as an honored guest in her family's house, she felt determined to come up with a more logical explanation for his disappearance. She couldn't tell her parents, "He just ran away."

She was thankful her misadventure had not lasted more than a day as the setting sun helped to light her trip back to the city's entrance. Her friend, Camillus, had long since gone home, replaced by another temple guard with whom she had no acquaintance. Melita reached into the pouch attached to her sash and produced her tessera.

The gate guards let her in without incident other than their askew glances at her disheveled appearance.

When she left their field of vision, she picked up her pace and headed straight home. Maybe her parents had already been released from their ordeal.

When she arrived, the house stood empty. She searched every room. Darkness.

The clamor of raised voices drew her attention toward the center of town, and she left the house without cleaning herself in search of what she feared to be an incident involving her family or their fellow disciples.

Halfway to the center, a group of dark figures approached, blocking her path.

Melita hid in the shadows and waited for them to pass.

The first thing she noticed was the group's melancholy state. Then, a familiar silhouette. "Mother?" She bolted from the darkness and hugged her parents.

Rena studied her daughter's stains. "Melita, are you hurt? We thought the worst. Where have you been? Is Yamin with you?"

"It's a long story."

Sabinus gathered the others. "Let's get back home and eat something. It's been a long day, and it will be wiser to share there."

Minutes later they arrived at home. After lighting lamps and gathering water to wash, Melita met her parents and the others in the main room.

Sabinus swallowed a gulp of his wine. "Melita, let's hear it."

Melita wanted to know what happened with her parents first but obeyed her father. Now was not the time to argue. "When we arrived at noon, only one house remained mostly intact. The others—"Tears welled. "I saw at least one person who'd been killed."

Rena gasped and put her hand to her mouth. "Killed? By the gods."

"The gods had nothing to do with this, Mother. Charis said it was slavers."

"Charis. Was she alright?"

"Yes, just scrapes and bruises. If she hadn't been so old, they might've taken her too. Others her age escaped with battered bodies."

"The children?"

"Just the able-bodied men. It was terrible. Wailing and children's cries echoed through the settlement."

"From the west." A male housemate spoke through gritted teeth. "No way any of the eastern groups would be bold enough to attack so close to a Decapolis city."

Sabinus grunted in agreement. "Did they take any livestock?"

"I don't think so. Animals still wandered about."

"No livestock. Definitely slavers."

"After we found Charis, Yamin went to find other survivors. That's when I asked her who had done this? She was so confused. But I helped her stand and we sought others."

"And Yamin?"

"The last I saw of him was near the edge of the settlement. He'd walked behind a burned house. I turned to Charis. When I looked for him again . . ." Her eyes swelled with tears. "I called for him, searching the entire settlement."

"Charis asked me if I knew why he would leave."

A far-off look clouded her eyes as the memory overtook her.

A plume of smoke blew past Melita at the settlement. She searched the surrounding hills for any sign of Yamin. "I don't know what happened, Charis. One moment he was walking over there and the next— My parents aren't going to like this. Any of this."

Charis spoke while tirelessly tidying up the remains of her small mud home. "Perhaps it was those who attacked us."

"You told me they were slavers. Why would they take Yamin?"

"Like all thieves, Melita, they're opportunists. They're taking advantage of the distractions the rebels create in the city to move on more vulnerable sources of labor."

Melita frowned. "Distractions provided by people like me and my parents."

"You mustn't blame yourself, deary. No one could've foreseen this."

"But if not for our beliefs, our blasphemy, they wouldn't have been brash enough to attack so close to the city."

"What of your friend? Is it possible he just—left? I mean, after seeing this, I can imagine how some might feel overwhelmed."

"No. Yamin has seen much worse in his life than this. You should hear his story, Charis." She scanned the perimeter again. "He was going to tell you all, before . . ."

Charis embraced her and wiped Melita's tears with her scarf.

Rena reached out and held her daughter's hand. "There's nothing you could've done, Melita. Is there anything else you can recall?"

Melita sniffled. "As I traveled back along the trail to the main road, I found the tessera Yareb gave to Yamin."

"Yareb!" Sabinus grabbed the edges of the table. "*He's* part of this story? No wonder everything—"

"No, Father. You don't understand. Yareb helped us get out the city when the guards were questioning everyone. He listened to Yamin's story about Jesus, and in return he gave him the tessera. One of the guards was Camillus."

"From the temple?"

Rena gasped. "Melita, you did not—"

"I just used my influence to get us past. Yamin was so nervous. If it'd been anyone else, we'd never have gotten out."

Sabinus calmed but the vein on his forehead told Melita he was still quite upset. "I've always said you keep some colorful company, Melita. This time your choice in friends was incredibly fortunate."

"Unlike your choice in Amphion."

He harrumphed. "And that brings us to our story."

Melita sat upright. "Yes, are we going to be all right? Are we safe now?"

Sabinus took another sip of his wine and began to his story.

Melita listened but could not help her mind wandering off wondering what happened to Yamin.

48

Darkness, pain, a tingling down the neck. The flash of a man leaping from the shrubs. Crude voices, unfamiliar, grasping from the suffocating darkness.

"Where are we?"

"Help me."

"We're lost."

Yamin's throat tightened.

Then another spoke, devoid of malice, from the light. *The hardest part of telling an experience is admitting your sins. Bare your soul . . .*

The voice faded as Yamin stirred. It filled him with a peace that conflicted with his aching head. *That's it.* That's the missing portion from my story for people to believe. "I have to admit my sins."

A firmer voice now spoke, this time corporeal, present. "I don't think that's going to help you in your current situation."

Yamin opened his eyes. Intersecting slats of iron surrounded him and four other young men. Great spoked wheels creaked as they rolled over stones on the unpaved road. He always felt sorry for the poor souls he witnessed in such a state. Now he found himself one of them. And no less poor.

An exceptionally violent bump dug the uneven flooring of the slaver's wagon into Yamin's rib forcing him to sit upright.

The others looked with brief uncaring glances.

The firm voice spoke again from outside his mobile prison. "Welcome back. Hope you ate earlier because there's nothing for two days." The slaver dressed in brown robes and black leather boots—the same that Roman soldiers wore—sat on the driver's bench.

I've gone longer. Yamin thought back to his time spent in the tombs when an occasional insect or unwary sparrow formed his meager daily nutritional intake. He scanned the faces of his fellow captives. "Are you all from that settlement back there?"

One man, not much older than Yamin, nodded slowly. "They lit our houses on fire to distract us. Then picked us off one by one in the chaos."

"And I just happened to be—"

"In the wrong place at the right time." The slaver chuckled. "Right time for us, anyway."

Yamin's fellow captive banged on the cage once with his fist.

"Save your strength, slave. You'll need it where we're going." He half-pointed to the east. A plume of gray-yellow smoke rose ominously from over the horizon. The setting sun reflected from its billowing form like brushed gold on fire.

Yamin remembered the dust storm he endured on The Lukka, and a shiver ran down his spine. He had not envisioned a challenge like this as part of his mission from Jesus.

"But I'm a Roman citizen. You can't enslave a citizen."

The slaver's eyes widened then squinted. "Really? Where's your tessera?"

Yamin patted his robes. Nothing.

The slaver scanned Yamin and prodded his fellow guard while gesturing to his own wrists. "Looks like you've seen time as a slave before, or at least a prisoner."

Yamin sighed in defeat. "You have no idea."

Two days later, Yamin found himself making vain attempts with his clothing to filter the air from the acrid scent of rotten eggs. Sulfurous plumes of hot gas crossed the uneven road before them. He scanned the surroundings and found it a barren wasteland of sharp volcanic stone. His captors had taken his only pair of sandals. *No escape through that*—he looked at the other captives' feet—*for any of us.*

A meager camp greeted them at the base of a sprawling volcano enveloping the horizon as if an ancient titan had dropped his carbon-black shield here during battle. Dark rock and sand spread out all around and sparkled in the setting sun like a field of diamonds. To Yamin's surprise, steaming water issued from a spring under a pile of giant boulders. He smacked his lips in anticipation since they had provided nothing to drink along the journey.

"Time to get some work out of you." The leader and three other captors gathered around the back of the cart. He unlocked the hasp on the door, and it creaked open under its own weight.

Yamin's angry cellmate bolted through the egress.

He watched wide-eyed as the men parted to give the escapee leave.

The man ran no more than ten steps then fell to the ground writhing in pain. He held up one of his feet. Blood trickled from multiple cuts in his sole.

The men laughed.

The leader threw him a pair of wooden sandals with leather straps. "These won't be comfortable, but they're better than what the ground has to offer for many miles in every direction. Get used to it."

They laughed again, and another guard passed out the same to the other captives in the cart. "Put them on and get out."

Once they gathered the five captives and made them sit huddled together, the presumed leader of the slavers spoke. His worn, brown leather coverings made him look like the blacksmith Yamin and Dar had watched on occasion in Hippos. "I am Kain. You are no doubt wondering what is expected of you while in my service." His gruff voice echoed off the boulders.

A brisk wind blew through the camp swirling the nearby plumes of gas into ghostly gyres. Yamin's skin chilled.

One of his fellow slaves spoke. "I'm a skilled artist. What good am I to you in this god-forsaken land?"

"Yes, and I'm a farmer. I haven't seen anything growing since yesterday."

Kain produced a wicked grin through thick facial hair. "You've all been moved up in the ranks of society."

The men laughed.

"Now you're miners."

Yamin had heard terrible stories from the well-traveled sailors on The Lukka of what happens in mines serving the Empire. Did these men work for the Emperor, or were they a rogue enterprise? The Imperial cinnabar mines in Hispania had been infamous for the brutality and death rate of slaves. *Are we going to be mining cinnabar?* Numbness spread as the realization of his predicament took hold. How could he possibly continue to serve Jesus if kept a slave?

The guards fed them moldy bread and warm water from the spring. The warm liquid tasted like the plumes of gas they rode through earlier and Yamin had a hard time keeping it all down on an empty stomach. He knew he needed to drink, and he certainly did not want to upset his captors.

Several minutes passed. The slavers then walked the five men around a pile of boulders to an area covered in bright yellow encrusted rocks. Giant cracks in the earth spewed more of the gas Yamin had seen earlier. His head swam.

One of his fellow prisoners passed out, overcome by the noxious fumes.

Kain ignored the sick man and spoke. "As you just witnessed, stay downwind of the plumes at all times. Gather as much of the yellow sulfur chunks as you can carry in the baskets." He pointed off to the side where roughly a dozen large-weave baskets had been piled. "Bring the full baskets to the cart waiting where you ate your daily meal. If you work from sunrise to sunset without any problems, eventually you'll be moved to a more—agreeable operation." He walked back around the boulders and left the five men alone.

Yamin did not move, nor did the other three who still stood, until Kain disappeared behind the rocks. He then walked over to help the unconscious man get to his feet. "Stay out of the gas plumes."

The man shook his head to clear it and coughed before nodding.

Another man asked, "How long is *eventually*?"

Yamin racked his brain. Was there any chance of escape from this hellish scenario into which they thrusted him? Could he trust these men if he did come up with an idea? He decided the best option was to get to know them before making any decisions. What better way than working side-by-side? "We better get started. I don't feel like being on the receiving end of that whip." He walked to the pile of worn baskets and picked one up.

The others reluctantly followed.

Yamin approached a steaming orifice and bent to inspect the rocks. He picked one up. It seared his hand, and he dropped it. The rock fell into the crevice and clinked as it bounced off the walls for quite some time before the sound faded. He blew on his burnt fingertips and looked sheepishly at the others. "I guess we should pick them up farther from the openings."

The men worked for hours before the sun rested on the horizon.

Yamin imagined what the heat would be like here in the summer months. His thirst overrode his desire to talk to anyone on the final walk back for the night.

Kain waited for them at the spring. "You did good your first day. Just finish out the month, and you'll be on your way to better conditions."

"A month?" The man who cut his feet earlier turned and threw up his hands. "We'll never survive a month out there. And you know it."

Kain shrugged his leather-bound shoulders and walked away.

Another slaver motioned for them to sleep in a makeshift lean-to near the water.

Inside, Yamin found poorly constructed sleeping mats and soiled linens. No food. "I guess we have to wait until tomorrow for our next morsel."

The others found their places for the night.

The man with the injured feet ended up next to Yamin. He winced as he took his wooden sandals off.

Yamin tore some strips from the bottom of his robe which was of a far sturdier fabrication than the other men's clothing, and handed them to him. "I'm Yamin, son of Eber, from Hippos."

The man returned a half-smile for the offering. "I'm Amiy." He took the strips and wrapped them around his feet. "Thank you."

The others introduced themselves before they all fell into uneasy rest.

49

The month's passing seemed a year to Yamin. He lost all the weight he had gained after his salvation. Bouts of diarrhea plagued them all. The demonic energy he once experienced would be helpful, but he had not desire for its return. Instead, his daily prayers to Elohim fueled him when the other men faltered.

During the second week, the man who had collapsed on the first day succumbed to the unhealthy conditions. It started with daily bloody noses. Several of them had developed the same symptom, but none as bad as he. The man collapsed and stopped breathing while wrestling his fifth basket of the day around the boulders.

They did not find him for nearly an hour, and no one could have helped. Yamin demanded to see Kain. "He needs a proper burial." His boldness cost him his daily allotment of moldy bread.

Fortunately, Amiy shared his meager portion. "Your prayers have helped me survive this ordeal."

Yamin felt a surge of joy, albeit fleeting. After they ate, he gathered the remaining workers' attention but spoke in hushed tones. "I've a story to share. It's one that's given me the strength to prevail through trials like this."

"You mean, you've been in situations like this before?"

"Let me tell you my experience, and you can judge for yourself." Yamin spoke to them with a newfound energy. How he discovered an opportunity to carry on his mission during this time was itself a miracle. He made sure to mention that Jesus arrived when he least expected help and his situation seemed hopeless.

And this time, he remembered to tell them of his personal transgressions. The ones not contrived by the demons. How he had coveted Dar's life, hated his parents baseless superstitions and ignorance, and how his anger with Baniy and the other fishermen on the sea grew to uncontrollable levels. "No one is without sin, blameless. It was when I thought rescue seemed too far out of reach, that Jesus stretched out his hand and released me from my chains."

Having nothing to lose, the men clung to Yamin's story of salvation. For the next two weeks of their initial trial, they treated each other as close friends, if not brothers. Yamin regretted not being able tell the dead man before his demise. He thought of how the guards dragged the man's lifeless body into the dunes. And as the four survivors continued to unearth sulfur that would eventually end up in Roman physicians' medicines or circus pyrotechnic displays, they watched as vultures soared in descending circles to feed on the man's remains. Yamin wondered what beliefs that man had and if he would meet Elohim in the afterlife.

Yamin had not been entirely sure a month's time passed. It was only when he overheard the guards speak of how terrible the past month had been for themselves, that he realized it grew close to being March. He left the city with Melita at the end of January, his last reference point. He listened as the two guards complained over their hot porridge.

"... never gives us a break. If it weren't for the heat coming from these rocks, we'd have frozen to death out here."

"That's why I always ask for different work in February. Nothing good ever happens in this cursed month."

"And when we show up with one worker short, which one of us will suffer the punishment?"

"They can't blame us for that, can they?"

"Just wait. We'll probably get sent right back here instead of, well, any place better."

"Yeah, nothing much worse than this volcano. Maybe a ship. I get awfully sick on the water."

Yamin slept in peace, hoping this situation might get better soon, at least for him and his fellow captives.

Two days later, at sunset, the familiar caged transport cart lumbered across the barren field of sharp stones. Even the single ox powering it seemed to hate its job. Thick tears and saliva oozed from its face and coagulated blood sealed a fresh wound just above his right front hoof.

The two guards he had overheard speaking loaded the four workers into the cart shortly after sunrise the next morning.

The weakened men strained to pull themselves up inside.

As Yamin entered, he asked the guard, "Where to now? Rowing a slave ship?"

"I don't like your insolence, boy." The guard kicked Yamin's leg inside and slammed the door.

Several hours passed. Fortunately, the trip around the outskirts of the sprawling volcanic no-man's land offered the men a midday respite from the daily drudgery. Biting northerly winds forced them to huddle close together. Yamin's clothing had worn so they now offered less protection from the elements.

Another work camp appeared before them. But this one already had over a dozen slaves. Some used hammers to crack the volcanic stone into movable pieces. Others carried the chunks to a pile. And still others loaded it onto a wagon. Another older man sat by the fire tending to several boiling pots and various bowls of unrecognizable liquid.

It can't be gold or some other precious metal. Yamin turned to whisper to Amiy. "What stone around here is so valuable they need slaves to mine and process it?"

Amiy frowned and shook his head gently.

Yamin scanned the workers trying to stay positive. *More to tell about Jesus.* He cracked a diminutive smile.

One of the new guards, a tall man with a trapezoidal beard, rapped the side of the cage. "What're you so happy 'bout?" He spoke Greek with a strange accent. "Ya' think'n this'll be easier'n the sulfur pit?" His deep laugh turned the heads of the other slaves. "Time to test yer spirit."

The four new arrivals poured from the cage and sat as before, in a tight group on the ground.

Kain addressed them. "I hope you remember I run these mines and everyone answers to me." He adjusted his leatherbound shoulders and continued. "All of you have survived the First Obedience. This is the second and Final Obedience. If you can surv—*work* well until the summer months, you'll be freed. If you become a problem, you'll never leave." He searched the men's faces. "Do you understand?"

Yamin and the others weakly nodded.

Kain motioned to another guard.

The guard made them stand and follow him to a lean-to like the one at the sulfur pit. Hot porridge steamed from within an iron kettle.

Yamin's stomach growled.

The old man stationed there scooped some into a clay bowl. "Eat and rest. Tomorrow you'll mine obsidian." His voice cracked.

Glad to have the break and a hot meal free of mold, at least any visible, Yamin sat and gave thanks to Elohim in hushed tones. The others joined him.

Not all his fellow captives came from a similar spiritual background. In fact, all three had been devout polytheists who denied the existence of the Hebrew god even after Yamin shared his story with them. Only after seeing how Yamin carried himself, after knowing why he did so, did they begin to change their allegiance to a single God of provision rather than a multitude of silent and unforgiving entities.

Yamin's faith grew in the knowledge that his obedience to Jesus helped others.

About two weeks later, the miners discovered the truth behind the nature of their captivity. As outlooks go, theirs became grim. And Yamin helped cause it.

50

Amiy and Yamin worked side-by-side most days. They had become as close as could be, and their bond of friendship made the other slaves jealous. Though Yamin accepted and treated all his fellow laborers equally, they frowned at anyone having joy in their predicament.

Yamin noticed their looks of contempt and grunts of displeasure. His concern grew, so he spoke to Kain on their behalf. He dumped a pile of sharp black-green volcanic glass at Kain's feet as Kain waited for and counted each of the workers to finish the day at sunset. "Sir, may I speak to you about a concern?"

"Nothing you consider a concern is worth my ear."

"But the men, sir. They're—unhappy."

Kain roared with laughter and refused to address Yamin's concern.

Yamin joined his three friends for the evening meal.

"What did you say to him?"

"I told him the workers were unhappy."

Amiy almost spit out his mouthful of porridge. "Unhappy? Of course, we're unhappy. Do you need details, Yamin?"

One of the other men spoke. "They're jealous of your contentment."

"They blame *me*?" He thought hard about it. But the man's words struck truth. Yamin knew what covetousness felt like. He remembered feeling that way about Dar's happiness. He now felt ridiculous for having treated his friend that way. And he understood the men's feelings. *Should I feel guilty because I am at ease and they are not?* But did he make a mistake by approaching Kain? The already tasteless meal in his hands suddenly became more so.

Right before sunrise, Yamin stirred awake at the sound of raised voices. He knew the rule about making any disturbances before the sun peeked above the horizon and hoped the other workers remembered too. He listened.

"The truth won't be good, Kain. You've already given them the false hope of freedom. Penalizing them for being unhappy won't make it better for us."

"I'm punishing them because of that boy's impudence. I won't share our plans. But they will learn that questioning my authority doesn't go unpunished. We need them alive and obedient until these wagons are filled."

"Think of another idea, Kain. Don't jeopardize what's worked so far."

The sun hung directly overhead and sweat beaded on Yamin's forehead. Not sure if the ever-warming daily temperature caused his perspiration or at any moment Kain would let loose his punishment, Yamin focused on shattering stone into shards.

A scream.

Yamin whipped his head around.

A boulder had slipped and fell onto Amiy's leg, pinning him.

Several others joined Yamin in shifting the great rock just enough to extract him.

Yamin inspected Amiy's leg and found nothing but superficial scrapes covering the entire surface. The combined wounds oozed enough blood for them to seek help. Yamin supported him as he hobbled to the main camp.

One of the guards accompanied them to the fire pit. Typically, the nightly cooking fire consisted of nothing more than small twigs. But now a larger fire burned planks of sawed wood.

Yamin looked for the source of fuel and found the rusty slaver cart dismantled in a scrap pile nearby.

He remembered Kain's overheard dark promise. *We're not being released. That's how Kain's punishing us?* The sentence did not fit the crime. Yamin's mind now went to another place. Escape.

An older slave, made to tend the fire and prepare the meals, sat near a lesser fire with a collection of small iron cookware with wide shallow bottoms. Each contained varying thicknesses of a milky-white liquid. One boiled away on a bed of glowing red embers. "Bring him here." He motioned to Yamin and Amiy to sit, then produced yet another tiny metal bowl. He positioned himself over Amiy's injured leg and dabbed a dry, sticky white paste on the oozing wounds.

Yamin and Amiy watched wide-eyed as the bleeding of each wound stopped with every touch.

The man continued his treatment. "Haven't you noticed the white deposits when moving rock out there?"

They nodded.

"Alum. We collect that too and ship it off with the other material. Other than stopping bleeding, I don't know what else it does. Guess I'll leave that for the physicians to play with." He put the bowl down. "All done."

Amiy thanked the man and allowed Yamin to walk him back to their lean-to for the evening meal. The others had already gathered.

As they ate, Yamin tested their powers of observation. "Have any of you noticed that no new slaves have arrived in weeks?"

They shook their heads and shrugged their shoulders while shoveling porridge in with their bare hands.

"Of the sixteen originally here when we arrived, only twelve are left. They won't be able to keep up production if they don't replace their workforce, right?"

Amiy swallowed hard. "What're you getting at, Yamin? Is there something you know?"

Yamin lowered his voice. "They're not freeing us."

The oldest man bolted upright and spoke louder than Yamin preferred. "What do you mean they're not freeing us?"

Others around the camp stopped their quiet conversations and looked toward Yamin's group.

Yamin lowered his head and sighed. "Keep your voices down. The last thing we want is to provoke the guards any further."

The older man continued. "You've already done that. This is your fault."

"I was only trying—"

"Should've kept your mouth shut. Then we'd be free to go when this is over. Now, who knows what they'll do to us?"

The only transport was the weekly cargo cart delivering cooking fuel and food and, on the return trip, took some raw sulfur and obsidian to some unknown destination in the west.

Yamin had two goals: return the promise of his fellow slaves' freedom before the heat of summer did them in, and get himself on that transport so he could continue his mission.

Yamin slaved tirelessly over the next two weeks to impress Kain and initiate reparations for the workers. After a particularly rainy day, he approached Kain upon dropping his last load of obsidian ore. He bowed his head out of respect. "Sir, it has come to my understanding that I have made a mistake. I would like to apologize for my impudent behavior." He glanced up to judge Kain's reaction.

Kain showed no interest in hearing what Yamin had to say and scanned the perimeter as if Yamin did not exist.

Yamin went on. "We've provided honest work every day, even in bad weather. Is there any chance you can reinstate the men's freedom? When the time comes, that is." He took a step back continuing to bow his head.

A beetle crawled on the rocky ground between them.

Kain stomped on it with his marred, black leather boot.

Yamin did not want to push his luck any further and backed away once more.

When he started to turn, Kain replied. "It seems you've created this problem all by yourself."

Yamin nodded slowly.

"I'll agree on two conditions. One is *you* stay with me as payment.

My personal slave." Kain produced a wry smile. "Pay for their freedom by giving up yours."

Yamin's jaw dropped. He had a hard time believing anyone worked out here in the summer months. He had an equally difficult time thinking he would survive such an ordeal. Who, in their right mind, would agree to watch over him while he worked? *He must be joking.* "And—and the other—sir?"

Kain looked into his eyes. "The other is you accompany me on the next shipment run."

Looking at the growing mound of ore, Yamin expected that to be sooner than later. He would be sure to get some of his answers on such a trip. Who ordered the raw materials? What are they used for? And, more importantly, would this ease his escape?

And freedom, via escape or manumission, for all the men had become complicated with the dismantling of the prisoner wagon. With all the ore, they would never fit in the cargo cart. The men certainly could not walk out, barefoot or on their painfully awkward wooden shoes. Yamin felt Kain had ulterior motives.

Two weeks later, the change from the wet season to dry was hard to miss. As if someone dammed the skies and added fuel to the sun, the climate shifted almost overnight.

At sunrise, and without warning, Kain addressed the group. "As promised for your hard work, you are now released." He turned and motioned for Yamin to climb into the loaded transport with him and two other guards.

Yamin half-turned to Amiy and whispered, "I'm coming back for you."

Kain called for him. "Hurry up now, personal servant. You'll have a rough ride sitting on jagged ore."

Yamin scowled at him. A second larger wagon, hooked to four oxen, lined up to follow them.

"You could always join your friends."

Both wagons had been loaded to capacity with black-green obsidian, yellow sulfur, and white alum. And these were no ordinary wagons. Of sturdy Roman design, they had undercarriages and a pivoting front axle for easy maneuvering. *Were these men working for the Empire?*

Yamin approached and wrestled himself onboard. He sat behind Kain who took up position on the driver's bench next to a large man who held the reigns.

Amiy's look of concern placed a weight on Yamin's chest. The others looked on with shocked and angry faces.

"Wait! How will we get out of here?"

"You can't leave us without food!"

Yamin had no choice. He made a deal and planned to adhere to it. As the cart pulled away, he called to Amiy. "I'm sorry. I don't have time to explain." He threw his pair of wood sandals to them. Hopefully, they could get use out of them to leave this horrid place. "Amiy, tell them the story!"

Amiy held up his hand in a halfhearted farewell gesture.

He turned to Kain. "That was cruel."

Kain laughed. "We got what we needed. And they got what was promised. A deal is deal."

The other guards joined in the sinister merriment.

He looked at Yamin. "And I got an indentured servant."

Yamin crossed his arms and knit his brow. "Where are we going?"

"The Great Sea, of course. To sell our merchandise to the highest bidder."

Not sure who worked for who nor the true intentions of these men, Yamin knew he needed to get away from them as soon as possible. He devised a plan. As soon as they entered an area with water and plants, he would make his move. And somehow get back here to rescue his friends.

51

Shackles prevent movement. And Yamin found them to be the biggest deterrent to enacting his escape. *Demons would make quick work of these chains.* But being here was preferable to having them back. Being anywhere, with nothing but Jesus' mission to occupy his time, is better.

The mission.

He closed his eyes and prayed in silence. *Lord, I'm still here. I've not faltered, even though the circumstances have been less than desirable. As sure as Jesus is my savior, I will continue to tell the people of Decapolis you are the one true God by sharing my story. Please let me share it now.*

"Kain, may I speak?" It had been hours on the first day of their journey, and he said nothing until now.

"Aim it over the edge if you need to go."

"That's not what I was going to ask, but now that you mention it . . ." Yamin relieved himself. It reminded him of his months on The Lukka. Once finished, he addressed his captors again. "How long is our journey?"

They ignored him.

"I'm only asking because I'd like to tell you a story. You know, to pass the time."

Kain laughed and elbowed his neighbor who held the reigns. "Up for a story, Porcius?"

The pudgy man snorted. "Sure."

Yamin took a deep breath and proceeded to weave his story into the most beautiful tapestry of visions so far.

The men sat mesmerized and did not speak during the entire telling, which lasted over an hour. Several minutes into the telling, Kain ordered the other cart to come along side so they could hear as well.

Yamin embellished where it did not interfere with his interaction with Jesus. His initial goal was to teach these men about the Lord's power to forgive and save. The flourishes had the purpose of gaining favor in their eyes. Maybe they would afford him just enough freedom to make escape that much easier. Either way, he would succeed.

First, he made sure neither of the men had been to Hippos. He painted the city as having walls of polished marble and fountains of effervescent spring water bubbling from the very streets. Baniy was envisioned as having crossed eyes and only one tooth. He made Captain Adjo a muscled, jewelry-clad, shirtless swashbuckler who believed his cat had been reincarnated from his deceased wife. And, as impossible as it may seem, Yamin built upon the story of the ancient and mysterious Maltese caves. He sensed fear in the men as he told them of bones still dripping with flesh and blood, a room filled with writhing insects, and booby traps made of spikes, deadfalls, and poisonous gas.

After everything he had experienced since the death of his parents, he found it easy to add colorful metaphors like, "colder than a basement mikveh in January," or "more confused than a pair of oxen tied backwards to a wagon."

This had the determined effect of lightening Kain's mood. And at the first nightly stop on their journey, he released Yamin from his fetters. "Your scars lend evidence to your tale. Truth or not, you're no stranger to irons."

"As I said in my story, I've been bound in more ways than one. Spiritual shackles hold many of us prisoners, Kain."

All the while, Yamin could not help but think of the prisoners they left behind and their difficult trial of escaping from that veritable death sentence. He made the deal with Kain to save their lives but ended up dooming them instead. Did they leave immediately? Staying put would certainly mean a slow demise from starvation and exposure.

After sunset, they settled around the fire with their evening meal. Kain sought details. "Thinking of your story, Yamin, you're one tenacious Jew. Never heard such a tale, especially from one of your kind."

"Oh, I'm not a Jew. Like I told you, I'm from Hippos."

"Rather dedicated to converting others to believe in the Hebrew god for not being one of their lofty moralistic tribesmen."

"And you sound rather prejudiced. Is there something I should know?"

"Other than Tiberius kicked all the Jews out of Rome years ago for trying to proselytize upper-class citizens?"

Yamin chuckled under his breath when he thought about how pleased Sabinus and Rena would be to hear that. "Nothing wrong with a higher moral code. Did it work? I mean, did any convert?"

"Don't know. I heard a rumor 'bout a woman named Flavia—"

Porcius spat something undesirable from his last mouthful of porridge into the fire. "Her name was *Fulvia,* and she was my cousin's friend's wife's sister."

Kain and Yamin squinted at Porcius, as did the two other men.

"It's true." Porcius leaned forward so the fire lit up his round face. "They tricked her into donating gold and purple dye meant for the temple in Jerusalem. But they stole it instead."

Kain rolled his eyes, as if he had been in similar bewildering conversations with Porcius before. "Let's hear it, Porcius."

Porcius whispered loudly. "I think it was the Isis cult."

Yamin and Kain looked at each other with confused expressions.

"It was the same time they kicked out all those astrologers too. Remember, Kain? Oh, and those who worshipped Bacchus. Then they sent away the—"

"And this has to do with our conversation how?" Kain's voice carried a feigned reprimand.

"I thought we were talking about why the Jews got kicked out of Rome." He looked at Kain and then at Yamin. "No?"

Yamin and Kain shared a chuckle. But Yamin withdrew his with a quiet sigh of frustration. *Keep it up, Yamin. They're lowering their guard.*

An owl's mournful, reed-like whistles echoed into a nearby ravine. Shortly after, another called from farther away. Yamin wondered what they said to each other. Were they trying to convince other owls to join their cause? To turn them away from old beliefs? Or were humans the only creatures on Earth so inclined to this behavior?

"You've given us much to think about, Yamin." Kain threw another piece of dismantled prisoner transport onto the fire. "I don't have to lock you up tonight, do I?"

Porcius produced a set of shackles.

Yamin grabbed his wrist and rubbed it. "I have no idea where we are, have no food or water, and nothing on my feet."

Kain looked at Porcius and nodded once. "I think we're good here."

Porcius stood and headed into the shadows. Moments later the sound of falling chains onto volcanic glass in the back of the wagon rang with melodic clinks.

Yamin prayed silently to Elohim. He gave thanks for the daily provision. But more so for answered prayers. Not only had he exacted the first stage of his escape from slavery, or whatever one would call this scenario, but he had sparked the embers of belief in the Lord. Had he made *God-fearers* of these men? Only time would tell. But he was not going to wait around to find out if the seeds he planted would germinate.

By the end of the day tomorrow, he would be on his way to freedom. Then on to help those he left behind.

52

By early morning on the third day, the sluggish, two-wagon caravan had reached the first Decapolis city. Canatha's outline stood in the distance through a thinly wooded area saturated in a sea of fog.

Yamin's heart leapt. He knew Melita slept inside those walls. He hoped, anyway. Was there any way to get a signal to her? Maybe he could sneak off and get lost in the misty forest before they even knew he had left. If he was going to help Amiy and the others, he had to do something soon before they perished.

He sought out each of the four slavers and found them in their respective places. Kain and Porcius sat in the front of him, and the other two men drove the load of ore behind him.

Over the course of the trip, Yamin had learned little about this load's destination and even less about who owned it. Kain's shrewd behavior thwarted Yamin's many attempts at gathering information. If he could figure it out, then maybe he could use that information against Kain.

So far, only Porcius had proven at all helpful. Last night, Yamin had just returned with a bundle of grass and twigs for kindling. They also made him prepare the food.

He wondered why. *I could poison them all. But since I haven't any poison . . .*

He combined course wheat flour with water, honey, and some old cheese in a pot then boiled the mixture over the fire.

Even if he had found something to spoil their meal, they watched him with caution while seated around the fire.

"Can't wait for some real food." Porcius shoveled porridge into his mouth with his hand like a blacksmith throwing wood into a furnace. "Had we driven through the night, we'd be eating roast chicken and warm bread by now."

One of the other men replied, "And who'd drive the oxen? You fell asleep twice with the reigns in your lap." He laughed, and the other men joined him.

Yamin sat with them and ate. "I wager if I had the right ingredients, I could make the best loaf of bread you've ever eaten."

"We don't gamble with slaves." Kain took being a taskmaster to a higher level.

Porcius lowered his hand from his mouth for the first time. "No, Kain, let the boy talk."

Yamin looked at Kain.

Kain nodded once for him to continue.

"You've all heard my story. But there's quite a bit I left out." Yamin knew how intrigued they had been the first time. He baited the hook once more. "Before my first demon ever took hold of me in Hippos, I learned how to cook and bake bread. Women's work, I know. But it has served me well."

"No wonder a demon found a home in you." Kain harrumphed and looked at the men. "He made a good wife!" Laughter erupted.

Yamin remained stoic. "My parents had both become too ill to cook. It was either take over for them or be stuck eating pickled fish for every meal."

Porcius licked his hand clean after emptying his bowl. "I'd have been fine. I love pickled fish."

"You love pickled anything." Kain threw his bowl at Porcius. "You'd eat a pickled dog."

Porcius absorbed the men's laughter.

Even Yamin chuckled under his breath. "Now, after I met Jesus, I was able to hone those skills while staying with friends along the road and in places like Raphana and there," he motioned to the city, "in Canatha."

Porcius asked wide-eyed, "You skipped Capitolias? It's too bad. They have the best *globuli* there."

"Had to pass it on my way to Canatha." Yamin never liked cheese curds anyway.

"Well, you're in luck. We're heading there tomorrow and should arrive by daybreak."

Kain punched Porcius in the arm.

One of the other men spoke. "We'll have to push the animals hard to make it by then, Kain."

"So be it. With the gold we make from these two loads, we'll buy a whole herd of new ones. New wagons, women, clothes, more slaves—"

Porcius picked up Kain's bowl and inspected it for any leftovers. "Uh, we didn't buy the *last* slaves."

The men laughed.

Yamin continued to eat. *I'll be in the city before sunrise. Melita must have made it back all right.*

A rooster's crow from a nearby farm froze Yamin's steps. He crawled away from the fire's edge an hour ago, and now the sun peaked over the horizon promising to cut through the thick fog before long. *They must know I'm gone by now.* After checking his surroundings, he stood and ran toward the city.

The ground here proved far more forgiving than that which surrounded the volcano. He planned to ask Sabinus for a pair of sandals as soon as he arrived. He prayed everyone made it back to the house after their ordeals. It had been almost two months now. Things must have calmed since then.

When he reached the gate, the guards still accosted travelers as they did when he and Melita left. *Not good.* He subconsciously patted the folds of his grubby robe half expecting the tessera to still be there. *Maybe I can find Melita's friend again. What was his name? Camel? Callistus? Camillus! Right.* He could almost taste the hot meal waiting—

He stirred hours later in the back of Kain's wagon, shackles secured at his ankles and wrists.

Porcius shifted in his seat. "He's awake."

Kain spoke without looking back. "You're not the first slave who's tried to run away, boy."

Yamin pretended to not listen. His head ached from the blow he must have received on approach to the city gate.

"You don't know what kind of trouble you've caused me. When we found you'd ran, we pushed the oxen hard. Two collapsed. You better hope we make Capitolias by dark." He turned to Porcius. "Maybe finding a buyer before the Great Sea would be best."

Darkness shrouded the landscape as Capitolias' silhouette against an orange twilight served as the only sign the city still stood in their path.

In time, Yamin overheard them say their contact planned to meet them outside the gate. Everything about their transaction seemed legitimate, but he doubted capturing citizens for servitude, abandoning them, and leaving them to die had any legal standing in the eyes of Roman law. He had not known many slaves closely, having already been at the lower end of the social ladder. Sure, the aristocrats in Hippos had them, but they lived better lives than Yamin and his family. Even they looked down on him every time he had walked through the city with Dar.

If only there was some way to prove my citizenship.

Porcius huffed. "No one there, Kain."

"I see that." Kain thought for a moment. "Set up camp near the cistern and get these animals watered. I'll go inside and find him."

The men ordered Yamin to stay put. He held up his shackled arms and smirked.

"You'll be lucky if Kain doesn't sell you off with the merchandise."

If only I could be so blessed.

Kain returned within the hour. "Sleep well, men, for tomorrow we'll be handsomely paid!"

Yamin shivered throughout the night. His captors provided no covering, and his robes stopped offering adequate protection from the elements weeks ago. The morning rays of sunshine aided his recovery, but he needed food.

Cooking fires sprouted up all around him as the Capitolias residents and visitors stirred in their camps outside the gate. A market stretched out along the city's wall, and sellers busied themselves preparing to tout their wares.

Kain's buyer approached.

Busy place for a transaction. Let's see how Kain handles this.

"Please, sir. Just a morsel. I've not eaten in days." Yamin jostled the iron shackles and curled out his lower lip. He knew how destitute he must have looked.

Some passersby glanced his way, but no one spoke to him.

Kain swung his head and glared at Yamin to be quiet.

Yamin had seen slaves chained before, and beggars he knew lied when they should be working to earn their denarii. What could he possibly say to make someone think twice about walking away?

Why not the truth? "I—I'm a Roman citizen. My name is Yamin, son of Eber, born in Hippos of Decapolis. He abducted me and abandoned others two days east of here."

Kain motioned for Porcius and the other men to silence Yamin.

The would-be ore purchaser looked at the commotion and squinted in suspicion.

"Quiet, slave." One of Kain's men kicked Yamin in the gut knocking the air out him.

As Yamin coughed and gagged, a stately woman approached.

The businessman delayed turning over the gold to Kain. "What goes on here, Kain? Is there truth to these accusations?"

At this point, several onlookers had stopped to witness the disturbance.

Kain chuckled nervously. "Of course not. This brigand was

caught stealing food from my men while we worked collecting the rare product you see in these wagons. Are you going to believe a slave over a fellow merchant?"

The stately woman positioned herself between Kain and Yamin. Her bright ultramarine dress and crisp white head covering blew in the breeze attracting just as many stares as did Yamin's distraction.

The crowd of spectators now grew to more than twenty.

"I'll need to inspect the loads more carefully." The businessman motioned for his associates to look through the wagons' contents.

"I—I'll throw in the wagons." Kain nervously craned his large neck to keep an eye on the inspectors. "They're Roman. And—and the tools, animals, even the servant."

The men finished their inspection and signaled positively to their employer.

The businessman motioned for his aid to hand over a plain wooden box to Kain. "I see nothing awry here."

Kain reached for the payment.

"Stop!" The woman in blue stood over Yamin and bent to lift his chin and look into his eyes. "I will pay you double what he's asking for this piece of the merchandise."

Yamin spoke only loud enough for the strange woman to hear. "I'm not merchandise."

She winked at him and whispered, "I know, dear." Her defiance in the face of men and the onlookers impressed Yamin. She turned and spoke directly to Kain. "Do you accept?"

Kain looked at the merchant.

The merchant shrugged his shoulders. "I would take that offer. He's too skinny for my line of work."

Kain smirked at the woman. "Take him."

She produced double the amount of gold anyone would pay normally for a slave twice Yamin's strength and apparent health.

Kain held out his hand.

"May the Lord be with you. Farewell." She dropped the coins, and they clinked in his meaty palm.

Kain signaled to Porcius to free Yamin.

Yamin had no idea who this woman was and feared he might now be in a worse situation than the one he just left. But her look of genuineness and impeccable timing could only be of God. Her blessing upon Kain also gave Yamin a sense this woman was more than what she seemed.

She escorted Yamin into the city. Her rapid pace kept him struggling to keep up.

A numbness spread over his body such that he could not find the will to talk. He had been saved a second time and tried to wrap his head around the situation. One thing was certain. He would finally get to carry out the mission in this town.

Before long they approached a small but elegant house near the center of the city.

Yamin looked hard at that narrow crisscrossing streets. *I could make a break for it.* But would being a runaway slave be worse than what he was now? What *was* he now?

"Before we enter my house, I must introduce myself, Yamin. My name is Dita. And it's time to celebrate your unshackling."

53

A middle-aged man and woman greeted them with smiles as Yamin and Dita entered the foyer.

"We have another. Let's go." Dita spoke with the commanding voice of a centurion.

And the couple in her house answered her commands like soldiers, never questioning the order or even blinking an eye. *What power does she have over them?* Yamin wondered.

The pair approached. They moved to take Yamin's sandals and replace them from a collection of slippers near the door only to find him barefoot. They stared at Yamin wide-eyed.

Yamin smirked. "It's been a long couple of months."

They whisked him to the back of the house where a stone bath lined with marble tile waited.

The man introduced himself. "I am Adrastus."

His well-groomed appearance made Yamin feel a tinge of embarrassment.

Adrastus motioned to the woman as she departed. "My wife, Cordula." He helped Yamin remove his tattered clothing and aided him into the bath. He then produced fresh linen clothes.

When they finished, Cordula returned and escorted Yamin back into the main room where a meal of fresh fruit, bread, and warm lentil stew waited on a low table surrounded by multiple cushions.

Dita's absence confused him. He thanked his rescuers, if that is what they were, and after a few minutes of quiet eating he gathered up the courage to ask, "Where's Dita? I have a few questions."

Adrastus put more bread on Yamin's dish. "She had other matters needing her attention. Is there something I can help you with?"

"Where do I start?"

"You could start with what any former slave should ask if they come through that door."

"And what would—wait. Did you say, *former slave?*"

Cordula topped off Yamin's cup of wine. "We're both former slaves."

"But—I thought—is that what she meant when she said, *unshackling?*"

Cordula moved away from the table. "She likes to have fun."

Dita entered the room. "And still take the business of freeing the abused very seriously." She smiled at Yamin. "Sorry for the subterfuge, Yamin. But the local magistrate doesn't appreciate my particular line of work."

"Which is?"

"Liberating poorly treated slaves."

"You mean, I'm actually free?" Tears welled in Yamin's eyes.

"I can't save everyone, but here's *your* letter of manumission. It's what I've been preparing while you've enjoyed the morning meal. "Once I've filed it with the city magistrate, your freedom will be official."

Yamin took a deep breath. "Then, as much as I'd like to stay and repay your generous gift, I must leave." He stood.

Adrastus bolted upright.

Dita stopped him from acting with a wave of her hand. "If this is about what you said outside the gate this morning—about the others left behind—we're prepared to offer assistance. But first, sit and tell me why we should help you."

Yamin wished he had the time to tell the whole story. How would she believe him otherwise? "If you promise to help me rescue them, I promise to tell you the whole story—on the way."

Dita motioned for Adrastus to leave.

Yamin hoped it was to prepare for their departure.

Dita sat next to him. "Please, you need your strength." She looked into Yamin's eyes deeply. "There's something about you, isn't there?"

Yamin choked on a piece of fruit. "How do you mean?" This woman was twice Yamin's age. *I hope there aren't any strange attachments to this gift of freedom.*

Dita must have seen the worried look spread across Yamin's face, as she chuckled lightly.

"Yamin, I haven't been freeing slaves for very long. But in the past few months, I've come to know when one of my new recruits knows more than they should at their age. For example—"

She gently took hold of Yamin's wrist and held it up. Cordula gasped.

"These scars are far too extensive to have formed in just the last two months."

Yamin did not pull away. His wounds provided no source of embarrassment for him. They only served as evidence. "You're right. But I have no doubt that your story of how you came to be a rescuer of slaves is equally entertaining."

"I would say more enlightening than entertaining."

"Then perhaps we do share something in common."

Adrastus entered. "Ready."

Yamin stood.

Dita followed. "Then let's go."

The first night on the trail back to the volcano taxed Yamin's mental stamina. He tried his best to calculate how long it would take to meet up if they traveled all night, and the men had left the mining site immediately after he had sacrificed himself for them.

He hoped he would have the chance to tell his friend Amiy why he appeared to have abandoned them. He prayed it was not too late.

Yamin informed Dita while he navigated. "It would take about three days to walk from the volcano to Capitolias. If they left right after me, we should meet somewhere in the middle before sunrise tomorrow."

Adrastus drove the two oxen. He gave Dita a knowing look. "Seems right to me."

Dita surveyed the landscape. "You say it becomes so rocky that one can't walk without sandals?"

Yamin nodded. "And all they had were slave shoes."

"Only slightly better than barefoot." Adrastus coaxed the animals to speed up.

Dita agreed. "Since we have some time, I think we should share our stories now."

Yamin's heart fluttered. "As my host, you should go first."

"I will have to agree."

Yamin had hoped his audience would be larger than Dita and her aide. He adjusted his seating position to get more comfortable. *Whatever her story is, mine has got to be better.*

As Dita's story unfolded, Yamin felt his jaw drop farther and farther. She spoke of Jesus and the miracles he performed in Jerusalem. One in particular concerned a young woman named Pericope, and how Dita, herself, had been a slave. Born into slavery. And because of what Jesus had done through Pericope, she had been freed.

What are the chances both of our tales would be about the same Savior?

"I found the gold my former masters had stolen. It took days of hiking in and out of ravines, buried deep in shadow, but I found it. Large clay jars full of gold coins. It was then I knew the Lord approved of my plan."

"What plan?"

Adrastus spoke without taking his eyes off the ever-narrowing trail ahead. "To free people like you and me."

Yamin understood now. "Our stories are one in the same."

Dita scoffed.

"I too have been enslaved." He held out his scarred arms. "And Jesus saved me when I thought all was lost."

The shock on Dita's and Adrastus' faces put a smile on Yamin's.

He shared his story. Twice he had to remind Adrastus to stay on the trail, as his account often distracted the driver from his task.

Dita pause for a moment, deep in thought. "This must have been only months before Pericope's encounter."

Yamin thought about how long ago his meeting with Jesus had occurred. "I barely figured out the timing for this trip. But I'll agree with your assessment if you'll tell me how long you've been about the business of freeing slaves."

"Well, young man. You are only the third."

"Adrastus and Cordula?"

She nodded.

Adrastus smiled. "I'm surprised she told you about the gold."

"I usually save that part."

Yamin nodded. "Probably wise."

Adrastus shook the reins. "She didn't tell me until last week."

"But don't ask any more about it." She gave both men a stern look. "I've made certain the bulk of it will never be found by anyone but myself, so it matters not."

"Won't those who lost it come looking for it?"

"I left some where it had fallen. Amongst the rotting carcasses of two oxen." Her face scrunched up. "Didn't think I'd ever get that smell out of my clothing or my nostrils. Hopefully, if they do succeed, what remains will be enough to satisfy their avarice. As for me, the gold's purpose is clear—to rescue the abused and, with their help, spread the word of Jesus' miracles. Because their salvation is bought not by gold, but by the acts of the Lord."

As the sun touched the horizon, Yamin strained to see any sign of the abandoned miners in the distance.

A shuffle of rocks to the left made them swing their heads. Malevolent whispers from the right made Yamin's skin crawl. Shadows moved all around them.

Adrastus slowed the wagon and spoke softly. "Bandits, mistress."

Yamin cursed his misfortune. *Dear Lord, what have I gotten myself into now?*

54

The mysterious figures stopped moving.

Yamin took the chance. He reached to Adrastus and grabbed his shoulder.

Adrastus pulled on the reins and stopped the wagon. The crunching of the wheels on jagged stone came to a halt.

Yamin whispered to Dita. "Let's see who's out there." He stood and called out greetings in Latin, Greek, Aramaic, and even Hebrew. "Heus! Ya! Shlama! Shalom!"

Dita whispered, "I think you've covered them all."

"I know the Egyptian too, but I doubt they speak it."

A silhouette appeared to the left. "Yamin?"

"Amiy? Thank the Lord." Yamin jumped from the driver's bench and walked to his limping friend.

They embraced. "We thought you'd left us for dead."

"I'm sorry. It was the only way. It was my fault."

"Explain later. Right now, we need help. We had to abandon two to their deaths. The others can barely walk."

In minutes, the remaining seven slaves had been collected and sat or lay in the back of the wagon. The night air chilled them.

Dita produced coarse linen blankets from under the driver's bench. "We'll look after your wounds and provide a hot meal when we get back. But for now ..." She handed out bread and dried fruit.

Yamin poured water into a clay cup, and the men passed it around drinking heavily.

On the return trip, one of the men refused to eat or drink. He curled into a ball and stopped breathing. The others looked hopelessly at the thin, lifeless body. There was nothing they could do.

Where the trail met the road, Yamin and Adrastus dug a shallow grave. When they finished, both stood in silence. Adrastus spoke while keeping his eyes on the grave. "I'm thankful to have met you, Yamin. Before, it was just Dita's word, and I wasn't too sure about her truthfulness. Her sincerity about freeing slaves was genuine. But now I believe without any doubt that Jesus is real."

Yamin nodded and turned to walk back to the cart. "Faith so powerful surpasses even my own."

"How can that be? You've seen Jesus and been given a gift by his power."

"Have you and your wife not been given similar gifts by his power, albeit indirectly? If people can believe even though they've never seen him, how much greater their faith."

Upon returning to the others at the cart, Adrastus proclaimed his desire to return to his wife as fast as possible so she could be told Yamin's story. "You can all rest. I'll have us home by midday tomorrow."

By the next evening, the men's wounds had been cleaned and dressed. They rested in small groups on mats around the house as they outnumbered Dita's available rooms.

Two of the miners, Leander and Seleucus, sat alone in a dark corner whispering.

Yamin tried to recall as much as he could about the men. He wanted to trust them all to be gracious guests, but he just didn't know them well enough.

Amiy sat against the opposite wall with two others. None were quick to rise when Dita entered. Their feet remained too sore to stand on.

She scanned the large central room and met each of her newly rescued guests' eyes. She smiled.

Yamin felt the sincerity in her expression. Helping others in need always filled him with joy as well. He jumped when she turned to him and held out her hand. "Come, Yamin. We have much to discuss."

Yamin nodded to Amiy and locked eyes momentarily with Leander who squinted oddly in return before turning back to his pale-skinned friend Seleucus.

Dita led Yamin into the courtyard. Much smaller than the yards at Sophus' workshop or Sabinus' home in Canatha, only benches sat against the walls and sparse plants grew from cracks in the hard packed ground. As they sat on a bench, darkness shrouded their faces while their feet remained illuminated by the faint oil lamp's light spilling from the doorway.

Dita sighed. "I've a decision to make, Yamin. Since you are the only one in our present company to have witnessed Jesus' miracles besides myself, I feel you are the one I can trust most."

Yamin shifted uncomfortably in his seat. "What of Adrastus? You told him of the gold."

She placed her hand on his. "I feel I've taken on more than I can handle. Adrastus and Cordula, even though they are only two, they were the first two in my plan to rescue many. But the sacrifices I had to make. . . The task is far more dauting than expected. Just when I started to rethink my goals, I felt drawn outside the city and found you."

He wanted to say, "*It must have been Elohim who sent you.*" But he held his tongue. *Who am I to presume the Lord's plans?* Besides, he didn't want to sound entitled or haughty. Instead, he sheepishly admitted how fortunate he had been. "You were in the right place at the right time. And I'm grateful."

"But now? Look at them, Yamin. I've gone from two to ten in a matter of days. I can't just release them into the streets with no prospects."

"Why not? Those men have been torn from their families. Ripped from the lives they once had. I bet they can't wait to leave."

She pondered for a moment. "Did you tell all of them your story? Back at the volcano?"

"I had many chances. But like everywhere I've told it, there's a marked division between those who accept it as the truth and those who remain skeptical. Some to the point of anger."

She nodded, and a grim look spread across her face.

"You're worried about sharing your story with them? You did such a wonderful job relaying it to me on the road."

Dita smiled.

"I'd hold back the gold part for now. You took a chance by not knowing me very well, and it paid off. But I'd not take any more chances with this lot. Once you've given them hope and provided coverings for their feet, you can set them free and move on to a more acceptable pace of rescuing the suffering."

"Thank you, Yamin. I knew you'd be helpful." She stood. "But I'm asking you to stick around after I let them go. I believe that working together, you and I can make a bigger difference than I ever imagined. You are definitely a Godsend."

Goosebumps spread down Yamin's arms. *This is a turn I never expected my mission to take. But it makes so much sense at this moment. I couldn't access Capitolias before, but now I've been given a chance.* He thought of Amphion and how his duplicity had seriously disrupted Yamin's plans in Canatha. *I'll be more cautious this time.*

He thought of Melita, and not for the first time in these past two months. Not knowing if she had made it back to her parents ate at him. He planned to go back when the chance presented itself.

He followed Dita inside and sat with Amiy once more. Dita stood in the midst of the men and spoke. "I know you are all tired, but at least your wounds are tended and your bellies full. And now, I choose to inform you that your freedom is given." She waited for the news to sink in.

Yamin detected weak smiles from the men, who had been as unsure as Yamin only shortly before regarding this strange woman's intentions. He was not even sure if she had the rights to the men's ownership. Were they slaves or abductees?

Dita continued. "You are free to stay here until you feel well enough to travel back to where your lives once were." She glanced Yamin's way and nodded once. "I only ask this. You've heard Yamin's story of salvation. But you've not heard my own. I was once a slave, born into slavery, until just recently actually. Now a free citizen of Decapolis and of the Roman Empire, I can travel where I want, purchase what I desire, including slaves such as yourselves—and I can free whomever I wish.

"All of you except Yamin have been brought my way by circumstances I never intended. But I believe the Lord Elohim had His almighty hand in leading us all to this very moment. His interventions have brought Yamin to you, me to Yamin, and then you to freedom. This can't be coincidence." She looked around at the men. Their tired eyes fought to focus on her.

Leander yawned loudly.

Yamin shot him a corrective look.

Dita conceded. "For now, rest. Sleep in the comfortable knowledge that you are free from the dreadful situation you have endured by the hands of evil men. Dream of better circumstances, and tomorrow, when you wake to a hearty meal, I will entertain you with a tale I now know was meant to be told with Yamin's for all to hear."

She retired to her quarters leaving Adrastus to watch over them Yamin watched as Adrastus and Cordula extinguished the oil lamps and secured the doorways. Safe in his surroundings, he fell fast asleep. He'd not slept this well for months. He dozed so soundly, he did not hear the bumps and jostles of two men leave after midnight and take with them all of Dita's gold.

55

Leander never planned on being anyone's servant, paid or not. He wasn't even a resident of that stupid settlement outside Canatha when the slavers attacked. Swindling coins from the old ladies by weaving a tapestry of lies to play upon their sympathies had worked well in the past. And if not, robbing them at knifepoint proved successful as a backup plan.

Waking up in the back of that cart with Yamin and the others helped him develop a stout cover story as to how he ended up there with them. And although he found Yamin's narrative entertaining, it was not enough to dissuade him from his own greed-filled ambitions.

While Dita addressed the men, Leander spoke in hushed tones to his friend Seleucus. "I don't care if your feet hurt. Look at mine. This *woman*—" His disdain for the opposite sex showed itself by the stressed hisses accompanying those words. "She must have real money to dress like that and own a house like this. When we were bathing, I caught a glimpse of where I'm sure she keeps her money."

Seleucus, dim-witted as he was, nodded along. He had found protection with Leander while working at the volcano and never left his side since. Seleucus had been an outcast due to his odd, diminished pigmentation. Being captured and made to work with others had been an improvement from his life of rejection, destined to wander the countryside begging. Finally, somebody wanted him for something. And since Leander didn't fit in with the other men due to his complete lack of belief in anyone but himself, the two bonded readily in the sulfur fields.

Leander elbowed Seleucus. "Are you listening to me or her?"

Seleucus blinked several times. "You, definitely you."

They waited for everyone to settle in for the night. Leander watched the candle Cordula had left lit on the table. It burned at a constant rate allowing him to guess how many hours passed before making their move for the gold.

He shook Seleucus awake. Without a word, they rose taking small steps to avoid noise, but also to keep from wincing in pain.

Leander found the gold exactly where he thought it to be. Years of practice looking for nothing but the shortest distance between himself and another's money had given him adequate sense for it. More than once he had to redirect Seleucus to the task. But that proved nothing more than keeping him from bumping into furniture or tripping over the other men as they slept.

The leather satchel was not as large a stash as Leander had hoped for, but he could not chance searching any further without sounding an alarm. Besides, the bag contained more gold than he had ever held in his hands before. And keeping Seleucus quiet was a task at which he needed practice.

He motioned for them to leave. The locking mechanism on the front door squeaked then clicked at their escape. They left the door slightly ajar and hobbled off into the night with their ill-gotten fortune.

After several minutes, their bandages grew filthy from the dusty streets, and they had to stop before leaving the city. Both men fell asleep in a narrow alcove separating two parts of a three-part religious center. Known as the Temple of the Capitoline Triad, this worship venue honored Jupiter, Juno, and Minerva. And it was there that the two men were found the next morning.

"You can't sleep here, *rusticus*." Obviously not a morning person, the temple guard kicked Seleucus' feet. "Especially this *monstrum*."

The guard's partner laughed.

"Leave him alone." Leander moved between them and the groggy Seleucus. "We are simply resting."

"No one rests on the temple. Now move along before we call the soldiers for your blasphemous conduct."

"Blasphemous? We're not the ones spreading lies about god-men walking around the countryside casting out demons and—"

"What is this you speak of? God-man? Who speaks this way? Are they in the city?"

Leander looked at Seleucus.

Seleucus looked as confused as ever.

Leander gave the guards directions to Dita's house, mainly as a distraction from getting arrested himself. He had no idea what the consequences would be or what it would mean if Dita and Yamin were caught for religious sedition. He did not care.

"Adrastus, they took the gold!" Dita turned to Yamin.

He could not tell if her countenance indicated sorrow or regret. Either way, he sensed her disappointment. Not sure if an apology was appropriate, he decided to offer condolences. "I guess you didn't need to tell them about the gold anyway." He shrugged and bit his lip nervously.

Adrastus took on a protective stance by raising his shoulders. "You brought these men into Dita's home, and it is your—"

"No, Adrastus." Dita held up her hand. "Do not be so quick to judge Yamin. This is as much my own fault as anyone else's."

The time to apologize arrived. "I'm sorry for the inconvenience." He thought back to his deal with the doctor who tried to save his father's life. "I can offer you my services—inasmuch as its worth for your efforts—and your loss."

Dita smiled. "Adrastus, have Cordula hand out the travel supplies to the others and send them on their way." She turned to Yamin.

Amiy now stood by his side. He had walked over after overhearing the troubling discussion.

Dita continued. "Yamin, you are free to go with them, but I would ask you to stay with us for a little longer. If it makes you feel better, I accept your offer for assistance. But only temporarily and only to help me discern future liberations."

"I've still work to do here in Capitolias. That sounds agreeable."

"You'll be compensated, of course."

Yamin's brow furrowed. "I don't understand. Didn't they take all the money?"

She let out a small chuckle. "A drop in the bucket, Yamin. I've enough gold to buy a thousand slaves. But it means our first task is to take a trip south."

"South? To where?"

"Jerusalem."

56

Yamin could not help but think of Melita in Canatha and Dar back in Hippos. A trip to Jerusalem would mean he could still spread the word of his encounter with Jesus at Gadara and Pella. But he would have to backtrack east to visit Philadelphia and Gerasa before crossing the Jordan to Scythopolis. Only then would he be done and in position to return to his friends, his mission accomplished.

He calculated the entire trip would take no more than a few weeks, barring any more unforeseen incidents and continued good weather. The time included stayovers in all six cities. Too bad his map had been taken when he was captured. Instead, he drew in the sand from memory the layout of the cities he had yet to visit, his landmarks being the Jordan, the Sea of Galilee, and Hippos.

He explained it to Dita. "We only need to stay long enough to tell my—*our*—stories in each city."

Adrastus craned his neck to view the map. "I would say this to be a wise plan, but we have no money to stay in these places. It would be better to leave visiting cities for another time."

Dita and Yamin looked at him.

"Maybe tell stories to people on the road?" Adrastus sheepishly offered.

Cordula half turned from her chore of readying supplies for the remaining freedmen. She nonchalantly added, "*We* have money."

Dita's eyes widened.

"It's true. Isn't it, Adrastus? We've saved almost everything you've paid us these past months."

A look of worry spread over Adrastus' face.

Dita saw it and put her hand on his shoulder. She whispered, "I'll consider it a loan and pay you back—with interest."

He smiled.

Yamin stood. "Then it's settled. When do we leave?"

"Since we've exhausted our supplies here with this latest incursion of guests, I'd say as soon as possible."

Moments later, Dita escorted the men to the front of the house and spoke. "Your lives before you were made slaves await you. I'm sorry I couldn't provide more. In payment, I only ask this: that you share my story and Yamin's with your friends and family. This good news that the Lord Elohim has sent a savior in the name of Jesus must be told to everyone you meet. It is because of His good deeds that you are now free. Go, and use that freedom to serve Him."

Amiy stood at the front. After Dita's farewell speech, he addressed Yamin. "You've been a good friend, Yamin. I have half a mind to join you in your mission. But I have family that need me at home."

"Thank you, Amiy. May the Lord bless your travels."

The two embraced. Yamin watched the men walk off. Their new sandals left numerous prints in the dusty street. *Time to make prints of our own.* He looked up to see a group of soldiers headed with purpose in his direction.

He turned to find Dita.

She was already making for the door. "You better hurry inside, young man." They entered the house and bolted the door. "Let's hope they didn't see us."

Yamin's heart pounded. "Let's pray they're not looking for us all."

Bang! Dust flew from the edges of the entrance.

Adrastus had already found Cordula. He whispered to Dita. "What do they want?"

From outside, an authoritative voice penetrated the closed door. "We have reports you are harboring a seditionist, a blasphemer against Rome, within your walls. Open or we will enter by force."

"No time to discuss the hows and whys." Yamin tugged at Dita's sleeve and the others followed. "Where does your courtyard lead?"

"Wait." Dita turned a corner in the back of the kitchen. "This way."

Behind the large clay oven, a shelving unit hid a narrow doorway. As they entered, Dita explained. "In my final days as a slave, I learned how fast moments of serenity and security can turn to those of panic and danger. When I first purchased this house, I also bought the adjacent smaller one just for this reason." Dita asked for help as she pushed a heavy wooden piece of furniture to expose the secret escape just slim enough to squeeze through one at a time.

They all passed through and pulled the furniture back into place behind them when the front door crashed onto the floor.

Dita whispered in the dark. "It cost a bit of gold for the labor and took a few days but was worth the effort wouldn't you say?"

They felt their way through the dark neighboring house as the sounds of rummaging next door diminished. There they stayed, huddled in a corner, until the soldiers left minutes later.

"A few probably remain in case we return." Yamin stretched. "Does this place have a back door?"

They snuck into the alleyway behind the row of houses.

Dita sighed. "There's no way we can access the cart and oxen from here."

Adrastus picked up his supplies. "I guess we walk." He looked at Yamin. "Looks like we'll have time to stay in your cities after all."

Mid-morning brought warm spring sunlight, and the air along the road south held less moisture. As the dry season approached, Yamin yearned for the Galilean shore. He kept the memory of his home, only a short distance northwest of here, fresh in his mind while traveling through Decapolis.

The image of Melita's face inspired him to keep moving forward. The faster this mission was done, the sooner he could return to her. Would she go back to Hippos with him? Or was she too fixated on adventure? Yamin did not mind discovering new places, but he wanted to settle down. These past couple of years had been a whirlwind of newness, and he needed a rest.

Sabinus and Rena's voices echoed in his mind as well. Every time he spoke to anyone on the road who would listen to his story, their words rang in his ears. Most of his traveling audience were pleasantly entertained while they journeyed alongside Dita's entourage. Some regarded Yamin's advances as a nuisance and shooed him away. He counted them as *the other half* and moved on to the next opportunity.

In Gadara, they found a modest inn and slept in a single room. Happy to have escaped persecution at the hands of the unforgiving Capitolias guard, Dita questioned how they found out. "We had only just arrived. And no one left the house."

"Except for those two who robbed you." Adrastus rolled over attempting to get comfortable next to Cordula. "I knew that pale fellow was strange."

"Oh, Adrastus." Cordula swatted his arm.

He chortled. "Could they have told anyone after sneaking off?"

"I can't imagine they had enough time to do anything." Yamin yawned. "It had only been a few hours, and we were no threat to them."

Dita neatly folded the ends of the linens around her bed essentially tucking herself in. "It will always remain a mystery. I like to think the Lord had other plans for us all and wanted some action in our steps."

"We'll see what tomorrow brings." Yamin decided to find the local rabbi first thing in the morning. He had good fortune with such leaders in the previous cities and hoped it held true here.

"The Lord is already there." Dita turned over and blew out the single oil lamp in the room.

57

The morning greeted the travelers with a panorama of the surrounding countryside, something they had not seen when arriving at dusk yesterday. The hillsides fell away on three sides of the city exposing the wide verdant Jordan River valley and the mountains to the southwest separating them from Jerusalem. Another sight, an open-air theatre, much like the one Yamin found on Malta, stood behind their inn. Its bright colonnades and archways with clean lines reflected the newness of its construction.

A calmness spread over him as he ate a breakfast of wheat pancakes with dates and honey. The last two months had been a living nightmare. Different than that of being possessed, of course. And he would take the living over the dead any day. Had he found his place now? With all the political and religious upheaval in these so-called autonomous cities of Decapolis, it was hard to tell. *Is this the path I need to be on? Jerusalem is not in Decapolis. But I can't thanklessly abandon Dita after what she has done for me. Is not Jesus' mission more important?*

Dita startled him from his thoughts. "Are you ready, dear?"

Careful to not let slip his concerns, Yamin decided to stay on the current course until the next city, Pella. Then he would have to decide if his mission could wait until after his debt to Dita was paid or not.

They made straight for the local synagogue after breakfast. Yamin sensed Dita's excitement as she walked next to him. He too felt elation kindling yet another spark in a dark corner of their world.

Adrastus and Cordula had fallen behind. Over his shoulder, Yamin witnessed Adrastus stop to speak to a clothing merchant. He took hold of Dita's arm and stopped her to wait for them to catch up.

Adrastus approached with a sullen face and whispered his news.

"No synagogues?" Yamin spoke a little too loudly and several citizens, pompous and proper, turned up their noses at the mention of anything Jewish.

Adrastus continued to keep his voice low. "I've asked several merchants, and they all say the same thing. The last of the Jews were scoured from the streets months ago."

"Scoured? To where?" Yamin could not help but think if he had not been waylaid by the slavers, he could have contacted the local rabbi before their forced removal. His skin flushed.

"They say the outer villages. The only remaining synagogue was converted to a stable, I think."

"You *think*?"

"Well, he had a strange accent. I think he said stable." Adrastus looked at Cordula for confirmation.

She shrugged her shoulders. "Maybe?"

Yamin's hopes at making a change in this city diminished.

Dita took his arm in hers. "We'll find them. We'll find someone to share with before we leave."

Yamin sighed. "You're right. But tolerance seems to be at a low point here."

Dita nodded and held Yamin's arm a little tighter.

As they walked through the city, shoppers drifted along the street in a steady tide from counter to counter buying, bargaining, and browsing the market's goods.

One building stood out from the rest in that it had an arched façade instead of straight lines. Various loaves of fresh bread lined its storefront counter. And inside the stall selling the bread stood —

"Melita?"

"Yamin?" Melita's smile beamed. She sped around the display and leapt at him. "What are you doing here?"

Her joy spread to the others in a wave of relief.

Yamin grabbed hold of her, and they embraced. He studied her face as if making sure it was truly his friend. "I could ask the same."

"My parents—we—I thought you were dead."

"I thought you were going to say I ran away."

"At first, but I know you too well. I knew there must have been another reason. But you do have some explaining to do."

Yamin looked around the shop. "As do you."

They both chuckled uneasily.

Dita stepped up. "I believe we all deserve explanations."

"Forgive me, Dita." Yamin stepped back and made the proper introductions.

"Saved you? Another savior, huh? Yamin, you're the most unfortunate and, at the same time, fortunate man I know."

"You have no idea. Let me tell you what happened, and then you can tell me how you ended up here."

Melita called inside for another worker to take her place at the counter. "Come, my parents are going to be so surprised." She motioned for Adrastus and Cordula to follow them.

As they entered, a grand room welcomed them. A mill ground grain into flour, and ovens glowed with embers of charcoal. The smells made Yamin wish he had waited for breakfast.

"Our house is up those stairs." Melita pointed. "It's not like what we had in Canatha but—"

"Yamin!" Sabinus entered from a back door carrying a basket. He placed it on the stone floor and held his arms out. Rena spun from toiling near the ovens and gasped. After their heartfelt reunion, Yamin's party joined Melita and her parents at a table in the great room.

Yamin looked around the interesting space. "This doesn't look like any bakery I've seen."

Sabinus passed around a basket of bread. "That's because it used to be the synagogue."

Yamin slowly turned to look at Adrastus and squinted. "How can you confuse stable for bakery?"

Adrastus shrugged. "What can I say? I'm not very good at translating."

Dita snorted while controlling a laugh.

Rena filled their cups with wine. "After being forcibly removed from Canatha, we decided to head for our associates in Jerusalem. But when we arrived here, this opportunity presented itself."

"And how convenient it was." Sabinus held up his cup. "To fortuitous circumstances and the reuniting of friends."

Yamin felt Melita's stare. They locked eyes, and a warm feeling spread through his chest. His palms started to sweat. He cleared his throat. "And all thanks to the Lord Elohim."

"And just when we thought your story was all we needed a few months ago." Sabinus sipped his wine. "Melita tells me you've another tale to tell."

"As do I." Dita's formal posture and sudden seriousness sent a coolness through the oven-warmed room.

Yamin shifted in his seat. "Yes, we've been sent running from our previous location too. My mission, as you're all aware, still continues, even after what I've endured these past two months."

"Endured?" Melita's concerned look warmed Yamin with its sincerity.

Yamin proceeded to share his ordeal, and much to Sabinus and Rena's delight, did not skip any of the gory details. Melita adhered to every word.

Of all the times Yamin had shared a story, any story, until his final days, this remained his most memorable one. It even surpassed his memories of telling fishing stories to his mother when his father had taken him out on the lake for the first time. He could not remember anyone caring more about his welfare than Melita at this moment. And it placed a decision in his path.

Dita interrupted where their two stories became one. Yamin motioned for her take over the telling. She began her part of the story with the woman Pericope and how she had come to the task of rescuing abused slaves. But she refrained from any mention of gold.

When she finished, Yamin gave her a knowing wink. *A wise exclusion of the facts.* After what happened with Leander, trust became as precious as the gold she needed for her mission. After living with Melita and her family for over a month, Yamin knew he could trust them. But he knew Dita could not.

Melita had been sitting to Yamin's right since they gathered at the low table. Halfway through his story, her hand found his. He clung to it, exploring every feature with his fingertips from her knuckles to the fine ridges of her prints. He memorized it all.

And at that moment, Yamin fell in love.

More unexpected than anything that had happened to him in these past tumultuous years, this feeling confused him. Elation battled disappointment. *What about my mission? Would she join me? Could I expose her to the dangers involved? Or is this the Lord releasing me from my assigned task?*

Sabinus' voice snapped him back to attention. "A noble cause, Dita. I, myself, don't believe in owning slaves. Not that we could afford any, right Rena?"

Rena smiled. "Yes, husband. And we've found—other uses for slaves in our line of work."

Dita's brow furrowed. "And that would be?"

Yamin tensed.

Sabinus answered for her. "You see, slaves will often propagate news faster than others not so in-line with local beliefs and rituals."

A pensive look spread over Dita's face.

Rena added, "Simply put, they have a willingness to help spread the word."

"And what word would that be?"

Sabinus poured more wine into Dita's cup. "Melita, would you explain to our guests how we found a home here in Gadara?"

Melita squeezed Yamin's hand then released it from under the table. "Of course, father." She turned to Yamin. "Yamin knows only up to the day he was taken. When I returned home, I thought things would return to normal. Instead, we found our welcome to be just another false promise from Amphion. He may have tried to serve on our side but was overwhelmed with the pressures from the temple leaders. It was either make a bold statement of his faith, *their faith*, by producing results or be utterly shunned and ousted from society. He chose the former, and my family was the result." She placed her hand on Sabinus' shoulder. "They seized our home and possessions and escorted us out of the city in broad daylight for all to see. An example of what happens to non-conformists."

Yamin sighed. "I must accept some of the blame for what happened. Amphion may not have shown his true self had I never met you on the road and stayed in your home." He did not mean for his comment to entice sympathy. He received it, nonetheless.

"Nonsense, boy." Sabinus motioned for Melita to continue. "The best part is coming."

"Everything for a reason, Yamin." Rena placed her hand on Sabinus' other shoulder.

Melita continued. "They took everything. We had my parents' traveling experience and the road before us. Nothing more."

"Well—" Rena smiled slyly.

"Mother, let me, please. I'm getting there." She smiled at Yamin. "I've told the story of our travels several times before, and she always thinks I'll forget this part. I was in tears. First, Yamin disappeared and now we were homeless."

Yamin could not resist. The happiness he found in her caring for him so spread a smile across his face. Once he realized its inappropriateness, he reeled it in.

"We left the others behind. They weren't implicated so didn't suffer in our public removal. It was just my parents and me. Then the rain started."

58

City Administrator Crius paced the floor of his palatial home near the temple of Neptune. Clearly the patron god of the sea influenced the designers of this house where he now found himself the new master. The mosaic on which his wide sandals tread depicted an enormous green glass and gold image of the deity riding a chariot through the waves pulled by two regal horses with serpentine mermaidesque tails.

Crius studied the tines of Neptune's trident, inlaid with glints of blue glass, for what he figured to the be thousandth time. "Your news vexes me, Sostratus."

Sostratus, the local Roman Commander, oversaw the auxiliary regiment made up of citizens. His gray hair spoke of time served for the Empire. He stood in respectful attention at the edge of the Neptunian tile arrangement.

"The numbers of refugees from our neighboring cities in the Decapolis grows daily." Crius finally stopped marching and met eyes with Sostratus from the across the round room. "And you want me to give an order to block their entrance to Gadara?"

"My men are spread thin, Praefect."

"What of our economy? Less visitors means less taxes."

"With respect, these are not the kind of visitors you seek. They are not coming to browse the markets or trade goods. They come for aid."

Crius thought for a moment then chuckled nervously. "Where? Where have they been going since we opened our gates months ago?"

"As I've reported weekly, Praefect—"

Crius raised an eyebrow of caution toward the commander. Sostratus shifted his weight. "—since your arrival, that is, there have been several arrests, others simply beg at the gates, and some stay a few days then pass through. Some have even obtained employment."

"Employment? Mixing with our populace? I hope they're Roman citizens, commander. Are you checking for tessera?"

"Yes, Praefect."

"And faithful? They're not Jews, are they?"

"I think my men have made it clear to any newcomers. They're place is in the villages outside our walls."

Crius nodded and produced an agreeing grunt. "We must continue to maintain a pocket of decorum in our fair city."

"Yes, Praefect."

"You say some have taken up residence and are working?" Sostratus nodded.

"Just to be sure, tell me where."

Sostratus thought for a moment. "A prominent example would be the new bakery, in the former Jewish synagogue."

Crius' eyes widened. "Interesting. Very interesting."

The cramped quarters on the second floor above the bread ovens welcomed Dita and her party. Her reservations about staying in the city another night diminished when she watched Yamin's reactions at dinner. *What am I to do with him? He seems to be in good hands with these people, and Melita appears to enjoy his company immensely.*

But this city's religious restrictions were as harsh as any other in Decapolis. She wondered if coming this way from Jerusalem had been a good idea in the first place. The trip to pick up a new supply of hidden temple treasure had taken her northwest, so she deemed that as good a direction as any to look for those in need of rescuing. But would moving around all the time be the norm?

Would sacrificing geographic stability be worth her efforts to save the abused? She hoped so.

Dita stared up through the small window into the spring night sky. Sparse clouds swept by making the myriad of stars blink in and out of view. Yamin slept near the door. Adrastus and Cordula lay entwined in the corner opposite the window. As they slept, their soft rhythmic breaths calmed her until sleep tugged her eyelids.

A shuffle at the entrance snatched her moment of serenity. A hand from the darkness beyond the doorway pierced the beam of starlight. Yamin's hand reached out and the two grasped each other. *Melita.* Dita could not decide if she was trouble or another wave of salvation for Yamin.

She made it her plan to find out before determining what to do with him. Legally, she still owned him.

Yamin's heart leapt when Melita's face appeared in the doorway. She pulled him up, and they whisked themselves quietly down the uneven stairs.

A single oil lamp on the table projected flickering shadows all over the room.

Melita sat and produced a loaf of intricately woven bread and ripped it in two. "It's time. Sit." She sighed and pulled over a small bowl of yellow etrog fruit.

Yamin sat at the end of the table next to her and eyed the food. "Time for what, a midnight snack?"

She handed him half the loaf. "In lieu of a Knot of Hercules."

"A wha—"

"*Shhh.*" She touched the tip of her finger to his lips. "Here." She handed Yamin a knife with a short triangular blade and handle made of bone. "Cut one in half."

Yamin sighed and sliced the yellow citrus in unequal halves. A droplet of juice orbisculated into his eye. He brought his hand up to his face to rub the sting away and nearly stabbed himself in the other eye in the process.

Melita stifled a laugh. She held up the other half of the loaf and one half of the etrog with her elbows on the table then motioned for him to do the same.

He blinked hard and followed her lead. He trusted her and expected only good to come from whatever this enigmatic ritual was she performed for him.

She took a deep breath. "We've known each other for months. You lived in my parents' house, we've taken walks, worked hand in hand." Tears welled up in her eyes. "And when you were taken—" She lost her composure.

Yamin put down the food and took her hands in his. "I know. I feel the same way. Don't cry. Everything's all right now, yes?"

Melita sniffled and wiped her tears on the sleeve of her white tunic. "Yes, everything's all right now. I used to live my life as if nothing were miraculous. Just upheavals and interruptions. Disappointments with an occasional string of good luck. And now, thanks to you, I see miracles everywhere." She picked up the food again.

"Oh." Yamin did the same.

She took a deep breath. "I'm stating my desire to be betrothed to you."

Yamin froze. *Betrothed?* Marriage had been the furthest idea from his mind since, well, forever. He knew he loved her but never brought the emotion to this conclusion.

Melita pushed the halves of her bread and fruit to Yamin's halves making them whole again. "I want to join you in your mission."

The desire to kiss her overwhelmed him. He launched his upper body across the narrow table until his lips met hers.

Melita hungrily returned his affection as they embraced.

A voice from the back of the room snapped them out of their moment of contentment. "Well, I guess that does it."

They jumped away from each other and squinted at the interloper. Dita had witnessed their private impromptu engagement ceremony. She walked over and plopped herself down next to Yamin with a quiet grunt. "Now, what do we do with you?" She turned to Melita and studied her with a penetrating gaze. "With both of you?"

59

The next morning, Yamin woke to Adrastus and Cordula mildly disagreeing in their corner of the room. Dita had apparently risen earlier. Sunlight now streamed through the window onto her empty sleeping mat.

Yamin's stirring silenced the couple. Adrastus produced a weak smile. "I hear the news is good, Yamin."

Cordula remained stoic.

"Dita?"

Cordula harrumphed. "Now, you'll be staying here, I guess."

He had not thought about what happens next. But that did seem to be a logical possibility. He propped himself up on his elbows. "Maybe. That upsets you?"

Adrastus stood. "We had plans of leaving on our own. Dita said we were free. We only stayed with her this long out of respect. She needs help to accomplish her goals. Once she found you, well—"

Cordula finished for him. "We figured you'd stay with her for a while. You know, take our places."

"And now you feel you're stuck. If I stay here, that is."

She nodded.

Yamin stood to meet Adrastus' eye. "I can make no promises. You'll have my answer by noon." He left to find Melita. Before speaking to Dita, he needed to know more about what his wife-to-be expected him to do.

When Yamin entered the kitchen, the pungent aroma of

fermented dough filled his nostrils. Melita had already started working before sunrise, as was expected by her parents. Rena mixed ingredients in a large wooden vessel while Sabinus tended to the already busy storefront. The sounds of the marketplace in the street flooded the room and stirred excitement, and hunger, in Yamin.

He announced his arrival. "What's for breakfast?"

Rena smiled sarcastically and thrust a lump of gooey herb-infused dough into his hands. "After the morning rush. Bring this to Melita. She'll show you what to do with it."

Happy to oblige, Yamin strode over to the two large clay ovens where Melita arranged different loaves inside with a long, dark, wooden spatula. "Good morning."

Melita stopped and smiled softly at him. "Welcome to what my world's been reduced to."

He looked around. "I've been in worse worlds. This one's not so terrible."

Yamin helped for about an hour until the crowd outside diminished.

Adrastus and Cordula spent that time sitting at the table and studying the action.

Sabinus entered. "Melita, hope you've eaten." He motioned for her to take his place at the counter. He sat at the table with Rena and their guests.

Melita sighed, grabbed some bread and fruit from the table, and motioned for Yamin to join her.

A cool morning breeze met his face as he stepped into the small sales area. Several baskets of bread surrounded him. Melita plopped onto a low stool. He searched for another and when he came up short, he sat at her feet.

They ate in silence for a minute before Melita spoke. "They're not going to be happy."

"Who?"

"My parents—when I tell them about us."

"Why not?" Yamin's voice carried into the street and several shoppers looked his way. He lowered his stature and repeated sotto voce. "Why not?"

Melita placed the food on the ground and joined him cross-legged on the floor. "Your parents are gone, so decisions like marriage and going where you want are much easier for you."

Yamin could not disagree. But why had she performed that ritual last night if she had not thought of the consequences beforehand? "You think they'll not allow you to leave with me?"

"They need me. This is our life now. It's too hard spreading dissent when you've been exiled from every major city, and it's only getting worse. We're playing with our lives at this point."

"I need to leave, Melita. And you heard Dita last night. She's released me. I'm free to continue my mission. *Our* mission."

She stood to collect money from a female customer for two loaves.

"You make that much for a loaf?"

"Two loaves, but yes."

"Your parents are doing well, then."

"And that's why staying is necessary. They are trying to save enough to leave and start doing what they did before."

"But last night you said you wanted to join me." His brow furrowed. "Hadn't you thought that out before betrothing yourself to me?"

The shiny coins in Melita's hand reflected the mid-morning sunlight. "I think I have a solution—to everyone's problem."

Later, after midday, Dita returned from her survey of the city.

Melita had just finished giving Adrastus and Cordula a thorough tour of the workings of the bakery, and they all sat at the table for the midday meal.

Sabinus poured the wine. "And what do you make of Gadara, Dita? Thinking of calling it home?"

Dita scoffed. "Sorry, that was not meant for you, but for the idea of staying in one place long enough to call it home. Having been a slave as long as I can remember, I've never had a home to speak of. I believe I've come to like a more transient way of things."

"We enjoy the home base idea. Even though finding one permanent has been challenging."

"This looks well enough." Dita scanned the room. "If I were so inclined, I would ask to hire on. How miraculous it would be to work as a free person and earn wages."

Adrastus put down his cup with a thud. "I am glad you brought that up, Dita. You see, Cordula and I," he looked at Yamin then back to Dita, "we've decided to stay here and do just what you suggested."

Dita's jaw dropped. "You mean, you're leaving me?"

Yamin swept in to save Adrastus from having to defend himself. "That's because Melita and I have decided to stay with you. As long as I can complete my mission through Decapolis."

Now it was Sabinus and Rena's jaws that dropped.

Rena gasped when she realized what Yamin had said. "You mean, *you're* leaving *us?*"

Sabinus stood and spoke to Melita. "You can't. We need you here."

"Father, Adrastus and Cordula will more than twice replace me." Melita turned to her mother. "You've been wanting more help. Trustworthy help."

No one spoke for moment.

Melita helped her mother stand and pulled her parents to the side. She motioned for Yamin to join them. When he did, she took her parents' hands in hers. "Yamin and I performed the ceremony last night."

Yamin, expecting the worst, readied himself by withdrawing from Sabinus' reach ever so slightly.

Sabinus took Rena's other hand and sighed. "You promise to uphold our beliefs?"

Rena shook off their hands, took a step back, and raised her voice. "No, Sabinus."

"Mother, I—"

Sabinus raised his hand to stop Melita from continuing. He looked at his wife. "We knew this day would come."

Rena eyed Yamin then met her husband's gaze. "His mission. It's dangerous."

"No more than ours has ever been."

"But Melina never had to endure such perils."

"Until recently, Mother." Melita walked over and took her hands in hers once more. "I've learned much about being discreet. We'll be careful."

Tears welled in Rena's eyes. "You promise to visit?"

Melita smiled and hugged her mother. "Of course."

"Then we better celebrate."

Sabinus walked to the counter, brought in the baskets, and closed the door. "Come, Yamin. We can afford to take a holiday for the rest of the day. Rena, more wine."

Evening approached, and the household had spent the afternoon telling stories and speaking of what the future held until a forceful knock on the door sobered them.

Sabinus stood. "Probably a regular customer wondering why we're closed so early." He opened the door to find an Imperial Commander standing with several soldiers and a stuffy city official.

The Commander took a step forward. "I, Sostratus, have been sent by Praetor Crius to inquire regarding the status of your employment and occupation of this dwelling." He stood aside to allow the city official access to Sabinus.

The official approached, studied the surroundings and Sabinus, then jotted something onto a piece of parchment. "Your purpose in this establishment?"

Sabinus stammered as Rena approached and stood just behind him to one side. "I have the proper documents for occupation here, I can assure you."

"That is not what I asked." The self-important functionary stomped his foot. "What is the purpose of this establishment? I see no wares, no signage. And you smell of wine."

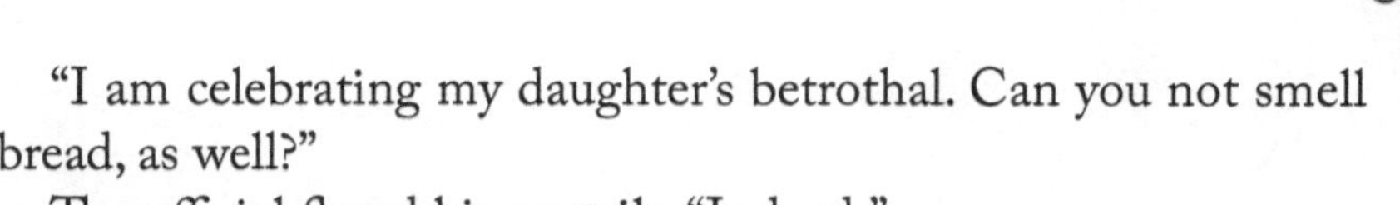

"I am celebrating my daughter's betrothal. Can you not smell bread, as well?"

The official flared his nostrils. "Indeed."

"This is a bakery, a fine one at that. We've been working here for almost two months. We pay our taxes. Why the investigation? Why now?"

Yamin's heart raced. *This is about me. Please, Lord, don't let this be about me.*

Melita must have noticed Yamin's worry. She took his hand and whispered, "We have a back door."

That's when Adrastus grabbed a basket of bread, handed another to Cordula, and headed for the counter. He burst into the scene and started setting up the sales area pretending to not notice the men.

Cordula caught on fast. "Bread! Fresh bread! Oh, forgive the intrusion, my masters." She backed away sheepishly.

Adrastus did the same.

The official scrutinized them then jotted down something else on the parchment. He turned to Sostratus and nodded once.

Sostratus approached Sabinus. "Felicitations." He turned and led his men away.

Sabinus waited until the men turned a corner before hugging Adrastus. "Oh, you're going to fit in here quite nicely."

"Thank you, Master. I mean, thank you."

"Sabinus is fine." He turned to face the others in the main room. "Now, where were we?"

60

The next morning Yamin and Melita accepted a barrage of fare-wells from Melita's parents, as well as from Adrastus and Cordula. Yamin promised he would protect Melita with his life. "We'll try to find the Jewish settlement outside the city before moving on to Pella. I wish I could give you more information about when we'll be back, but—"

"We know, son." Sabinus hugged him. "We're not going anywhere."

Rena beamed. "And when you get back, we'll have the public ceremony." She turned to Sabinus. "Maybe in June?"

The couple departed with Dita. All were weighed down with food, water, and extra clothes.

A brief, light rain shower met them outside the city while they cautiously inquired of settlers about the location of the banished Gadara rabbi and his followers. They met with little success. The people's guarded replies made Yamin's teeth clench every time. *Will someone turn us in just for asking?* He contemplated his next move, but not without involving the women.

"I feel we need to leave."

Dita took their lack of success as an omen. "We won't last long without my funds. And if we ask the wrong person, we'll get that commander hunting for us."

Melita shuddered. "And that would lead them back to my parents."

Yamin sat on a rock and sighed. "I've been feeling the same for a while now. But how am I supposed to carry out my mission if I can't tell anyone here about Jesus?"

Melita sat next to him. "My parents aren't going anywhere, Yamin. They have established themselves in the community and, when the time's right, will use their skills and your story to disrupt the system."

Yamin jumped from the rock. "That's just it, Melita. I don't want to disrupt *anything*. But everywhere I go, that's what happens. Jesus told me to share my experience, to tell everyone in my home what the Lord had done for me. Decapolis is my home. But every time I do, people get hurt. Why?"

Dita stood by as poised and calm as ever. In a soft voice she answered him. "Because Jesus *is* disruption—to the non-believer. He's a thorn in the side of the oppressive status quo, the ultimate ingredient for change."

"But how do you change something so powerful? When so many are offended by the simple mention of a miracle or a single god?" He plopped back down onto the rock with a huff. How could he continue his mission? He did not wish to subject Melita to the dangers involved in spreading the word of Jesus. He balled his fists.

A flash of twisted possession gripped his chest. A legion of voices rang out for an instant, all screaming in discorded terror. His eyes widened, and his heart fiercely beat. Only a memory. But enough to snap him out of his downward spiral of negativity. *Thank you, Jesus.*

Melita grabbed his arm and spoke softly. "We'll figure this out together, my love."

My love. No one had referred to him in such a way since his mother. And he felt nothing as strong since his brief encounter with Jesus. His heart melted, and he fell to his knees when he understood what a miracle Melita herself had become. *We need to pray.* He reached out to take Melita and Dita's hands.

They joined him on the sandy ground. Drying grass and weeds crunched under their weight, releasing their herbal scents.

"Elohim, the one true god, thank you." Yamin drew in a deep

breath and slowly released it. It was the deepest gratitude he had ever imagined. Yes, his salvation from demonic control had been miraculous. But when the miracles kept coming, when the gift of a new life allowed the miracles to be visible— "You've provided time and again. And we've heeded your wisdom. Forgive me when I've doubted you."

Dita interjected when he paused. "Bless our travels and our missions, Elohim."

Yamin gave Melita's hand a gentle squeeze to let her know it was all right to add something.

Melita hesitated, cleared her throat, and stammered. "I—we—"

Yamin squeezed her hand again and looked at her. He mouthed, "You can do it."

She followed Yamin's lead and took in a deep cleansing breath before proceeding. "I agree with what they said." She opened one eye and sought condonation from Yamin.

He nodded and motioned for her to continue.

She took another great lungful of air and started again. "My parents believe in one god, a man-god, who walks the Earth with us. If Yamin says that Jesus is this god, your servant, then I'd have to agree. Since meeting Yamin, I've been privileged to many blessings. I can only assume they've been provided by you for your holy purpose."

Yamin eyes widened. *The miracles.*

Melita must have sensed his surprise and opened her eyes. "What? Did I say something wrong?"

Dita chuckled. "No, dear. You did just fine."

Yamin produced a contented smile. "Amen."

They stood.

"Now what?" Melita scanned their surroundings.

Dita sighed. "No sign of your rabbi anywhere, Yamin." She met his eyes. "I have a suggestion that might help."

Yamin squinted, first at Dita's comment, then over her shoulder to a rising commotion from the city gate in the distance. Several soldiers pushed their way through the travelers on the road then into the nearest row of tents.

Melita lowered her stature. "They're looking for someone."

Yamin studied his wife-to-be's face and wondered how he would be able to continue without incessantly worrying about her safety. He grabbed Dita's and Melita's sleeves and tugged them in the direction away from the soldiers. "Dita, let's hear your idea."

By sunset, they reached the outskirts of the next Decapolis city to the south, Pella. This is where Yamin would say good-bye to Melita and Dita. Parting ways had been Dita's plan to allow him to continue his mission and keep Melita away from any of the negative consequences typically involved in the telling of his experience.

The difficult terrain had tired them out, so their priority was finding an inn. Sabinus provided Melita with enough money to stay in luxury, but Dita's wisdom prevailed and they settled on modest accommodations not far from the city's nymphaeum, a semi-circular monument surrounding a voluminous natural spring.

The constant sound of flowing water helped lull Yamin to sleep. But it was the proximity to Melita that calmed his spirit the most. Every breath of hers, the rising and falling of her torso against his, was like a soothing breeze. It reminded him of how it felt sailing his father's boat on the Sea of Galilee. When all was still, a warm wind would stir the mirror-like surface and rock the vessel ever so slightly reminding him he was still alive and able to sense his surroundings no matter what negative emotions plagued him.

He caressed her arm, the minute details etching themselves into his mind through gifted tactile senses. He wished Dita had not been in the same room this night and already longed for the day he would be reunited with Melita in Scythopolis, the last of the cities on his mission.

Yamin dreamed of what life would be like for himself and Melita once all this was complete. Would Dita have found others to help her? Would Hippos welcome him back? Would he ever see Jesus again? He had rehearsed what he would say to him since he had begged to leave in his boat. He longed to introduce Melita to him.

Before falling asleep, Yamin imagined what Jesus would say after hearing about his adventures.

You have done well, my faithful servant.

6 1

Melita's reluctance to leave Yamin the next morning soon faded after Dita's persuasive argument. Meeting up in a few weeks seemed tolerable considering the possible alternative. There was no way she could resist Dita's logic after all the terrible incidents she and her family had been through recently.

"You two have a destiny together," Dita told her. She looked off to the west over the Jordan River valley. "I see you having children and living out the rest of your lives in peace spreading news of Elohim's miracles." She turned to Yamin. Her motherly smile contrasted with their drab surroundings. "And I am grateful to have been a part of it."

Yamin could not argue either. He never wanted to leave Melita's side but the dangers outweighed her temporary absence from his life. After hearing Dita speak, he envisioned traveling back to Hippos, reestablishing his family's hold on their small parcel of land, and rebuilding. Although he did not want to live as a subsistence fisherman any longer. He would have to supplement his income by learning a new profession, but something still related to the sea he had called home for most of his life.

As they walked through the city, they found Pella's religious tolerance to be greater than that of any other Decapolis stronghold he had visited so far. Not sure if it meant the farther south a city lied, the more tolerant or if it had been pure chance. Perhaps it was the proximity to Jerusalem in comparison to those farther north and closer to Rome. Either way, Yamin felt he could move slowly in his search for a synagogue. Sluggishness also had the advantage of increasing time spent with Melita.

Dita had wandered off earlier to pursue her own agenda for the time being. Yamin wondered if this city would produce any slaves in dire need of manumission. He could not help but double his duty and be watchful for such individuals. He knew Dita would be doing the same for him.

He then remembered that Dar's little sister had been relocated here after their mother died. He kept one eye out for any sign of her, as well.

After learning from a friendly textile merchant about the location of the synagogue, they turned west toward the valley. Before they reached their destination, a young mother and her daughter stopped them in the narrow street.

"Please, alms?" The thin woman sheltered her young daughter in the folds of her soiled dress.

The child recoiled upon their approach yet kept her face and her innocent expression purposely visible.

Melita gave Yamin a sly look.

He caught on and nodded.

Yamin and Melita wore nice clothes. Certainly not those of aristocrats, but not peasant's either. Any destitute person would assume they had coins to spare. Yamin felt drawn to them, regardless of Melita's unspoken warning.

He had never interrogated anyone before, so determining if this woman had been forced to beg for another's benefit would be a challenge. "Why do you need the money, woman?" *That came out wrong.*

The woman's eyes grew wide, and she turned to walk away.

Melita reached out her hand. "Wait. He didn't mean to pry."

The woman stopped.

Melita continued. "It's just, before we give money to strangers, we want to know it'll be used for good."

As if practiced, the woman spun an unbelievable tale of disasters leading her to this state of existence. "My husband was a master mason, often hired by city leaders to head up new construction."

Yamin's brow furrowed. "Where is he? What has become of him?"

The woman held her hands over her daughter's ears and whispered. "Dead."

Melita let out a tiny gasp.

Yamin fingered a coin in his bag and continued his investigation as kindly as he could. "Is this money going all to you?"

The woman squinted at him. "What do you mean?"

He scanned the nearby doorways and alley entrances. "Is someone forcing you to beg for their benefit?"

The woman hesitated then stammered.

"Yamin! Can't you see she's trying to feed her child?" Melita turned to the woman. "What's your name, dear?"

Before the woman could answer, a slovenly man squeezed through a doorway and interrupted. "What's the meaning of your interrogations? Give her money or leave."

Melita backed away and reached for Yamin's hand.

Yamin took her hand and addressed him. "Are you her husband?"

"I told you, he died." The woman did not try to cover the child's ears this time. Tears welled in her eyes.

The thin man's styled beard conflicted with his simple attire. He yanked the child from the woman and attempted to grab the woman's. He lowered his voice but not enough to prevent Yamin and Melita from hearing. "I've told you time and again. No chatting. Get the money or walk away."

The woman cringed, and the child began to cry.

He turned to Yamin. "What are you looking at? Keep moving and mind your business."

Yamin tugged at Melita until she followed him. "We have to find Dita. She can help that woman."

They sped away but made sure to remember how to find their way back to that doorway.

It was not long before they found Dita. She was talking to a temple guard when they approached. "...next to the inn, you say?" Dita pointed west.

The guard nodded.

Dita thanked the man and turned with a smile. "I found the synagogue. It's right—"

"We know where it is." Yamin kept his voice low. "We have a more pressing issue that needs your input."

He explained to her on the way back.

Dita stopped walking. "Yamin, I hate to disappoint you, but I don't have enough money to make an offer to buy a slave, let alone two."

"She's right." Melita sighed. "We only have enough to get us to Jerusalem."

"After that, I could buy all the slaves in this city."

Yamin thought for a moment. He let out a forceful sigh. He knew how close he had come to missing out on Dita's saving him. Minutes either way and he would now be the slave of another, still missing out on his mission and still separated from Melita. "Then you two had better be on your way before they move on. I'll find the local rabbi, if he exists, and head immediately to Gerasa after."

Dita handed him some of their traveling money. "Don't worry. I'll take good care of her." She hugged him. "We'll come back this way and find that woman and child."

Yamin took Melita in his arms. "It's taking all I've got to keep you from staying with me."

"I know, my love." She kissed him deeply.

Yamin watched as the women walked downhill toward the valley gate. The noon sun illuminated the myriad of blooming wildflowers outside the city's walls. He hoped their journey would be nothing less beautiful and worry free.

His visit with the local Jewish leader proved fruitful. The rabbi begged for Yamin to stay the night in Pella and speak to his people. But Yamin knew if he lingered, his rendezvous with Melita could be jeopardized. Gerasa called to him. Sharing his testimony solely with the rabbi would have to suffice.

The road south also led Yamin farther east. With the distance from Jerusalem came the same religious intolerance he found in Gadara and other Decapolis cities to the north. The rabbi in Pella had warned him but Yamin wished to keep higher expectations for success. He was too familiar with miracles now to let someone's pessimism distract him from his efforts.

As experience had shown, the roads between cities provided the best audiences, and he shared his story with as many who would take time to listen. And as much as Philadelphia's name suggested, brotherly love kept itself only to those who followed local philosophies. The barren rolling hills surrounding its high stone walls mirrored the welcome he received. Those who did not swear to their gods were turned away at the gates. Yamin had been refused entry and accepted the inevitable.

He spent the next couple of days roaming through the surrounding villages and fields for anyone who would hear his story. And although most welcomed him, their hospitality waned when the completion of his story tore the audiences in half.

Days passed, and Yamin's funds dwindled. He never stopped thinking about reuniting with Melita and wondered how their journey progressed. All the people started to look the same as he searched for his betrothed's visage in every face.

The journey to Scythopolis had been the longest intercity trip in his travels so far, as he chose less frequented roads to the west to shorten the distance. Crossing both the Jabbok and Jordan Rivers, as well as traversing desert and mountainous terrain sapped his energy and diminished his resources. He pushed himself toward his meeting with Melita.

Nightfall halted Yamin's arrival south of the city so he made camp by the Jordan. He had run out of food the day before. The spring harvest of barley had begun and Yamin took advantage by collecting what he could as he passed the fields, as well as a few handfuls of legumes. At twilight, he threw them and some sage into a small cooking pot filled with river water and started a humble fire at the shoreline.

Leaves crunched under footfalls up the bank's incline. Yamin turned his head and squinted in the direction of the sound. Nothing. *Probably a lost goat.* Other traveler's small fires sprung up along the shoreline generating a wave of released tension through his body. Fears of being abducted again waned. The number of travelers out here surprised him. But he thanked Elohim for the blessing. No one would dare collect slaves in such a populated area. But bandits did not care about crowds. Always the opportunists.

The more people expelled from the cities, the more opposition the Roman leaders created against their occupation. Thievery had grown to be the easiest method of rebellion. Yamin, credit awarded to his demons, lived nearly two years as a thief.

Another rustle of leaves from behind.

Takes one to know one. He reached for a nearby rock and pulled it closer to his side.

A splash sounded from the water's edge.

They had surrounded him.

A young couple and their two small children turned a corner from upstream. The eldest child, maybe four years old, walked barefoot in the shallows. The man attempted to collect water in a leaky goatskin bag. He then glanced Yamin's way and approached. "Hallo!" His clothes fared better than Yamin's. His short thick beard made Yamin's look juvenile.

Yamin loosened his grip on the rock.

A series of twigs snapped in the bushes behind him and his grasp tightened once more.

The visitor inspected the noise through the fading light over Yamin's head but did not seem to find the source. "I see you've an intact skin." Firelight flickered on the man's face.

Yamin nodded then handed it to the stranger. "I am Yamin, son of Eber."

The man accepted the skin. "And I am Yuval. I'd rather not mention my father's name."

"I once had similar reservations when introducing myself."

Yuval motioned for his family to join him. "Father was criminal. I wasn't."

His wife scooped up the younger child and the other clung near her side as they approached.

"My wife, Dodi."

Dodi plopped the child down and sat next to the fire. "Thank you for your hospitality." She placed a basket next to her and retrieved foodstuffs from within. She handed unleavened bread to Yuval than peered inside his cooking pot. "You've quite a Passover meal already prepared here, Yamin."

Yamin's brow furrowed. "Passover? What's that?" *Are they asking me to pass my food over to them?*

Yuval broke a piece from the bread and handed it to him. "Well, we assumed from your name—"

Dodi handed small pieces to each child on either side of her. "Yamin is a Hebrew name. But you know this, yes?"

He chuckled. "Never given it much thought." His parents worshipped all sorts of gods, and he knew their ancestry had been a jumble of ethnicities. But what difference did it make to these people that his name was Jewish?

"I guess it would best be described as meaning *on the right hand*." Yuval thought for a moment. "Have you an affinity for things on the right side?"

Yamin put the bread between his legs on his robe and sat back supported by his hands. *Right side. The* starboard *side.* He knowingly nodded to himself then felt the couple's anticipatory stares. Ignoring Yuval's question, he asked one of his own. He sat upright again, picked up the bread, and held it out. "And what is this Passover?"

Yuval proceeded to tell the story of how Elohim rescued the ancient Jews from captivity in Egypt over a thousand years ago. He and the children listened intently as Yuval unwound the ancient tale of Moses with colorful mannerisms and voices. Dodi prepared the remaining food and made additions to Yamin's soup.

"Another miracle of Elohim I've not heard of. Thank you for sharing."

Yuval proceeded to pray, first in Hebrew then in Aramaic for Yamin's benefit. He held up the bread and took a bite. Dodi and the children followed.

Yamin ate. Cheerfulness welled up in him, and he laughed out loud.

Guarded smiles spread over Yuval and Dodi's faces.

Yuval asked, "Are you all right?"

"Very well, thank you. It's just that I miss my wife and, well, I'm happy to have been blessed by your company tonight. I've had a lonely couple of weeks."

Dodi handed Yamin a small wooden bowl filled with his own amended soup and more bread. "As are we."

Yamin thanked Dodi then turned to Yuval. "You've shared your story. May I share one of my own?"

Dodi looked at the children then at Yuval.

Yuval nodded. "Is it appropriate for children's ears?"

Yamin knew it was not. Telling the story still gave him chills, and demonic possession would evolve nightmares in anyone. "Do they speak Greek?"

Dodi laid the children to rest on mats near the fire as Yamin began to share his experience. When he reached the end, Yuval and Dodi had expressions he had seen before in many others. Wonderment mixed with fear.

Yuval spoke first. "We had hoped to make it to Jerusalem and the temple before Passover began. Now I'm glad we didn't."

"Yuval!" Dodi swatted his arm. "My parents are sick. You know we couldn't have left earlier."

"If we had, we'd have missed this chance of hearing about another of Elohim's miracles." He turned to Yamin. "They are so few these days it seems."

Dodi checked on the children. "Earlier, you mentioned a wife. What happened to her? If you don't mind us asking."

Yamin looked up at the sprawling band of stars above their heads and sighed. "I met her after my salvation. In my travels through Decapolis. At first, I wasn't interested in a spouse. But the Lord put her in my path too many times for it to be just coincidence."

Dodi smiled then laid next to her children. "Where is she? I pray no harm befell her."

"Oh, no. Nothing like that. She's helping a friend—with an errand. I'm supposed to meet her here," he motioned toward the city, "in the next couple of days during the fertility festival time."

"We just passed through the city and witnessed the celebration firsthand." Yuval produced a small wineskin and offered it to Yamin. "We'll drink a blessing to our wives."

Yamin took a sip. The strong wine surprised him, and he coughed upon swallowing it. "You're—not *from* Scythopolis?"

"Oh, no. We've traveled from Tiberias, on the shore—"

"On the shore of the Sea of Galilee! I'm from Hippos!"

"Then we are practically neighbors."

Yamin helped himself to another sip of wine. "I watched the sun fall behind your city countless times."

"And I've watched it rise from behind yours more times than I can count as well." Yuval smiled. "Let's drink to our cities on the lake."

They settled down for the night around the small fire as Yamin's eyelids grew heavy from drink. His mind wandered back to his time working on his father's boat, right before he traveled west. He turned to Yuval and asked sheepishly, "You aren't by chance a fisherman, are you?"

Yuval had already fallen asleep.

Yamin was not sure he wanted to know the answer.

63

Yamin woke with a slight headache. He looked around for his guests. Or had *he* been *their* guest? He found Dodi tidying up and Yuval occupying the children near the river's edge. A gentle breeze carried a thin whisp of gray smoke from the embers of last night's fire into his nose. The acrid scent offered no improvement to the pain in his temple.

He cleared his throat then spoke to Dodi. "What does your husband do for a living?"

"He's a shipwright."

Her nonchalant reply sent a wave of relief over him. "So, *not* a fisherman."

"Ha! They owe him more fish than we can eat in a year."

Yuval approached. "What's so funny?"

Yamin stood and straightened his clothes. "I'm just happy to have met someone with an interest in boats."

Dodi scoffed. "Interest? More of an obsession."

"Hey!" Yuval shot her a playfully chiding look then whispered loudly to Yamin. "She's right. I love my boats."

"I have experience building myself." Yamin exaggerated but wanted to keep the conversation going.

"Oh, really? On the lake?"

"Well, more maintenance than anything. My father's old boat kept me busy."

Dodi stood and called the children over. "I think we're ready."

Yuval gave Yamin a hug.

"May Elohim bless your journey, your mission, and your marriage."

"Thank you. You as well."

"And if you find yourself in Tiberias, please visit. I think you'll know where to look."

They parted ways as the family continued south along the river to Jerusalem, and Yamin headed for Scythopolis in hopes of meeting Melita any day now.

Three days passed. No Melita. No Dita. And no friendly faces.

Yamin met no one here with sympathy for his cause. Several people listened, and discussions among the listeners ensued but nothing like he had experienced in the other Decapolis cities.

Some people slipped him some coins, enough for food, but not lodging, so he spent his nights by the road south of the city with an eye open for any passersby. Once he thought he spotted Melita and Dita riding in a cart—just strangers.

The combined festivals of *Fordicidia* and *Vinalia Priora* had passed and so had Yamin's hope for Melita's safety. *Something must have happened to them. Were they robbed? Did bandits steal Dita's gold and* . . . He could not bear to think of anything horrid happening to his love.

He wandered aimlessly through the streets of this largest of the Decapolis cities. His drive to complete his mission diminished, replaced with fear and anxiety. He drifted south, down into the valley where stood a theatre and amphitheater. In the theatre, two actors recounted the tale of Romulus and Remus in celebration of yet another Roman festival. The hedonistic behavior of these people angered Yamin. *Don't they know none of it matters?*

The summer months turned to fall and news of the death of Livia Drusilla, former Emperor Augustus' wife, brought lament to the whole empire. He had no need to visit the theatre now, as actors, both professional and amateur took to the streets pretending to be her ancestors. This drove many of the citizens to wail loudly in their public display of grieving. Some extreme showmen even tore out their hair and scratched their faces to one up their neighbors.

Their false sense of sorrow for a luminary they never knew disgusted Yamin. But he still could not tear himself away from the city where he was to meet Melita. *Melita.* The name only brought pain now instead of joy.

Then the voices. Not from within. But from others when they passed nearby. Others who reveled in drink and lusted after one another. Their faces contorted in pain from their demons. Only he could see them.

"Still here."

"Ready for us again?"

"We can help dull the senses."

Every time he heard them, he relied on his salvation experience with Jesus to drive the demonic speech away. He prayed to Elohim. But he grew tired. Living on scraps and begging of the kindness of others wore thin as well. He knew if he could fill his days with work on the water again, he could at least pretend to not feel remorse for his loss. Would he find friends in Hippos?

Yuval! Yamin remembered the invitation to visit Tiberias. Maybe he would offer him an apprenticeship at least.

On the final morning of September, nearly six months since last seeing Melita, Yamin departed Scythopolis for home.

As he moped through the northern gate, a familiar voice called his name from behind. Dita, still wearing blue, albeit a different set of clothes than last he saw her, rushed to meet him.

His heart stopped. He looked through the throngs of travelers for Melita to no avail. When Dita caught him, he could not speak. Words of anger and delight rose to the tip of his tongue but he could not decide which to release. His energy had been sapped. Finally, all he could ask was, "Melita?"

Dita caught her breath. Her voice matched her haggard expression. "I—I don't know."

64

Yamin fell to the side of the road and landed next to a food vendor's tent. The scent of dill and other cooking herbs wafted up and made his stomach turn. He nearly retched.

Dita supported his shoulders. "I'm so sorry for being away so long, Yamin."

"What happened? I waited." Tears welled. "I waited."

"We tried to send word so many times. But we had no way of knowing—"

"We? She's *alive?*"

"What? Of course, she is."

Yamin's head swam with a jumble of emotion. He almost screamed. But he grabbed Dita and hugged her with all his might. "Thank you, Lord. Another miracle. Thank you, Jesus."

After a moment, Dita struggled gently to free herself from his grasp. "I don't know how far behind me she is. Could be a day. But she's on her way. Come, let me explain." She motioned for some men who accompanied her to help Yamin up, and they led him back into the city.

"No, I can't go back in there. Too many voices. Not without her."

Dita's brow furrowed. "Yes, you can. Come, I've already secured a house for our stay. I left a man at the gate to receive Melita upon her arrival. We've been scouring the city for almost two days searching for any sign of you, asking everyone if they've spoken to you, heard of you even. It's a miracle I found you at all after so much time."

A *miracle.* "Something made me stay until now."

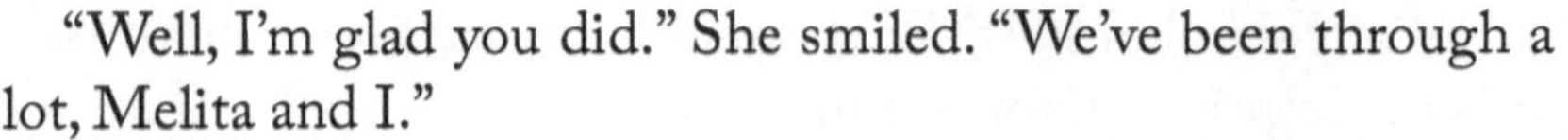

"Well, I'm glad you did." She smiled. "We've been through a lot, Melita and I."

A tinge of anger rose within him. "Better be a good story. I've been in anguish. Still am, to be honest."

A few minutes' travel had them at the house. From the front door, the acropolis dominated the hilltop in the distance at the city's center. With the fine location and the manpower to aid her, Yamin knew Dita must have gotten to the hidden treasure and then rescued some abused slaves along the way. But what else had happened so monumental as to keep Melita from returning for months?

Dita gave orders for a bath and a meal. "You'll want to get cleaned up before—"

"No, Dita." Yamin sat on a simple stool just inside the door. "Tell me now." He took a deep breath. "Please."

"Right. Of course." She dismissed the help but not before ordering water and some fruit and bread. She knelt on the floor in front of him. "We should pray first."

Yamin grabbed his knees and squeezed. "Dita—" He closed his eyes. "You're right. We should."

One of the men brought a pillow for her to sit on along with the food and water.

Yamin took a long drink from a decorative clay vessel then closed his eyes. "Elohim, your path is not easy. Thank you for the strength to carry on through this trial." He opened his eyes and spoke to Dita. "I heard them."

"Who? Who did you hear?"

"The demons."

Dita gasped. "They're—back?" She withdrew her head from his slightly.

He shook his head then chuckled. "No, my faith kept them at bay. That's the one thing I've learned through this absence from Melita."

Dita let out a sigh. "Are you ready?"

"I need to know where she's been."

"Where should I start? With running for our lives from thieves or being imprisoned for two months?"

"Imprisoned? How—"

"I'll start at when we left you."

"At the end of March."

"Right. Wow, we *have* been gone a long time. It didn't seem that long with everything we've been through."

Yamin squeezed his knees again.

"All right. Here goes. After we left you in Pella, we realized we were being followed by the same two fellow slaves of yours from the volcano."

"Leander and that pale one."

"Seleucus."

"Right. Never cared too much for either, and they've proven why."

"We did not know it was them at first. Only that those two men never left our trail. Whether we veered left or right, they followed."

"What did you do?"

"Melita decided we should hide and wait for them to come around. But they figured out our plan and caught us from behind. Well, Leander figured it out. Seleucus, poor soul, couldn't figure his way out of a room with three walls."

"Did they hurt you? Melita?"

"They wanted the gold. They had already wasted what they stole from me, and like everyone else who handles money poorly, they wanted more to waste on their frivolity and sinful escapades."

"But you never told them about the rest."

"We used their belief that I had more to fill them full of promises and reassurances along the road to Jerusalem. When we entered the city, which is where I told them the treasure had been hidden, we simply turned them over to the authorities."

"Well, that couldn't have been much of a delay."

"You'd think that was the end. But they told the centurion everything they knew about the slave releases, the gold I had, and your story, what little they remembered of it. Their suspicious nature drove them to investigate. They forced us to remain in the city under their watchful eye until they had all the information they needed to make a decision."

"What decision?"

"The decision to let us go, arrest us, or whatever they wanted. Their watchful eyes kept us for two months. After about a week, Melita hatched a plan to escape, but it failed and they kept us even more tightly watched. We couldn't even leave our room at the inn. It might as well have been prison."

"Did they hurt her?"

"A few bruises, but not from the guards. From her falling out the window."

Tears welled in Yamin's eyes. "It's all my fault. I'm sorry, Dita."

"Your fault? You can't blame yourself for another person's poor decisions. Even though your choice to turn left or right can change the course of the future, what others do is their own responsibility."

"But if I hadn't rescued those men from—"

"No! No, Yamin. You mustn't go down that path. Otherwise, we'd question every decision we've ever made and be afraid to ever step out our doors."

"You're right. I know you're right."

She smiled at him. "I know. Now, where was I."

"Two months."

"Right." She shifted her position on the pillow. "The questioning slowed over the two months until finally they unlocked the door for good. We insisted that the other men had lied, but I sensed someone's personal greed had kept us detained for so long. Melita was distraught. She pined for you and cried herself to sleep nightly with the thought of what you must have been going through in her absence."

"As did I. Fearing the worst brought out the worst. Only my faith sustained me."

"As it should have. I retold my story to her often to keep her spirits up. And together we pieced together your story until we thought we had it right, just as you told it."

Yamin felt a rush of warmth rise inside him. "That's good."

"It was good. Because after they released us, we told that story to as many who would listen. And that led to us making connections to find those in need of my *special* services."

"You spent time rescuing slaves? But couldn't you have done that alone? Melita knew I was waiting here. Why didn't she—"

"It wasn't that easy. When we first were freed, she sent several messages via courier to Scythopolis. We addressed them to you in every inn we could find word that existed there. We even sent letters to the local magistrate with promise of reward money. But when we never heard back, we assumed you had moved on back to Hippos. Melita took that as a comfort and planned on heading straight there for you when we finished our business."

"Business?"

"Jerusalem was the last place I served as a slave before finding myself free. I still had some connections in the right places, and with Melita's help—her being assured in her mind about your whereabouts—we took to the business of freeing those in need."

Yamin could not believe what he heard. But the more he thought about it, the happier he became that everything had turned out well, and Melita had been as distraught as he in his absence. *She still loves me.*

"We freed fifty-four slaves, Yamin. Fifty-four. Can you believe it? But we had to leave as summer came to an end. The local aristocracy got wind of our doings and made the sale of any slaves to anyone other than their own nearly impossible. We were pushed out, for now." She produced a cunning smile.

The door flew open and nearly knocked Yamin from his stool.

A man entered. "Mistress Dita, I've brought her."

Melita, weathered from her travels, swept into the room. Her clothing, the same blue as Dita's only dustier, carried on it the scent of flowered perfume. "Yamin? Yamin!"

He leapt from his seat and into her arms. They both cried with exhausted tears. Kisses flowed between them.

Yamin pulled back and looked deeply into her amber eyes. "You're really here. Thank the Lord, I've found you."

"I think *I* found *you*."

He chuckled. "Yes. Yes, you did."

65

A month later, Yamin and Melita found themselves in Tiberias at Yuval and Dido's spacious lakeside home. Dita first brought them back to Gadara where Sabinus and Rena planned an enormous feast for their marriage by the lake. Their original vows of marriage made months ago had no legal force on their own. They were more a personal agreement between the couple. As a result, the wedding itself, known as the "*affectio maritalis*," was a mere formality to prove to the community that the couple intended to live together.

On their wedding day, Yamin lead a procession to Yuval and Dido's home, where Melita was then escorted by her bridesmaids to meet her future husband. She wore a *tunica recta*—a white woven tunic—belted with the elaborate "Knot of Hercules." Her hair had been carefully arranged under an orange wedding veil. Matching orange shoes adorned her feet.

After the official marriage contract had been signed, the enormous feast that Melita's parents had planned commenced. The day ended with a noisy procession to the couple's new home, a humble outbuilding on the lakefront property.

Yamin stared deeply into Melita's eyes. "Are you ready?"

"Always."

He swept her off her feet and lifted her into his arms.

"Oh!" Melita chuckled.

Yamin proceeded to carry her over the threshold.

"You should know I'm not that superstitious."

Yamin stopped short of the entrance while everyone looked on from a distance. "If you trip while walking inside, I'd never hear the end of it. So, play nice."

"Bad omens are for old ladies." She glanced at her mother over his shoulder and smiled. "But why start off with any doubts."

Dita waved then parted ways with them there, but not before repaying Melita and providing a hefty wedding gift of gold.

Yuval took Yamin under his wing as a shipwright's apprentice, and Yamin could not have been more delighted to serve him.

Yamin beamed as he watched Melita enjoy sharing the domestic duties with Dodi. Not having the pressure of working for one's parents made it an ideal situation. Seeing her care for the children drove him to truly desire some little ones of their own for the first time in his life. And after a visit across the great lake to visit Dar and Althea, seeing their newborn child made the longing even greater.

He pulled Melita aside one afternoon while she helped prepare dinner. He was covered in sawdust and she in flour. "You're beautiful, wife."

"So are you, husband."

They both smiled.

"You know what Yuval told me today? A long while back he found an old, abandoned fishing boat with a broken mast box just north of here on the shore."

Her eyes widened in disbelief. "No, he didn't."

"True story. He even used some wood from the keel to build another boat for a customer. Said it was *a rare find*."

She pulled him closer. Sawdust rubbed off him and onto her robes. Flour sprinkled from her onto his arm.

She studied his rough hands, still scarred from his trials. "Are you happy here, Yamin?"

"Of course. Why do you ask?"

"You know. Your mission. You told me that you never felt like you truly finished."

"Oh, I don't know." He turned to the doorway overlooking the shipyard and the Sea of Galilee beyond. The late afternoon sun bathed the eastern coast surrounding Hippos with a golden hue. "I'm working on a plan to continue the mission—until the very end."

"The end?"

"Well, *our* end anyway. You know how stories go. One person tells another and so on. I have a good feeling mine will be around for a long time."

Epilogue

The turbulent, unforgiving Sea of Galilee sent gusts of wind ripping the tops of the waves to shreds and lacing the dark water with a satin foam.

Dita, the vessel's only passenger, sat comparably impetuous at the bow as coarse strands of gray hair escaped their linen covering and dripped lake water down her neck. Cold spray splashed over the side and landed upon her wrinkled face. She held fast in defiance.

Yamin tacked the boat ever so slightly leeward to alleviate the constant barrage attacking his traveler. He gripped the tiller tighter with both hands. "Hold on!"

A wave crashed over the bow and nearly swept Dita away.

It then struck Yamin. The frigid water temporarily blinded him. Half expecting her to be lying in the bottom of the boat, he opened his eyes.

There she sat, stalwart as ever, an angel of mercy having freed over a thousand abused captives, including himself, who fell victim to their Roman owners' oppression.

She never did let a rough passage like this upset her.

Being the sole crewman on this worn, wooden vessel would have presented a maritime challenge to an ordinary sailor, even under calm conditions. Yamin was no ordinary sailor. The boat's size, its jury-rigged sail and ropes, and its sensitive rudder took getting accustomed to. But he built this boat nearly twenty years ago when he started his shipwright's apprenticeship. It was his first of many, each built with passion and the rest sold with pride.

He laid his palm upon the thinning warped seat next to him and pulled up a tiny sliver of wood. His view of the material remained incomplete until he could touch it. He was grateful for the ability to get more out of his surroundings than most people. He had lost that God-given talent once and made too many mistakes because of it.

Thoughts of repairing the seat ran through his mind.

The large square cloth over their heads filled with a sudden gust and snapped to attention. Yamin contemplated lowering the sail when the eastern shoreline appeared before them through the stinging spray. *Almost there.*

Dita shifted her position.

He did too in anticipation of getting her to dry land.

Yamin thanked the Lord for Dita every day by working hard as a shipwright and ferryman. It provided a sort of restitution. One of her stipulations for being given his freedom all those years ago. He relived the memory.

"When you leave and again enter the world on your own," she had frequently reminded him, "you have the responsibility to live a righteous life. A life others can look upon and wonder how you learned to live this way. And you will tell them the story I have told you in addition to your own.

While adjusting the mainsail before making landfall, Yamin thought back to the day when he departed as a newly married man with a second chance at life. He recalled their last conversation.

"Leaving you, Dita, is—" His chest tightened. She reminded him of his mother. The sorrow threatened to draw forth old memories he didn't want to return. *Such darkness.* Yamin shuddered.

Dita's eyes softened. "Your path is your own to choose, Yamin. You will continue to serve Elohim well. This recent trial— You never stopped trusting the Lord by putting him first, and in doing so you found success."

And now, two decades later, she was again in his presence. Her demeanor remained unchanged over the years. Only the frailty of her aged body betrayed the passage of time. But her determination remained as resolute as ever.

Somehow, he knew this encounter would be their last. Yamin allowed himself a tight-lipped smile. *She's still making a difference in the lives of others.*

The wind calmed near the edge of the great lake as the boat's hull cut through the chop. With a scraping sound his land-loving customers relished, the boat made landfall.

No one to meet them. Just as he had predicted.

Perhaps the older residents here still remembered when on this very beach a legion of demons in a herd of swine leapt to their deaths into the lake. Little did they realize the miracle they had witnessed. Little did they know the changes in so many people that occurred because of their unwilling animal sacrifice.

Yamin lifted the grey stone anchor from the floor of the boat and heaved it over the starboard side. He preferred starboard. The many years of tossing the anchor overboard had worn a rut in the gunwale. He recalled attaching this piece of wood after learning from Yuval, now deceased, who had taught him the skill of softening boards by soaking them in warm water before bending.

After securing the boat, Yamin offered to carry Dita to dry land.

"Allow me some dignity." She scowled at the waist deep water. With a sigh, she flicked a glance his way. Her head scarf sat limp upon damp silvered hair. "If you insist."

Once on the beach, they grasped each other's hands and prayed, giving thanks for all the Lord provided.

"Father," Dita continued, "Yamin and I part ways again to continue the journey you've set before us." They raised their heads simultaneously and gazed at each other's faces. "Please provide us with the wisdom to overcome temptation and the fortitude to carry on, despite the obstacles that come our way."

They finished together. "Amen."

They spoke no other words as their wet hands separated from each other's.

Dita walked up the hillside leading east to Canatha.

Yamin moved a foot toward her—then paused. *No. Your life is in Tiberias.* Traveling no longer appealed to him. And she alone needed to complete this final task. Was it one last effort to liberate captives? Yamin did not know. Perhaps she moved this time to aid those bound in spirit rather than those bound by chains.

He no longer needed to wander to carry out his mission. Being a ferryman provided him a captive audience. One that came to him and would sit to be entertained for the time it took to travel from one side of this enormous lake to the other. One or two hours, depending upon his passenger's destination. More than enough time to share Dita's and his stories.

Word of mouth was the best source of advertisement, and travelers from all walks would tell their acquaintances about the ferryman who tells stories. Stories of such intrigue and hope they *must* use his service, if for nothing more than to drown the boredom of the voyage.

Yamin had learned much from Dita, making it easy to hold their attention. She witnessed several miracles in her time. And almost everyone in the region had now been aware of, whether they believed them or not, the marvels involved with Jesus's crucifixion, resurrection, and ascension almost twenty years ago.

As he entered the boat, he recalled the marvels once more. He smiled as warmth flowed through his body, despite the chill brought on by his moist robes.

He turned to see if Dita had gone. He looked up and down the beach and saw no one other than a single fisherman to the north securing his boat for the evening. A lone seagull cried from its rocky perch.

He considered staying here for the night in case Dita needed him. But time was short. He had an arrangement with a regular customer for a morning transit. Yamin looked forward to spending a couple of hours with his old friend, Thomas.

A couple of hours. He harrumphed. A long-gone sailor once spoke to him about the concept of time. *If I had only listened to Baniy's advice. Where would I be now?*

He hoisted the sail to embrace a calming west wind. His need for tacking lessened. *Oh, the things that led me to this point in my life.*

His journey had been fraught with pain and fear in the beginning, only to be rewarded with the peace and joy he felt now. *Everything is as it should be.* He would do it all again to come to the wisdom which he now possessed.

Yamin's own story was another he would share with his passengers, but only when he sensed their readiness to accept it. His was a darker, more frightening tale than any other he told. His friend Thomas had yet to hear the beginning. *I think it might be time for him to know how it started.*

Two hours later, Yamin reached the western shore. The sun had nearly set. He anchored a few boat lengths from the beach and dined on dried and pickled fish, day-old bread, and a small portion of wine that would probably turn to vinegar if left until morning.

He preferred nights on the boat. The gentle rocking lulled him to sleep and kept unsavory characters from bothering him. But nothing matched nights at home with Melita. His two children, now grown and starting families of their own, occupied his thoughts. He would see them all tomorrow before the sabbath sundown.

Calls from the shore at dawn roused him from his sleep. Thomas was early. *As usual.*

Yamin hoisted the stone anchor and poled the boat as close to shore as he could. Wavelets in the water's surface reflected the rising sun's light.

Thomas nearly leapt into the water and onto the bow of the boat. "Good morning, Yamin, my old friend."

Yamin reached out a helping hand. "And to you, Thomas." He waited for his guest to get comfortable. "Have you eaten breakfast?"

"Just." He sniffed the air inside the small vessel. "And if all you have to offer is pickled sardines—" Thomas waved his hand in front of his nose and smiled.

Yamin chuckled and shoved off the boat toward the east. The calm sea made sailing a challenge. He set up the oars and rowed for a few minutes.

Thomas stroked his gray beard. "Any new stories to share on this, my final trip across the sea?"

Yamin stopped oaring. "Final trip? What do you mean?"

Thomas looked off toward the east. He removed his sandals and hung them over the side of the boat. Slapping them together, he generated a small dust cloud that hung in the still air. A gentle breeze spread ripples across the water and swept the tiny particles away.

"You're moving on, then?"

Thomas nodded. "East, to India. The Lord calls, and I must go. A story would be greatly appreciated."

Yamin sensed the strengthening wind and pulled on the halyard to hoist the sail. He reached out for the mainsheet and rubbed the fibrous flax cordage, its structure now fully evident to him. Remembering when the lines on his father's vessel were fashioned out of everything from old linen clothing to the hides of animals, he watched as the western shoreline faded away.

I miss that old boat.

Jeff Keene II holds degrees in biology, chemistry, and linguistics. His writing path began when his high school teacher assigned him the task of creating an original screenplay. Twenty-five years later, that screenplay was published as a short story in a Long Island newsletter. But the writing bug really began when developing a textual criticism about a New Testament story in a master's level seminary course in 2012. Since then, Jeff has had the undying urge to write about unnamed characters in the Bible who've met Jesus.

He has served as a volunteer firefighter where he suffered a line-of-duty injury resulting in the loss of his right foot below-the-knee, worked on a NOAA research vessel for 17-days at sea, and even applied to the NASA Teacher in Space program. He currently serves as a public school teacher.

Jeff lives with his wife, Andria, in Central Florida. They have two adult children.

Connect with Jeff online at:
https://peglegpenman.com

www.ingramcontent.com/pod-product-compliance
Lightning Source LLC
Chambersburg PA
CBHW031306210726
48287CB00005B/1438